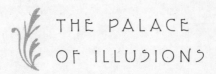

THE PALACE
OF ILLUSIONS

Chitra Banerjee Divakaruni's books include the bestselling novels *The Mistress of Spices*, *Queen of Dreams* and *Sister of My Heart*, the prize-winning story collections *Arranged Marriage* and *The Unknown Errors of Our Lives*, and the 'Conch Bearer' series for children.

She teaches creative writing at the University of Houston and divides her time between Houston and the San Francisco Bay area.

THE

PALACE

OF ILLUSIONS

A Novel

CHITRA LEKHA
BANERJEE DIVAKARUNI

PICADOR

First published 2008 by Doubleday,
an imprint of The Doubleday Broadway Publishing Group,
a division of Random House, Inc., New York

First published in India 2008 by Picador

First published in paperback 2009 by Picador
an imprint of Pan Macmillan Ltd
Pan Macmillan, 20 New Wharf Road, London N1 9RR
Basingstoke and Oxford
Associated companies throughout the world
www.panmacmillan.com

ISBN 978-0-330-45853-5

Book design by Maria Carella
Photo of peacock feather by Siede Preis/Photodisc/Getty Images

9 8 7 6 5

A CIP catalogue record for this book is available
from the British Library.

Printed and bound in India by Replika Press Pvt. Ltd.

Visit *www.picador.com* to read more about all our books and
to buy them. You will also find features, author interviews and
news of any author events, and you can sign up for e-newsletters
so that you're always first to hear about our new releases.

to my three men

Abhay

Anand

Murthy

always

Who is your sister? I am she.
Who is your mother? I am she.
Day dawns the same for you and me.

From *Innana's Journey to Hell*,
3rd Millennium BCE,
translated from Sumerian by N. K. Sandars

ACKNOWLEDGMENTS

My deepest thanks to:

My agent, Sandra Dijkstra, and my editor,
Deb Futter, for guidance

Antonya Nelson and Kim Chernin
for encouragement

My mother, Tatini Banerjee, and my mother-in-
law, Sita Divakaruni, for good wishes

Murthy, Anand, and Abhay for love

Baba Muktananda, Swami Chinmayananda, and
Swami Vidyadhishananda for blessing.

Like many Indian children, I grew up on the vast, varied, and fascinating tales of the *Mahabharat*. Set at the end of what the Hindu scriptures term Dvapar Yug or the Third Age of Man (which many scholars date between 6000 BCE and 5000 BCE), a time when the lives of men and gods still intersected, the epic weaves myth, history, religion, science, philosophy, superstition, and statecraft into its innumerable stories-within-stories to create a rich and teeming world filled with psychological complexity. It moves with graceful felicity between the very recognizable human world and magical realms where yakshas and apsaras roam, depicting these with such exquisite surety that I would often wonder if indeed there was more to existence than what logic and my senses could grasp.

At the core of the epic lies the fierce rivalry between two branches of the Kuru dynasty, the Pandavas and the Kauravas. The lifelong struggle between the cousins for the throne of Hastinapur culminates in the bloody battle of Kurukshetra, in which most kings of that period participated and perished. But numerous other characters people the world of the *Mahabharat* and contribute to its magnetism and continuing relevance. These larger-than-life heroes, epitomizing inspiring virtues and deadly vices, etched many cautionary morals into my child-consciousness. Some of my favorites, who play prominent roles in *The Palace of Illusions*, are: Vyasa the sage, at once the composer of the epic and a participant at crucial moments in the action; Krishna, beloved and inscrutable, an incarnation of Vishnu and mentor to the Pandavas; Bheeshma, the patriarch who, bound by his promise to protect the Kuru throne, must fight against his beloved grandsons; Drona, the brahmin-warrior who becomes teacher to both the Kaurava and Pandava princes; Drupad, the king of Panchaal, whose desire for vengeance against Drona activates the wheel of destiny; and Karna, the great warrior, who is doomed because he does not know his parentage.

But always, listening to the stories of the *Mahabharat* as a young girl in the lantern-lit evenings at my grandfather's village home, or later, poring over the thousand-page leather-bound volume in my parents' home in Kolkata, I was left unsatisfied by the portrayals of the women. It wasn't as though the epic didn't have powerful, complex women characters that affected the action in major ways. For instance, there was the widowed Kunti, mother of the Pandavas, who dedicates her life to making sure her sons became kings. There was Gandhari, wife of the sightless Kaurava king, who chooses to blindfold herself at marriage, thus relinquishing her power as queen and mother. And most of all, there was Panchaali (also known as Draupadi), King Drupad's beautiful daughter, who has the unique distinction of being married to five men at the same time—the five Pandava brothers, the greatest heroes of their time. Panchaali who, some might argue, by her headstrong actions helps to bring about the destruction of the Third Age of Man. But in some way, they remained shadowy figures, their thoughts and motives mysterious, their emotions portrayed only when they affected the lives of the male heroes, their roles ultimately subservient to those of their fathers or husbands, brothers or sons.

If I ever wrote a book, I remember thinking (though at that time I didn't really believe this would ever happen), I would place the women in the forefront of the action. I would uncover the story that lay invisible between the lines of the men's exploits. Better still, I would have one of them tell it herself, with all her joys and doubts, her struggles and her triumphs, her heartbreaks, her achievements, the unique female way in which she sees her world and her place in it. And who could be better suited for this than Panchaali?

It is her life, her voice, her questions, and her vision that I invite you into in *The Palace of Illusions*.

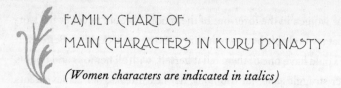

FAMILY CHART OF
MAIN CHARACTERS IN KURU DYNASTY

(Women characters are indicated in italics)

Satyavati m. Shantanu m. *Ganga*

Ambika and *Ambalika* m. Vichitravirya   Bheeshma

Gandhari m.   Dhritarashtra (the blind king)

Duryodhan, Dussasan,
and 98 other brothers
(THE KAURAVAS)

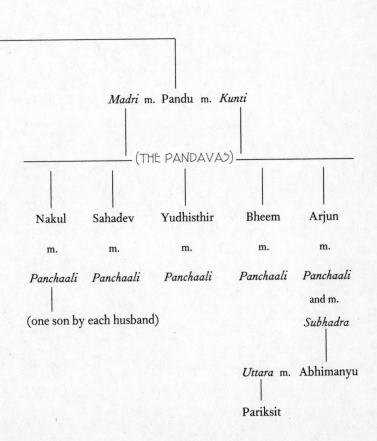

Madri m. Pandu m. *Kunti*

(THE PANDAVAS)

Nakul	Sahadev	Yudhisthir	Bheem	Arjun
m.	m.	m.	m.	m.
Panchaali	*Panchaali*	*Panchaali*	*Panchaali*	*Panchaali*
				and m.
				Subhadra

(one son by each husband)

Uttara m. Abhimanyu

Pariksit

OTHER MAJOR CHARACTERS

ASWATTHAMA: Drona's son

DHRISTADYUMNA: Brother of Panchaali (often referred to as Dhri)

DRONA: Teacher of warcraft for the Kaurava and Pandava princes; teacher of Dhristadyumna

DRUPAD: King of Panchaal, father of Panchaali (Draupadi) and her twin brother Dhristadyumna; onetime friend and now enemy of Drona

KARNA: Best friend of Duryodhan and rival of Arjun; king of Anga; as an infant he was discovered floating on the Ganga river and was brought up by Adhiratha the chariot driver

KEECHAK: Sudeshna's brother and commander of the Matsya army

KRISHNA: Incarnation of the god Vishnu; ruler of the Yadu clan; mentor to the Pandavas and Arjun's best friend; dear friend to Panchaali; brother of Subhadra, who marries Arjun

SUDESHNA: Virat's queen; Uttara's mother

VIRAT: Aged king of Matsya; Uttara's father

VIDUR: Chief minister of Dhritarashtra and friend to the orphaned Pandavas

VYASA: Omniscient sage and composer of the *Mahabharat* who also appears in it as a character

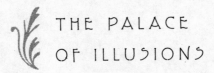

THE PALACE
OF ILLUSIONS

fire

Through the long, lonely years of my childhood, when my father's palace seemed to tighten its grip around me until I couldn't breathe, I would go to my nurse and ask for a story. And though she knew many wondrous and edifying tales, the one I made her tell me over and over was the story of my birth. I think I liked it so much because it made me feel special, and in those days there was little else in my life that did. Perhaps Dhai Ma realized this. Perhaps that was why she agreed to my demands even though we both knew I should be using my time more gainfully, in ways more befitting the daughter of King Drupad, ruler of Panchaal, one of the richest kingdoms in the continent of Bharat.

The story inspired me to make up fancy names for myself: Offspring of Vengeance, or the Unexpected One. But Dhai Ma puffed out her cheeks at my tendency to drama, calling me the Girl Who Wasn't Invited. Who knows, perhaps she was more accurate than I.

This winter afternoon, sitting cross-legged in the meager sunlight that managed to find its way through my slit of a window, she said, "When your brother stepped out of the sacrificial fire onto the cold stone slabs of the palace hall, all the assembly cried out in amazement."

She was shelling peas. I watched her flashing fingers with envy, wishing she would let me help. But Dhai Ma had very specific ideas about activities that were appropriate for princesses.

"An eyeblink later," she continued, "when you emerged from the fire, our jaws dropped. It was so quiet, you could have heard a housefly fart."

I reminded her that flies do not perform that particular bodily function.

She smiled her squint-eyed, cunning smile. "Child, the things you don't know would fill the milky ocean where Lord Vishnu sleeps—and spill over its edges."

I considered being offended, but I wanted to hear the story. So I held my tongue, and after a moment she picked up the tale again.

"We'd been praying for thirty days, from sun-up to sundown. All of us: your father, the hundred priests he'd invited to Kampilya to perform the fire ceremony, headed by that shifty-eyed pair, Yaja and Upayaja, the queens, the ministers, and of course the servants. We'd been fasting, too—not that we were given a choice—just one meal, each evening, of flattened rice soaked in milk. King Drupad wouldn't eat even that. He only drank water carried up from the holy Ganga, so that the gods would feel obligated to answer his prayers."

"What did he look like?"

"He was thin as the point of a sword, and hard like it, too. You could count every bone on him. His eyes, sunk deep into their sockets, glittered like black pearls. He could barely hold up his head, but of course he wouldn't remove that monstrosity of a crown that no one has ever seen him without—not even his wives, I've heard, not even in bed."

Dhai Ma had a good eye for detail. Father was, even now, much the same, though age—and the belief that he was finally close to getting what he'd wanted for so long—had softened his impatience.

"Some people," she continued, "thought he was going to die, but I had no such fears. Anyone who wanted revenge as badly as your royal father did wouldn't let go of body and breath so easily." She chewed ruminatively on a handful of peas.

"Finally," I prompted her, "it was the thirtieth day."

"And I for one was heartily thankful. Milk and rice husk is all very well for priests and widows, but give me fish curry with green chilies and tamarind pickle any day! Besides, my throat was scraped raw from gabbling all those unpronounceable Sanskrit words. And my buttocks, I swear, they were flat as chapatis from sitting on that freezing stone floor.

"But I was scared, too, and stealing a glance here and there, I saw I wasn't the only one. What if the fire ceremony didn't work the way the scriptures had claimed it would? Would King Drupad put us all to death, claiming we hadn't prayed hard enough? Once I'd have laughed if someone had suggested our king might do that. But things had changed since the day when Drona appeared at court."

I wanted to ask about Drona, but I knew what she'd say.

Impatient as mustard seeds sputtering in oil, that's what you are, even though you're old enough to be married off any day now! Each story will come in its time.

"So when your royal father stood up and poured that last pot of ghee into the flames, we all held our breath. I prayed harder than I'd ever done in my life—though it wasn't for your brother I was praying, not exactly. Kallu, who was cook's apprentice then, had been courting me, and I didn't want to die before I'd experienced the joys of having a man in my bed. But now that we've been married for seven years—" Here Dhai Ma paused to snort at the folly of her younger self.

If she got onto the subject of Kallu, I wouldn't hear the rest of the story today.

"Then the smoke rose," I interjected, with experienced dexterity.

She allowed herself to be pulled back into the tale. "Yes, and a spiraling, nasty-smelling black smoke it was, with voices in it. The voices said, *Here is the son you asked for. He'll bring you the vengeance you desire, but it'll break your life in two.*

"*I don't care about that,* your father said. *Give him to me.*

"And then your brother stepped from the fire."

I sat up straight to listen better. I loved this part of the story. "What did he look like?"

"He was a true prince, that one! His brow was noble. His face shone like gold. Even his clothes were golden. He stood tall and unafraid, though he couldn't have been more than five years old. But his eyes troubled me. They were too soft. I said to myself, *How can this boy avenge King Drupad? How can he kill a fearsome warrior like Drona?*"

I worried about my brother, too, though in a different way. He would succeed in completing the task he was born for, I had no doubt of that. He did everything with such meticulous care. But what would it do to him?

I didn't want to think of it. I said, "And then?"

Dhai Ma made a face. "Can't wait till you appear, eh, Madam Full of Yourself?" Then she relented.

"Even before we'd finished cheering and clapping, even before your father had a chance to greet your brother, you appeared. You were as dark as he was fair, as hasty as he was calm. Coughing from the smoke, tripping over the hem of your sari, grabbing for his hand and almost sending him tumbling, too—"

"But we didn't fall!"

"No. Somehow you managed to hold each other up. And then the voices came again. They said, *Behold, we give you this girl, a gift beyond what you asked for. Take good care of her, for she will change the course of history."*

" *'Change the course of history'*! Did they really say that?"

Dhai Ma shrugged. "That's what the priests claimed. Who can tell for sure? You know how sounds boom and echo in that hall. The king looked startled, but then he picked the two of you up, holding you close to his chest. For the first time in years, I saw him smile. He said to your brother, *I name you Dhristadyumna.* He said to you, *I name you Draupadi.* And then we had the best feast this kingdom has ever seen."

As Dhai Ma counted out the feast foods on her fingers, smacking her lips in happy remembrance, my attention veered to the meaning of the names our father chose. Dhristadyumna, Destroyer of Enemies. Draupadi, Daughter of Drupad.

Dhri's name fell within the bounds of acceptability—though if I were his parent I might have picked a more cheerful appellation, like Celestial Victor, or Light of the Universe. But Daughter of Drupad? Granted, he hadn't been expecting me, but couldn't my father have come up with something a little less egoistic? Something more suited to a girl who was supposed to change history?

I answered to Draupadi for the moment because I had no choice. But in the long run, it would not do. I needed a more heroic name.

Nights, after Dhai Ma had retired to her quarters, I lay on my high, hard bed with its massive posts and watched the oil lamp fling flickery shadows against the pocked stone of the walls. I thought of the prophecy then, with yearning and fear. I wanted it to be true. But did I have the makings of a heroine—courage, perseverance, an unbending will? And shut up as I was inside this mausoleum of a palace, how would history even find me?

But most of all I thought of something that Dhai Ma didn't

know, something that ate at me like the rust corroding the bars on my window: what really happened when I stepped from the fire.

If there were voices, as Dhai Ma claimed, prophesying my life in a garbled roar, they hadn't come yet. The orange lick of flames fell away; the air was suddenly cold. The ancient hall smelled of incense, and under it, an older smell: war-sweat and hatred. A gaunt, glittering man walked toward my brother and me as we stood hand in hand. He held out his arms—but for my brother alone. It was only my brother he meant to raise up to show to his people. Only my brother that he wanted. Dhri wouldn't let go of me, however, nor I of him. We clung together so stubbornly that my father was forced to pick us both up together.

I didn't forget that hesitation, even though in the years that followed King Drupad was careful to fulfill his fatherly duty and provide me with everything he believed a princess should have. Sometimes, when I pressed him, he even allowed me privileges he kept from his other daughters. In his own harsh and obsessive way, he was generous, maybe even indulgent. But I couldn't forgive him that initial rejection. Perhaps that was why, as I grew from a girl into a young woman, I didn't trust him completely.

I turned the resentment I couldn't express toward my father onto his palace. I hated the thick gray slabs of the walls—more suited to a fortress than a king's residence—that surrounded our quarters, their tops bristling with sentries. I hated the narrow windows, the mean, dimly lit corridors, the uneven floors that were always damp, the massive, severe furniture from generations ago that was sized more for giants than men. I hated most of all that the grounds had neither trees nor flowers. King Drupad believed the former to be a hazard to security, obscuring the vision of the sentries. The latter he saw no use for—and what my father did not find useful, he removed from his life.

Staring down from my rooms at the bare compound stretching below, I'd feel dejection settle on my shoulders like a shawl of iron. When I had my own palace, I promised myself, it would be totally different. I closed my eyes and imagined a riot of color and sound, birds singing in mango and custard apple orchards, butterflies flitting among jasmines, and in the midst of it—but I could not imagine yet the shape that my future home would take. Would it be elegant as crystal? Solidly precious, like a jewel-studded goblet? Delicate and intricate, like gold filigree? I only knew that it would mirror my deepest being. There I would finally be at home.

My years in my father's house would have been unbearable had I not had my brother. I never forgot the feel of his hand clutching mine, his refusal to abandon me. Perhaps he and I would have been close even otherwise, segregated as we were in the palace wing our father had set aside for us—whether from caring or fear I was never sure. But that first loyalty made us inseparable. We shared our fears of the future with each other, shielded each other with fierce protectiveness from a world that regarded us as not quite normal, and comforted each other in our loneliness. We never spoke of what each one meant to the other—Dhri was uncomfortable with effusiveness. But sometimes I wrote him letters in my head, looping the words into extravagant metaphors. *I'll love you, Dhri, until the great Brahman draws the universe back into Himself as a spider does its web.*

I didn't know then how sorely that love would be tested, or how much it would cost both of us.

blue

 Perhaps the reason Krishna and I got along so well was that we were both severely dark-skinned. In a society that looked down its patrician nose on anything except milk-and-almond hues, this was considered most unfortunate, especially for a girl. I paid for it by spending hour upon excruciating hour being slathered in skin-whitening unguents and scrubbed with numerous exfoliants by my industrious nurse. But finally she'd given up in despair. I, too, might have despaired if it hadn't been for Krishna.

It was clear that Krishna, whose complexion was even darker than mine, didn't consider his color a drawback. I'd heard the stories about how he'd charmed his way into the hearts of the women of his hometown of Vrindavan—all 16,000 of them! And then there was the affair of Princess Rukmini, one of the great beauties of our time. She'd sent him a most indecorous love letter asking him to marry her (to which he'd promptly and chivalrously responded by carrying her off in his chariot). He had other wives, too—over a hundred, at last count. Could the nobility of Kampilya be wrong? Could darkness have its own magnetism?

When I was fourteen, I gathered up enough courage to ask Krishna if he thought that a princess afflicted with a skin so dark that people termed it blue was capable of changing history. He smiled.

That was how he often answered my questions, with an enigmatic smile that forced me to do my own thinking. But this time he must have sensed my confused distress, for he added a few words.

"A problem becomes a problem only if you believe it to be so. And often others see you as you see yourself."

I regarded this oblique advice with some suspicion. It sounded too easy to be true. But when the festival of Lord Shiva approached, I decided to give it a try.

On this particular night each year, the royal family would go in a procession—the men in front, the women behind—to a Shiva temple and offer their prayers. We didn't go far—the temple was situated within the palace grounds. Still, it was a grand spectacle, with the entire court and many of the prominent citizens of Kampilya accompanying us, dressed in their glittery best—exactly the kind of event that brought out my worst anxieties. I'd make excuses of ill health so I could stay in my room, but Dhai Ma saw through them and forced me to participate. Miserable among a crush of women who chattered among themselves and ignored me, I'd try to make myself invisible. The other princesses with their bright faces and cheerful banter made me feel doubly awkward as I slouched behind them, wishing Dhri were with me. If someone addressed me—a guest or a newcomer, usually, who didn't know who I was—I tended to blush and stammer and (yes, even at this age) trip over the edge of my sari.

But this year I allowed a delighted Dhai Ma to dress me in a sea-blue silk light as foam, to weave flowers into my braid, to place diamonds in my ears. I examined Queen Sulochana, the youngest and prettiest of my father's wives, as she walked ahead of me, carrying a platter filled with garlands for the god. I observed the confident sway of her hips, the elegant grace with which she inclined her head in response to a greeting. *I, too, am beautiful*, I told myself, holding

Krishna's words in my mind. I tried the same gestures and found them surprisingly easy. When noblewomen came up and complimented me on my looks, I thanked them as though I was used to such praise. People stood back, deferential, as I passed. I raised my chin proudly and showed off the line of my neck as young courtiers whispered among themselves, asking each other who I was, and where I'd been secreted all these years. A visiting bard stared at me admiringly. Later, he would make up a song about my unique comeliness. The song caught public fancy; other songs followed; word traveled to many kingdoms about the amazing princess of Panchaal, as mesmerizing as the ceremonial flames she was born from. Overnight, I who had been shunned for my strangeness became a celebrated beauty!

Krishna was much amused by the turn of events. When he came to visit, he teased me by playing the tunes of the most extravagant songs on his flute. But when I tried to thank him, he acted as though he didn't know what I was talking about.

. . .

There were other stories about Krishna. How he'd been born in a dungeon where his uncle Kamsa had imprisoned his parents with the intention of killing him at birth. How, in spite of the many prison guards, he'd been miraculously spirited away to safety in Gokul. How, in infancy, he killed a demoness who tried to poison him with her breast milk. How he lifted up Mount Govardhan to shelter his people from a deluge that would have drowned them. I didn't pay too much attention to the stories, some of which claimed that he was a god, descended from celestial realms to save the faithful. People loved to exaggerate, and there was nothing like a dose of the supernatural to spice up the drudgery of facts. But I admitted this much: there was something unusual about him.

Krishna couldn't have visited us often. He had his own kingdom in distant Dwarka to rule, and his many wives to placate. Additionally, he was involved in the affairs of several monarchies. He was known for his pragmatic intelligence, and kings liked to call on him for counsel. Yet whenever I had a serious question, something I couldn't ask Dhri, who was too straightforward for the knotted ways of the world, it seemed that Krishna was always there to provide an answer. And that too is a puzzle: why did my father allow him to visit me freely when he had kept me segregated from other men and women?

I was fascinated by Krishna because I couldn't decipher him. I fancied myself an astute observer of people and had already analyzed the other important people in my life. My father was obsessed by pride and the dream of getting even. He had absolute notions of right and wrong and adhered to them rigidly. (This made him a fair ruler, but not a beloved one.) His weakness was that he cared too much about what people might say about the royal house of Panchaal. Dhai Ma loved gossip, laughter, comfort, good food and drink, and, in her own way, power. (She routinely terrorized the lower servants—and, I suspect, Kallu—with her razor tongue.) Her weakness was her inability to say no to me. Dhri was the noblest of all the people I knew. He had a sincere love of virtue but, sadly, almost no sense of humor. He was overly protective of me (but I forgave him that). His weakness was that he believed completely in his destiny and had resigned himself to fulfilling it.

But Krishna was a chameleon. With our father, he was all astute politics, advising him on ways to strengthen his kingdom. He commended Dhri on his skill with the sword but encouraged him to spend more time on the arts. He delighted Dhai Ma with his outrageous compliments and earthy jests. And me? Some days he teased me until he reduced me to tears. On other days he gave me lessons on the precarious political situation of the continent of Bharat, and chastised me if my attention wandered. He asked me what I thought of my place in the world as a woman and a princess—and then challenged my rather traditional beliefs. He brought me news of the world that no one else cared to give me, the world that I was starving for—even news that I suspected would be considered improper for the ears of a young woman. And all the while he watched me carefully, as though for a sign.

But this I would recognize later. At that time, I only knew that I adored the way he laughed for no reason, quirking up an eyebrow. I often forgot that he was much older than me. Sometimes he dispensed with his kingly jewels and wore only a peacock feather in his hair. He was fond of yellow silk, which he claimed went well with his complexion. He listened with attention to my opinions even though he usually ended up disagreeing. He had been a friend of my father's for many years; he was genuinely fond of my brother; but I had the impression that it was I whom he really came to see. He called me by a special name, the female form of his own: Krishnaa. It had two meanings: *the dark one*, or *the one whose attraction can't be resisted*. Even after he returned to Dwarka, the notes of his flute lingered in the walls of our cheerless quarters—my only comfort as Dhri was called away more and more to his princely duties, and I was left behind.

milk

It was my turn to play storyteller. And so I began. But was *began* the right word? Hadn't Dhri and I been telling each other this story ever since we were old enough to realize the menace at its heart?

Once a boy came running in from play and asked, Mother, what is milk? My friends say it is creamy and white and has the sweetest taste, second only to the nectar of the gods. Please, mother, I want milk to drink.

The mother, who was too poor to buy milk, mixed some flour in water, added jaggery, and gave it to the boy.

The boy drank it and danced in joy, saying, Now I, too, know what milk tastes like!

And the mother, who through all the years of her hardship had never shed a tear, wept at his trust and her deception.

. . .

For hours the storm had flung itself at our walls. The ill-fitting shutters that covered the windows hadn't managed to keep out the gusts of freezing rain. The floor was slippery with wetness and the carpet at our feet sodden. I sighed, knowing it would smell of mold for weeks. The lamps flickered, threatening to abandon us to darkness. From time to time, a moth dived into a flame with a sizzling sound, a brief burning smell. On such nights, when the sudden crack of thunder flung our hearts up and down in startled exhilaration, Dhri and I told each other stories to keep our minds occupied. For though our days were overcrowded with lessons, our evenings stretched before us bare as a desert. The only one who ever shattered their monotony by his visits was Krishna. But he came and went without warning, taking mischievous pleasure in his unpredictability. The stories kept us from wondering too much about the rest of Drupad's family—his queens, and the other children whom we saw only on state occasions. What were they doing? Was our father in their lighted, laughing chambers? Why didn't he invite us to join them?

Dhri shook his head. "No! No! The story must start earlier."

"Very well," I said, hiding a smile. "When King Sagar discovered that his ancestors had been burnt to ashes by the anger of the great mendicant Kapil . . ."

At other times my brother took my teasing equably, but now it irritated him. It was as though the story made him regress into a younger, more anxious self. "You're wasting time," he scowled. "You know that's too early. Start with the two boys, the other ones."

. . .

Once in an innocent time, the son of a brahmin and the son of a king were sent to the ashram of a great sage to study. Here they spent many years together, growing into the best of friends, and when it was time for each to return to his home, they wept.

The prince said to his schoolmate, Drona, I will never forget you.

Come to me when I become king of Panchaal, and all I have will be yours as well.

The brahmin embraced the prince and said, Dear Drupad, your friendship means more to me than all the riches in the treasury of the gods. I will hold your words in my heart forever.

Each went his way, the prince to learn the ways of the court, the brahmin to study further with Parasuram, the renowned scholar-warrior. He mastered the arts of war, married a virtuous woman, and had a beautiful son. Though poor, he was proud of his learning and dreamed often of the day when he would teach his son all he knew.

Until one day the boy came home from play asking for milk, and his wife wept.

. . .

Were the stories we told each other true? Who knows? At the best of times, a story is a slippery thing. Certainly no one had told us this particular one, though it was the tale we most needed to know. It was, after all, the reason for our existence. We'd had to cobble it together from rumors and lies, dark hints Dhai Ma let fall, and our own agitated imaginings. Perhaps that was why it changed with each telling. Or is that the nature of all stories, the reason for their power?

Dhri was still dissatisfied. "You're looking at the story through the wrong window," he said. "You've got to close it and open a different one. Here, I'll do it."

. . .

A young prince inherited a troubled kingdom, a court filled with intrigue, legacy of a complacent king who had trusted his nobles too much. After much strife and bloodshed, when the son managed to es-

*tablish his power over these same nobles, he promised himself that he
would not repeat his father's error. He ruled well but watchfully, making closer friends with justice than with mercy. And always he listened
for whispers and mocking laughter, which to him were the forerunners of
insurgence.*

. . .

"You're too partial," I complained. "You're always trying to
make him look good, pretending he wasn't at fault."

He shrugged. "He *is* our father, after all! He deserves some
partiality!"

"I'm taking back the story," I said.

. . .

*One day, while the king held court, a brahmin came into the hall
and stood in front of him. The king was surprised to see that though his
clothes were threadbare, the man did not look like a supplicant. He stood
as straight as a flame, his head held high, his eyes shining like agates. A
submerged memory half rose in the king's mind, and sank again. Around
him he could hear murmurs, courtiers wondering who the stranger was.
He ordered a councillor to lead the stranger to the treasury, where each
day gifts were given to the needy, but the brahmin shook off the man's
hand.*

*Drupad, he said, his voice reverberating through the hall, I am no
beggar! I come to hold you to your promise of friendship. Once you
asked that I should come and live with you, that all you had would be
mine also. I do not want your riches, but I ask that you find a place for
me at your court. You will gain much from this, for I will share with you
the secret science of warfare that my guru taught me. No enemy would
dare to approach Panchaal with me at your side.*

I paused, knowing Dhri wanted the next part.

. . .

Like lightning an image etched itself against the king's eyelids, two boys embracing, wiping their tears at parting time. That old, dear name was on his tongue, Drona. *But behind him, people were laughing, pointing at the mad brahmin—for surely he was mad to speak with such presumption to the king!*

If Drupad acknowledged him, if he stepped down from the royal dais and took him by the hand, would they laugh at him, too? Would they think him weak and fanciful, unfit to rule?

He could not risk it.

Brahmin, he said sternly, how can a learned man such as you claim to bespeak such folly? Do you not know that friendship is possible only between equals? Go to the treasury door, and the gatekeeper will see to it that you get enough alms to live a comfortable life.

Drona stared at him for a moment. Drupad thought he could see his body shaking with rage and disbelief. He braced himself, thinking he would shout—lay a curse upon him, maybe, like brahmins were known to do. But Drona merely turned on his heel and left. None of the courtiers, when questioned later, knew where he went.

For days, weeks, perhaps months, Drupad could not taste anything he ate. Regret layered his mouth like mud. At night, lying sleepless, he considered sending messengers across the country, secretly, in search of his friend. In the morning it always seemed a foolish notion.

Dhri stopped. Having shaped our father's motivations the way he wished them to be, he was willing to let me tell the rest.

. . .

Time is the great eraser, both of sorrow and of joy. In time, the incident grew dim in Drupad's memory. In time, he married and fathered children, though none turned out to be as gifted a warrior as he had hoped.

The old rebellious nobles died or retired to their ancestral villages. The new ones respected or feared him, so that he believed himself to be safe. For him this was the same as happiness.

Until one dawn, before the sun was up, he was awakened by the sentries on the palace walls blowing their horns. The Kaurava army was at the gates of Kampilya.

Drupad was mystified. He'd had little to do with the Kaurava clan, whose kingdom lay to the northwest, in Hastinapur. From what he'd heard, their blind ruler, Dhritarashtra, was a quiet, careful man. Why would they attack him without provocation? He gathered his own formidable forces, and when he marched on the intruders, he was further mystified to find that the leaders of the foray were mere teenagers—the Kaurava princes, he gathered. What folly had possessed them? It was easy enough to rout their army. But as he turned his chariot back in victory, a new chariot approached him, moving so fast that he could not tell from where it came. A cloud of arrows flew from it, darkening the entire sky, cutting Drupad off from his army and causing his horses to rear up in alarm. Before his charioteer could calm them, a young man had leaped from the other chariot onto his. His sword was at Drupad's throat.

We do not wish to harm you, the young man said. But you must come with my brothers and myself as our prisoner.

. . .

Dhri laid a finger on my lips. For some paradoxical reason, he wanted to narrate the moment that pained him most, that laid bare his longing.

Even in mortal danger, Drupad could not but admire the young man—his poise, his courtesy, his skill at arms. A fleeting yearning rose up in him: if only he were my son.

"Don't say that!" I interrupted angrily. "You're the best son a father could ever desire. Aren't you giving up your entire life to get King Drupad what he wants—senseless though it is?"

"Go on with the story," he said.

. . .

Who are you? Drupad asked. And why have you attacked me when I have no enmity with you?

I am Arjun, son of the late King Pandu, the young man said. I have captured you at my guru's bidding.

Who is your guru?

A flash of proud love illumined Arjun's face. He is the greatest teacher of warcraft, he said. He taught us princes for many years. Now our studies are complete, and for his dakshina he has asked that we capture you. You must know of him. His name is Drona.

. . .

I paused here to picture the moment. How would Arjun have looked? How would he move? Was he good-looking as well as brave? Krishna, to whom he was related through some convoluted family tie, had mentioned his many accomplishments from time to time, piquing my interest. Though I would never confess this to Dhri (I sensed his unspoken jealousy), for me Arjun was the most exciting part of the story.

Dhri nudged me with a scowl. He was good at guessing my thoughts. "Go on."

. . .

A king was made to kneel at the feet of a brahmin.

A brahmin said to a king, Your land and life belong to me. Who is the beggar now?

A king said, Kill me, but do not mock me.

A brahmin said, But I do not wish to kill you. I wish to be your friend. And since you said that friendship was possible only between equals, I needed a kingdom. Now I will give you back half your land. South of the river Ganga, you will rule. The north will belong to me. Are we not truly equal, then?

A brahmin embraced a king, a king embraced a brahmin. And the anger that the brahmin had carried smoldering within him all these years left his body with his out-breath in the form of dark vapor, and he was at peace. But the king saw the vapor and knew it for what it was. Eagerly, he opened his mouth and swallowed it. It would fuel him for the rest of his life.

. . .

I was hoping Dhri would let it be, but he was like a hunting dog at a boar's throat: "And then?"

Suddenly I was tired and heartsick. I thought, I shouldn't have chosen this story. Every time I spoke it, it embedded itself deeper into my brother's flesh, for a story gains power with retelling. It deepened his belief in the inevitability of a destiny he might have otherwise sidestepped: to kill Drona. Yet like a scab that children pick at until it falls to bleeding, neither of us could leave it alone.

And then you were called into the world, Dhri. So that what started with milk could end one day in blood.

There was more to the story. Whose blood, and when, and how many times. All that, however, I would learn much later.

"What do you think Drona looks like?" Dhri asked.

But I had no idea.

. . .

Years later, after my marriage, I met Drona in the Kaurava court. He held our hands—for Dhri was with me, too—in his firm grasp and looked into us with his hooded eagle eyes. He knew of the prophecies by then. Everyone did. Still, with great courtesy, he said, Welcome, son. Welcome, daughter. I was breathless, unable to reply. Behind me, Dhri made a small sound in his throat. And I knew that he saw what I saw: Drona looked exactly like our father.

cosmology

"What is the form of the world?"

The prince recited, "Above are the heavens, abode of Indra and the gods who sit around his throne. There, in the center of the seven worlds peopled by celestial beings, lies the milky ocean on which Vishnu sleeps, waking only when the earth grows overburdened with unrighteousness. Below it stretches our earth, which would tumble into the great void if it were not supported upon the hoods of Sesha, the thousand-headed serpent. Further below is the underworld, where the demons, who hate the light of the sun, have their kingdom."

The tutor asked, "What is the origin of the four castes?"

"When the Supreme Being manifested Himself, the brahmin was born from his head, the kshatriya from his arm, the vaishya from his thigh, and the sudra from his foot."

"What therefore is the duty of the kshatriya?"

"The warrior-king must honor men of wisdom, treat other kings with the respect due to equals, and rule his people with a firm yet merciful hand. In war he should be fierce and fearless until death, for the warrior who dies on the battlefield goes to the highest of heavens. He must protect anyone who seeks refuge with him, be generous to the needy, and keep his given word though it lead to his destruction."

"And . . . ?"

My brother faltered, forcing me to offer assistance from behind the curtain. "Forefathers," I hissed. "Vengeance."

"And most of all," Dhri took a breath and continued, "he must bring renown to his forefathers by avenging the honor of his family."

Through the gauze of the curtain I could see the tutor frown. The holy thread that hung across his bony chest quivered with agitation. Though he was alarmingly learned, he wasn't much older than us. The curtain was there because otherwise my presence flustered him so much that he was quite unable to teach.

"O great prince," he said now, "kindly ask your sister princess to refrain from prompting you. She is not helping you to learn. Will she be sitting behind you in your chariot in battle when you need to remember these important precepts? Perhaps it is best if she no longer joins us during your studies."

He was always trying to discourage me from attending Dhri's lessons—and he wasn't the only one. At first, no matter how much I begged, King Drupad had balked at the thought of me studying with my brother. A girl being taught what a boy was supposed to learn? Such a thing had never been heard of in the royal family of Panchaal! Only when Krishna insisted that the prophecy at my birth required me to get an education beyond what women were usually given, and that it was the king's duty to provide this to me, did he agree with reluctance. Even Dhai Ma, my accomplice in so many other areas of my life, regarded the lessons with misgiving. She complained that they were making me too hardheaded and argumentative, too manlike in my speech. Dhri, too, sometimes wondered if I wasn't learning the wrong things, ideas that would only confuse me as I took up a woman's life with its prescribed, restrictive laws. But I hungered to know about the amazing, mysterious world that extended past what I could imagine, the world of the senses and of that which lay beyond them. And so I refused to give up the lessons, no matter who disapproved.

Now, not wanting to antagonize the tutor further, I made my voice contrite. "Respected teacher, my apologies. I promise not to interrupt again."

The tutor stared fixedly at the ground. "Great prince, kindly remind your sister that last week, too, she promised us the same thing."

Dhri hid his smile. "Most learned one, please forgive her. As you know, being a girl, she is cursed with a short memory. Additionally, she is of an impulsive nature, a failing in many females. Perhaps you could instruct her as to the conduct expected of a kshatriya woman?"

The tutor shook his head. "That is not my area of expertise, for it is not fitting that a celibate should think too much on the ways of women, who are the path to ruin. It would be better if the princess learns such things—and others as well—from the large and daunting lady who is her nurse and who can, one hopes, discipline her better than I. I will recommend this excellent course of action to your royal father."

I was dismayed by this sudden turn in events. No doubt my father, armed with the tutor's complaints, would try once again to dissuade me from attending the lessons. Now we'd spend a great deal of time arguing—rather, he would rant and I would be forced to listen. Or worse: he would order me to stop, and I would be forced to obey.

Additionally, I resented the tutor's declaration that women were the root of all the world's troubles. Perhaps that was why, when he gathered up his palm leaf manuscripts and rose to leave, I pushed the curtain aside and gave him a brilliant smile as I bowed. The effect was better than I had hoped. He jumped as though stung;

manuscripts fell, helter-skelter, from his hands. I had to pull the end of my sari over my face to hide my laughter, although I knew there would be trouble later. But inside a current surged through me at the discovery of a power I didn't know I had.

Dhri shot me a remonstrative look as he helped the tutor pick everything up. Later he would say, "Did you have to do that!"

"He was being so difficult. And all those things he accused women of—you know they're not true!"

I'd expected my brother to agree but instead he gave me a considering look. With a shock I realized that he was changing.

"Besides, it was just a smile!" I continued, but with less confidence.

"The problem with you is, you're too pretty for your own good. It'll get you into trouble with men sooner or later, if you're not careful. No wonder Father's been worrying about what to do with you."

I was surprised—first at the news that my father spared me any thought, and second at my brother's compliment, backhanded though it was. Dhri never commented on my looks; nor did he encourage me to comment on his. Such useless talk, he believed, made people vain. Was this another sign of change?

But I merely said, "How is it that Father never worries about you? Is it because you're so ugly?"

My brother refused to rise to the bait. "Boys are different from girls," he said with stolid patience. "When will you accept that?"

. . .

In revenge, the tutor shot a last comment at me from behind the safety of the door that led to the passage. "Prince, I have recalled one rule of conduct which you may tell your sister: A kshatriya woman's highest purpose in life is to support the warriors in her life: her father, brother, husband, and sons. If they should be called to war, she must be happy that they have the opportunity to fulfill a heroic destiny. Instead of praying for their safe return, she must pray that they die with glory on the battlefield."

"And who decided that a woman's highest purpose was to support men?" I burst out as soon as we were alone. "A man, I would wager! Myself, I plan on doing other things with my life."

Dhri smiled, but halfheartedly. "The tutor wasn't totally wrong. When I leave for the final battle, that's what I'd like you to pray for."

The word moved over me like a finger of ice. Not *if* but *when*. With what chill acceptance my brother spoke it. He left the room before I could contradict him.

I thought of the husband and sons that everyone assumed I would have someday. The husband I couldn't visualize, but the sons I imagined as miniature versions of Dhri, with the same straight, serious eyebrows. I promised myself I'd never pray for their deaths. I'd teach them, instead, to be survivors. And why was a battle necessary at all? Surely there were other ways to glory, even for men? I'd teach them to search for those.

I wished I could teach this to Dhri as well, but I feared it was too late. Already he had started thinking like the men around him, embracing the world of the court with open arms. And I? Each day I thought less and less like the women around me. Each day I moved further from them into a dusky solitude.

. . .

Dhri was given other lessons, though these I couldn't share.

Late mornings, he fought with sword and spear and mace with the commander of the Panchaal army. He learned to wrestle, to ride horses and elephants, to manage a chariot in case his charioteer was killed in battle. From the nishad who was my father's chief hunter, he learned archery and the ways of forest people: how to survive without food or water, how to read the spoor of animals. In the afternoons, he sat in court and observed my father dispensing justice. Evenings—for a king must know how to use his leisure appropriately—he played dice with other noble-born youth, or attended quail fights, or went boating. He visited the homes of courtesans, where he partook of drink, music, dance, and other pleasures. We never discussed these visits, though sometimes I spied on him when he returned late at night, his lips reddened from alaktaka, a garland around his neck. I spent hours imagining the woman who had placed it there. But no matter how much sura he drank or lotus fiber he ate, each morning my brother was up before daybreak. From my window I would see him bathe, shivering, in the cold water he insisted on drawing, himself, from our courtyard cistern, ignoring Dhai Ma's remonstrations. I would hear him chanting prayers to the sun. *O great son of Kashyap, colored like the hibiscus, O light of lights, destroyer of disease and sin, I bow to you.* And then, from the Manu Samhita, *He who has not conquered himself, how will that king conquer enemies?*

Some evenings, Dhri didn't go out. Instead, closeted in with one minister or another, he learned statecraft: the art of preserving a kingdom, of strengthening its borders, of allying with other rulers—or subduing them without battle, of recognizing spies who may have wormed their way into the palace. He learned also the differences between righteous and unrighteous war, and when to use each. These were the lessons I most envied him, the lessons that conferred power. They were the ones I needed to know if I were to change history. And so I cajoled Dhri shamelessly, forcing him to share reluctant bits with me.

"In righteous war, you fight only with men that are your equal in rank. You don't attack your enemies at night, or when they're retreating or unarmed. You don't strike them on the back or below the navel. You use your celestial astras only on warriors who themselves have such weapons."

"What about unrighteous war?"

"You don't need to know about that!" my brother said. "I've told you too much already. Why do you want all this information, anyway?"

. . .

One day I said, "Tell me about the celestial astras."

I didn't think he'd agree, but he shrugged. "I guess there's no harm in telling you, since you'll never have anything to do with them. They're weapons that must be invoked with special chants. They come from the gods and return to them after being used. The most powerful ones can be used only once in a warrior's lifetime."

"Do you have an astra? Can I see it?"

"They can't be seen, not until you've called them. And then you must use them right away; otherwise their power might turn against you. They say that some, like the Brahmastra, wrongly used, can destroy all of creation. In any case, I don't have any—not yet."

I had my suspicions about the existence of such astras. They sounded too much like tales old soldiers would make up to impress novices.

"Oh, they're real enough!" he said. "For instance, when Arjun captured our father, he used the Rajju astra to enclose him in an invisible net. That's the reason the Panchaal forces couldn't rescue him, even though he was only a spear's length away. But very few teachers know the art of summoning them. That's why Father has decided that when the time is right I must go to Drona in Hastina-pur and ask him to accept me as his student."

I stared at him in shock. Surely he was joking! But my brother never joked.

Finally I managed to say, "Father has no right to humiliate you this way! You must refuse. Besides, why would Drona agree to teach you when he knows you'll use the knowledge to try and kill him?"

"He'll teach me," my brother said. He must have been tired, for he sounded bitter, which was rare for him. "He'll teach me because he's a man of honor. And I'll go because it's the only way I can fulfill my destiny."

. . .

I don't wish to imply that King Drupad neglected my educa-tion. An unending stream of women flowed through my apartments each day, attempting to instruct me in the sixty-four arts that noble ladies must know. I was given lessons in singing, dancing, and play-ing music. (The lessons were painful, both for my teachers and me, for I was not musically inclined, nor deft on my feet.) I was taught to draw, paint, sew, and decorate the ground with age-old auspi-cious designs, each meant for a special festival. (My paintings were blotchy, and my designs full of improvisations that my teachers frowned at.) I was better at composing and solving riddles, respond-ing to witty remarks, and writing poetry, but my heart was not in such frivolities. With each lesson I felt the world of women tighten-ing its noose around me. I had a destiny to fulfill that was no less momentous than Dhri's. Why was no one concerned about prepar-ing me for it?

When I mentioned this to Dhai Ma, she clicked her tongue with impatience.

"Where do you get all these notions? Your destiny as important as the prince's!" She rubbed brahmi oil into my scalp to cool my brain. "Besides, don't you know, a woman must be prepared for her destiny in a different way."

Dhai Ma herself taught me the rules of comportment—how to walk, talk, and sit in the company of men; how to do the same when only women are present; how to show respect to queens who are more important; how to subtly snub lesser princesses; how to intimidate the other wives of my husband.

"I don't need to learn that!" I protested. "My husband won't take another wife—I'll make him promise that before I marry him!"

"Your arrogance, girl," she said, "is only exceeded by your optimism. Kings always take other wives. And men always break the promises they make before marriage. Besides, if you're married off like Panchaal's other princesses, you won't even get a chance to talk to your husband before he beds you."

I drew in a sharp breath to contradict her. She gave me a challenging grin. She relished our arguments, most of which she won. But this time I didn't launch into my usual tirade. Was it a memory of Krishna, the cool silence with which he countered disagreement, that stopped me? I saw something I hadn't realized before: words wasted energy. I would use my strength instead to nurture my belief that my life would unfurl uniquely.

"Perhaps you're right," I said sweetly. "Only time will tell."

She scowled. It wasn't what she was expecting. But then a different kind of grin appeared on her face. "Why, princess," she said, "I do believe you're growing up."

. . .

The day Dhai Ma told me I was ready to visit my father's wives to test my social skills, I was surprised by the excitement that surged through me. I hadn't realized how much I craved companionship. I'd long been curious about the queens—especially Sulochana—who flitted elegant and bejeweled along the periphery of my life. In the past I'd resented them for ignoring me, but I was willing to let go of that. Perhaps, now that I was grown, we could be friends.

Surprisingly, although the queens knew I was coming, I had to wait a long time in the visitor's hall before they appeared. When they did arrive, they spoke to me stiffly, in brief inanities, and wouldn't meet my eyes. I drew on all my speaking skills, but the conversations I began soon disintegrated into silence. Even Sulochana, whose blithe grace I had so admired during the festival of Shiva, seemed a different person. She responded to my greetings in monosyllables and kept her two daughters close to her. But one of them, a charming girl of about five years with curly hair and her mother's shining complexion, squirmed away from Sulochana and ran to me. Her eye must have been caught by the jeweled peacock pendant I wore—I'd dressed with care for the visit—for she put out a finger to touch it. I lifted her onto my lap and unclasped the chain so she could play with the pendant. But Sulochana snatched her away and slapped her so hard that red finger marks marred the child's fair cheek. She burst into bewildered tears, not knowing why she was punished. I stared at the queen in shock, my own face tingling with shame as though I were the one who'd been slapped. Soon afterward, Sulochana retired to her chambers with excuses of ill health that were clearly false.

When we reached my rooms, I couldn't hold back my tears. "What did I do wrong?" I asked Dhai Ma as I wept against her ample bosom.

"You did fine. Ignorant cows! They're just scared of you."

"Of me?" I asked, startled. I hadn't thought of myself as particularly fearsome. "Why?"

She pressed her lips together, angrier than I'd ever seen her. But she couldn't—or wouldn't—give me an answer.

I began to notice things, though. My maidservants—even those who had been with me for years—kept their distance until summoned. If I asked them anything of a personal nature—how their families were, for instance, or when they were getting married—they grew tongue-tied and escaped from my presence as soon as they could. The best merchants in the city, who routinely visited the apartments of the queens, would send their wares to me through Dhai Ma. Even my father was uneasy when he visited me and rarely looked directly into my eyes. I began to wonder whether Dhri's tutor's nervousness at my interruptions had a less flattering cause than my beauty. And whether my lack of friends and visitors was due not to my father's strictness but to people's wariness of someone who wasn't born like a normal girl and who, if the prophecy was correct, wouldn't live a normal woman's life.

Did they fear contagion?

Already the world I knew was splitting in two. The larger part, by far, consisted of people like Sulochana who couldn't see beyond their little lives of mundane joys and sorrows. They suspected anything that fell outside the boundaries of custom. They could, perhaps, accept men like Dhri who were divinely born, to fulfill a destiny shaped by the gods. But women? Especially women who might bring change, the way a storm brings the destruction of lightning? All my life, they would shun me. But the next time, I promised myself as I wiped my angry tears, I would be prepared.

The other group consisted of those rare persons who were themselves harbingers of change and death. Or those who could laugh at such things. They wouldn't fear me, though I suspected they might well hate me, if the need arose. So far, I knew only three such people: Dhri and Krishna—and Dhai Ma, transformed by her affection for me. But surely there were others. As I chafed in my father's palace, I longed to find them, for only they could provide the companionship I ached for. I wondered how long I would have to wait before destiny brought them into my life, and I hoped that when it did so, one of them would become my husband.

smoke

Early in my life, I learned to eavesdrop.

I was driven to this ignoble practice because people seldom told me anything worth knowing. My attendants were trained to speak in elaborate flatteries. My father's wives avoided me. King Drupad only met with me in settings designed to discourage uncomfortable questions. Dhri never lied, but he often kept things from me, believing it his brotherly duty to shield me from unpleasant facts. Though Dhai Ma had no such qualms, she had the unfortunate habit of mixing up what actually happened with things that, in her opinion, should have occurred. Krishna was the only one who told me the truth. But he wasn't with me often enough.

So I took to eavesdropping and found it a most useful practice. It worked best when I appeared engrossed in some mindless activity, such as embroidery, or pretended to sleep. I was amazed at all the things I learned in this manner.

It was how I discovered the sage.

. . .

The sairindhri was braiding my hair in the five-rivers design when I heard one of the maids say, in a squeaky, excited whisper,

"And he promised I'll be married on full moon day in the month of Sravan—"

"So?" Dhai Ma responded scathingly from the next room, where she was setting out my clothes. "Fortune-tellers are always predicting weddings. They know that's what foolish girls want to hear most. That's how they get fatter fees."

"No, no, respected aunt, this sadhu didn't take any money. Also, he didn't just make vague promises. He said I'd marry a man who tends the king's animals. And as you know, Nandaram, who works in the stables, has been courting me! Didn't I show you the silver armband he gave me last month?"

"It's a long leap from an armband to the wedding fire, girl! Come Sravan, we'll see how accurate your holy man was. Now set out that blue silk sari carefully! And watch how you handle the princess's breast cloth. You're crushing it!"

"But he told me about my past, too," the maid insisted. "Accidents and illnesses I had when I was a girl. The year my mother died and what her last words were. He even knew about the time Nanda and I—" here her voice dipped shyly, leaving me to guess at details.

"You don't say!" Dhai Ma sounded intrigued. "Maybe I'll go see him. Ask him if that good-for-nothing Kallu will ever change his ways, and if not, what I must do to be rid of him. What did you say the Babaji's name was?"

"I didn't ask. Truth to tell, he scared me, with a beard that covered his whole face and glittery red eyes. He looked like he could put a curse on you if you made him angry."

"Princess," my sairindhri said, bowing. "Your hair is done. Does it please you?"

I picked up the heavy silver-backed mirror while she held another one behind my head. The five-stranded braid hung glossily down my back, sparkling with gold pins. I could smell the fragrance of the amaranths woven into it. It was beautiful, but it only made me dissatisfied. What use was all this dressing-up when there was no one to admire me? I felt as though I were drowning in a backwater pond while everything important in the world was happening elsewhere.

What if the prophecy at my birth was wrong? Or: what if prophecies only became true if you did something about them?

I decided that I'd accompany Dhai Ma to the holy man.

. . .

"Absolutely not!" Dhai Ma exclaimed. "Your royal father will have my head—or at the very least my job—if I take you outside the palace. Do you want your poor old nurse to starve by the roadside in her old age?"

"You won't starve," I said. "Kallu will take care of you!"

"Who? That no-good drunkard? That—"

"Besides," I interjected deftly, "my father doesn't have to know. I'll dress up as a servant maid. We can just walk to—"

"You! Walk on the common road where every man can look into your face! Don't you know that the women of the Panchaal royal family are supposed to remain hidden even from the gaze of the sun?"

"You can get me a veil. It'll protect me from men and sunshine, both at once."

"Never!"

I was reduced to pleading. "Please, Dhai Ma! It's my one chance to know what my future holds."

"*I* can tell you what your future holds. Severe punishment from your royal father, and a new Dhai Ma, since this one's life will be prematurely terminated."

But because I was the closest thing she had to a daughter, or because she sensed the desperation beneath my cajolery, or maybe because she, too, was curious, she finally relented.

. . .

Swathed in one of Dhai Ma's veils and a skirt several sizes too large, I knelt in front of the sage, touching my head awkwardly to the ground. My entire body ached. To get to the banyan grove where the sage was residing, we'd had to ride in a palanquin through the city, then cross a lake on a leaking ferry boat, then sit for hours on a rickety bullock cart. It taught me a new respect for the hardiness of commoners.

I was startled by a rumble like a thundercloud. The sage was laughing. He didn't look too frightening. In his lined, cracked face, his eyes shone mischievously.

"Not bad, for a princess!"

"How did you know?" I said in chagrin.

"I'd have to be blind not to see through such a terrible disguise. At least the old woman could have given you some clothes that fit! But enough of that. Eager to learn your future, are you? Did you ever think how monotonous your life would be if you could see all that was coming to you? Believe me, I know! However, I'll oblige you both—in some part. You first, old woman."

He informed a delighted Dhai Ma that Kallu would perish soon in a drunken brawl, that she'd accompany me to my new palace after marriage, and that she'd bring up my five children. "You'll die old and rich and cantankerous as ever—and happy, because you'll be gone before the worst happens."

"Sadhu-baba," Dhai Ma asked in concern, "what do you mean by *the worst*?"

"No more!" he snapped, his eyes turning tawny, making her

cower. "Princess, if you want your questions answered, you must step inside the circle."

I hadn't noticed the thin circle etched into the ground around him. Dhai Ma grabbed at my skirt, whispering about witchcraft, but I didn't hesitate. Inside the circle, the earth felt hot against my blistered soles.

"Brave, eh?" he said. "That's good—you'll need it." He threw a handful of powder onto a small fire. A thick smoke rose until I couldn't see anything outside the circle.

"What's that?" I gasped.

"Curious, too!" His voice was approving. "I made it myself, from resin and neem leaves and a few other select ingredients. It keeps the mosquitoes away."

In the smoke, shapes—humanlike, yet not human—rose and fell as though caught in a wind current.

"What are those?" To my embarrassment, my voice trembled.

"Ah, that's the other thing the mixture does—call up the spirits. You may ask them your questions."

Far within the banyan grove, I heard a jackal howl. Coldness passed over my skin like ghost breath. For the last few days, I'd been longing for this moment. Why, then, did a strange reluctance silence me now? It came to me that I didn't trust the sage enough to reveal to him my secret desires.

Later I would wonder, was it because of this lack of faith that the spirits answered me so obliquely, in riddles that were more hindrance than help?

"Scared, princess?" the sage taunted. "Maybe you'd better step out and return to your safe palace—"

"No!" I cried. "Ask your spirits if I will get what I desire."

A smile—feral or condescending?—glinted through the sage's beard. "And do you even know what that is, child?"

Stung, I retorted, "I'm no child, and I do know what I want! I want to leave a mark on history, as was promised to me at my birth."

"Very commendable! But there are other things—perhaps unknown to you—that you crave more. No matter. The spirits will see into your heart and answer accordingly."

He clapped his hands and the spirits swirled faster. Yellow whispers came to me through the smoke.

You will marry the five greatest heroes of your time. You will be queen of queens, envied even by goddesses. You will be a servant maid. You will be mistress of the most magical of palaces and then lose it.

You will be remembered for causing the greatest war of your time.

You will bring about the deaths of evil kings—and your children's, and your brother's. A million women will become widows because of you. Yes, indeed, you will leave a mark on history.

You will be loved, though you will not always recognize who loves you. Despite your five husbands, you will die alone, abandoned at the end—and yet not so.

After the voices fell silent, I sat stunned. Much of what they said—the part about five husbands, for instance—confused me. The rest filled me with despair.

"Oh, don't look so dejected," the sage said. "How many women can claim to be envied by goddesses? Or become queen of queens?"

"I don't want them if it means the other parts will be true as well. What good is it to own the most wonderful palace in the world if I'll have to lose it? And all those deaths! I refuse to be the cause for them, especially Dhri's."

"You don't have a choice, my dear."

"I'll enter a hermitage! I'll never marry—"

His crooked teeth flashed. "Destiny is strong and swift. You can't trick it so easily. Even if you hadn't come seeking it today, in time it would have found you. But in your case, your own nature is going to speed its process."

"What do you mean?"

"Your pride. Your temper. Your vengefulness."

I glared at him. "I'm not like that!"

"Even the wisest don't know what's hidden in the depths of their being. But here's something to console you: Long after you're gone, men will remember you as the most amazing queen this land has seen. Women will chant your name to bring them blessing and luck."

"Much good that'll do me when I'm dying alone, tortured by guilt!" I said bitterly. "Men might value fame above all things. But I'd rather be happy."

"You'll have happiness, too. Didn't you hear the spirits say you'll be loved? Besides, I have a feeling you'll grow to feel differently about fame!"

His jocularity angered me, but I controlled myself because I needed his help. "I've heard that great seers have the power to change the future they foretell. Please—can't you shape mine so that I don't harm those dearest to me?"

He shook his head. "Only a fool meddles in the Great Design. Besides, your destiny is born of lifetimes of karma, too powerful for me to change. But I'll give you some advice. Three dangerous moments will come to you. The first will be just before your wedding: at that time, hold back your question. The second will be when your husbands are at the height of their power: at that time, hold back your laughter. The third will be when you're shamed as you'd never imagined possible: at that time, hold back your curse. Maybe it will mitigate the catastrophes to come."

He poured water on the fire, extinguishing it with a hiss, a signal for me to leave. But then, glancing at my unhappy face, he said,

"You've borne the harshness of the prophecies well, so I'll give you a parting gift—a name. From now on you'll be known as Panchaali, spirit of this land, though in your wanderings you'll leave it far behind." He turned to a thick book made of palm leaves and opened it.

"What are you writing?" I couldn't help but ask.

He ran a hand through his thick mane, exasperated. "The story of your life, if only you'd stop interrupting it. And of your five husbands. And of the great and terrible war of Kurukshetra that will end the Third Age of Man. Already you've kept me from it for too long. Go now!"

. . .

"Done so quickly?" Dhai Ma asked. "He didn't have much to tell you, did he?"

"What do you mean?"

"Why, you barely stepped in, then stepped out. I'm glad, though." She dropped her voice as she pulled me toward the waiting cart. "These sages with their sorcery—you never know what they might do to a young virgin."

Inside the sage's circle, had time taken on a different gait? I climbed onto the cart, too preoccupied to feel its jolts. I peered through the shadows of the banyan one last time. The gloomy light played tricks on me: it seemed that there were two figures sitting inside the circle. One of them was the sage. The other—why, he appeared to have an elephant's head! The cart lurched away before I could point him out to my nurse.

"What did he say?" Dhai Ma was all curiosity. "Nothing bad, I hope. You look so solemn. I knew this heat would be too much for you! Remind me to get you some green-coconut water when we go through the bazaar."

I pondered what to tell her. "He prophesied that I'd have five husbands," I said finally.

"Five husbands!" She slapped her forehead in disgust. "Now I know he's a fake! Why, in all my years I've never heard of a woman with more than one husband! You know what our shastras call women who've been with more than one man, don't you? Though no one seems to have a problem when men sleep with a different wife each day of the week! Can you see your royal father, proper as he is, ever allowing something scandalous like that?"

I hoped she was right. If that part didn't come true, then perhaps the others wouldn't either.

Dhai Ma heaved a sigh. "He probably made up the bit about Kallu dying, too! I'll probably be the one to perish first, the way that man tortures me day and night. What a waste of time this was! Oh, my aching back! Wait till we get back to the palace. I'll give that maid a box on her ear that she won't forget for the rest of her life."

. . .

Each night I thought of my name. Already I'd insisted that everyone address me by it. *Princess Panchaali*. A name strong like the land, a name that knew how to endure. It was what I'd been waiting for. No matter what else came to pass, I would always thank the sage for giving it to me. I thought also of the palace the spirits had promised me. Most magical, they'd called it. I wondered how I would ever gain such a palace.

I didn't want to contemplate the other prophecies—they were too disheartening—but they knocked against my heart. I understood, suddenly, the unspoken questions the spirits had answered: Who would I marry? Would I ever be mistress of my own home? Would I find love? Were these the kinds of desires hidden in my heart? How puerile they were, things my maids might have wanted!

Was I then no better than the women who surrounded me, wrapped in the cocoons of their unimaginative lives, not even knowing enough to want to escape? It was a mortifying thought.

Other nights I considered the mystery of the book the sage showed me, the story of my life. How could such a book be written before I'd lived the incidents it described? Did this mean that I had no control over what was to happen?

Surely it wasn't so. Otherwise, why did he take the trouble to warn me?

. . .

I didn't speak to the sage again for many years, though I heard of him from time to time. I learned his name: Vyasa the Compendious, because of the many hefty books he'd written. Vyasa the seer, born on a dark island of a union between an ascetic and a fisher princess. On my wedding day, I would see him in the marriage hall, seated on my father's right, his placement revealing an importance I hadn't guessed at. He'd gaze at me, blinking mildly, as though he'd never seen me before. When I'd make my first great mistake, his expression would remain unchanged, so that I wouldn't realize the enormity of what I'd done until it was too late.

Later, among my wedding gifts, I'd find a wooden box. When I'd open it, a familiar smell, wild and bitter, would rise from the powder inside. I'd use it in Khandav, and later in the Kamyak forest. Thrown on fire, it warded away insects, just as he'd promised, and nightmares as well. On those nights, my rough bark-bed seemed softer. But no matter how much I called for them—for by now I had other, wiser questions—the spirits did not return to me again.

incarnations

The palace was in turmoil because Sikhandi had returned.

My maids gathered in corners and corridors, whispering fervently, but they scattered like sparrows when I approached them. Dhri was shut up in council with our father, so I had no way of asking him. And Dhai Ma, when she finally appeared, wringing her hands, was so distraught that I could hardly get any sense out of her.

"But who is Sikhandi? And why is everyone so afraid of her?"

"She is—was—oh, I don't know how to say it!—your royal father's eldest daughter, then she did something terrible and King Drupad sent her away. Now she's returned. They say for the last twelve years she's been in a forest somewhere, performing the strictest austerities—eating only leaves of the holy bel tree, standing neck-deep in freezing water all winter, that kind of thing—so that now she's been turned into a great and dangerous warrior."

I was intrigued by this sister whose existence had been hidden so successfully. (What else, I would wonder later, had they been keeping from me?) I'd never met a woman who was a dangerous warrior. "I'd like to see her," I said.

"Well, I guess that's a good thing," Dhai Ma muttered, "because

Sikhandi wants to see you, too. This afternoon, in fact. Only—she isn't really a woman anymore."

"Do you mean she no longer behaves like one?" I asked. Dhai Ma had a lengthy compendium of rules as to how women should behave. For years she'd tried to din them into my head. Already I felt sympathy for the unknown Sikhandi.

But Dhai Ma sped off, with more hand-wringing, to ensure that the noon meal befitted the dignity of a great and dangerous warrior. She paused only to inform me that Dhri, who usually ate with me, would not be here because Sikhandi had expressed a desire to speak with me alone.

I waited with some excitement to view my sudden-found sister. I wondered what she looked like. Was her body hard and muscular, her arms scarred from weapons? Or was it her heart that had changed so that it no longer shook at the thought of killing? How had she survived in the forest—for she must have been just a girl when she left? What terrible crime could she have committed for our father to banish her at that tender age? And why did she want to speak with me, alone? Perhaps finally I'd have in her what I'd so longed for: a friend with whom to whisper and laugh about silly things, to exchange ornaments and confidences, to tell my secrets— even that of the spirits' prophecy, which I held inside me like a dark, jagged rock.

. . .

Sikhandi walked with a panther grace, light and assured on the balls of his feet. Yes, *his*. What I'd interpreted as Dhai Ma's expression of disapproval was the literal truth: Sikhandi, who was born a woman, was now a man! Clearly, he wished there to be no misunderstanding about this: he was clothed only in a white cotton dhoti, his wiry upper body bare, his nipples flat and burnished as copper coins. He carried a bow, which he leaned against the wall before approaching me. His cheekbones were like knives. His almond-shaped eyes gave him a foreignness that was not unattractive. Around his neck hung a garland of white lotuses.

Silently he put out his hands to touch my cheeks. I hesitated—he was a stranger, after all—but then I allowed it. His fingers were slim, like a woman's, and callused from stringing a bow. A shiver went through me as they grazed my face. I noticed that we were the same height, and somehow this consoled me for the loss of the sister he was supposed to be.

He smiled past the shadows in his almond eyes. He stood on tiptoe to kiss my forehead. "Little sister," he said. "I thank you from the depth of my soul for what you'll do for me."

. . .

Sikhandi stayed with me for a day and a night, and in that time he told me his story.

He said: Have you heard the fable of the donkey that wrapped himself in a lion's hide so the other animals would fear him? Or of the wolf that hid under sheepskin so he could mingle undetected with his prey? I feel like both sometimes. A fake—or a hidden menace.

No, I didn't pray to the gods to be changed. I'd lost faith in them a lifetime ago. This time I invoked a yaksha. He appeared in the sky with his burning demon sword. When he heard what I wanted, he laughed and plunged it into me. The pain was unbearable. I fainted. When I awoke, I was a man. And yet not completely so, for though my form was changed, inside me I remembered how women thought and what they longed for.

I had to be a man, because only a man can do what I must accomplish—kill the greatest warrior of our time.

Yes, someone greater even than Drona.

His name is Bheeshma the terrible. He is guardian of Hastinapur and granduncle to that prince, Arjun, who defeated our father, and Drona's friend. Tangled indeed is the web of this world!

This garland? You've noticed it doesn't fade? I've worn it for twelve years now. I was six when I found it hanging on the palace gate and placed it around my neck. Our father cried, What have you done, you foolish, unlucky girl! But I hadn't taken it in childish fancy, as he supposed, and nothing he did would make me put it back. Finally he banished me so that the ill luck rising from my action wouldn't haunt his house.

Oh, he and I are father and child indeed! We both live for vengeance.

When I wore the garland, my previous life, which I had remembered only in glimpses, fell upon me like a flood.

First I remembered my death upon a pyre: flesh melting, eyelids burnt away, the skull bursting. And through it all: my impatience to be gone. Because without death there is no rebirth, and without rebirth I could not kill Bheeshma.

The god Shiva himself had promised me that in my next life I would kill him whom no man had defeated before.

My name? In that body I was Amba, the princess of Kasi, the rejected one.

Very well, the story from the beginning, then. We three sisters, princesses of Kasi, were to marry. My father arranged a swayamvar, inviting all the kings of the land, so that we could choose our husbands. I already knew the man I wanted: King Salva, who had wooed me for a year.

The garland for Salva was in my hands when Bheeshma descended on us like a plague. He forced the three of us onto his chariot and took us, terrified, to Hastinapur, to marry us to his younger brother.

When I'd recovered wits and breath, I told him, I love Salva. I can't marry your brother.

The brother said, A woman who has embraced another in her heart is not chaste. I do not wish to marry her.

Bheeshma said, Very well, I will send you back to Salva.

But when I went to him, Salva said, Bheeshma has taken you by the hand. You've been contaminated by his touch. You belong to him now.

I said, If someone grasps my hand against my will, how does that make me his? I said, I'm the one who decides to whom I belong.

In the sandalwood days of love I'd thought that if I could not have Salva, I would die. Now I discovered that a woman's life is tougher than a banyan root, which exists without soil or water. For Salva forced me to return to Bheeshma, and still I lived.

I told Bheeshma, My happiness has crumbled into dust because of you. Marry me so that at least my honor can be saved.

Bheeshma said, Forgive me. In youth I promised my father I would never marry. I cannot go back on my word.

I said, What is a dead vow, compared to a living woman's ruin?

He didn't answer. When I looked on his serene face, hatred filled me with its black haze, more hatred than I'd ever thought I could feel.

Abandoned and shamed, I went from court to court, seeking a champion who would battle Bheeshma, but all were afraid of him. I went to the Himalayas in my despair and performed austerities so that the gods would help me. Years passed; my youth fell away. The gods were reluctant to interfere because Bheeshma was the son of

Ganga, goddess of the sacred river. Finally, the child-god Kartikeya took pity and appeared before me with this garland. He said, If you can find someone to wear it, he will defeat Bheeshma.

My hopes rekindled, I went back to the kings with the everlasting garland. But the cowards! In spite of a god's assurance, they were still afraid. Even King Drupad, known in that time as a champion of the weak, dared not accept it. In disgust I flung it on his palace gate and went to my death.

The humor of the gods is cruel; or perhaps they see more than we do. I was reborn as Drupad's daughter. The moment I set eyes on the garland-that-never-fades, my past returned to me, and with it my rage. I took the garland for myself, determined to do on my own what no man dared do for me.

Remember that, little sister: wait for a man to avenge your honor, and you'll wait forever.

. . .

Later I asked Krishna, "What Sikhandi said about his past life, was it really true?"

Krishna shrugged. "He believes it to be so. Isn't that what truth is? The force of a person's believing seeps into those around him—into the very earth and air and water—until there's nothing else."

Oh, it was hard to get a direct answer from Krishna!

"Could he really have been Amba in a previous incarnation?" I persisted. "Or did he—through some strange empathy—feel her sorrow so deeply that he resolved to avenge her?"

"We all have past lives," Krishna said, though that wasn't what I'd asked. "Highly evolved beings remember them, while lesser souls forget."

"No doubt you remember yours."

"I do! Once I was a fish. I saved mankind from the great flood.

Once I was a boar. I lifted Earth out of the primordial waters with my tusks. Once, as a giant tortoise——"

"Wait!" I interrupted. "Those are the incarnations of Vishnu! I read about them in the Puranas."

He lifted his shoulders and spread his hands. "There's no fooling you, Krishnaa! In you, I've met my match!"

I eyed him with suspicion. I never could tell when he was joking.

Then he said, "I remember your last life, too."

I tried to feign indifference, but I couldn't keep it up. "Tell me!" I cried.

"You were just as impatient then. In meditation, you invoked Shiva. He came and stood in front of you, silent and blue as moonlight. You asked for a wish to be granted. He smiled. You asked for it again——and again. Five times you made your wish before he had the chance to say yes. Therefore, in this life, you will have what you wanted five times over."

Five. The word beat upon my heart, and the warnings of the sage, which I'd managed to push to the back of my mind over the last months, stung me again like poisonweed.

"What was my wish?" I asked, my throat dry.

"Haven't you had enough of prophecies yet!" Krishna said. His eyes, bright with amusement, were like black bees.

. . .

King Drupad had invited Sikhandi to stay with him, but Sikhandi politely excused himself. (Drupad tried, unsuccessfully, to disguise his relief at this.) However, when Sikhandi said that he would like to stay with my brother and me instead, I sensed our father's uneasiness. Perhaps he was worried that Sikhandi would be a corrupting influence! But I was delighted. Something about Sikhandi drew me to him. Was it his easy acceptance of me? His own unusual life? He bore his destiny so casually, it made me worry less about Dhri's and mine. He made me realize the existence of possibilities I hadn't dreamed of.

We whiled away his short visit in eating and storytelling and playing at dice (for Dhri had taught me this most unladylike pastime). We laughed a great deal, often at the littlest things. I composed poems and riddles to entertain my brothers and watched as they practiced with swords.

Dhri bested Sikhandi easily, then asked with concern, "How are you going to defeat Bheeshma?"

"I don't have to defeat him," Sikhandi said. "I just have to kill him."

Reluctant to let him leave my life, I tried to tempt Sikhandi to remain longer. Was it because one day (if the prophecy about my husbands was true) I, too, would cross the bounds of what was allowed to women? I promised to write a poem in his praise, to let him win at dice, to have Dhai Ma cook his favorite fish curry. Dhri offered to teach him the newest wrestling holds.

Sikhandi shook his head, his eyes regretful. "Thank you for making me so welcome," he said. "All my life, people have been glad to see me leave."

Dhri gave him his favorite horse and the best spear in the armory. I gave him sweet laddus to eat on the way, and a yak-hair shawl against the approaching winter. In its folds I had secreted gold coins. I imagined his face when he'd discover them on a cold and hungry day in an unfriendly town.

But he would take nothing.

"To start my penance," he explained, "I must travel light, living off only what the land yields."

"Penance!" I cried. "For what? It's others who should be doing penance for all the ways in which they've let you down."

"To kill the greatest warrior of one's time is a terrible deed," he said, "no matter what the cause. It weakens the foundations of society. It's worse when it's done through trickery—and that's what I'll have to resort to, because certainly I don't have the skill to achieve it otherwise. I'm atoning for it in advance, as it's very likely that I, too, will die in the process."

Under the shadow of the palace gates, Dhri said, "Brother, you've been both woman and man. You must know secrets that others don't. Share some of your wisdom with us."

Sikhandi's lips twisted in a bitter smile. "Yes, I've learned a few things along the way, though now that I'm neither man nor woman they can't do me any good. But here's one that may be of use to you: the power of a man is like a bull's charge, while the power of a woman moves aslant, like a serpent seeking its prey. Know the particular properties of your power. Unless you use it correctly, it won't get you what you want."

His words perplexed me. Wasn't power singular and simple? In the world that I knew, men just happened to have more of it. (I hoped to change this.) I would have to ponder Sikhandi's words.

But I had something else to ask before he left. I grasped his hands one last time, feeling those calluses. I'd tried to soften them with a paste, but he'd stopped me. "What's the use?" he'd said. "I'll just have to grow myself some more."

"When we first met," I asked, "why did you thank me?"

"I thanked you because you'll help me fulfill my destiny."

"How?"

"You'll bring about the Great War where I'll meet Bheeshma and kill him." His face darkened. "But I should have begged your pardon instead for all the humiliation you'll suffer before the war, and all the sorrow afterward. And much of this you'll endure, sister, because your destiny is linked with mine."

fish

I sat stubbornly under a jamun tree in my garden, trying to concentrate on a volume of nyaya shastra. It was a large and laborious book that set out the laws of the land, which my brother was currently studying. (Soon after Sikhandi's visit, Father had terminated my lessons with his tutor, declaring that I needed to focus on more feminine interests.) Around me summer unfurled its drowsy petals in a conspiracy to distract me. Insects sang. Luscious purple jamuns dropped lazily onto thick grass. The paired cry of bright birds pulled at my chest, releasing a strange restlessness. (Was this a feminine interest?) My companions, daughters of courtiers, clustered themselves under canopies hoisted to protect our complexions. (They'd been inflicted on me after Sikhandi's visit by my father. He hoped they would be a good influence, but they merely annoyed me.) They murmured gossip, chewed betel leaf to redden their lips, exchanged recipes for love potions, pouted, giggled without reason, and emitted suitably feminine shrieks if a bee orbited too close. From time to time they sent me beseeching glances. If only I'd decide to go back inside the palace! This pitiless sun—even with a canopy, it was so bad for the skin! They'd have to spend hours soaked in yogurt and turmeric paste to counter its ravages!

I ignored them sternly and continued to read. The book, which described in diligent, morose detail complicated laws concerning household property—including servants and wives—caused my eyelids to droop. But I was determined to learn what a king was supposed to know. (How else could I aspire to be different from these giddy girls, or from my father's wives, who spent their days vying for his favors? How else could I be powerful in myself?) So I ignored summer's blandishments and battled with the book.

But I was fated never to finish learning nyaya shastra. For even as I turned the page Dhai Ma came from the palace, waddling as fast as her bulk would allow. Out of breath and wheezing, her face an alarming red, she shooed my companions away. Then she whispered the news in my ear (but in her excitement she was so loud that everyone heard): my father had decided—Sikhandi's visit must have stirred up a veritable storm of anxiety in him—that I was to be married next month.

. . .

Ever since the prophecy, I'd thought intermittently of marriage—at times with excitement or resignation, at times with dread. I sensed, vaguely, that it was a great opportunity—but for what I wasn't sure. I'd imagined that it would be similar to the weddings of my father's other daughters: arranged by elders. But Dhai Ma informed me I was to have a swayamvar. Eligible rulers from every kingdom in Bharat would be invited to Panchaal. From among them, my father had announced, I would choose the man I was to marry.

After the initial shock, I was filled with exhilaration. I ran to find Dhri. "I can't believe I'm going to pick my own husband!" I cried. "Why didn't you tell me?"

"Don't get so excited," he replied glumly. "Something always goes wrong in a swayamvar—either while it's happening, or later."

I felt a twinge of foreboding, but I refused to let Dhri's words ruin my mood. He was too cautious. Sometimes I told him that the gods must have got mixed up when they pushed us out from the fire. He should have been the girl, and I the boy!

"I wish Father hadn't made this decision so hastily," he said.

"You're just jealous that I get to choose my own spouse when you don't!" I joked. As a matter of fact, Dhri was quite taken with the neighboring princess to whom our father had betrothed him. I'd surprised him a couple of times, gazing solemnly at her portrait, which he kept hidden behind a stack of scrolls. But a question gnawed at me: Why would our father, who delighted in control, allow me so much freedom?

"Is it really going to happen?" I asked Dhri. "Or is he going to suddenly change his mind?"

"It'll happen. He's sent out a hundred messengers to invite the most important kings. Pleasure palaces are already being built for them and—"

But Krishna—when had he entered the room?—laughed, startling me.

"Oh, it'll happen, Krishnaa, but it may not be what you're imagining. Truth, like a diamond, has many facets. Tell her, Dhristadyumna. Tell her about the test."

· · ·

This was what they'd planned, my father the king, along with his ministers and priests, for the good of Panchaal and the honor of the house of Drupad: before the wedding, there would be a test of skill. The king who won it would be the one I'd garland.

"Why even call it a swayamvar, then?" I cried. "Why make a spectacle of me before all those kings? It's my father, not I, who gets to decide whom I'll marry."

Dhri looked unhappy, but he spoke firmly. "No, fate will decide that. It's not an ordinary test that Father's setting your suitors. They must pierce a fish made of metal, revolving high on the ceiling of the wedding hall."

His support of our father made me angrier. "What's so difficult about that? Isn't that the first thing warriors learn, how to hit a moving target? Or do your enemies sit on the battlefield, waiting for your arrow to come and find them?"

"There's more to it," he explained, his voice patient. "They can't look directly at the target but only at its reflection in a pool of whirling water. They must shoot five arrows through a tiny hole in a shield to hit the target. Nor can they use their own weapons."

"They must use the Kindhara, the heaviest bow in existence," Krishna added helpfully. "Your father borrowed it, after much supplication, from the gods. There's only a handful of warriors in the world today strong enough to lift it up, and fewer still that can string it."

I glared at them both. "Wonderful!" I said. "So he's set them an impossible task! Is he mad?"

"Not impossible," Krishna said. "I know someone who can accomplish it. Arjun, the third Pandava prince, my dearest friend."

"Arjun?" I said in surprise. "You never told us he was your dearest friend!"

"There are many things I haven't told you," Krishna said, quite unapologetic.

Dhri's eyes were eager. "Is he really the greatest archer of his time?"

"I think so," Krishna said. "He's handsome, too, and a great favorite with the ladies. I think our Krishnaa will like him!"

His words had made me curious, though I wouldn't give him the satisfaction of seeing that. "Why would our father want me to marry the man who humiliated him?" I asked.

"Arjun didn't humiliate him!" Dhri said quickly. "He was only following Drona's orders. A warrior has the greatest respect for the man who defeats him in battle."

Men! They lived by strange rules. I wanted to ask Dhri why our father hated Drona so much, then, since Drona had been the mastermind behind that defeat. But I allowed myself to drift to more pleasant thoughts. To be the beloved of the greatest archer of our time. To be the woman whose smile made his heart beat faster, whose frown wounded him almost to death, whose advice guided his most important decisions. Could this be the way I was meant to change history?

Krishna smiled slyly, as though he knew what I thought. Then he said, "If he should come, if he should win, what a great victory it will be for Panchaal!"

I didn't like the sound of that. "What do you mean, for Panchaal?"

"Don't you see?" Krishna said. "Once he's married to you, Arjun can't fight against your father. He can never be Drona's ally again."

My mouth filled with ashes. How foolish I'd been, dreaming of love when I was nothing but a worm dangled at the end of a fishing pole.

"Father designed the test to lure Arjun to Panchaal, didn't he?" I said. "Because he'd been defeated by Arjun, he couldn't send a marriage proposal directly to him without losing face. But the swayamvar—it's the perfect opportunity! He knew a warrior like Arjun wouldn't be able to resist such a challenge. Power—that's all he cares about, not his children." I'd long suspected this. Still, I was surprised at how much it rankled to articulate it.

"Panchaali," Dhri started, "that's not true!"

"Why won't you ever admit the truth?" I spoke bitterly. "We're nothing but pawns for King Drupad to sacrifice when it's most to his advantage. At least I'm just going to be married off. You—he's willing to push you to your death just so he can have his revenge."

As soon as I'd said the words I was sorry—and not only because Dhri looked as though I'd slapped him. Dhai Ma said one could call up a man's death by speaking of it. Had I brought my brother bad luck because I couldn't control my tongue? I said a quick prayer for his safety though I wasn't much for praying.

Krishna touched my shoulder. "Your father isn't as heartless as he seems, my dear. He's just convinced that your happiness lies in being the wife of Bharat's greatest hero. And for Dhri, he's convinced his happiness lies in avenging the honor of his family."

Even as Krishna spoke, I seemed to smell blood and burning. I was ashamed of my petty worries. The future that awaited Dhri was so much worse than anything I'd ever have to face! I wondered if it would break him or harden him, and which would be worse. I wondered if I'd prayed for the wrong thing.

"As for being pawns," Krishna was saying, "aren't we all pawns in the hands of Time, the greatest player of them all?"

. . .

At night I considered what Krishna had revealed, and why he'd pricked the bubble of my romance no sooner than it had formed. He was trying to teach me something. Was it to be aware of the dark motivations that lay behind seemingly benign actions? Was it to not let myself be carried away by emotion, to see myself instead as part of a larger political design that would affect the fate of Bharat? Was it to teach me how to wear the armor of caution so that no one could reach past it to break my heart?

Important lessons, no doubt. But I was a woman, and I had to practice them—as Sikhandi had suggested—in my own way. I would approach the problem aslant. No matter what my father's intention, I could still make Arjun's heart beat faster. I could still influence how he thought. Perhaps Time was the master player. But within the limits allowed to humans in this world the sages called *unreal*, I would be a player, too.

sorceress

One morning, the sorceress arrived.

But why do I call her that? She looked no different from the women who sold their wares in the marketplace, with the pleats of her blue sari tucked, peasant fashion, between her legs. A faint smell of salted fish wafted from her.

"Who are you?" Dhai Ma demanded. "How did you get past the guards?"

She had a star tattooed onto her chin and muscled arms with which she moved Dhai Ma—not ungently—out of her way. Dhai Ma stared, her mouth agape at the woman's effrontery. I expected her to shout for the sentry or berate the woman with her usual belligerence, but she did neither.

"I've been sent," the sorceress said to me, "to fill some of the bigger gaps in your largely useless education."

I didn't protest. (Secretly, I agreed with her estimation of my lessons.) I was interested in seeing what she had to offer.

"Who sent you?" I asked. I had a suspicion it was Vyasa the sage. He, too, came from fisher-folk.

She grinned. Her teeth were very white in her dark face, their edges sharp and serrated. "Your first lesson, princess, is to know

how to sidestep questions you don't want to answer. You do it by ignoring them."

The rest of that week she taught me how to dress hair. She
taught me how to wash it, oil it, comb the tangles out of it, and braid
it into a hundred different designs. She had me practice on her and
rebuked me sharply if I pulled too hard, or snagged a tress. Her hair
was kinky and unruly, difficult to handle, so I received many such
admonishments. I took them with unaccustomed meekness.

Dhai Ma puffed out her cheeks in disapproval. "Ridiculous!"
she said emphatically (though not, I noticed, in the sorceress's hearing). "Whoever heard of a queen braiding someone's hair—or even
her own, for that matter?" But I felt the sorceress had her reasons,
and I worked hard until she declared herself satisfied.

. . .

The sorceress taught me other unqueenly skills. She made me
lie on the floor at night, with only my arm for a pillow, until I
could sleep under those conditions. She made me wear the cheap-
est, most abrasive cotton saris that chafed my skin until I grew
used to them. She made me eat what the lowest of my servants ate;
she taught me to live on fruits, then water, and then to fast for days
at a time.

"That woman's going to be the death of you!" Dhai Ma wailed.
"She's wearing you down to skin and bone." But this was not true.
The sorceress had taught me a yogic breath that filled me with energy so that I needed no other sustenance. The breath made my
mind one-pointed, and I began to glimpse subtleties that had been
invisible to me before. I noticed that her lessons went in opposites.
She taught me adornments to enhance my beauty. She taught me
how to make myself so ordinary that no one would spare me a sec-

ond glance. She taught me to cook with the best of ingredients and the most meager. She taught me potions to cure illness and potions to cause them. She taught me to be unafraid of speaking out, and to be brave enough for silence. She taught me when to lie and when to speak the truth. She taught me to discover a man's hidden tragedies by reading the tremor in his voice. She taught me to close myself off from the sorrow of others so that I might survive. I understood that she was preparing me for the different situations that would appear in my life. I tried to guess what shape they might take, but here I failed. I failed also in this: though I knew all that she taught me was important, in my vanity I only learned the ones that flattered my ego.

. . .

Toward the end, she taught me seduction, the first role a wife must play. She demonstrated how to send out a lightning-glance from the corner of the eye. How to bite, slightly, the swollen lower lip. How to make bangles ring as I raised my arm to pull a transparent veil into place. How to walk, the back swaying just enough to hint at hidden pleasures.

She said, "In bed you must be different each day, sensitive to your lord's moods. Sometimes a lioness, sometimes a trembling dove, sometimes a doe, matching its partner's fleetness."

She gave me herbs, some for insatiability, some for endurance, some for the days I might want to keep a man away.

"What about love?" I asked.

"The stalk of the blue lotus, ground into honey, will make a man mad for you," she said.

"That's not what I meant."

She gave me the name of an herb to arouse my own desire.

"No. Teach me how to love my husband, and how to make him love me."

She laughed out loud. "I can't teach you that," she said. "Love comes like lightning, and disappears the same way. If you're lucky, it strikes you right. If not, you'll spend your life yearning for a man you can't have. I advise you to forget about love, princess. Pleasure is simpler, and duty more important. Learn to be satisfied with them."

I should have believed her and modified my expectations. But I didn't. Deep in my stubborn heart I was convinced I deserved more.

. . .

There were two final gifts the sorceress gave me: a story and a parchment. The story was the tale of Kunti, mother of Arjun. The parchment was a map of Bharat's many kingdoms.

In her youth, the sorceress told me, Kunti was given a boon by the irascible sage Durvasa, whom she'd managed somehow to please. Whenever she wanted, she could call upon a god, and he would gift her with a son. It was a strange boon, not without its drawbacks, but it came in handy when her husband Pandu couldn't provide her with children. Thus her eldest, Yudhisthir, was the son of the god of righteousness, her second, Bheem, the son of the god of wind, and Arjun, the son of Indra the king-god. Once, King Pandu's other wife, Madri, begged and begged Kunti to loan her this boon, and Kunti did. Thus, Nakul and Sahadev, sons of the twin healer-gods, were born.

"Do you believe that men can be born from gods?" I asked.

She gave me a look. "As much as they can be born from fire! But my believing is not important, nor yours. That's not why stories are given to you."

The sorceress was a good storyteller. She brought Kunti's lonely existence alive so I could look into its lightless crevices. Adopted by her uncle, the childless king Kuntibhoj, she had no brothers to cherish her, no sisters to confide in, no mother to turn to for consolation. Her marriage to Pandu—one of political convenience—wasn't happy. Almost immediately he took the beautiful Madri as his second wife and lavished his affection on her. Soon afterward, Pandu was cursed by a brahmin. He left his kingdom in the hands of his blind brother, Dhritarashtra, and went into the forest to do penance. As faithful wives, Kunti and Madri, too, left the comforts of the court and accompanied him (though perhaps they shouldn't have bothered—the curse stipulated that if Pandu touched a woman in desire, he would perish). Years passed. The children appeared. But one day Pandu, no longer able to resist, embraced Madri. He died. The guilt-ridden Madri chose not to live on. Kunti, devastated though she must have been both by her husband's death and his last act, gathered all her willpower. She brought the five princes back to Hastinapur, making no distinction between her own children and those of her rival. She was determined that no one would cheat them out of their inheritance. For years she struggled, a widow alone and in disfavor, to keep them safe in Dhritarashtra's court until finally, now, they were grown.

I wanted to tell the sorceress how moved I was by Kunti's sufferings and her courage, but she forestalled me. "Don't let the waves of your emotion drown you," she said, fixing me with eyes that were cold as agates. "Understand! Understand what drove a woman like her. What allowed her to survive when she was surrounded by enemies. Understand what makes a queen—and beware!"

I didn't pay the sorceress much attention. With the arrogance of youth I thought that the motives that drove Kunti were too simple to require careful study.

Only when we met would I realize how different she was from my imaginings. And how much more dangerous.

. . .

The map was a thick crinkled sheet the color of skin. Before this (though the tutor had spoken of it) I'd never seen the shape of the country I lived in, a triangle that narrowed downward in a wedge that drove itself into the ocean. It was made up of so many kingdoms that I thought I'd never learn them all. The rivers and mountains were easier: I enunciated their names as I traced them with my finger. When I touched the peaks of the Himalayas, my hand tingled, and I knew that those icy ranges would be significant in my life. I looked wonderingly at the kingdom of Panchaal and the dot that was Kampilya. It was a strange feeling, to locate myself for the first time in the world.

"I had this map made just before I came," the sorceress said. "But it's already outdated." She passed her hand over the parchment, and it seemed that the boundaries of the kingdoms shifted, some growing larger, some shrinking. A few disappeared altogether while others changed names.

"The kings are always fighting," she said. "All they want is more land, more power. They tax the common people to starvation and force them to fight in their armies."

"Surely there must be some good kings," I argued, "who care for their subjects." I was thinking of Krishna, though I knew little of how he governed his lands.

"Too few," she said, "and they're tired with fighting. In this Third Age of Man, the good are mostly weak. That is why the earth needs the Great War, so she can start over."

There it was again: the Great War, the words like nails scraping my lungs. Hesitantly I said, "I was told I'd be the cause of the war."

She looked at me. I thought I saw pity in her eyes. But she merely said, "There are many causes for such a gigantic event."

I persisted. "I was told that a million women would be widowed because of me. It wrings my heart to think that I'll cause so much suffering to those who are innocent."

"It's always been that way. When did the innocent not suffer? In any case, you're wrong in thinking of woman as an innocent species." She waved her hand again and the map flickered. It seemed to me that I was looking into a hundred homes, humble and kingly both. I heard the voices and thoughts of women, bitter and bickering. Some wished death and disease on their rivals, others wanted control of their household. Some berated children with words that left scars on their hearts. Some beat servant girls or forced them out, penniless, into the jaws of a ravenous world. Still others whispered their discontent into their sleeping husbands' ears all night, so that the men, waking in the morning, acted out the anger that festered within their wives.

"As you see," the sorceress said, "women contribute to the world's problems in a hundred insidious ways. And you, who will be more powerful than most, could wreak greater havoc if you aren't careful. I've taught you some better alternatives—if only you can keep them in mind and not get swept away by passion!"

"I can!" I said, with the confidence of the untested. I knew I was intelligent—wasn't Dhai Ma always complaining about how overly smart I was? I knew enough to control passion. I visualized myself as a great queen, dispensing wisdom and love. Panchaali the Peacemaker, people would call me.

The sorceress laughed. That's the last memory I have of her, bent over and clutching her sides until tears ran from her eyes.

portrait

The artist had set up the paintings, each covered by a silk veil, by the time I entered the hall. Dhri was already seated, his brow crumpled in a frown, and though he nodded at me, he didn't smile. He hadn't touched the mango juice that Dhai Ma had set beside him. Palpable as heat, his anxiety made me anxious, too. But I'd have to wait until we were alone to find out the problem.

The artist had visited Kampilya before. When it was time for Drupad's other daughters to be married, he came to paint their likenesses so that they could be sent to kings with whom my father wished to form alliances. But today he'd brought with him the portraits of the leading kings of the land for me to examine. This way, when I faced my suitors in the wedding hall, I would know who each one was.

I'd hoped to find Krishna here. I was depending on him to tell me the secrets a potential wife needs to know, information the artist was sure to skip over, either from ignorance or fear. Which king had a hidden disease, who was haunted by a family curse, who was a miser, who had retreated from battle, and who was too stubborn to do so. It was mystifying how Krishna knew such things. But he was nowhere around. Probably, I thought with some annoyance, he was in his palace by the sea, enjoying the company of his wives.

The artist uncovered the first portrait. "This is the noble Salya, ruler of the southern kingdom of Madradesh," he intoned, "and uncle to the Pandava princes."

I stared at the king, whose elaborately fashioned crown didn't quite hide the whiteness of his hair. His face was good-humored, but his girth betrayed his fondness for the easy life. Under his eyes, the skin sagged.

"He's old!" I whispered to Dhri in distaste. "He probably has daughters my age. Why would he want to come to the swayamvar?"

My even-tempered brother shrugged. "It's a challenge, as you yourself said, and men find it hard to turn down challenges. But he's no danger to us. He's not going to win."

I appreciated Dhri's choice of a pronoun that coupled our fates, but I found slim comfort in his confidence. If Salya won, I thought with a shudder, he would claim me, and I'd have to go with him, as mute and compliant as the purse of gold a winner carries away at the end of a wrestling match.

The artist uncovered other portraits. Jarasandha, king of Magadha, with his live-coal eyes. (I'd heard Dhri's tutor say he kept a hundred defeated kings chained in a labyrinth under his palace.) Sisupal, his friend—his hooked chin topped by a sneering mouth— who ruled over Chedi and had a long history of disputes with Krishna. Jayadrath, lord of the Sindhus, with his sinister, sensuous lips. I saw king after king until their faces blurred. Many, I knew, were decent men. But I hated them all for coveting me, and I prayed that each would fail.

The long afternoon teetered between boredom and dread. I was waiting for one face alone. I wanted to see if I'd visualized it accurately. Probably not. Doesn't the imagination always exaggerate— or diminish—truth?

When the artist uncovered the last and largest painting, I sat up, certain that it was Arjun's.

But he said, "Here is the mighty Duryodhan, crown prince of Hastinapur, with the scions of his court."

So this was the notorious Kaurava prince, Arjun's cousin! The tutor had whispered to Dhri that he'd hated the Pandava brothers, his dead uncle's sons, from the day they'd arrived at the court, his competitors for the throne he'd believed from birth to be his. There was some talk that he'd tried to drown one of them when they were still children.

Duryodhan was handsome in a muscle-bound way, though I didn't care for the willful set of his mouth. Encrusted with jewels, he occupied a throne decorated with gold lotuses. Something about the way he leaned forward, his right hand fisted, exuded discontent. To his left sat a man who was a pale, petulant copy of him.

"His younger brother, Dussasan," the artist explained.

The brothers made me uncomfortable, though I couldn't have explained why.

"Remove the picture," I commanded, and then, as my eyes were caught by the figure on Duryodhan's right, "No, wait!"

Older than the prince and austere-faced, the man sat upright, his lean body wary, as though he knew the world to be a dangerous place. Though in the midst of a court, he seemed utterly alone. His only ornaments were a pair of gold earrings and a curiously patterned gold armor unlike anything I'd seen. His eyes were filled with an ancient sadness. They pulled me into them. My impatience evaporated. I no longer cared to see Arjun's portrait. Instead, I wanted to know how those eyes would look if the man smiled. Absurdly, I wanted to be the reason for his smile.

"Ah, you are looking at Karna," the artist said, his voice reverent, "ruler of Anga, and best friend of Duryodhan. It is said that he is the greatest—"

"Stop!"

The single, sibilant word startled us all. Krishna was standing in the shadow of the doorway. I'd never seen him look so angry.

"Why are you showing the princess that man's picture? He's no prince."

Flustered, the artist covered up the painting with shaking hands, begging Krishna's pardon.

I was bewildered. Why was Krishna so vehement? What was it about this man that made him react in this uncharacteristic manner? Something in me was drawn to defend the sad-eyed Karna. "Why do you say he's that? Isn't he king of Anga?"

"It was a kingdom gifted to him by Duryodhan," Krishna said, his voice like metal, "as an insult to the Pandavas. He's just the son of a chariot driver."

For the first time, I was unconvinced by his words. A man who sat with such unconcern among princes, a man who had the power to perturb Krishna, had to be more than merely a chariot-driver's son. I turned to Dhri to check. His eyes flickered and fell. Ah, there was a secret, something Krishna wasn't telling me! I'd have to extract it from my brother later.

Krishna said, brusquely, "Don't you have any other portraits?"

"I have your majesty's likeness," the artist stammered, backing from the room, "and that of your illustrious brother, Balaram. A million pardons! I will bring them at once!"

Heat rose to my face. Did Krishna want to be one of my suitors? I'd never thought of that possibility. All these years he'd been to me as the air I breathed—indispensable and unconsidered. But today I sensed that there was more to him than the jesting self he'd chosen, until now, to reveal to me. This new Krishna, his eyes stern with anger, his voice like an arrow—I was certain he could pass the swayamvar test if he wished it.

How would it be to have him as my husband? An uneasiness rose in me as I turned the thought around in my mind. I loved him— but not in that way.

Krishna smiled his old, mocking smile. "Don't worry, Krishnaa," he said. "I'm not going to compete against my friend Arjun. Nor will Balaram. We know your destiny leads you elsewhere."

It was embarrassing to be so transparent. I looked down at the patterned marble of the floor, determined to give away nothing else.

"But I'll be there," he said. "On that crucial day, I'll be there— to keep you from choosing wrongly."

My eyes flew to his face. What did he mean? Bound as I was by the contest, what was left for me to choose?

His eyes were cool and inscrutable. Behind him, Dhri gazed out at the burnished afternoon and stifled a yawn. Had I imagined Krishna's words? Or had he spoken them inside my head, only for me to hear?

. . .

The artist reentered, bent under the weight of two silver-framed portraits that Krishna waved impatiently away. "Why haven't you shown the princess the pictures of the Pandavas?" he demanded.

The artist hesitated, clearly afraid of Krishna's wrath, but finally he whispered, "Your Highness, they're dead."

My heart thudded loudly, out of rhythm. What was he saying? And why didn't Krishna or Dhri contradict him? Could it be true? Was this why Dhri had looked so anxious?

"What have you heard?" Krishna asked, far too calmly.

"There was a fire," the artist said. "All the tradesmen on the road were talking about it. In Varanavat, where the five princes had gone for a holiday with their mother, the poor widowed Kunti. The guest-house they were staying in burnt to the ground. People found nothing but ashes—and six skeletons! Folks are thinking it was murder. Some say the house was built of lac, designed for easy burning. But of course no one dares to accuse Duryodhan!"

"That's what I heard, too," Dhri cried. "What a loss for all Bharat!"

My head whirled. Part of me was aghast at the terrible thing that had happened to the Pandavas and their mother, but a larger part could think only of myself. Fear makes us selfish. If Arjun was dead, what would happen to me? If no king was able to pass the test, the swayamvar would be a failure. My father would be denounced for setting his guests an impossible task. I'd be forced to live out the rest of my life as a spinster. But worse things could happen. The insulted kings could decide to band together in a war against my father and divide the spoils of the fallen kingdom—including me—among them.

"Krishna," Dhri's voice held a tremor. "What are we to do? Is it too late to call off the swayamvar?"

"Dear boy!" Krishna answered, with inexplicable good humor, "hasn't that earnest brahmin who labors over your studies taught you anything? Princes must not panic until they've tested the truth of a rumor for themselves."

"But the skeletons—"

Krishna shrugged. "Bones may belong to anyone." He signaled to the artist to bring the portraits of the Pandavas.

"How can you be certain?" Dhri asked. Then his eyes widened. "Have they sent you word?"

"No," said Krishna. "But in my heart I'd know it if Arjun were dead."

I wanted to believe him, but I was racked by doubt. Can hearts know these things? I was sure that mine was incapable of such subtle perceptions.

"Here are the five Pandava brothers," the artist announced, uncovering the portrait with a flourish, revealing the man we were all hoping would be my husband.

. . .

Later Dhai Ma said, "He's too dark, and his eyes have a stubborn look. The oldest brother, what's his name, Yudhisthir—now *he* looked much calmer. Did you see how he sat in the painting, plump and regal, smiling with those even white teeth? Maybe you'd better marry him. He's going to be the king, after all—that's if their old uncle ever hands over the throne."

"Arjun is taller!" I spoke with pert brightness, trying to dispel another face with its ancient, sad eyes that kept coming to my mind. "And didn't you see his battle scars? That proves how brave he is."

Dhai Ma wrinkled up her nose. "How could I miss them? They were like earthworms all over his shoulders. If tall is what you want, I say you go for the second brother, that Bheem. Those muscles were quite a sight! I've heard he's easy to please, too. Just give him a large and tasty meal, and he's yours for life!"

"Didn't you say that was how Duryodhan tricked him as a child? Gave him poisoned rice pudding and then, when he became unconscious, threw him into the river? Arjun would have been too intelligent for that. I can tell by the sharpness of his nose, his chiseled chin."

"Chiseled!" Dhai Ma made a rude sound. "It's cleft in two, and you know what that means: a roving eye. Such men are trouble from start to finish, and don't I know it! If it's good looks you're after, why not choose one of the two youngest, the twins. Eyes like lotus petals, skin like gold, bodies like young shal trees." She smacked her lips in approval.

"For heaven's sake, Dhai Ma, they're far too young for me! I prefer the mature, masterful kind."

She gave an exaggerated sigh. "Then I guess you're stuck with your Arjun. At least try not to be fool enough to give him mastery over you. But your brain is probably too addled with romance to retain anything I'm saying."

"I suspect I'll have to take you along when I'm married, so you can remind me," I said, and we laughed together. But the laughter faded quickly. The jokes fell from us; only the uncertainties we'd tried to hide beneath them remained. Dhai Ma put an arm around me. Did she guess how my heart balked inside me like a horse that refuses to follow its rider's commands? How I longed to speak to her of that other, forbidden name: Karna. Outside, night birds called to each other as they looped through the inky night, their pensive cries close, then far, then unexpectedly close again.

births

I wanted to know what Kunti looked like. I thought it would be wise preparation, in case she turned out to be my mother-in-law. Perhaps her face would give me a clue as to what lay inside. (I hadn't forgotten the sorceress's warning.) But the artist didn't have a picture of her. He sent me, with apologies, a different portrait: that of Gandhari, Duryodhan's mother and Arjun's aunt.

The portrait was small, about a handspan square, and ill-executed, as though painted by an apprentice. Perhaps there wasn't much demand for the pictures of women, once they were married off, even if they were queens. Dhai Ma and I pored over it, trying to make out her features, but they were mostly obscured by a thick white blindfold.

"You know the story," Dhai Ma said. "When she heard that she was to marry the blind Dhritarashtra, she tied it over her eyes, declaring she didn't want to enjoy the pleasures her husband had been deprived of. They say she's never removed it since."

I'd heard the story—or, more accurately, the song that had been composed in honor of her devotion to her husband. (From time to time, my father sent bards to my apartments, hoping that their songs would instill appropriate attitudes in me and warn me off dangerous ones. Thus far, I'd also been subjected to the lives of Savitri, who heroically saved her husband from the clutches of Lord Death; Sita, who was eternally faithful to her husband, even when abducted by a demon king; and Devyani, who, in spite of her father's warnings, insisted on falling in love with the wrong man and was left brokenhearted.) Between ourselves, though, Dhai Ma and I agreed that Gandhari's sacrifice wasn't particularly intelligent.

"If my husband couldn't see, I'd make doubly sure to keep my own eyes open," I said, "so that I could report everything that was going on to him."

Dhai Ma was of a different opinion. "Maybe the thought of marrying a blind man disgusted her—but being a princess she couldn't get out of the match. Maybe she did this so she wouldn't have to look at him every single day of her life."

The portrait must have been an old one. In it, Gandhari looked pretty in a lost, girlish way. Tendrils of hair fell over her forehead, and she had a listening air, as though she was trying to compensate for her lost sight. I wondered if there were days when she regretted her decision to opt for wifely virtue instead of the power she could have had as the blind king's guide and adviser. But she'd made a vow and was trapped in the net of her own words. Her mouth was strong, though, and her pale, beautiful lips balanced disappointment with resolution.

Gandhari's marriage, although she'd given up so much for its sake, was—like Kunti's—not a happy one. (Later I would wonder if that was what gave them strength, both these queens. But perhaps I'd got the cause and effect mixed up? Perhaps strong women tended to have unhappy marriages? The idea troubled me.) Dhritarashtra was a bitter man. He never got over the fact that he'd been passed over by the elders—just because he was blind—when they decided which of the brothers should be king. Though he claimed to love his younger brother—and possibly did, for he was a strange and contradictory man—he must have been delighted when the curse-blighted Pandu withdrew into the forest. The goal of Dhritarashtra's life was to have a son who could inherit the throne after him. But here a problem arose, for in spite of his assiduous attempts, Gandhari didn't conceive for many years. When she finally did, it was too late. Kunti was already pregnant with Yudhisthir.

A year came. A year went. Yudhisthir was born. As the first male child of the next generation, the elders declared, the throne would be his. Dhritarashtra's spies brought more bad news: Kunti was pregnant again. Now there were two obstacles between Dhritarashtra and his desire. Gandhari's stomach grew large as a giant beehive, but her body refused to go into labor. Perhaps the frustrated king berated her, or perhaps the fact that he'd taken one of her waiting women as his mistress drove Gandhari to her act of desperation. She struck her stomach again and again until she bled, and bleeding, gave birth to a huge, unformed ball of flesh.

"The palace was in an uproar," Dhai Ma said, "people running around wringing their hands, crying that this was the work of demons, the blind king sitting stunned on his throne while Gandhari lay in a faint. But luckily a holy man showed up. He cut the ball into a hundred and one pieces, and called for vats of butter, one for each piece. He sealed the pieces in the vats and cautioned that they shouldn't be opened for a year. And that's how Duryodhan and his brothers—and their sister Duhsala—were born. Maybe that's why he's such great friends with Karna, who also came into the world in a strange way."

Heat rose to my face at the sudden mention of Karna's name. To hide it, I quipped, "Doesn't anyone have normal births anymore?"

Dhai Ma gave me a sharp glance. But if she had a question, she didn't ask it. Was it because she didn't know what to do with the answer? "You're a fine one to talk!" she snorted, and then went on with the story. "Most people think that Adhiratha, a chariot driver, is Karna's father. But one of our stable boys that used to work in Hastinapur a while back told us a different story. Adhiratha found Karna on the river Ganga one morning when he'd gone there to pray, floating in a wooden casket. He was just a week old then.

"That part isn't so uncommon. Once in a while, a noblewoman will get in trouble and dispose of the evidence this way. But there was something special about this child. He had gold rings in his ears, and the gold armor that covered his chest—why, you couldn't take it off. It was part of his body. Adhiratha believed the gods had answered his prayers and sent Karna to him because he didn't have any children."

Maybe Adhiratha wasn't completely wrong. I remembered the otherworldly expression on Karna's face in the portrait. He looked as though, sometime, somewhere, he'd been touched by a divine hand. I wished there had been a way for me to buy that portrait, to secret it away, to look at it whenever I wanted. But of course such an action was impossible. A princess has no privacy.

Dhai Ma shot me another glance before heaving her body off the floor. "I'd better get to work. And you're late for your dance lesson, as usual." At the door she paused. This time the warning in her voice was a serious one. "Sometimes I talk too much. If you know what's good for you, you'll put that story out of your mind and behave in a way that doesn't bring shame to your royal father."

I knew what she was referring to, and she was right. But my disobedient heart kept going back to Karna, to that most unfortunate moment in his life. We'd both been victims of parental rejection— was that why his story resonated so?—but my suffering couldn't compare to his. Over and over I imagined the mother who had abandoned him—for I was sure that it was she and not the gods that had set him afloat on the river. Against my closed eyelids, I saw her as she bent to the water to cast the child—her own sweet, sleeping flesh—into its night currents. In my imagination, she was very young, and the curve of her turned-away face was a little like Gandhari's, though that was a silly thing to think. She didn't weep. She had no tears left. Only fear for her reputation, which made her draw her shawl more closely over her head as she watched the casket. Just for a moment; then she'd have to hurry back. She'd left all her jewelry in her bedchamber, had clothed herself in her oldest sari. Still, it would be a disaster if the city watchman discovered her so far from her parents' mansion at a time when only prostitutes are abroad. She choked down a cry as the bobbing casket disappeared around a bend in the river. Then she walked home, her steps only a little unsteady, thinking, At least it's done.

My heart ached for both mother and child, because even I who knew so little of life could guess that such things were never done. For the rest of her life, she would wonder where her son was. Passing every handsome stranger, she'd ask herself (just as he would, walking by women he didn't know), Could this be—? Each morning when they woke—in the same town, or kingdoms apart—their first thoughts would be of each other. In anger and regret, they'd both wish she'd had the courage to choose another way.

scorpion

 Dhri said, "I'm telling you this against Krishna's wishes."

"Why doesn't he want me to know?"

"You'll see soon enough. Now listen."

. . .

The story begins with the great tournament in Hastinapur, where Drona has decided that the princes, who have come of age, are ready to demonstrate their battle skills.

The arena thrums with anticipation; the citizens, noble-born and commoner, are anxious to see what the princes are capable of. After all, one of them will be their future king. Already there are factions. Some cry out Duryodhan's name, for he is dashing, brave, and generous to a fault. Even today, riding to the tournament, he threw handfuls of gold coins into the crowd until his purse was empty. But others secretly pray that the highest prize will go to one of the five Pandava brothers, those fatherless boys brought up on the fringes of the court by an uncle who only pretends to wish them well.

And it seems that the gods are not as deaf as we customarily accuse them of being. For look, here at the end of the day is Arjun's name being announced as the greatest of the contenders. He has shot fire arrows into the air and then quenched them with rain arrows. He has sent snake arrows slithering toward the crowd, and then, just before they struck the terrified viewers, plucked them from the ground with eagle arrows. His sleep arrows have enveloped them in dreams; his rope arrows have bound their hands and feet; his arrows of enchantment have made them cower in front of monsters more terrifying than any they could have imagined. Shining with pride, his teacher claims that these are only the minor weapons he has learned to use! The others are too powerful, too sacred, to be called on except in serious battle.

But just as his uncle, the blind king, gets to his feet (very slowly, some note) with the prize garland, an unknown youth in golden armor appears in the arena. He asks permission to take part in the tournament, and then skillfully replicates every feat of Arjun's. The crowd is silenced by amazement. Then it breaks out in cheers, and Duryodhan cheers the loudest.

The stranger brings his palms together and turns his face to the sky, offering prayers to the sun. He thanks the crowd with a modest bow. Then, in courtly speech, he invites Arjun to single combat. The winner, he suggests, will be the champion.

The crowd applauds at the prospect of this grand spectacle. The three old men sitting by the king in the royal pavilion—Bheeshma, the grandfather; Drona, the teacher; and Kripa, the royal tutor—glance at each other in dismay. This is an unforeseen danger, a risk they do not wish Arjun to undertake, for to their experienced eyes it is clear that the stranger is as good as—and perhaps better than—the Pandava prince whose reputation they hope to establish today.

Do you know this youth? Bheeshma asks. Kripa shakes his head, but Drona pauses, a considering look on his face. He whispers something.

Let the combat begin, says the blind king, raising his scepter, but Kripa leaps to his feet.

There are procedures to be obeyed first, he says. The lineage of the contestants must be established, for a prince may be challenged to single combat only by another prince. We all know Arjun's parentage. But, valiant stranger, kindly tell us your name, and from which princely house you are descended.

The stranger's face flushes. My name is Karna, he says. Then, so softly that all in the assembly must strain to hear, But I do not come from a princely house.

Then, according to the rules of a royal tournament, you cannot battle Prince Arjun, says Kripa, his voice kind. If he feels triumphant, no one notices; he has long learned to hide such emotions.

Wait! cries Duryodhan, springing up in outrage. Clearly this man is a great warrior. I will not let you insult him like this, using an outdated law as your excuse! A hero is a hero, no matter what his caste. Ability is more important than the accident of birth.

The citizens approve of these sentiments. They cheer lustily.

Duryodhan continues, If you insist that it is necessary for Karna to be a king in order to battle Arjun, then I'll share my own inheritance with him! He calls for holy water and pours it over the stranger's head. To the cheers of the crowd, he says, King Karna, I now pronounce you ruler of Anga, and my friend.

Karna embraces him fervently. I'll never forget your generosity, he says. You have salvaged my honor. Earth may break asunder, but I will not forsake you. From this moment, your friends are my friends, and your enemies my bitterest foes.

The crowd roars its admiration. This, they tell each other, is how heroes should behave!

The three old men exchange looks of concern. Things have not worked out the way they planned. The upstart Karna has found popularity even without vanquishing Arjun. And Duryodhan has found a powerful ally. Now the two archers, fierce in battle stance, face each other in the arena. Who knows what the outcome of this contest will be?

There's a small commotion in the pavilion built for the women of the palace. One of the queens has fainted—perhaps from heat, perhaps from the prolonged tension. Is it Gandhari, the blind king's wife? Is it Kunti, distressed at this challenge to her son? Before the truth can be ascertained, the people's attention is caught by an old man who limps into the arena. From his clothing it's clear that he belongs to a lower caste. Is he a blacksmith? No, say those who know such things. He's a chariot driver.

He heads for Karna and—wonder of wonders—Karna sets aside his bow to touch the old man's feet.

Son! the newcomer cries. Is it really you, back after so many years? But what are you doing here, among these noble princes? Why is there a crown on your head?

With infinite gentleness, Karna takes the old man's hand and guides him to a corner, explaining as he goes.

The crowd is stunned, silent. Then whispers and jeers begin to be heard, especially among the Pandava faction. Sutaputra! Voices hiss. Driver's son! From the pavilion, Bheem's voice booms disdainfully, Drop your bow, pretender! Go get yourself a whip from the royal stables instead!

Karna's hand tightens around his bow. Arjun! he calls. But Arjun has already turned his back on him and is walking away. Karna stares after him. It is the supreme insult—one for which he'll never forgive Arjun. From this moment on, they will be arch-enemies.

Who knows what might have happened then, but the sun chooses this moment to dip beneath the horizon. A relieved Drona gives the signal, and trumpeters sound the call for the end of the tournament. The crowd disperses reluctantly, buzzing with dissatisfaction and gossip. The Pandava brothers are joined by the three old men; together, they make their way to their modest dwelling where Kunti is resting (it was she who fainted), discussing the day's strangeness as they go. Duryodhan takes Karna with him for a night of carousing at his palace. Later that evening he'll put his own necklace, a rope of pearls and rubies, around Karna's neck and say, thickly, I declare you the true champion! If those cowards hadn't stopped the fight, you would have rubbed Arjun's face in the mud. Ah, these Pandava vermin who are always plotting to steal my kingdom! Would that I had a friend who might rid me of them!

And Karna will hold himself very straight and reply, When the time comes, I will do so for you, my liege and my friend—or I will die trying.

. . .

"So that's how Karna became a king," I said. "Why didn't Krishna want me to know?"

Dhri said, "He felt that it would make you too sympathetic to Karna. And that would be dangerous."

"Dangerous? How?"

"Arjun isn't the only one who can pass the swayamvar test."

The pulse in my throat started hammering. Guiltily, I turned away, facing the dark garden. "You mean Karna could do it, too?"

"Yes. He plans to come to the swayamvar, along with Duryodhan. He plans to win you. We must not allow it."

I wanted to ask: If he were, indeed, as wondrous a hero as Arjun, why should it matter if I married him instead of the Pandava prince? Wouldn't he be as great an ally for Panchaal? Why was Krishna so against him? Was it just that he favored his friend Arjun? There were other secrets here. But I sensed that my uncomplicated brother did not know them. So, instead, I asked, "How can you stop him? If he wins, aren't we honor-bound by Father's oath?"

"The honor of family is more important than other kinds of honor," my brother said. He waited a moment, as though daring me to disagree. "I'll think of a way. Krishna will help me. You, too, must do your part."

I didn't want to argue with Dhri, but I wasn't ready to turn against Karna, not even for the sake of family honor. Instead I asked, "Adhiratha said Karna had been gone for many years. Do you know where he'd been?"

Dhri nodded grimly. "The lost years of Karna's life: that's the most important part of the story, and the main reason I'm telling it to you."

. . .

Early in life Karna demonstrates a passion for archery. At sixteen—still believing he is Adhiratha's son—he goes to Drona, the foremost teacher in the land. He confesses that he is lowborn and begs to be accepted as his student. But Drona is busy with princes. I will not teach a chariot-driver's son, he says. Disappointed, insulted, Karna vows he will learn from one who is greater than Drona. He leaves the city for the mountains and finally, through great effort and even greater luck—though whether the luck is good or bad is uncertain—he finds the ashram of Parasuram.

"Drona's own teacher," I whispered. "Didn't he once erase the entire race of kshatriyas from the earth because they'd grown corrupt?"

Dhri nodded.

Since truth hasn't served him well, Karna does not risk it again. He tells Parasuram that he is a brahmin. Seeing his potential, the sage agrees to teach him. In time Karna becomes the best of his students, the most beloved, the only one to whom Parasuram imparts the invocation for the Brahmastra, the weapon that no one can withstand.

The day before he is to leave Parasuram's ashram, Karna accompanies his teacher on a walk through the forest. When a tired Parasuram wants to rest under a tree, Karna offers his lap as a pillow. As the old man sleeps, a mountain scorpion creeps from its hole and stings Karna repeatedly on the thigh, drawing blood. The pain is intense, but Karna does not want to disturb his teacher. He sits unmoving—but blood spurts from his wound onto Parasuram's face and wakes him. In rage Parasuram curses his favorite student.

. . .

Shock forced me to interrupt. "But why?"

Dhri said, "Parasuram realized that a brahmin could never have borne so much pain in silence. Only a kshatriya was capable of that. He accused Karna of having deceived him. And though Karna told him that he didn't belong to the warrior-caste but was merely a charioteer's son, Parasuram wouldn't forgive him. He said, Just as you've deceived me, so will your mind deceive you. When you need the Brahmastra the most, you'll forget the mantra needed to call it up. What you've stolen from me will be of no use to you in the hour of your death."

I was outraged. "Didn't Karna's years of devoted service mean anything to Parasuram? What of his love for his teacher, because of which he bore the scorpion's sting? Wasn't that worth some forgiveness?"

"Ah, forgiveness," Dhri said. "It's a virtue that eludes even the great. Isn't our own existence a proof of that?"

. . .

A disconsolate Karna makes his way back down the mountain, having gained and then lost that which he'd set his heart on. It is night. Resting in the woods outside a village, he hears a beast lumbering toward him. His mind in turmoil, he shoots an arrow at the sound. From the beast's dying cry, he realizes he has killed a cow, that most sacred of animals.

I shut my eyes. I didn't wish to hear any more of this story. I willed Karna to walk away from the fallen animal before he was discovered as its killer. I knew he wouldn't.

In the morning he finds the owner of the cow, confesses his deed, and offers compensation. But the enraged brahmin says, You killed my cow when she was defenseless. You, too, will die when you have no means of protection. Karna pleads with him to change his curse. I'm not afraid of dying, he says. But let me die like a warrior. The brahmin refuses.

. . .

"How could Karna bear to keep on living after all these misfortunes?" I whispered.

Dhri shrugged. "Suicide is the coward's way. And whatever his faults, Karna isn't a coward.

"I told you this story against Krishna's advice for two reasons. One is that the unknown is always more fascinating than the known."

(But in this my brother was mistaken. Nothing has more power over us than the truth. Each painful detail of Karna's story became a hook in my flesh, binding me to him, making me wish a happier life for him.)

"But also," Dhri continued, "I want you to realize that Karna is cursed. Anyone joined to him will become cursed, too. I don't want that to happen to you—because you're my sister, but also because you're born to change history. You don't have the luxury of behaving like an ordinary starstruck girl. The consequences of your action may destroy us all."

I was annoyed at being pressed in this way. But even more, I was frightened by the conviction in his voice. All this time, I hadn't known that he'd taken my destiny as seriously as his own. Still, I spoke lightly. "I'm glad you have so much confidence in my power! But remember what Krishna said? We're nothing but pawns in Time's hands!"

"Even a pawn has a choice," my brother said. "The day Sikhandi left for the forest, I longed to go with him. To leave the palace behind without a backward glance. To live out my life in peace under the trees. To escape the bloody fate toward which I've been pushed every moment since I was born. I could have done it. Sikhandi would have hidden me so skillfully that the entire Panchaal army wouldn't have found me. But I chose not to."

"Why?" My throat was dry. How wrong I'd been all this time, thinking I knew my stoic, resigned brother.

"Two reasons held me back," Dhri said. "One was you."

"I would have gladly come with you," I protested hotly. "If you'd only asked—"

"The other," he interrupted, his harsh voice scraping against my ears, "was myself."

. . .

Through the long night, out of love for Dhri, I tried harder than ever before to bar Karna from my mind. But can a sieve block the wind? Fragments of stories floated in my head, women who had saved their husbands by countering their ill luck with their virtue. Perhaps I could do the same for Karna? In the midst of that hope a regret leaped up like a leopard. Why hadn't Dhri sidestepped his fate when he had the chance! I imagined him carefree under a canopy of gigantic mahogany trees, his brow erased of the creases that marred his handsomeness. But the next moment I was proud of his resolution—the way I had been of Karna for facing the angry brahmin. I knew I should not compare them, that my loyalty should be aimed only toward my brother. Yet as I swayed between sleep and waking, the two men began to melt together in my mind. How similar their nature and their destinies were, pressing them both toward tragedy, forcing them into acts of dangerous nobility. No matter how skilled they were at battle, ultimately it would not help them because they were forever defeated by their conscience. What cruel god fashioned the net of their minds this way, so they could never escape it?

And what traps had he set up for me?

song

Coiled on the silver tray like a white snake, the wedding garland was as thick as my forearm. I regarded it warily as though it might, at any moment, decide to strike.

"What's wrong now?" Dhai Ma said. "Why is your face like a blackened pot?"

"It's too heavy," I said. I imagined placing it around a neck. I could clearly see the corded, straining muscles, though the rest of the face was frustratingly blank.

"Ridiculous!" Dhai Ma said. "If he's a true hero, he'll be able to bear its weight.

"And yours, too," she added with a wink.

Attendants buzzed around me. A little more lotus pollen to burnish the bride's cheeks; the end of the wedding sari, white and gold, arranged cleverly to accentuate the swell of her breast while creating a virginal effect. An old woman rubbed paste of sandalwood on my navel with a sly smile. Bangles, waistband, anklets, a jeweled nose ring so massive it had to be held up by a chain attached to my hairdo.

"I feel like I'm in battle armor," I told Dhai Ma.

"You are," she said. "Enough dillydallying, now! Your royal brother's about to wear out the corridor with his pacing."

Dhri was waiting outside my rooms to walk me to the wedding

hall, where the kings had already gathered. He looked severe in his ceremonial silks. I noticed the scabbard on his hip, carved with flying beasts.

"Why the sword?" I asked.

Dhai Ma said, "What a question! Don't you know it's the brother's sacred duty to protect his sister's virtue? He'll have his hands full today, with all those dirty old men drooling over you."

"Your vulgarity never ceases to amaze me," Dhri told her. She laughed and gave him a cuff on the ears, then hurried off to bully her way into the best seat in the royal attendants' area.

But I knew the real reason for the sword. He expected trouble.

. . .

I heard it under the bluster and music, the announcement of the newly arrived: neighs, trumpetings, the clink of weaponry.

Dhri said, "The kings have brought their warriors. They're lined up outside. But don't worry. The entire Panchaal army, too, is armed and ready."

"Thank you for letting me know," I said. "Now I feel completely calm."

"Did anyone ever inform you," he said, "that sarcasm is unbecoming in brides?"

When I stepped into the wedding hall, there was complete, immediate silence. As though I were a sword that had severed, simultaneously, each vocal cord. Behind my veil I smiled grimly. Savor this moment of power, I told myself. It may be your only one.

. . .

First Dhri showed me the kings who had come only to watch, the ones I didn't have to fear.

"Look, Krishna."

There he was, my friend, my exasperation, conversing with his brother as though he were at a country fair. The jaunty peacock feather on his crown dipped as he raised his hand in a gesture that could be a benediction or a careless hello.

Across the hall, spectators were grouped according to caste. The vaishya sector was marked by a blue banner painted with a merchant ship. The sudra banner depicted farmers harvesting wheat. The brahmins had the best seats, up front, with fat, tassled bolsters to lean on. Their banner, a priest making a fire offering, was made of white silk.

Now Dhri pointed out the important suitors. I tried to match them to their portraits, but they seemed older, heavier, their features flattened by age and perhaps anxiety. To lose in front of this great assembly—even though all but one of them must—would be such a public dishonor. Its sourness would flood the mouth for years. By my brother's rust-edged tone, I knew the ones who were most dangerous—not because they might win, but because of what they might do when they lost.

"Arjun?" I finally asked.

"Not here."

I marveled at how he'd learned to make his voice expressionless. He went on to name other names. When he stopped, I asked, "Is that all?"

He understood the question beneath the question. His eyes showed his displeasure. "Karna has come."

Dhri didn't point him out, but I found him. Next to Duryodhan, half hidden behind a marble pillar. My heart beat so hard, I was sure Dhri would hear. I longed to look into Karna's face, to see if those eyes were indeed as sad as the artist had portrayed, but even I knew how improper that would be. I focused instead on his hands, the wrists disdainfully bare of ornaments, the powerful, battered knuckles. If my brother had known how badly I wanted to touch them, he would have been furious. Duryodhan made a comment—probably about me—and his companions slapped their knees and guffawed. Karna alone (I noted with gratitude) sat still as a flame. Only the slightest thinning of his lips indicated his disapproval, but it was enough to silence Duryodhan.

Dhri was calling me to the dais, his voice so sharp that my attendants stared in surprise. I went, but all the way loyalty and desire dueled inside me. If Arjun wasn't here, what right did Krishna and Dhri have to insist that I not choose Karna?

A trumpet sounded. The contest had begun.

. . .

Later, long after a forest was razed and a palace filled with wonders built in its place, after the game of dice, after treachery and loss, banishment and return, after the war with its blinding mountains of bones, bards would immortalize the swayamvar where, some claim, it all began. This is what they would sing:

In that hall perfumed with hopes and decorated with anxieties, where pride played the wedding flute and anger the drum, the greatest kings of Bharat were unable to lift the Kindhara bow from the ground. Of the handful that could aim and shoot, none was successful in piercing the fish eye. Jarasandha missed it by the width of his little finger, Salya by the width of a bean seed, and Sisupal by the width of a sesame seed. When Duryodhan shot his arrow, a cheer rose from the audience, but the steward examined the target and proclaimed that the Kaurava prince had missed it by the width of a mustard seed.

Now only Karna was left. Like a lion he rose to his feet. Light glinted on his armor as on a golden mane. He turned eastward to pray to the sun. He turned northward to bow to his teacher, for such was his greatness that he bore him no grudge in spite of his curse. He joined his palms in respect as he approached the mighty Kindhara, and when he lifted it—as easily as though it were a child's bamboo bow—all the assembly murmured in amazement. When he pulled on the bowstring to test its resilience, a deep and musical vibration spread through the hall, as if the bow was singing. Even Draupadi held her breath, entranced. But then, as if in reply, came a sound like thunder. The earth herself began to tremble, and one could hear, in the distance, the cries of jackals and vultures. The brahmins shook their heads at these omens and whispered into each other's ears, What calamity will befall us should this man win the contest? Krishna himself sat up in his seat, and the great Vyasa who, it is said, had foreseen the entire history of the land in meditation, watched Karna with alertness, for he recognized this moment as one where the course of history hangs balanced between good and ill.

But Dhristadyumna, who stood at the side of Draupadi, took a step forward and said, Renowned though you are for your skill, Karna, my sister cannot have as her suitor a man of a low caste. Therefore I humbly request you to return to your seat.

Karna's eyes flashed like ice in sunlight, but he had learned much since the tournament at Hastinapur. His voice was calm as he replied, It is true that I was brought up by Adhiratha, but I am a kshatriya. My guru, Parasuram, saw this with his inner eye, and cursed me for it. That curse gives me the right to stand here today among these warrior kings. I will take part in this contest. Who dares to stop me?

In response, Dhristadyumna drew his sword, though his face was pale as a winter evening and his hand shook, for he knew he was no match for Karna. But the honor of his house was at stake, and he could do nothing else.

Then, out of the silence that shrouded the marriage hall, a voice rose, sweet as a koel's song, unbending as flint. Before you attempt to win my hand, king of Anga, it said, tell me your father's name. For surely a wife-to-be, who must sever herself from her family and attach herself to her husband's line, has the right to know this.

It was Draupadi, and as she spoke, she stepped between her brother and Karna, and let fall her veil. Her face was as striking as the full moon after a cloudy month of nights. But her gaze was that of a swordsman who sees a chink in his opponent's armor and does not hesitate to plunge his blade there. And every man in the assembly, even as he desired her, thanked his fate that it was not he who stood before her.

In the face of that question, Karna was silenced. Defeated, head bowed in shame, he left the marriage hall. But he never forgot the humiliation of that moment in full sight of all the kings of Bharat. And when the time came for him to repay the haughty princess of Panchaal, he did so a hundredfold.

. . .

I don't blame the bards for what they sing. In a way, things occurred just as they describe it. But in another way, they were completely different.

When Karna issued his challenge and my brother stepped forward with his hand on his sword, a haze of panic blurred my vision. Something terrible was close to happening. There was no one, other than I, who might be able to stop it. But what should I do? I looked at Krishna, hoping for direction. It seemed to me that he pointed with his chin, but what was he urging? Behind him Vyasa frowned. He had warned me of this moment, though my wheeling mind couldn't recall his words. Hadn't he said I'd be the cause of my brother's death? I gritted my teeth and took a deep breath. I would not give in to fate so easily.

Dhri unsheathed his sword and braced his shoulders. Karna leveled his arrow—the one he'd chosen to pierce the target—at my brother's chest. His eyes were beautiful and sad and unfaltering, the eyes of a man who always hits what he aims at.

My mind went blank except for one memory: the moment I'd stepped from the fire unwanted and Dhri had gripped my hand, claiming me. He had been the first one to love me. Everything paled before that fact: the newborn tremor in my heart when I looked at Karna, the numbness that I knew would replace it when he turned from me in anger.

Later, some would commend me for being brave enough to put the upstart son of a chariot driver in his place. Others would declare me arrogant. Caste-obsessed. They'd say I deserved every punishment I received. Still others would admire me for being true to dharma, whatever that means. But I did it only because I couldn't bear to see my brother die.

Can our actions change our destiny? Or are they like sand piled against the breakage in a dam, merely delaying the inevitable? I saved Dhri, yes, so that he could go on to perform heroic and terrible deeds. But death is not so easily cheated. When it came for him again, its shape was so much worse that I wished I'd let it snatch him away at the swayamvar, where at least he would have perished with honor.

This much I'm certain of: Something did change in the moment when I asked Karna the question that I knew would hurt him the most, the only question that would make him lay down his bow. When I'd stepped forward and looked into his face, there had been a light in it—call it admiration, or desire, or the wistful beginnings of love. If I'd been wiser, I might have been able to call forth that love and, in that way, deflected the danger of the moment—a moment that would turn out to be far more important than I imagined. But I was young and afraid, and my ill-chosen words (words I would regret all my life) quenched that light forever.

scar

 My feet were bleeding. I'd never walked barefoot on common streets, over thorns and stones. I stared at the man striding ahead, the cheap white shawl that covered his wiry back, and wondered if he was who I suspected. An hour ago I'd put a wedding garland around his neck. The punishing sun beat upon my head, dizzying me. We hadn't spoken since we left the palace. My throat was parched. I'd eaten nothing all day, as was customary for brides, and afterward he'd refused to stay (churlishly, I thought) for the wedding feast.

"I must return to my family," he'd said. "They'll be worrying." In reply to my father's questions, he stated that he was not at liberty to speak of them, or give us his name.

My father controlled his temper with effort. "Let us bring your family here," he said. "They can live in whichever of my palaces you wish them to have. Half the kingdom, after all, is yours, according to the marriage contract."

The man said he had no need of palaces. He asked that I shed my finery, inappropriate for a poor brahmin's wife. The maids brought me a cotton sari. I handed my gold ornaments to Dhai Ma, who was crying. I kept only the necklace of shells which he'd placed around my throat.

"At least let us give you a chariot," my brother cried in consternation. "Panchaali isn't used to—"

"She must learn it now," he replied.

Each footstep on the cracked, burning path was agony. I was too proud to ask him to slow down, even when I stumbled and fell. Gravel tore at my knees through the thin cotton of my sari. There were cuts on my palms. I bit at my lips to keep in tears of pain, of anger at my husband's indifference. An insidious voice inside me said, Karna would never have let you suffer like this. But that was no longer correct. If he saw me now, he would have laughed with bitter satisfaction.

I rose and gritted my teeth. I placed one foot after the other. *I can survive this*, I said to myself, the way Dhri might have. But it hurt too much. I couldn't keep it up. Besides, it was foolish, what I was trying to do. I was a woman. I had to use my power differently.

I found a banyan by the side of the road and sat down in its shade. I stretched out my throbbing feet. Perhaps it was a good thing that I was so exhausted. My tiredness was a screen that shielded me from my fear, from caring about what my husband (how strange that term) would think. I took a deep breath and crossed my arms. I watched his receding back and waited to find out how soon he'd notice I wasn't following him—and what he'd do then.

. . .

This is how I came to be in such a predicament:

Karna had left. The hall was abuzz with the dissatisfaction of unsuccessful kings. Duryodhan shouted that the test was unfair. Impossible. And besides, he wasn't going to put up with this insult to his friend. "Let's leave in protest," he cried to the other kings. But someone else—I think it was Sisupal, his face suffused with outrage, yelled, "Why should we leave so easily, without giving Drupad something to remember us by?" Dhri's back grew stiff. I saw him signal the commander of the Panchaal army.

Then the brahmin said, "May I try?"

My head was still awhirl with what I'd done to Karna. There was a pain in my chest, as though someone had taken my heart in his hands and was wringing it. I noticed, without much interest, that the man's long hair was gathered in a traditional topknot. White home-spun covered his slender shoulders. He seemed young. His smile re-vealed strong, straight teeth—a rarity among the poor. The kings laughed mockingly, but the brahmins cheered.

"A brahmin is higher-born than any prince," one of them de-clared. "He has the right."

Someone else shouted, "And don't underestimate the power of prayer! It might well prevail where muscles failed!" Glares were ex-changed between the brahmins and kshatriyas in an age-old power struggle.

A relieved Dhri motioned the young man forward.

The brahmin chanted something—a prayer, perhaps, though his tone was not one of supplication. In a motion so rapid that his arm was a streak of light, he lifted the bow. Shot. Before I could take in a breath, the shield cracked in two and fell with a clang, and the fish, still revolving slowly, hung askew from the ceiling, its brass eye pierced by the brahmin's arrow.

The commoners erupted in cheers, though the kings were omi-nously quiet. Dhri grasped the man's hands; my father descended from his throne; the priests hurried to the dais; my attendants rushed forward, strewing flowers and gabbling wedding songs. Someone thrust the garland into my hands. The brahmin was very tall. He had to bend down so I could raise the garland over his head. Who was he? Krishna might have known, but in the press of people, I couldn't find him. How could a brahmin be so skilled with the bow? I tried to check if he had any battle scars, but the shawl covered his shoulders. Dhai Ma had stories where gods came to earth, disguised, to marry virtuous princesses, but I doubted that I was sufficiently virtuous for that. I tried to look into his face, but it was deliberately angled away. One of the kings blew his battle conch. It was echoed by others. Hurry, Panchaali, Dhri whispered. Why wouldn't the man meet my eyes? I stood on tiptoe and numbly dropped the garland around his neck. Was this even a proper wedding, conducted with such unseemly haste? He slipped a chain made of cowrie shells, such as poor village women wear, over my head. Against my skin, the shells were like cold, minute fists. And so I was married.

The fight started almost immediately. Twenty kings, perhaps more, rushed at my stranger-husband. He disappeared under the flashing of swords. I stared at the roiling mass of men and weapons. I should have been more worried—for my new husband as well as myself—but I couldn't bring myself to care. Dhri shouted orders as he parried and thrust, but a group of kings had barred the doorway, preventing our soldiers from entering.

Impossibly, the stranger emerged from the sea of weapons unscathed. Even the shawl around his shoulders hadn't been disturbed. I expected him to look grim. Instead, a fierce glee filled his face. He thrust me behind him and aimed an arrow at the melee. I thought I heard him speak. The arrow split into a hundred points of light, the dots of light connected, and a sizzling net fell onto the kings. They flailed around, falling drunkenly over each other. It was the perfect punishment. When he aimed again, the kings guarding the doorway broke rank and fled.

"Lady," the stranger said, his eyes politely lowered, "I apologize for the fright this must have caused you."

He was no brahmin, I was sure of that. Conjectures bubbled in my mind. I narrowed my eyes to better examine him. "I'm not so easily frightened," I said.

. . .

Soon after I sat down under the tree, my husband hurried back. He was scowling. He started to ask a question, then saw my feet. His face flushed. He knelt and examined my soles, his hands unexpectedly gentle, sure of what they were doing. He fashioned a cup of leaves and fetched me water from a nearby pond to drink. He fetched me more water to wash my feet, then tore a strip from his shawl and bandaged them. He apologized for not noticing my troubles. He was distracted by many worries. When I asked what they were, he shook his head.

I stared at his face, trying to match it to the one I'd seen in a painting a lifetime ago. But that face had sported a moustache, a crown, jeweled earrings, long, flowing locks, oiled and perfumed. This face, thin and sunburned, with its raised, ascetic cheekbones, the hair pulled severely back, confused me. There was only one thing I could think of doing.

Quickly, before I lost courage, I pulled the shawl from his shoulders. There they were, the battle scars! Daringly, I touched one that ran across his taut upper arm. His eyes flew to my face. Strange—they looked so like another pair of eyes! How could this be? But no, I had no right even to think this question. I'd destroyed that part of my life. This was now my destiny. For the sake of my family and the prophecy at my birth, I had to make the best of it.

"Are you Arjun?" I asked.

He didn't answer, but he smiled, and a little of his severity fell away. That should have pleased me, but my heart weighted down my chest like a dead thing. Still, I forced myself to not remove my hand. I am his wife, I told myself. Against my fingers, the scar was puckered and harder than I had imagined, as though the shard of an arrow were still lodged inside the skin. I ran my nail over it as the sorceress had instructed and heard the sharp intake of his breath. Why should that make my face grow hot with guilt?

He said, "If I were Arjun, would that make you happier?"

I managed an even tone. "I'm no longer a princess. I'm your wife, and content with my lot, whoever you may be."

"Most commendable." There was a teasing spark in his eyes.

I risked the next words, treading the dangerous territory of the half-truth. "But I have thought often of Arjun since Krishna spoke to me of his powers."

He turned from me, looking over to the side. His brow was corrugated, the line of his lips hard. What if he wasn't Arjun, as I'd so hastily presumed? Why hadn't I heeded Dhai Ma's warning that forwardness would be the ruin of me? Most warriors, after all, had battle scars. Who could blame my stranger-husband if he was furious right now, hearing another man's praise on his new wife's lips?

But when he spoke, it was with courtesy and some charm, and I realized that whatever troubled him had nothing to do with me. "I cannot reveal my identity without my family's permission. But I'll tell you this: I too have thought of Panchaali since Krishna described her many virtues to me!"

For the rest of the way he held my arm, supporting me as I limped along. He didn't speak further, and I was thankful for the silence. My mind was trying to encompass all that had happened in the last few hours. Now that I was sure of Arjun's identity, I knew that everyone who cared for me—Dhri, Dhai Ma, my father, Krishna— would be delighted at how things had turned out. I was married to a man who was the greatest warrior of his generation. He would become one of my father's staunchest allies. In the Great War, he would protect my brother as he attempted to fulfill his destiny. Courteous, noble, brave, handsome, he would be a fit husband for me (and I a fit helpmate for him) as together we left our mark on history. Perhaps he would build me the palace I dreamed of, a place where I finally belonged.

I would no longer waste time on regret. I would turn my face to the future and carve it into the shape I wanted. I would satisfy myself with duty. If I was lucky, love would come.

That was what I told myself as we walked and walked, the hot day wilting around us, the pathway of stone and thorn taking me further each moment from everything that had been familiar to me.

brinjal

I bent over a smoky fire fueled by cow-dung, cooking brinjal curry under the watchful eye of my mother-in-law. The kitchen was tiny and airless. My back ached. The smoke made my throat burn. Sweat poured into my eyes. I wiped it off furiously. I wasn't going to give my mother-in-law the satisfaction of thinking that she'd reduced me to tears, though in fact I was on the verge of weeping with frustration.

She sat pristine in her white widow's sari, her hair blacker and glossier than it had any right to be (she was old, after all, with five grown sons), flicking stones from the cheap red rice that her sons had begged as alms. The heat didn't seem to affect her. At first I thought it was because she'd positioned herself in front of the single small window. But perhaps she had inner resources beyond what my eyes could see. A subtle disdain flickered under the composure that marked her face. It seemed to say, You find this difficult? Why then, you'd never have survived a hundredth part of what I've been through.

I'd entered a household full of mysteries, secrets that no one articulated. I'd have to use all my resources to try and decipher them. But one thing I knew already: from the moment she saw me yesterday, my mother-in-law regarded me as her adversary.

. . .

It had turned evening by the time Arjun and I entered a small settlement at the edge of town, with dilapidated mud walls pressed up against each other. I thought I'd prepared myself to accept hardship. But my heart fell as I noted the alleys stinking with refuse, the stray dogs with their open sores. It was all I could do to not clap a hand over my nose.

As we turned a corner, four young men, all dressed like Arjun as poor brahmins, joined us. I knew these must be the other Pandavas. From under my veil, I darted glances at their faces, but I couldn't recognize a single one. What art of disguise had they learned?

The brothers embraced Arjun and cuffed him on the shoulder, chiding him for not allowing them to help him in the fight. When they turned to greet me, their eyes were alight with curiosity and (I thought) admiration. Not sure how a new wife should behave with her brothers-in-law, I bowed my head and joined decorous palms, though I was equally curious. They were a lively lot, the two youngest ones miming how the defeated kings had run from my husband, the large, muscled one slapping his knees and doubling over with laughter while the eldest watched indulgently. My husband was pleased by their praise, though he didn't say much. At their approach, he'd let go of my arm, a fact I didn't care for.

The oldest brother—this would be Yudhisthir—urged us to hurry. "We're late!" he said. "You know how Mother worries." We turned the final corner and there was their hut, the meanest in the row. From the small kitchen window came the clink of pots.

The tallest of them—if I remembered right, his name was Bheem—winked at Arjun. "Mother's always so serious! Let's play a trick on her." Before the others could stop him, he called out, "Ma, come and see what we've brought home today."

"Son," said a woman's voice in a patrician accent, "I can't come right now or the food will burn. But as always, whatever you brought should be shared equally amongst all my sons."

The brothers looked at each other, embarrassed.

Yudhisthir frowned at Bheem. "You certainly have a way of getting into trouble—and dragging us along! Let me go and explain."

He disappeared through the low doorway. I thought he would be back soon, but he didn't return for a long time. The brothers waited in awkward silence. I sensed that they hesitated to invite me in without their mother's permission. I looked toward Arjun, but— perhaps deliberately—he was watching a plume of smoke rising from a nearby hut. I stood on the porch feeling parched and unwelcome, the regrets I'd chased away returning to descend on me like vultures. When my legs hurt too much, I sat down on the ground, leaned my back against the hut wall and closed my eyes. I must have dozed. When I opened them again, my mother-in-law loomed above me like a statue carved from ice. And though I'd had doubts about the identity of her sons, I knew at once that I was staring up at the widowed queen Kunti.

. . .

Kunti didn't believe in using spices. Or perhaps she just didn't believe in letting her daughter-in-law have any. She'd handed me a pulpy brinjal, along with a lump of salt and a minute amount of oil, and told me to prepare it for lunch. I asked her if I might have a bit of turmeric and some chilies. Perhaps some cumin. She replied, "This is all there is. This isn't your father's palace!"

I didn't trust her words. In the alcove behind her I could see bowls and jars, a pouch. On the floor sat a grinding stone, stained yellow from its last use. I swallowed my anger and chopped the brinjal on the dull cutting blade. I rubbed salt into it and dropped it into the pan. There was too little oil. The cow-dung fire burned too high, and I didn't know how to reduce it. In a few minutes, the pieces began to get scorched. I was about to give up and let them burn to blackness when, turning, I saw the smallest of smiles on Kunti's face. I understood. If the fish had been Arjun's test, this was mine.

. . .

This is what Kunti declared to her sons yesterday, before she said a single word to me: "All through my life—even in the hardest of times—everything I said, I made sure it was done. I told myself I'd bring you up as princes in the halls of your forefathers, and no matter how much harassment I faced, I held on to my promise. Sons, if you value what I did for you, you must now honor my word. All five of you must marry this woman."

I stared at her, my brain trying to take in what she had said. Was she joking when she said they must all marry me? No, her face made that clear. I wanted to shout, Five husbands? Are you mad? I wanted to say, I'm already married to Arjun! But Vyasa's prophecy recoiled upon me, robbing me of my protests.

I recognized, too, the thinly veiled insult in Kunti's words. *This woman*, as though I were a nameless servant. It angered me, but it also hurt. From the stories I'd heard about Kunti, I'd admired her. I'd imagined that if she did indeed become my mother-in-law, she would love me as a daughter. Now I saw how naïve I'd been. A woman like her would never tolerate anyone who might lure her sons away.

The brothers looked at me with speculation in their eyes. They didn't protest. Maybe they weren't used to contradicting their mother. Or maybe the idea wasn't as repugnant to them as it was to me. Only

Arjun blurted out, "Mother, how can you ask us to do this? It's contrary to dharma."

"Let us eat now," Kunti said. Underneath the serenity her voice was like steel. Here was woman's power at work! In spite of my fury, I felt a grudging admiration. "It's late. You're tired. We can discuss it tomorrow."

Arjun drew in his breath. I waited for him to stand up for me, to tell his mother that he and I were already husband and wife, committed to each other. She had no right to destroy that.

To my disappointment, he said nothing.

Now that she'd had her way, Kunti turned to me. She allowed herself to smile as she welcomed me with a bouquet of gracious words. But I felt the thorns underneath.

When it was time for bed, the brothers unrolled their mats and lay down, one beside the other. Kunti placed her mat at their heads and gave me the last, rat-nibbled one to lie on. I was to sleep near the brothers' feet, at a chaste distance. I considered refusing, but I was too weary. I'd save my rebellion for another day.

I drifted in and out of sleep all night, listening to the plaintive call of owls, watching the moon drag itself across the small window. I was uncomfortable, miserable, disillusioned—and most of all, angry with Arjun. I'd expected him to be my champion. It was the least he could have done after plucking me from my home. When inside me a voice whispered, Karna would never have let you down like this, I did not hush it.

The night seemed endless. Someone snored. Someone else shouted angrily in his dream. Once I thought I saw a man looking in through the window. To my blurred, homesick eyes, his face looked like Dhri's, though that was impossible. And a good thing, too. Dhri would have been enraged to see me like this, lying on the floor at the feet of these men—on my wedding night, no less, when my bed should have been piled with scented silks. When I should have been held close and cherished. But I was no longer my brother's to protect or indulge, I thought, tears of self-pity filling my eyes. I'd placed a garland around the neck of a man who hadn't even cared to tell me his name, and it had changed everything.

I was about to give in to despair when a thought came to me: This is what she's hoping for! The heat of that realization dried up my tears. I took a resolute breath, the way Kunti might have if she were in my place. I loosened my muscles, using the techniques the sorceress had taught. I no longer resisted the floor but let my body sink into it. One moment at a time, I told myself. What use was it to worry about the future, which might take a shape far different from what either Kunti or I wanted? And with that, sleep came to me.

. . .

"You're burning the brinjal," Kunti said, her voice kind. "Also, you've put in too much salt. Oh, look how red your eyes are! I should have guessed that a princess like you, brought up in luxury, wouldn't have any experience with cooking." She gave a patient sigh. "Never mind. You can scrub the pots while I repair the curry."

But I was ready now. "Respected mother," I said, bowing, "being so much younger, I know my culinary skills can't equal yours. But it's my duty to relieve you of your burdens whenever possible. Please let me do so. If your sons are displeased with the food, I'll gladly accept the blame."

I turned to the pot and covered it with a battered dish and focused on what the sorceress had taught me. I willed the oil to bubble up, the brinjal to soften. I prayed to the fire to hold back its power. I closed my eyes and imagined a rich paste of poppy seed and cinnamon coating the pieces. I didn't open them until the aroma filled my nostrils.

When at mealtime the brothers praised the brinjal for its distinctive taste and asked for more, I remained in the kitchen and let Kunti serve her sons. I kept my face carefully impassive, my eyes on the floor. But she and I both knew that I'd won the first round.

lac

 That first night, all my hopes fallen in ruins around me, I dreamed of the palace of lac, where my husbands were supposed to have burned to death. Of how it had come into being.

In my dream, I was a lac insect. Like my hundred sisters, I attached myself to a new twig and drank its sap. I had no eyes, so I focused my entire impassioned energy on drinking. I drank and grew and secreted resin red as mud until I was covered with it, until we were all covered. Within my shell I held still and grew, like my hundred sisters, and within me grew the eggs. The moon waxed full: once, twice, three times. The resin pooled and spread across the branches, turning them red until the tree seemed to be a dancing flame. The waiting villagers nodded. *Yes, soon.* The eggs hatched, a hundred new insects attached themselves to other trees, the villagers broke off the branches and scraped the resin clean and sent it to Varanavat where Duryodhan had ordered a palace to be built for his five cousins.

(And I? I died. No need to mourn me. My work was done.)

. . .

Palaces have always fascinated me, even a gloom-filled structure like my father's that was a fitting carapace for his vengeful obsession. For isn't that what our homes are ultimately, our fantasies made corporeal, our secret selves exposed? The converse is also true: we grow to become that which we live within. That was one of the reasons why I longed to escape my father's walls. (But— unknown to me—by the time I left, it was too late. The creed he lived by was already stamped onto my soul.)

Often I imagined my own palace, the one I would build some-day. What would it be made of? What form would it take? Krishna's palace in Dwarka was pink sandstone, the arches like the ocean waves that bordered it. It sounded lovely, but I knew mine would have to be different. It would have to be uniquely mine.

When I'd asked him what kind of palace he thought I should have, Krishna said, "Already you live within a nine-gated palace, the most wondrous structure of all. Understand it well: it will be your salvation or your downfall."

Sometimes his riddles were tiresome. I sighed. I'd have to wait for time to uncover the answers he wouldn't give me. But this much I knew already: my palace would be like no other.

But this night, lying in a hovel, I dreamed of the palace of lac, burnished like wings. Gods and goddesses were carved into its sills to lull its inhabitants into a belief of safety. When did the Pandavas discover its flammable truth? They told no one. Such a bitter be-trayal by their own cousin, their childhood playmate, must have hurt, but they secreted it deep within their bodies. They continued to laugh and sing and go boating on Varanavat lake. They invited the caretaker, the traitor Purochan, to a banquet, and did not poison his food. What gave them so much strength?

. . .

Years later, Sahadev, the youngest brother, the gentle chroni-cler of their lives, told me the rest of the story.

He said: "When she realized that Duryodhan had offered us this holiday at Varanavat in order to kill us, our mother went into her chambers and wept for a night and a day.

"We paced outside her room, not knowing what to do. She'd always been so strong, our foundation stone. When she came out, we rushed to comfort her. But her eyes were dry. She said to us, I've used up all the tears of my life so that they will not distract me again."

(In this, though, she was mistaken. A woman can never use up all the tears of her life. How do I know this? Because Kunti would weep again—and I would weep with her.)

"She sent word to Vidur, the blind king's chief minister, who was sympathetic to our cause. On his advice, she made us dig a tunnel that would run from the house to the forest, that would collapse after we'd used it, leaving no telltale trace. But she wouldn't let us escape until she felt the time was right. Meanwhile, each day she gave alms to the poor and opened our doors to homeless travelers so they might have a place to sleep.

"One night the nishad woman arrived with her five sons. They were traveling to the fair with their woven baskets and feathered arrows. My mother offered them food and all the wine they wanted. She invited them to sleep in the main hall though they would have preferred the stables. When they were asleep, she asked us to set the house on fire. We saw the perfection in her plan: the nishads' charred skeletons would be taken for ours; Duryodhan would believe he had succeeded in ridding himself of us. But we were distraught, too. They were our guests. They'd eaten our food; they'd gone to sleep trusting us. To kill them would be a great sin.

"Our mother looked us in the eye. I drugged the wine, she said. They'll feel no pain. As for the sin of killing them, I swear it will not touch you. I take it all on myself. For the safety of my children, I'll gladly forgo heaven."

Sahadev's eyes grew moist as he spoke. He'd forgotten that Kunti wasn't his true mother. The look on his face was more tender than anything he'd ever offered me. But for once I didn't begrudge it to Kunti. Could I have made that ultimate sacrifice, taking on damnation for my children?

Sahadev, if only you'd told me this earlier! For by this time Kunti and I (yoked together uneasily by our desire for Pandava glory) had frozen into our stance of mutual distrust. But had I known the story before, I would have tried harder to be her friend.

. . .

In my dream, Bheem applies the torch to the palace: doors, windows, threshold. Last of all, he flings it onto the roof of the caretaker's cottage where Purochan sleeps. The others are in the tunnel already. He vaults in after them, clangs shut the trapdoor. The fire buzzes like bees. The roof of the tunnel is hot to the touch. The palace walls buckle and fold. Lacquered tears flow down the cheeks of the gods. The Pandavas crawl on hands and knees in the mud, their ears alert for cries. But the blessed roar from the fire drowns all other noises. The palace explodes, a dark heart bursting. Those who run to look will later claim they saw a thousand insects soar into the sky on blazing wings.

boon

"Marry all five of you!" my father sputtered. "How can you, prince of a noble house, suggest such a heinous act?"

In the throne room, the air throbbed with tension. My father and Dhri sat on golden thrones. The five Pandavas sat across from them on silver seats, to remind them that they were honored guests but less powerful. In a corner, behind an embroidered curtain, Kunti and I sat on chairs of sandalwood. I'd graciously offered her the larger one. She'd accepted with a slight frown, not sure if my action was respect or ruse. But the size of a seat has little to do with the power of the person who occupies it. We all knew this.

Earlier in the day, Dhri had arrived with palanquins and musicians to take us to the palace. (It had, indeed, been him at the window last night; he and his men had been scouring the city for me.) He brought robes and jewels, horses. Fine weapons that brought a gleam to the brothers' eyes. And an invitation from King Drupad, who wanted to celebrate his daughter's marriage (which had been so hasty and unsatisfying) with a grand banquet where he could show off his new son-in-law.

"We are delighted to have gained the Pandavas as our relatives," Dhri said with an elegant bow. I tried to catch his eye, to indicate that I was less than delighted, but he was busy being gracious.

He loved courtesies and had had little occasion to practice them. The brothers looked relieved at having to shed their disguise. On the way to the palace, their kingly robes cast a glow on their faces. Even I had to admit that they rode like gods.

"Admittedly, this is an unusual arrangement. But how can it be heinous to obey one's mother?" Yudhisthir asked. "Haven't our scriptures declared, The father is equal to heaven, but the mother is greater?"

Not many men would have been able to make such statements sound convincing, but somehow Yudhisthir succeeded. Perhaps it was because we could see that he believed what he said.

"If we can't agree," he continued calmly, "that Panchaali should marry all five of us, then we brothers must take our leave, returning your daughter to your care."

I stared at him in outraged shock. King Drupad stiffened, and my brother's hand fisted around the hilt of his sword. To be sent back to her father's house was the worst disgrace a woman could face. When she was a woman of a noble house, such an insult could lead to a blood feud between the families. Was Yudhisthir oblivious of the danger in which his words had thrust the Pandavas?

"You can't do that!" Dhri exclaimed angrily. "My sister's life would be ruined!"

Arjun's eyes flew to his brother's face. His jaw was tense. He disagreed with Yudhisthir, I could see that. But out of respect for his brother—or perhaps because he knew that they had to stand together in this—he said nothing. I was disappointed, but in the pragmatic light of day, I didn't blame him as much as I had last night. Family loyalty was what had saved the Pandavas all these precarious years. How could I expect him to give it up for a woman he hadn't met until yesterday?

"To say nothing of the reputation of the royal house of Panchaal!" my father added. "Draupadi would most likely have to take her own life, and then we'd have to hunt you down and kill you in revenge."

"The choice is yours," Yudhisthir said, without heat. (Was that calmness a façade, or was he truly unshakable in the face of threats?) "An honorable life for the princess as a daughter-in-law of Hastinapur—or a death you force upon her."

"Honorable!" blustered my father. "Perhaps in Hastinapur such behavior's considered honorable, but here in Kampilya men will call Draupadi a whore! And if I should hand her over to the five of you, what will they call me? Perhaps death *is* a better alternative."

I didn't fear the fate they imagined for me. I had no intention of committing honorable self-immolation. (I had other plans for my life.) But I was distressed by the coldness with which my father and my potential husband discussed my options, thinking only of how these acts would benefit—or harm—them. My brother protested hotly, but they brushed his youthful words aside. Why didn't Arjun speak up in my defense? Surely, now that they were considering my possible death, he should have felt some responsibility? Some tenderness?

Ah, Karna! Was this my punishment for having treated you so cruelly? And where was Krishna, whose ill advice had lured me to this moment?

The rest of the Pandavas, stolid in their silence, didn't seem to care about what became of me. (In this assumption I was wrong. One of them had already begun to fall in love with me. Later he would tell me, I thought my chest would burst from the effort of holding in my angry words. If it had gone any further, I would have stood against my brother for your sake, even if it made me traitor to my clan. But in my agitated preoccupation with Arjun, I was blind to this.)

While the men negotiated—my father furiously, Yudhisthir with nonchalance—I examined Kunti from under my veil. (I wasn't required to wear a veil in my father's house, but it had its uses.) A small, triumphant smile flickered on her lips when she heard Yudhisthir quoting the scriptures in praise of motherhood. But a telltale artery pulsed in her throat. The Pandavas—hiding as they'd been from Duryodhan's long and lethal reach—had much to gain by forming an alliance with the powerful Drupad. They had everything to lose if they angered him. Knowing this, why hadn't Kunti laughed off her remark as a mistake and allowed the marriage to stand as it was? I didn't believe her claim that everything she said had to come true, or her honor would be lost.

Something else was at work here, something I'd have to puzzle out.

My father's eyes were the first to fall. "I'll send word to Vyasa, wisest of the wise," he muttered. "He knows the future as well as the past. We'll abide by his advice."

Yudhisthir graciously acceded; Kunti wiped a tiny bead of sweat from her temple; the Pandavas retired to their quarters. I retreated to my bedroom, pleading a headache to escape Dhai Ma's eager queries about my bridal night.

. . .

Vyasa sent a prompt verdict: I was to be married to all five brothers. My father was not to distress himself about how this would affect his reputation. This never-before-seen marital arrangement would make him more famous than a heap of battle victories. If people asked uncomfortable questions, he could blame it on the gods, who had ordained it lifetimes ago.

To keep me chaste and foster harmony in the Pandava household, Vyasa designed a special code of marital conduct for us. I would be wife to each brother for a year at a time, from oldest to youngest, consecutively. During that year, the other brothers were to keep their eyes lowered when speaking to me. (Better if they didn't speak at all.) They were not to touch me, not even the tips of my fingers. If they intruded upon our privacy when my husband and I were together, they were to be banished for a year from the household. In a postscript he added that he would give me a boon to balance the one that had landed me with five spouses. Each time I went to a new brother, I'd be a virgin again.

I can't say I was surprised by Vyasa's verdict. (Hadn't his spirits threatened me with such a fate years ago?) But now that it was to become an imminent reality, I was surprised at how angry it made me feel—and how helpless. Though Dhai Ma tried to console me by saying that finally I had the freedom men had had for centuries, my situation was very different from that of a man with several wives. Unlike him, I had no choice as to whom I slept with, and when. Like a communal drinking cup, I would be passed from hand to hand whether I wanted it or not.

Nor was I particularly delighted by the virginity boon, which seemed designed more for my husbands' benefit than mine. That seemed to be the nature of boons given to women—they were handed to us like presents we hadn't quite wanted. (Had Kunti felt the same way when she was told that the gods would be happy to impregnate her? For a moment, sympathy twinged through me. Then it was lost beneath a surge of resentment. If it weren't for her, I wouldn't be in this miserable situation.)

If the sage had cared to inquire, I'd have requested the gift of forgetting, so that when I went to each brother I'd be free of the memory of the previous one. And along with that, I'd have requested that Arjun be my first husband. He was the only one of the Pandavas I felt I could have fallen in love with. If he had loved me back, I might have been able to push aside my regrets about Karna and find some semblance of happiness.

. . .

I was married to the four other Pandavas, one after the other, in a long-drawn, tedious ceremony. I put my hands into each man's as the priest chanted the appropriate mantras and scattered yellow rice over us. A part of my mind noted the slight differences: Yudhisthir's palm was the softest; Bheem's was calloused from wielding the mace, which I'd learned was his favorite weapon, and it trembled in mine, surprising me; Nakul's hands were scented with musk; Sahadev's had an ink smudge on the middle finger of his right hand. I tried— not too successfully—to read these clues. It struck me that, during our hasty ceremony at the swayamvar, there had been no opportunity for Arjun and me to hold each other's hands.

The irony of that made me want to find Arjun, to see what he was doing. Angling my face discreetly under my veil, I discovered him sitting off to one side, staring deliberately into the distance as though he refused to be part of the festivities. I was shaken by the bitter downturn of his mouth. I hadn't expected him to care so much about the fact that I didn't belong to him alone. I must have made an involuntary movement, for he swiveled his head to look at me. His eyes were angry—as though I were the one who had chosen to marry his brothers, and thus betrayed him!

I lifted my veil and stared back, uncaring of what his brothers might think of my indecorous behavior. I had to send Arjun a message and knew this might be my last chance in a long time. According to Vyasa's dictum, we wouldn't even be able to speak privately to each other for the next two years. I was desperate to make him re- alize that this situation wasn't any more to my liking than his. That he keep in his mind, through the next two years, what we'd shared, frail though it was: that moment of tenderness on the road, his gentle hands on my injured feet. Only then could I hope to salvage our fledgling relationship. *I'll be waiting for you*, I tried to tell him with my eyes. But he averted his gaze. My heart sank as I saw that he'd made me the target of the frustrated rage that he couldn't express toward his brothers or his mother.

I blamed Kunti for this development. She knew her son's psychology: if he couldn't have me all to himself, he didn't want me at all. He would go through the motions of marriage, but he would keep his heart from me. And wasn't that exactly what she intended?

Afterward, Dhri tactfully whisked the four younger brothers off to a tiger hunt, my father sent opulent wedding announcements to everyone he knew, and Yudhisthir moved into my palace. I went to him reluctantly, still brooding over Arjun's unfair anger. But perhaps my own situation made me more patient with my husband than I would have been otherwise. When he made overtures of tenderness, I stopped myself from turning away. I would not make him the victim of my disappointment, I told myself. Kind, courteous, and well-read, he was easy to get along with, though I found him somewhat lacking in humor. (Only later would I discover other facets: his stubbornness, his obsession with truth, his insistent moralizing, his implacable goodness.) In bed, to my amused surprise, he was shy and easily alarmed. Slowly I realized that he had in his head a compendium of ideas (had Kunti put them there?) about what constituted ladylike sexual behavior, and—this was a longer list—what didn't. I could see that I'd have to dedicate significant energy to reeducating him.

It was going to be a long year.

grandfather

Dhri sent an urgent message: Yudhisthir and I were to meet him at the guard tower situated atop the city walls. When we climbed it, we saw a huge army approaching Kampilya.

Fear dizzied me. Only two weeks had passed since my swayamvar. Had the unsuccessful suitors returned for revenge? But Yudhisthir said, "Look, there's the banner of Hastinapur!"

"It seems that your uncle has sent an entourage to welcome you home!" Dhri said with an ironic smile.

"What else can he do, now that he's learned his nephews are alive and well—instead of reduced to ash and crumbled bone—and allied moreover to the powerful Drupad?" Yudhisthir said, his smile equally ironic. I was surprised. With his brothers, he was always the reasonable one, holding them back, chiding them when they cursed their Kaurava cousins. So he did have his secret darkness, my near-to-perfect husband!

But now he was leaning over the edge of the battlement, as delighted as a child at his first fair. "Look, Panchaali! Grandfather himself has come to fetch us!"

At the head of the army I saw a man on a white horse, his beard like the rush of a silver river. The sun, reflecting off his armor, was blinding. He dwarfed everyone around him.

So this was Bheeshma, grandfather to my husbands, the keeper of dreadful vows, the warrior to whose destruction Sikhandi had dedicated his life. Torn between detestation and fascination, I couldn't drag my eyes from him.

Yudhisthir glanced at me, his grin proud and boyish. "He does tend to take one's breath away, doesn't he!"

As usual he had read me wrong.

Bheeshma raised his hand in greeting—he must have recognized Yudhisthir. Even from that distance I felt his love, heavy and piercing as a javelin.

. . .

My father received Bheeshma respectfully enough, but he didn't mince his words. "Duryodhan almost killed them last time," he said. "Who's to say he won't succeed the next time around? I don't want my only daughter sent back to me in widow's white." He seemed more concerned about losing his new allies than about my marital misfortunes.

Bheeshma's eyes flashed at the insult. But he only said, "My life for their safety." He spoke with such simple force that even Krishna, whom my father had invited to the meeting, nodded.

"Let them go," he said to my father. "With the grandfather to watch over them, Duryodhan won't try anything—not for a while. Besides, how long can you keep them cloistered? They're heroes, after all."

When my father and his courtiers left the room, Bheeshma embraced Krishna. I hadn't realized they knew each other so well. My ignorance irked me.

"Now it begins, Govinda," Bheeshma said, calling him by a name I hadn't heard before. (How many facets were there to Krishna? I felt, with a kind of despair, that I'd never know them all.) The two men looked at each other, somber with a secret they wouldn't share with us. They made me feel like a child.

Then Bheeshma turned to Yudhisthir, cuffing him on the ear. "Scoundrel!" he scolded. "Why didn't you let me know that you were alive? When I thought you boys perished in the burning house, it almost killed me!" His tone was jocular, but his face showed the depth of his emotion. Deep grooves were etched around his mouth. All of a sudden, he looked his age. When he wiped his eyes, I couldn't stop myself from staring. I'd never seen a man—least of all a famous warrior—shed tears.

But in the space of a breath he shook off sorrow and took my hands in his. His face filled with genuine gladness. "Dearest granddaughter," he said, "I welcome you with all my heart to your new home!" No one had invited me into his life so convincingly. No one had been so eager to find a place for me in his home.

All this while, for the sake of Sikhandi, I'd decided to hate Bheeshma. But now I found I couldn't withstand his quicksilver charm. I felt my mistrust melting in the warmth of his smile. Perhaps, I thought, I was finally going where I belonged.

. . .

The Pandavas returned to Hastinapur in triumph, escorted by marching soldiers and painted elephants and musicians blowing on conches and horns. Kunti and I rode in a chariot resplendent with silk pillows and cloth of gold curtains. Behind us came a hundred men carrying chests filled with jewels, my father's parting gift. Kunti had a small, satisfied smile on her face—and why shouldn't she? Her sons were safer and wealthier than they'd ever been, with powerful relatives that Duryodhan would hesitate to anger. The whole of Bharat was abuzz with the story of my marriage to five brothers whose filial piety was such that they preferred to share a wife rather than break their mother's word. In our skirmish of wits, too, she had come out ahead, successfully destroying the bond that might have formed between Arjun and me had we only had each other—a bond that might have made him turn, in time, to me instead of her for counsel.

I swallowed the bitterness that rose like bile to my mouth. Our war wasn't over yet. I would bide my time, observing her, learning her weaknesses. Meanwhile, I would act to perfection my role of daughter-in-law.

"What's the palace at Hastinapur like?" I asked in my politest voice.

"It's very grand," she said, her voice dismissive. With no one else around, she didn't need to put on a show of pleasantness. "It's probably grander than anything you're used to."

. . .

Though I suspected Kunti's words, they fired my eagerness to see my new home. I fantasized about a structure that would, in every way, be the opposite of my father's fortress: airy and effulgent, with windows everywhere and doors opening onto generous balconies. Its walls would be shimmering red sandstone. Its gardens would be a celebration of color and birdsong. Situated on the topmost floor, my rooms would be washed by breezes carrying the distant fragrance of mango blossoms. From a balcony inlaid with marble I would look out over the entire city and know what was going on, so that when Yudhisthir became king, I could advise him wisely.

If Dhai Ma (to whom Kunti had taken a dislike, banishing her to the back of the procession with the other servants) had been in the carriage, she would have known right away what I was thinking.

She would have clicked her tongue and puffed out her bottom lip and warned me with one of her favorite sayings: *Expectations are like hidden rocks in your path—all they do is trip you up.*

. . .

Nothing could have been more different from my imaginings than the quarters allotted to Yudhisthir and me in Hastinapur. A block of rooms situated squarely in the center of the palace (to keep us safe, Kunti claimed), they looked out onto a courtyard filled with statues of dancing women frozen in torturous poses. The rooms themselves, though large, made me feel cramped. They were crowded with gaudy draperies, oversized bolsters, too-soft carpets that sucked at my ankles, and far more furniture than we had any need for. Intricate artifacts occupied every available surface. A flock of maids were always bustling around, dusting them and gawking at me. It almost made me nostalgic for the stern gloom of my father's court. Once I suggested that the décor might be simplified. But Kunti (whose rooms these must have been when she had arrived at this palace as a young bride) frostily informed me that every item here was sacred, having belonged at one time to King Pandu.

Though I felt stifled by my apartments, I was strangely reluctant to leave them. The palace itself was a curiosity, with its bulging gold domes and curlicued moldings, its doors embossed with beaten metal, its furniture massive enough to accommodate a race of giants. But beneath the gay pomp crouched something ominous and slavering that wished my husbands ill. Now it had turned its attention on me to ascertain if I was the weakest link in the Pandava chain. I felt it approaching, though I could not guess from which direction. It made me long to tunnel underground and hide—I, who'd chafed so impatiently to leave the safety of my father's house and plunge into history!

But as the newest royal daughter-in-law, I wasn't allowed to hide myself. On state occasions, I had to ride alongside Yudhisthir in his chariot. (At these I discovered, to my surprise, that I was popular. Something about my wedding had caught the public fancy. My appearances were greeted with much cheering, a fact that caused Kunti to teeter between pride and annoyance.) There were endless banquets among the extended family (the Kauravas loved to carouse) that I was expected to attend (appropriately veiled and chaperoned), though I had to leave these gatherings, along with the other wives, before the drinking and gaming started and matters grew interesting. Afternoons, Kunti would drag me with her to visit the other women in the palace. At these gatherings, the women spent much time in casual display of jewelry and clothing, or in making discreet references to their husbands' feats. When I didn't participate, they whispered maliciously about certain people who thought they were better than others because they were married to more than one man. It would have been amusing if I hadn't felt so lonely.

I hungered for someone with whom I could have an intelligent and frank conversation. Dhri had accompanied our party to Hastinapur, but as soon as he had met Drona and persuaded him to be his teacher, my father recalled him to Kampilya. It was our first separation, and I missed him dreadfully—his patience, his ability to understand me without words, his unwavering support of me even when he disapproved of my actions. I even missed his exasperation. I missed Krishna, too—the way in which his laughter helped lessen the gravity of my problems. I wished he would visit us. Though from Kunti's comments I gathered that here in Hastinapur a wife was not allowed to meet with men except in the company of her husband, I knew I'd find a way to see him in private. Talking to Dhai Ma would have helped me unburden myself, but Kunti made sure she was kept busy with errands. I couldn't gainsay her without engaging in a fight, and I wasn't ready for that yet. I was desperate enough to have welcomed even Yudhisthir, who had many interesting if unrealistic ideas about the world, but he was occupied by his own duties, and I saw him only in the bedchamber.

. . .

Of the people I'd met since moving here, most blurred into anonymity, but a few stood out. The blind king made a great show, whenever we met, of embracing my husbands and calling loudly on the gods to shower them with good fortune. He blessed me also with such platitudes as May-you-be-the-mother-of-a-hundred-sons, or May-your-wedding-sindur-forever-shine-on-your-forehead. (We knew, of course, that he'd like nothing better than to have the entire Pandava lineage perish.) My other husbands were barely able to tolerate his hypocrisy (Arjun would mutter under his breath, while Bheem's face turned an alarming shade of purple), but Yudhisthir would touch the old man's feet and inquire after his health with genuine affection. Was he a saint, or merely lacking in common sense? In either case, it was most annoying.

Then there was the blindfolded Gandhari, about whose wifely virtue so many songs had been composed. At first I dismissed her as docile and overly traditional. At the women's gatherings she expressed no opinions; at the family banquets, she focused her entire attention on her blind husband's needs. But after a few weeks of watching and asking around, Dhai Ma said, "Don't be fooled by her quietness! She's dangerous, with more power than most people realize, and one of these days she just might decide to use it." She went on to tell me how some god, pleased by Gandhari's devotion to her husband, had granted her a boon. If she ever took off her blindfold and looked at someone, she could heal him—or burn him to cinders.

I was impressed. I wouldn't have minded a boon like that. It was more useful than the ones I'd been given, and a lot less awkward.

"Watch out for her brother, too," Dhai Ma warned.

"Who? That Sakuni?" I'd seen him in court, sitting among Duryodhan's cronies, a thin, stooped older man with heavily lidded eyes. He'd given me a leering grin. I'd gathered from servant gossip that he had a penchant for dice and dancing girls. "You worry too much," I said to Dhai Ma.

"Someone has to," she said with asperity. "And it certainly isn't your royal oldest husband, who labors under the delusion that all the world loves him."

. . .

The one man I hadn't seen since I came to Hastinapur was Karna. I knew that at the request of Duryodhan, who considered him his closest friend, Karna spent much of the year in Hastinapur, leaving Anga in the care of his ministers. I knew also that soon after my swayamvar, Duryodhan had taken a wife and had urged Karna to do the same. But in this one matter he did not oblige his friend. When I heard my husbands wondering why, I had to exert all my self-control to keep my face calm, my breath even and uncaring.

I confess: in spite of the vows I made each day to forget Karna, to be a better wife to the Pandavas, I longed to see him again. Each time I entered a room, I glanced up under my veil—I couldn't stop myself—hoping he was there. (It was foolish. If he'd been present, surely he'd have turned away, my insult still a fresh gash in his mind.) I eavesdropped shamelessly on the maids, trying to discover his whereabouts. On the verge of asking Dhai Ma to find out where he'd disappeared to (for she had her ways of unearthing secrets), I bit back my tongue a hundred times. If she'd heard me pronounce his name, she would have known how I felt. And even to her who loved me as she loved no one else, I didn't dare reveal this dark flower that refused to be uprooted from my heart.

river

The grandfather invited me to join him for a walk along the banks of the Ganga.

"It's very pretty there," he said, smiling that deceptive, charming smile. "And it'll give us a chance to get to know each other better, away from the distractions of the court."

I assented, but with reluctance. The first few weeks after my arrival at Hastinapur, as loneliness tightened itself like a band of iron around my chest, I'd waited for him to contact me (for surely he knew that the rules forbade me from approaching him). He hadn't. Even when we met at banquets, he'd paid me scant attention beyond a greeting, affable though it was. I was surprised and hurt. I'd believed in the warmth of his welcome at our first meeting; I'd believed I'd found an ally in a house of strangers. But he had only been speaking the language of courtesy. Feeling like a fool, I decided I wouldn't trust him again. So by the time this invitation arrived, I no longer wanted him to know me better. And as for him, I was certain that he was far too wily to reveal himself to me.

· · ·

Even apart from my personal disappointment at him, the grandfather made me uneasy. I wished there was someone to whom I could confide this, but my husbands adored him. Even Kunti's impassive face took on a beatific glaze when she spoke of the many ways in which he'd helped her.

"He's the father we never had," Yudhisthir told me once in a rare burst of emotion. "He kept us safe through the years of our childhood. We were an embarrassment to the blind king, a thorn in his foot, a reminder that he was only a regent. He would have loved to hide us away in some provincial town, to bring us up like the sons of shopkeepers. By herself our mother couldn't have stopped him. But Bheeshma fought for us."

"If it weren't for him, Duryodhan would have had us murdered in our beds a long time ago," Bheem added.

I had so many questions. Was he really the son of a river goddess, as I'd heard, and did she really drown each of his seven older brothers at birth? The story said that she'd been about to drown him, too, when his father the king had stopped her. She'd left them then, her husband and her newborn, and disappeared into the water. Growing up, how did the boy think of his mother—with loneliness and longing, or with baffled resentment? Hating her, did he hate every woman? Was all his love transferred to his father, his king and savior?

His father fell in love again, as men tend to do. But the woman wouldn't marry him unless he could assure her that Bheeshma's sons would not dispute her children's claim to the throne. So that his father might have his wish, Bheeshma vowed to remain celibate all his life. He also vowed to protect the throne of Hastinapur, even with his last breath. The gods, who seem to like it when humans make unnatural sacrifices, gave him a boon for that: no one would be able to kill him unless he was ready to die.

I wanted to warn my husbands that one couldn't depend on a man who plucked frailty and desire so easily out of his heart. How could he have compassion for the faults of others, or understand their need? Keeping his word was more important to him than a human life. That's why he'd sent Amba away without a moment's hesitation. There might come a day when he'd do the same to us.

Then Arjun said, "He loved us."

We were in the chamber where Yudhisthir and I received guests. He was standing at a window that opened onto an ancient ashwattha tree that greedily sucked light from the room, its airborne roots hanging like matted hair. I couldn't see Arjun's face—the ornate draperies obstructed my view. But it didn't matter. The sorceress had taught me well. From the way his voice dipped low I knew what he'd never admit: throughout their childhood my husbands were famished for affection. Kunti had given them her entire steely devotion, but no tenderness. Perhaps she'd cut it out of her nature when she was left in the forest widowed and alone. Perhaps that was the only way she knew to survive.

Then Bheeshma entered their lives with his large lion's laugh. He carried them on his shoulders and hid sweetmeats in his room for them to find. He told them wondrous, terrifying stories late into the night. He praised their small achievements, which Kunti failed to notice, and bought them toys as good as the ones Duryodhan wouldn't share. When Kunti caned them for waywardness, he secretly rubbed salve on their cuts.

How could they not give themselves to him?

Love. There's no argument, no matter how strong, that can overcome that word. I was jealous of Bheeshma for inspiring such a devotion in my husbands—but he had helped me understand something about the Pandavas, something crucial. Your childhood hunger is the one that never leaves you. No matter how famous or powerful they became, my husbands would always long to be cherished. They would always yearn to feel worthy. If a person could make them feel that way, they'd bind themselves to him—or her—forever.

I held on to this knowledge like a traveler in a desert fists his hand around a gold-veined rock he has stumbled on, knowing there will be a time when it will prove valuable.

. . .

The grandfather had the charioteer drive us to a secluded part of the river some distance from Hastinapur. I sat stiffly in my corner as we traveled, wishing Dhai Ma was with us. I'd tried to bring her along, but he'd waved her away. *I'm too old for you to need a chaperone, my dear!* He'd laughed so hard that his hair, which fell to his shoulders, rippled like wind on water.

We started walking. Wildflowers bloomed along the river, round and yellow, with black centers. There were random piles of white stones. Even I, who preferred gardens to wilderness, could see their strange and asymmetric beauty. The domes of the palace gleamed against a purpling sky, made picturesque by distance. I couldn't take my eyes from the river's foaming rush. How much had happened here! Babies drowned, babies saved.

As I thought the words, I saw on the waters a bobbing casket, a gold-adorned child moving rapidly on the swirling foam. Even then he knew not to weep. As he passed us, he opened his eyes and fixed his gaze on me, though surely a newborn couldn't have done that.

Bheeshma shot me a keen glance. "What is it, granddaughter?"

"I thought I saw—" I broke off, shook my head. It was too difficult to explain. I feared it would give too much of myself away.

But Bheeshma gave an understanding nod. "The river holds many memories. She offers to you the ones you most long to know. But she's tricky like her currents. Sometimes she shows you what you wish to see, and not the actual truth."

He was waiting for a response, but I was saved by a group of tribal women who appeared down the path, balancing large loads on their heads. When they recognized the grandfather, excitement rippled through them. "Bheeshma Pitamaha!" they called in delighted tones. "Grandfather!" He must have walked here often, for they were not surprised to see him—nor, to my amazement, overly awed. They offered him small green bananas from their baskets and asked after his health. Was his gout better? Had the herbs they'd given him helped? He asked about their children, whose names he knew, and gave them silver coins. Later he shared the bananas with me. They were studded with large black seeds and not fully ripe. They made the inside of my mouth pucker up, though Bheeshma chewed his unperturbed way through several.

The women stared at me with great curiosity. After we passed them, they gathered under a mohua tree to point and giggle, speaking in the local dialect. I thought they said, Five? Are you sure? Five! There was envy in their eyes. But I may be wrong. Maybe it was sympathy.

. . .

It wasn't that I doubted the grandfather's love for the Pandavas—and, by association, myself—or his promise that he'd guard them with his life. But what if there came a time when he had to choose between this vow and that other, older one by which he'd lived his entire life: to protect Hastinapur against all enemies?

A well-meaning man, Dhai Ma liked to say, is more dangerous because he believes in the rightness of what he does. Give me an honest rascal any day!

. . .

"My mother," the grandfather said, staring at the river, "used to call me Devavrata."

"Your mother?" I was surprised into blurting. "But I thought—"

He smiled. "That my father had brought me up single-handed? Not quite, though that's the story he preferred to tell. She kept me with her until I was eight—my happiest years, I think. She taught me everything I know that's of any value. She still comes to me sometimes, here in the river, if I have a really serious problem or need her opinion."

I wasn't sure how to take his words. Did he mean them literally? Or did the river soothe his mind, helping him to think better? There was a boyish yearning on his weathered face. I felt he didn't speak like this often. Against my better judgment, it made me lower my defenses, so that when he asked me how I liked living at Hastinapur, I told him the truth.

"The palace makes me uneasy. Too many people there hate my husbands. It'll never be home to me."

He smoothed his beard. I thought I'd offended him. But perhaps he knew what it was to be hated, for he said, "You need a palace of your own. I should have thought of it earlier. I'll speak to Dhritarashtra about it. It's high time, anyway, that he announced an heir to the kingdom."

On our way back, I asked, a little self-consciously, "Did you tell your mother about me?"

"I did," he said. "She said you were a great flame, capable of lighting our way to fame—or destroying our entire clan."

My mouth went dry. Once again, when I least expected them, Vyasa's prophecies had returned to haunt me. "Why would she say that? How can I destroy the great house of the Kurus, and why would I want to do that when I'm part of them?"

Bheeshma shrugged. He didn't seem overly concerned. "I don't know. She loves to tease me with riddles. Don't look so worried! Sometimes what she says shouldn't be taken literally."

His casual kindness put me at ease. "I know someone like that, too," I said wryly, and it struck me with a pang how long it had been since I'd seen Krishna.

Bheeshma laughed his vigorous, delighted laugh. "Impossible, aren't they? They drive you insane, but you can't imagine life without them."

As he helped me up into the carriage with old-fashioned gallantry, telling me that we must do this again soon, I felt that a door had opened between us. I believed that in some inexplicable way I understood him better than people who had spent their entire lives around him. What I sensed, I liked and trusted. And so (not knowing that one day I would rue it bitterly) I relaxed, allowing him into my heart.

. . .

Bheeshma was, indeed, a man of his word. The very next day, in open court, he gave the blind king a severe tongue-lashing until the chastised Dhritarashtra agreed to hand Yudhisthir his birthright. He would divide the kingdom in two, he announced, his voice tremulous with largesse, and give the Pandavas the bigger half, leaving the smaller portion for his own son. From behind the curtain where the women sat, I was elated—more so for having been the catalyst for our good fortune. (I planned to make sure that my husbands learned of the part I'd played in it.) But Kunti, who knew the blind king better, pursed her lips. And rightly. The next day we discovered that he'd given my husbands Khandav, the most barren and desolate portion of the kingdom, keeping Hastinapur for his own Duryodhan. The younger Pandavas clamored to fight this injustice, but Yudhisthir said, "Wouldn't you rather live in your own home, even if it's a desert? Besides, it's an opportunity for us to make something out of nothing. To prove our worth."

Dhritarashtra held a rushed coronation for Yudhisthir, then promptly packed us off. Perhaps he feared we would change our minds about going.

"After all," he told Yudhisthir, "it's now your duty to govern your new subjects."

"Which subjects does he mean?" Bheem asked as we climbed onto the large and ornate chariot the king had given us as a parting gift. "The cobras or the hyenas?"

Our departure was a quiet one; only a meager entourage accompanied us. (Khandav had a bad reputation among the servants.) To my delight, we left Kunti behind. I don't know what Bheeshma had deduced from our talk at the river, but he persuaded her—and only he could have done it—that the journey would be too strenuous. Waving us goodbye at the palace gate, she looked astonished that her sons could go off to live their lives without her. Framed by the giant doorway, her figure appeared so small that I was ashamed of my jubilation. (But not for long. Perhaps as revenge, Kunti insisted that I leave Dhai Ma with her. "She'll keep me company until I'm able to join you," she said. Short of flagrant disobedience, I couldn't refuse.)

On the third day, the chariot, not the best of vehicles for barren desolations, broke down on the pocked and uneven road, leaving us stranded beside a clump of cacti. But amazingly, a few hours later, Krishna joined us. (How had he known we would need help?) He brought with him soldiers, food, tents, and several sturdy horses, and appeared unsurprised at the recent turn of events. He gave me a warm but too brief greeting, leaving all the things I longed to tell him waiting in my mouth. Watching him ride ahead, joking with Arjun and Bheem, I was happy and dissatisfied—and jealous of my husbands. In the past, whenever he visited, Krishna had given me his complete attention. Why should things be different now, just because I was a wife? The old restlessness from my girlhood that I'd thought I was done with—*if only I could have been a man*—rose in me as I watched them clap each other on the back. I pushed it away sternly. Wishful thinking was a folly. For better or worse, I was a woman. I'd have to find a woman's way to force him to notice me.

The landscape changed; the trees grew stunted; under our feet the earth turned yellow and foul-smelling. I sat sidesaddle behind Yudhisthir on a great black charger. I couldn't quite believe what a transformation my life had undergone—or that I had helped to bring about this new destiny we were living. If someone had told me a few days ago that I'd be rid of Hastinapur and traveling to my new kingdom with my husbands and Krishna and no mother-in-law, I'd have been delirious with excitement! But truth, when it's being lived, is less glamorous than our imaginings. Yudhisthir was not the best of riders, and the animal, recognizing this, yanked at his bridle, reared up, kicked out, and came to a stop at random moments. In between he bared his teeth and attempted to attack my husband's arm. I consoled myself with the thought that Yudhisthir was a good man. Righteousness come to earth, they called him. One couldn't expect such a virtuous personage to be a master horseman as well.

Truly it was a transient world we lived in. Yesterday in a palace, today on the road, tomorrow—who knew? Perhaps I would find the home that had eluded me all my life. But one thing was certain: the currents of history had finally caught me up and were dragging me headlong. How much water would I have to swallow before I came to a resting place?

In the midst of my elation, a thought twisted in me: with each moment, I was moving further from Karna. I would probably never see him again.

In my mind I heard Dhai Ma's voice—and perhaps because I missed her bullying love, I admitted that she was right.

It's the best thing that could happen to you, she said.

palace

The forest was still burning around us when my husbands called me to the make-shift canopy that had served as our home since we arrived in Khandav. I considered ignoring them. I was hot and irritable, and in the midst of putting together a meal with primitive, foraged foods. Our entourage—soldiers, mostly—weren't much help. Besides, I was uneasy. I kept hearing the cries of animals, though I knew that couldn't be. There weren't any animals left in the wilderness of Khandav—not since Arjun set the forest on fire. The lucky ones had escaped. The rest were dead.

Wind swirled ash along the ground. Smoke stung my eyes and coated my tongue. I looked for Krishna, then remembered that he'd ridden off in search of something. My husbands were speaking with a man I hadn't seen before. Where had he come from? He squatted on the ground. Around him he'd drawn lines with a stick. I couldn't tell what they were. I stared at him. He was short and stubby, dressed in skins. Rings of bone and gold pulled his earlobes down to his shoulders. He stared back, unblinking, as though I weren't the queen of this land but an intruder.

"Come, Panchaali," Yudhisthir said. When I joined him on the wooden plank where he sat, he hesitated before putting an arm around my shoulder. The other brothers looked away, embarrassed. Were they thinking that next year, or the next, one of them would do the same to me?

Better not to ponder such things.

Arjun leaned against his chariot, his face fire-flushed. "Respected lady," he said, "this is Maya." He kept his eyes on a distant column of smoke and used the formal mode of address. The anger he'd felt at my wedding to his brothers still festered inside him, though he hid it so well that only I was aware of it. If I spoke to him, he answered politely, in monosyllables. If I approached a place where he was, he found a reason to leave it. I wanted to shake some sense into him, but along with exasperation I felt sympathy. Sometimes when he didn't know I was watching, there was a starkness on his face, the look of a man who was consumed by jealousy and hated himself for it.

The ends of Arjun's long hair were singed. He was still carrying the giant bow that the god of fire had given him. It had a name, he had told us: Gandiva. From time to time, his hand caressed its curve as though it were a woman. I felt a sting, then chastised myself. I should be thankful he's consoling himself with a new weapon, I told myself, instead of looking for a new wife.

"He builds palaces for gods," Arjun continued, "and for the asura kings of the underworld. He's going to make us one, too—"

"—because Arjun saved him from the fire," Sahadev added proudly.

"A palace like no one has ever seen!" Bheem said, throwing open his excited arms. "I've asked him to build me a kitchen where a hundred cook fires may be lit all at once, without need of fuel."

Bheem loved to cook as much as he loved to eat. To my surprise, he'd been the one to help me most these last few days, doing the heavy work, cleaning the animal carcasses and roasting them over the open fire while I boiled rice and cut up fruits. When I tried to lift a heavy pot from the fire, he took it from me, not caring if our hands touched. Our first day in Khandav, he'd announced bluntly that Vyasa's laws, which were meant for palace living, were ridiculous now that we were stuck in the wilderness with only each other to depend on. He'd treat me as a man should treat his brother's wife, but he couldn't follow all those nitpicky rules. Whenever I needed assistance, he was going to provide it. If he figured out a way to make life in this hot, sweaty, insect-plagued jungle a little more bearable for me, he was certainly going to do it. And if Yudhisthir had a problem with that, he should banish him right now. My law-abiding husband hadn't been pleased, but ultimately he accepted what his brother said. I, on the other hand, had been most grateful at finding such a devoted champion. I silently sent Bheem my apologies for having dismissed him earlier as a boor, and at mealtimes, I heaped his plate higher than the others'.

"And stables with walls fashioned so cleverly that our animals will be warm in winter and cool in the summer," Nakul said. I had already seen, on the journey, how much he loved horses. He made us pause at regular intervals so that our mounts could be fed and watered. At night he walked among them, feeding them lumps of jaggery, making sure they were rubbed down. Even Yudhisthir's hell-raising charger nudged him gently with its massive head, whickering, and Nakul smiled as though he understood what it said. Once I overheard him declare that he trusted wild beasts more than any courtier he knew.

Did the massacre at Khandav forest torment him? I would never know. Though they must have disagreed with each other from time to time, my husbands never revealed their dissension to outsiders. (And in this matter, I was still an outsider.) Kunti had trained them well.

"We need a great chamber of crystal and ivory where kings can discuss statesmanship or listen to music," Yudhisthir proclaimed.

"Or play at dice?" Sahadev teased, because that was Yudhisthir's one weakness.

"We must have a dome that reaches up toward the sun, to amaze all men and proclaim the glory of the Pandavas," Arjun said, looking into the distance as though he could see things invisible to the rest of us. He clutched his bow as though he'd never set it down.

Bheem darted me a shy glance. "Shouldn't we ask Panchaali what she wants?"

And now I saw what in my distraction I'd missed earlier: he loved me. I found the knowledge oddly painful.

Yudhisthir nodded, reasonable as always, though by himself he wouldn't have thought to solicit my opinion. "You're right, brother. Tell us, Panchaali."

But when I opened my mouth to speak, my mind turned blank. Ash blew onto my face, settled on my skin, gritty as ground-up bone. I hadn't bathed for days. Why couldn't it have been Arjun who fell in love with me? He could have wrested my mind from the thoughts of a man who wouldn't stop occupying it even though I'd never see him again.

. . .

Later, when I asked why he'd killed all those animals, Arjun would say, "Agni wanted me to set the forest afire for him. I couldn't refuse a god, could I?"

But Krishna said, "How else could you have settled here? Built your kingdom? Gained all that fame? Changed the direction of history's wheel? Someone has to pay a price for that. You of all people should know this, Krishnaa."

He was right. In order for a victory to occur, someone had to lose. For one person to gain his desire, many had to give up theirs. Wasn't my own life—and my brother's—proof of that? But I refused to agree, to give Krishna that satisfaction. There was this, too: I wanted to believe that sometimes good may happen without bad biting its heels. I wanted to believe that sometimes the gods give us gifts and ask for nothing back.

He looked at me with a sigh, part sympathy, part exasperation. "Dear one," he said, "time will teach you what you refuse to learn from your well-wishers."

. . .

They were waiting for an answer, so I said the first word that came as I stared at the dead landscape.

"Water. I want water. Everywhere. Fountains and pools, ponds for birds to sport in."

I didn't believe the ugly little man in front of me could make it happen, but he nodded, a considering spark in his eye.

"I want a stream wending its way through the palace, with lotuses blooming all year," I added. I was being outrageous, but why not? Everyone else was asking for impossibilities—fires without fuel, towers that brushed the sun. ("But running water inside a home!" Kunti would gasp when she saw it. "Fool of a girl, didn't anyone teach you that it washes away good luck?")

"I do it!" Maya said. A gap gleamed between his crooked teeth as his lips pulled back in a grin. "I give you more: floors looking like rivers, waterfalls looking like walls. Doorsteps all glittery like melted ice. Only wise people see through Maya's truth. But few so wise! All cry: How great are royal Pandavas to live in such palace! How great Maya, maker of palace! But first you must give me right name for it."

My husbands argued. Yudhisthir wanted to name the palace after their dead father, but the others didn't share his filial piety for a man they didn't remember. Arjun wanted to name it in honor of Shiva, god of the hunt, his favorite deity. Nakul suggested we should call it Indrapuri, because wasn't it going to be a palace fit for the king-god? Sahadev feared that that would be too prideful.

"What does Panchaali think?" Bheem asked.

I looked at Maya. His fleck-brown eyes glittered. Later I'd wonder, was it malice I'd glimpsed in them? Along with gratitude, he must have harbored rage and sorrow, his home reduced to cinders around him, his companions dead or scattered forever.

He inclined his head as though he knew what I was thinking and approved of it. But perhaps it was he who sent the words into my mind.

If foreboding flew over me on scorched wings, crying for its dead mate, I didn't hear. I smiled with sudden elation, thinking, This is what I've been waiting for all my life!

I said, "This creation of yours that's going to be the envy of every king in Bharat—we'll call it the Palace of Illusions."

. . .

Maya outdid himself as he built. He magnified everything my husbands wanted a hundredfold, and over it all he laid a patina of magic so things shifted strangely, making the palace new each day even for us who lived there. There were corridors lighted only by the glow of gems, and assembly halls so filled with flowering trees that even after hours at council one felt as though one had been relaxing in a garden. Almost every room had a pool with scented water. Not all his magic was benign, though. Early in our stay, before we got used to looking at things a certain way, we bumped into walls built of crystal so clear that they were transparent, or tried vainly to open windows that were painted on. Several times we stepped into pools that were disguised as stretches of marble flooring and ruined our elaborate court attire. At those times I thought I heard Maya's disembodied, mocking laughter. But it all added to the allure of this palace that was truly like no other.

On the day the palace was done, Maya took Arjun aside.

"You save Maya life," he said, "so I give you warning. Live in palace. Enjoy. But not invite anyone to come see."

My husbands pondered over the cryptic words. What did Maya mean? Was it a trick? Had he slipped a curse into the foundations as he built them? Asuras were not to be trusted—everyone knew that. Still, they were reluctant to take him seriously. They'd waited so long for a place they could call home, a setting that proclaimed their worth. (How well I understood that craving!) They yearned to show it off—to friends and enemies both. (So did I, though only one man came to my mind.)

But Krishna said, "Maya is right. Everyone who sees this palace will want it for himself. Envy is dangerous. You'll have to deal with it eventually—but why call it down on yourself before its time?"

. . .

We didn't like what Krishna said, but we trusted his wisdom. So, reluctantly, we cancelled the grand celebration we'd planned. No doubt some people spoke ill of us, wondering at our inhospitality. (This distressed Yudhisthir; opinions were important to him.) Still, those who loved us came to visit anyway, even without an invitation, and they returned home with such amazing stories that others followed. Many stayed on, for Yudhisthir was a just and kind ruler. Soon a prosperous city grew up around Khandav. People called it Indra Prastha—that's how impressive it was. Minstrels began to make up songs about the unparalleled grandeur of the Pandava court. Slowly, the warnings we'd been given—by Maya, by Krishna, by Vyasa long ago—retreated into the lightless crevices of memory.

These were good years for me. I loved my palace, and in return I felt its warmth embracing me as though it were alive. Some of its serenity seeped into me, some wisdom, so that I learned to be happy with my lot in the world. (And now that I had such a palace, how could I be otherwise?) I took my place beside each of my husbands at the proper moment, and saw our pairings as movements in an elaborate dance. I saw my husbands, too, differently. They were a unit together, five fingers that complemented each other to make up a powerful hand—a hand that would protect me if the need arose. A hand that had gifted me this beautiful palace. Wasn't that sufficient to be thankful for?

My husbands, too, learned to appreciate my strengths. We were all surprised to discover that I had a good eye for matters of governance. More and more, Yudhisthir began to ask my advice when a tricky judgment had to be delivered. And I, having learned more of the workings of women's power, was careful to offer my opinion only in private, deferring to him always in front of others.

These were the years when I gave birth to my five sons, one from each husband: Prativindhya, Sutasoma, Srutakarman, Sataneeka, and Srutasena. (Their names were chosen by Yudhisthir, who favored hefty, polysyllabic appellations. Sometimes, when I was flustered by the children's clamoring, I'd get them confused.) I loved the boys dearly, but I wasn't particularly maternal. Or perhaps my energies were used up in being a wife five times over, and a queen besides. Fortunately, Dhai Ma, whom I'd rescued from Kunti's tyrant grasp, was more than happy to take them off my hands. She chased after them day and night, regaling them with invectives, but in truth she was far more indulgent with them than she'd ever been with me—a fact that they took full advantage of.

Dhri, who was busy helping my aging and increasingly cantankerous father rule his kingdom, visited me whenever he could.

Here, for a while, he could set aside his cares as he hunted and rode and argued boisterously with my husbands about gaming strategies, or wrestled with my boys and showered them with too many gifts, or strolled with me in the gardens that were my delight. Once, when we were by ourselves, he praised me for the way I handled my unconventional domestic situation.

"I didn't think you could have done it," he said. "You were so prickly about little things, always ready to rebel. Now you're truly a queen!"

I smiled. "If I am, I owe it to my palace."

When I repeated this to Krishna, he frowned. "Don't be so attached to what is, after all, no more than stone and metal and asura sleight of hand. All things in this world change and pass away— some after many years, some overnight. Appreciate the Palace of Illusions, by all means. But if you identify so deeply with it, you set yourself up for sorrow."

Out of my fondness for him, I didn't argue. But inside I knew I had nothing to fear. Maya had promised us that no human would be able to harm our palace, no natural disaster lay it low. No one could wrest it from us. As long as we—or our descendants—lived in it, it was indestructible, and in turn, it would protect us.

It was as close to immortality as I could imagine—and enough to satisfy me.

· · ·

I dreaded bringing Kunti to my palace and made excuses to delay it as long as possible. But finally she arrived, stepping from the carriage with an elaborate groan and disapproval stitched onto her prim, pursed lips.

As my husbands guided her through the palace, I steeled myself for criticism. But the palace must have worked its magic on her, for after a few superficial complaints she fell silent, and a childlike look of wonder came into her eyes. Once or twice I heard her laugh in delight as Sahadev or Nakul—strangely, they who were not born of her were her favorites—explained one of Maya's illusions to her. And though she never complimented me on the planning of the palace, her pleasure in it melted some of the aversion that had encrusted my heart for so long.

Kunti was a wise woman—wiser than me, if truth were told. In those first days, her shrewd eyes examined much more than the curiosities in the palace. She saw that in this place, I was mistress. Where my husbands had once relied on her, they now depended on me. She could not disrupt this state of affairs without causing her sons serious unhappiness. Perhaps the palace laid its calming finger on her, making her realize that she loved them more than she resented me. Had we remained in Hastinapur, in her husband's palace, I am sure she would have fought me fiercely for control. But the Palace of Illusions was my domain, and she accepted this, spending her days in the cool, fragrant garden (for here it was always cool) listening to the bulbuls sing.

Or was she a better actress than I gave her credit for, biding her time, waiting for the mistakes she knew I'd make?

wives

 I didn't win all my battles. My husbands
took other wives: Hidimba, Kali, Devika,
Balandhara, Chitrangada, Ulupi, Karuna-
mati. How naïve I'd been to think I could have prevented it! Sometimes there were political reasons, but mostly it was male desire. I
retaliated by locking myself up in my quarters, refusing food, and
throwing expensive objects at my husbands if they dared to approach me. My tantrums became almost as famous as Yudhisthir's
righteousness, and over the years not a few songs were composed
about Panchaali's jealousy.

In truth, I wasn't nearly as upset as I made out to be. I was a
practical woman. I knew I couldn't expect my husbands to remain
celibate while they waited for their turn as my spouse. I knew also
that I was special to them in a way that none of the syrupy beauties
they married later could ever be. I'd been at their side when they
were young and in danger. Marriage to me had protected them from
the murderous wrath of Duryodhan. I'd played a crucial role in
bringing them to their destiny. I'd shared their hardship in Khandav. I'd helped them design this unique palace, which so many
longed to see. If they were pearls, I was the gold wire on which they
were strung. Alone, they would have scattered, each to his dusty
corner. They would have pursued separate interests, deposited their

loyalties with different women. But together, we formed something precious and unique. Together, we were capable of what none of us could do alone. I finally began to see what the wily Kunti had in mind when she'd insisted that I was to be married to all of them, and though they never made my heart beat wildly, the way I'd hoped as a girl, I committed myself totally to the welfare of the Pandavas.

Still, it's never a good idea to let one's husbands grow too complacent. My displays of temper ensured that the Pandavas continued to regard me with a healthy respect. When I finally forgave them, they were appropriately penitent. It kept the number of their wives to a minimum and—what was more important—made the wives reluctant to visit the palace.

Only once was I truly shaken, when Arjun chose Subhadra, Krishna's sister, as his mate and carried her away in a wildly romantic chariot race, with her other brother, the irate Balaram, chasing after them. After they were married, Arjun brought her to me so she could pay her respects. He'd made her dress in a simple cotton sari, but it didn't hide her translucent beauty. Her lips trembled with nervousness. (She'd heard of the tantrums.) Drops of sweat shone on her temples like a circlet of pearls. Still, nothing could dampen the drunken love in her eyes—a look that was reflected on Arjun's face. He'd never looked at me that way, and never would. A pang went through me, remembrance of another man that I'd put away successfully for so long that I'd thought it was erased. And though one part of me sympathized with Subhadra's fear, the other part raged that she had so easily and thoughtlessly gained what I in spite of all my renown as the chief queen of the Pandavas would never possess. And so I turned from her, making deliberate, cutting remarks about seduction and betrayal until she was reduced to tears.

More than Subhadra (who after all owed me nothing), more than Arjun (whose perfidies I was used to by now), it was Krishna I felt had betrayed me. But when I accused him of having encouraged his sister to snatch Arjun from me, he was quite unabashed.

"Arjun's not like a nose ring that someone can snatch from you," he said sternly. "He comes and goes of his own will. Besides, you know that no matter whom else he marries, his commitment to you remains the same. But most important, out of their union will come a great warrior, and out of him will come a king even greater." He touched my shoulder, perhaps to lessen the harshness of his words. "Isn't that more important than the brief heartache you suffer?"

. . .

Over time, I found myself becoming friendly with the wives. (This was aided by the fact that they all chose to remain with their own people, in the kingdoms of their birth. Distance is a great promoter of harmony: a fact that women who find themselves in situations similar to mine should keep in mind.) Surprisingly, Subhadra became my favorite. On her visits, she put up with my petty tyrannies without complaint—bringing me water, combing my hair, even fanning me on hot afternoons—until I was shamed into desisting. Though no one could accuse her of weakness, she was more pliant than I. Perhaps that was why, when tragedy fell upon us both, she would handle it more gracefully. In the years of my misfortune, she would take my sons into her home, treating them no differently from her own child, deftly balancing affection and discipline. I would love her for that. But no, she'd made her way into my heart long before. Her mannerisms—the way she raised an eyebrow or burst into laughter or shook her head at a display of folly—were Krishna's, and watching her made me feel that he was by my side.

A decade passed thus, as in a dream. And as in a dream, I recall those years only faintly, the way one remembers the colors of a serene sunset. Is it always like this when life goes the way we want? My husbands and I grew older, richer, more comfortable with our good fortune. And with each other, so that when at the end of a year I went from one bed to the next, it no longer caused us awkwardness. Trade and industry and art prospered in our city. Our reputation spread across kingdoms. Our subjects, flourishing, blessed us in their prayers. We held in our palms all the things we'd once longed for. But deep down, though no one would admit it, we were a little restless, a little bored. The current of destiny seemed to have flung us ashore and receded. Not knowing that it was gathering in a tidal wave, we chafed in our calmness, wondering if it would ever claim us again.

afterlife

The boundaries of afterlife are even more complicated than the rules that pen us in on earth. Depending on their deeds, the dead can be dispatched to many different abodes. Fortunate brahmins are sent to Brahmaloka, where they can learn divine wisdom directly from the Creator. The best among kshatriyas go to Indraloka, filled as it is with pleasures both artistic and hedonistic. Lesser warriors must be content with the courts of the god of death, or the sun and moon deities. For evildoers, there are one hundred and thirty-six levels of hell, each corresponding to a particular sin, and each with its own set of tortures, such as tongue-tearing, being boiled in oil, or being devoured by ravenous birds, all of which our scriptures describe with great relish. Dhri's tutor was of the opinion that virtuous women were sent directly into their next birth, where, if they were lucky, they reincarnated as men. But I thought that if lokas existed at all, good women would surely go to one where men were not allowed so that they could be finally free of male demands. However, I prudently kept this theory to myself.

In any case, I knew enough to realize that there would be trouble when Sage Narad, who had paid us a surprise visit, said to Yudhisthir, "No, great king, while visiting Indra's court, I didn't see the spirit of your respected father there."

We'd dined on the finest fare our cooks could come up with at such short notice (for Narad had a discriminating palate)—from fried bitter melons and stuffed brinjals to lentils cooked to a buttery paste that melted in the mouth and thickened rice pudding bristling with almonds. Having eaten their fill, the men were now relaxing on silken cushions. I sat behind Yudhisthir, passing around a platter of silvered betel leaf and digestive spices and assessing the sage from under my veil.

With his slight build and his simple white clothes, Narad looked harmless, but he had quite a reputation. He had powerful family connections (emerging, it was said, directly from the brain of Brahma) and was a formidable devotee of Lord Vishnu. His favorite activity was to travel from court to court and world to world, collecting gossip and spreading mayhem. He had already contributed to the demise of several regimes, and was justly known as Narad Troublemaker. I wondered what he was planning.

"I did see him, however, in the court of the god of death," he added, cocking his head like a mischievous raven.

"But why is my father in Yama's court and not Indra's?" Yudhisthir asked, peeved by this slight to family honor.

"Your grandfather's there, too," Narad said, yawning delicately behind his hand. "But don't let it disturb you. They were quite comfortable, though the thrones there aren't as splendid as those in Indra's court, nor the cushions as easeful to the posterior. However . . ."

"What can we do to ensure that our ancestors enter Indra's court?" Yudhisthir interrupted.

"By a strange coincidence," Narad said, "that is just what I asked them. They said that if you performed the Rajasuya sacrifice, they'd be sent there."

"Then we shall certainly perform it!" Yudhisthir announced. "Tell us how it's to be done."

Narad wrinkled his brow, feigning anxiety. "It's too dangerous! First you must make all the kings of Bharat pay you tribute. And if they don't, you must battle and defeat them. And then you must hold a huge fire ceremony that they all have to attend."

I was skeptical about the entire endeavor. Even if there were lokas, what proof was there that the dead could be promoted from one to the next based on what we did here on earth? Yudhisthir, too, hesitated. He was a peace-loving man. But Arjun's eyes glittered and Bheem raised his fists high. Sahadev and Nakul sat intent and still. I doubted that they cared about ancestors or believed any more than I did in the lokas. However, Narad's story gave them the perfect opportunity to shake off their lassitude, polish their rusting battle skills, fill the royal coffers, and gain renown—and be lauded as dutiful offspring at the same time.

"When do we start?" Arjun asked.

"Let's not rush into things!" Yudhisthir said. "We'll send for Krishna. He'll advise us."

"Ah, Krishna, the master tactician!" Narad cried, clasping his palms. "How fortunate you are to have him as your friend! You do know that he's the incarnation of Vishnu himself, don't you?" He threw me a sly glance, checking to see if I believed this outrageous claim.

"Is he really an incarnation?" Arjun asked curiously. "He seems so . . . normal, always joking around with us—"

"He only reveals his divinity to those who are ready for it," Narad said, and though he spoke to Arjun, it was me that he fixed with his gaze.

I had dismissed Narad's words as another of his teasing tricks, but later, when I was alone, I couldn't stop thinking about them. What if I had presumed wrongly? What if there were, in truth, worlds upon worlds invisible to ordinary mortals the ways stars are in the daytime? What if the gods did come down, from time to time, to live among us and guide our destinies? Past the sleeping silhouette of Nakul, my current husband, beyond the dark window of my bedroom, a pale yellow moon hung low in the sky. What mysteries were hidden behind its pockmarked face? I could not decide if the laws of those worlds should supersede ours. If we should bow before the advice of a god-man even when it went against everything that made sense.

. . .

I watched Krishna carefully when he arrived. He didn't act particularly godlike. He teased me as usual, remarking that I'd put on weight (a blatant lie). He insisted that I cook for him and then claimed (another lie) that my milk-sweets were nowhere as good as the ones he'd grown up on in Vrindavan. When my husbands asked him about the Rajasuya, he was surprisingly amenable to the idea. He said the country was filled with corruption and needed shaking up. A carefully controlled bloodletting now might prevent a great carnage later on. He seemed to have forgotten his earlier warnings about envy.

Krishna helped my husbands create a strategy. They began by killing Jarasandha, the most feared ruler of the time—and incidentally, a longtime enemy of Krishna. (Bheem tore his body in two during a wrestling match, a feat he described to me later in delighted, excruciating detail.) They then released the many kings Jarasandha had imprisoned in his labyrinths and gave them back their kingdoms. This made my husbands so popular that wherever they went after that, they were greeted with friendship. Who knows what would have happened in Anga, Karna's kingdom? But Krishna adroitly avoided the problem by instructing Yudhisthir to send a courteous letter to the blind king, stating that out of respect for their uncle, the Pandavas would not challenge any of his allies. Not to be outdone in sophistry, the blind king sent back a flowery missive stating that he would be delighted if the Pandavas managed to gain the support of all the kings of Bharat and increase their father's fame. After they had been victorious and sent him an invitation, he wrote back that though he himself could not travel because of his infirmity, Duryodhan and his friends would be happy to attend the festivities at this palace of ours that everyone spoke of so highly.

Dhritarashtra's letter sent us into a frenzy of activity. We'd been prepared for a large gathering, but we hadn't thought that the Kauravas would come. Knowing that they would be here changed everything. My husbands strode up and down the palace, examining everything with a newly critical eye—the way they thought Duryodhan would. Even the mild-mannered Yudhisthir grew snappish. It was imperative that everything be perfect by the time the Kauravas arrived. Then they'd be forced to acknowledge how well their poor cousins—the ones they'd always insulted and ridiculed—had done.

And I? I threw myself into the preparations, holding nothing back, as a good wife should. It wasn't difficult. I, too, wanted Duryodhan to stare openmouthed at what they'd made of the wilderness. I, too, wanted him to be dazzled by all their treasures—including myself, their crown possession. It was the least my husbands deserved after all those years of struggle and shame, of fleeing in fear for their lives. If there was another reason why I forced my maids to work deep into the night, polishing and laundering, or spurred my cooks to create exotic new dishes for every banquet we would hold, or commissioned the royal tailor to design clothing more elaborate than anything we'd ever worn, or ordered the gardeners to coax each plant in my garden into blooming, I was careful not to examine it.

discus

The celebrations began well. My husbands were gracious and modest in their triumph, and they welcomed the visiting kings with ebullient enthusiasm. This was their first opportunity to be hosts, and they were determined to do it right. For their part, the kings appreciated the courtesy—not to mention the costly gifts that were heaped on them—and settled down to enjoying the festivities. But later we would realize that discontent had been simmering in many hearts from the very first. It's a rare man—and an even rarer ruler—that can remain untouched by jealousy in the face of a peer's sudden prosperity. All of us (except perhaps Yudhisthir) knew this truth. We should have been more vigilant, but we were all distracted, in different ways, by the presence of the Kaurava contingent.

The day I learned that what I both feared and longed for was about to happen—that Karna would be part of Duryodhan's party—I went into the small private courtyard that my bedroom opened onto, and sat among the ashwagandha plants with my back against the warm stone wall. Give me strength to do the right thing, I whispered, though to whom I don't know. I didn't put much trust in the gods. They were too involved in their own quarrels and weren't above employing trickery to get what they wanted. A soft afternoon wind sighed around me; the yellow ashwagandha blooms trembled, releasing their pungent, sweaty odor; it seemed to me that my palace was counseling me as it held me in its embrace. I thought it said that Karna's coming was my chance for reparation.

And so when Karna arrived, I put away passion and folly and the awkwardness that goes with it. I stood by my husbands and welcomed him the same way I welcomed the rest of the Kaurava party, without my voice trembling, or my gaze faltering. I created occasions where I could be hospitable to him. I was determined to erase, through graciousness, my past insult. We were none of us young and foolish as we'd been at the time of my marriage. We could put the past behind us.

But Karna wouldn't accommodate me. I'd assigned him one of our grandest guest chambers, with a balcony that looked out onto a lake that turned silver each night under the moon, but he gave it to Dussasan, choosing instead a small, spare room that opened only to courtyard walls. To everyone else's eye, his behavior was faultless. He accompanied Duryodhan to every public event—sacrificial ceremonies, dance performances, the discussions of courtly matters—and sat through them patiently, if not with pleasure. But whenever Yudhisthir planned an intimate gathering where I would play a part—a dinner in the private chambers for family, or an evening where we might recite poetry—Karna excused himself. If by chance we passed each other along a palace path, he responded to my warmest greetings with correctness—and nothing else. Slowly it came to me, with a sinking of the heart, that he was not going to allow me to redeem myself.

. . .

On the final day of the yagna, after Yudhisthir was crowned as the greatest among the kings of Bharat, he was expected to choose a guest of honor from among the assembled rulers. For many nights my husbands had been trying to decide who this should be. Should they recognize the oldest? The one with the largest territory? The one best known for his acts of charity? The one they wanted most as their ally? But they'd failed to agree.

Now in the assembly Yudhisthir said to Bheeshma, "Grandfather, everyone here will agree that you are the wisest among us. It is therefore fitting that you choose our guest of honor."

Standing behind him, I could see what Yudhisthir was too blind to notice: everyone did not agree with him. Though they didn't dare speak out against Bheeshma, he had many enemies. Some mistrusted him because of the oath he'd taken, which they considered terrible and unnatural. Others resented him because he kept them from carving the Kaurava kingdom up for themselves. Others hated him merely because he loved us.

When I realized this last bit, my hands grew shaky. All this time, tucked within the safety of my palace, I'd believed we were safe. I'd believed that as long as we wished no one harm, no harm would come to us. But envy had been lurking outside our walls all this while—and now we'd given it the perfect opportunity to creep in. It disfigured the faces in front of me as the kings whispered to each other, their facile friendship for my husbands evaporating with each word.

"Krishna!" Bheeshma announced, making me start. "Krishna should be the guest of honor."

His statement was like a stone tossed into a wasp's nest. The assembly exploded in an uproar. A few were pleased (my husbands could not contain their smiles), more were angry, but most were perplexed. I was perplexed, too, much though I loved Krishna. He was a relatively minor king, in spite of the colorful stories that surrounded him. What did Bheeshma know of him that I didn't?

Krishna, who had been sitting halfway down the hall with the rest of the Yadu clan, stood up. He didn't appear particularly elated. It has always been hard for me to read his chameleon expressions, but I thought he looked resigned. He joined his palms in acceptance of the honor and walked quietly to the dais. His demeanor affected the audience; they too, began to quieten. Yudhisthir gave a sigh of relief.

Then Sisupal, king of the Chedis, leaped up red-faced from his seat. I remembered him from the swayamvar—he'd been at the forefront of the disgruntled suitors who had tried to kill Arjun. He was a master at inciting others, lending credence to the shameful thoughts they'd pushed deep inside. My heart constricted as I wondered what he would do now.

Sisupal clapped his hands in derisive applause. "This is wonderful indeed! With so many great heroes in the assembly, the prize goes to a cowherd who became a king by treacherously killing his uncle! The man my friend Jarasandha sent running from the battlefield a score of times! The man who took his revenge by instigating Bheem to kill my friend through trickery! Such a man is to be honored above us all today! But what else can one expect in the court of a bastard king?"

There was a collective gasp. I didn't dare look at Yudhisthir's face. Arjun took a step forward, hand on his sword.

"Sisupal," Bheeshma said, controlling himself with effort, "you're a guest here, though you've obviously forgotten the courtesies you owe your hosts. I don't want the Pandavas to incur the sin of killing you, so I ask you to take back your gravely offending words."

"I don't take back what I say," Sisupal said, "particularly when it's true. Very convenient, wasn't it, all those gods visiting Kunti

and that poor eunuch, Pandu, in the forest? And speaking of eunuchs, did you ever wonder, all you great kings, why Bheeshma was so quick to take the oath that's made him so famous?"

With a roar, Bheem barreled his way to the front of the dais. But Bheeshma gripped Bheem's arm. He no longer seemed angry. He pointed to where Krishna stood by the dais. As always, Krishna carried no sword, but something I'd never seen—a disc with serrated edges—was in his right hand. The sun struck its surface, dazzling me, creating the illusion that it spun very fast around his forefinger.

"I promised to forgive you a hundred insults," Krishna said to Sisupal, his voice conversational. "You crossed that number long ago, but I was patient, knowing that you weren't too skilled at counting." He waited until Sisupal's roar of rage died away. "This time you've gone too far, insulting the grandfather. Still, I'll let it go if you apologize. This way Yudhisthir can complete his yagna in peace."

"Coward! Don't try to fool me with your honeyed words," Sisupal yelled, his words slurring with fury, "the way you lured my beautiful Rukmini away."

I vaguely recalled an old story—something about how Krishna's favorite wife had once been promised by her brother to Sisupal—but there was no time to sort out my thoughts. Sisupal had broken into a run, his sword leveled at Krishna. I clutched at Arjun's arm. (Yudhisthir was not much use at such times.) "Help him!" I cried.

He looked at me incredulously. "I can't interfere in Krishna's fight!"

"Don't worry, Panchaali," Yudhisthir said, patting my shoulder. "Remember what Narad said about Krishna's powers?"

Sisupal thrust his sword with sudden savagery at Krishna's belly. The blade moved so fast, it was a blur. I screamed and covered my face. Around me people were crying out in dismay. I felt a piercing

sorrow as though the blade had gone through my own body, then emptiness like I'd never felt before. It struck me like an iron fist, the realization that if Krishna wasn't in my life, nothing mattered. Not my husbands, not my brother, not this palace I was so proud of, not the look I longed to see in Karna's eye.

When did he start mattering this much to me? Or had it always been so, only I'd been impervious to it until calamity forced it to my attention?

"Panchaali," I heard Bheem call. "You can open your eyes now. It's over."

Indeed it was. Sisupal's head lay on the floor, spewing blood. I closed my eyes again hastily.

"Krishna chopped it off with his chakra," Bheem explained. "But the headless body kept moving forward, its sword still aimed at Krishna. It was something to see! It keeled over at the last moment, right at his feet. The strangest thing happened when the body fell. A light flashed from it and disappeared into Krishna! What do you make of that?"

I was too dazed to make sense of any of it—the outer occurrences, or the turbulence inside me. This time when I opened my eyes, I focused them on Krishna. He didn't look like he'd just killed a man. A slight smile danced on his lips, as though he was recalling an old and not unpleasant memory. Did it have anything to do with the light Bheem had mentioned—and had that been Sisupal's soul? His feet were splattered with blood.

"It isn't mine," he told me, seeing the expression on my face. "I'm not hurt." But that wasn't quite true. Blood dripped from the index finger of his right hand. (Could a god bleed?) He must have used it to fling the disc. (Of the disc itself there was no sign. I wouldn't see it again for many years.) I tore a strip off the end of my sari and bandaged the wound.

"Now you've ruined that abominably expensive sari," he said. "I'll have to get you a new one, although it's probably not going to be as fine. I'm a relatively minor king, after all!"

I stared at him in shock, then reddened. Did he know my other thoughts, including those about Karna?

Kings had leaped up from their seats. Some were protesting angrily. A few had drawn their swords. I thought I saw Narad crouched in a corner of the sabha, observing the chaos with a mix of dread and ecstasy on his face. An unhappy Yudhisthir was vainly calling for order. My other husbands climbed down into the audience, trying to calm people. Was that Karna I saw helping them, arms raised, his back like a giant tree trunk, keeping the roiling crowd away from the dais where I stood? But for once my attention slipped away from him.

If I wanted to tell Krishna what I'd felt, this was the time. (Why was it so important that I articulate for him my confused grief?) The ground felt unsteady under my feet. My face was hot. I'd never bared my soul to Krishna in this way. I was afraid he would laugh at me. Still, I said, "When I thought you had died, I wanted to die, too."

Krishna gazed into my eyes. Was it love I saw in his face? If so, it was different in kind from all the loves I knew. Or perhaps the loves I'd known had been something different, and this alone was love. It reached past my body, my thoughts, my shaking heart, into some part of me that I hadn't known existed. My eyes closed of their own accord. I felt myself coming apart like the braided edge of a shawl, the threads reaching everywhere.

How long did I stand there? A moment or an eon? Some things can't be measured. I know this much: I didn't want it to end.

Then his voice intruded into my reverie, laughter stitched into its edges, just as I'd feared. "You'd better not let my dear friends the Pandavas hear that! It could get me into a lot of trouble!"

"Can't you ever be serious?" I said, mortified.

"It's difficult," he said. "There's so little in life that's worth it."

There was no opportunity for further conversation, for this time the ground shook in earnest. The pillars of the sabha swayed. Though the magic Maya had woven into them kept them from toppling, people panicked, yelling as they ran. I thought I heard the cawing of ravens. Someone grabbed my arm. I struck out, then saw it was Bheem, his hair wild about his face.

"Steady there!" he said, rubbing his cheek ruefully. "Elder brother asked me to escort you to your quarters. This is no place for you."

I bristled at the comment, but Krishna gave me a gentle push. "Go, Krishnaa. We wouldn't want you to get hurt."

Bheem shook his head in dismay. "What an unfortunate end to our yagna! What will happen now? The priests are saying the earthquake is a bad omen. They're saying the gods are angry at Sisupal's death."

"Priests like to say such things," Krishna replied. He didn't seem too concerned about the anger of the gods.

As Bheem hurried me along, I noticed Karna. He'd been holding back the surging crowds that were trying to rush to the doorway near the dais, patient with their flailing terror. When he saw that I was safe with Bheem, he gave him a curt nod and turned to leave. I focused all my mental energy at his receding back, thanking him, willing him to look once at me. I know he must have felt the force of my wish—even Bheem glanced at me, his brow furrowed in perplexity. But Karna walked away, his footsteps as steady as though I'd never existed.

lake

Duryodhan was acting strangely.

The other kings had departed soon after Sisupal's death—most of them sullen-faced and disapproving, without observing the courtesies of leave-taking—but the Kaurava party lingered on. The rest of us wished them gone, but Yudhisthir was too polite to let us hint at this. Perhaps also, stung by the distrust of our other guests and disappointed at the unpleasant end to the yagna he'd so looked forward to, he was gratified that Duryodhan courted his company. That he was so fascinated by our palace. It pleased him to possess something his cousin admired, and he gave Duryodhan leave to wander where he wished.

As a result, I would come upon the Kaurava prince in unexpected places—in the kitchen, where he examined the cook fires with acute interest, or in the garden, where he interrogated the gardeners as to where we'd acquired certain plants. Soon I realized what he wanted: to build himself a similar palace. But when I expressed my indignation to my husbands, demanding that they stop him, they merely scoffed at his ambition. They pointed out that he'd never be able to accomplish such a task, not unless he got hold of an architect as skilled in magic as Maya, and how would he manage that?

"He'll just drain the coffers of Hastinapur," Arjun said, "and then burden the people with unjust taxes."

"Maybe they'll get so fed up, they'll rebel and depose him," Bheem said.

"Maybe they'll set up one of his saner younger brothers to become crown prince," Nakul said.

"No chance of that!" Sahadev cried. "You know how *blindly* our revered uncle dotes on Duryodhan." The four of them guffawed until Yudhisthir put an end to it.

I couldn't take Duryodhan's plans as lightly. We'd poured our hearts into designing this palace. It was an embodiment of our most intimate desires, our secret wishes. It was *us*. Every time I saw Duryodhan measuring a doorway with his eyes, or pointing at a floating stairwell while his uncle Sakuni jotted down notes, I felt violated—the more so because Duryodhan's smirk indicated that he knew exactly what was going through my mind.

The presence of Karna at such moments made things worse. He'd be standing beside Duryodhan, looking supremely uninterested. I'd already heard, through servants, that he'd repeatedly asked Duryodhan for his leave to return to Anga. But each time Duryodhan entreated him to stay, stating that he needed his dearest friend with him.

I knew I shouldn't care. Still, it hurt me that Karna was so keen to leave my palace, that none of its charms were able to entrance him. For the first time, it made me look at the palace with a doubtful eye, wondering if it was truly as special as we'd believed it to be. Or had Maya laid a spell not upon the palace foundations but on us, so that the beauties we doted on had no existence outside of our own longing?

But in this I was mistaken. The palace was fully as magical as Maya had claimed, and like all magical dwellings, it sensed its inhabitants' thoughts. In the next days, I would feel from it a coolness, a withdrawal. Later I would wonder, was its displeasure with me the cause of the accident that occurred, the accident that would have such far-reaching consequences?

If Duryodhan's days were spent reconnoitering, his nights were spent at elaborate revels that he organized. I resented these bitterly. They were a reminder that, no matter how important I was to my husbands, there would always be places where I couldn't accompany—or advise—them. But my uneasiness had causes more serious than a hurt ego. The reports I heard were disquieting—the scantily clad dancers, the expensive sura Duryodhan ordered in wagonloads and presented to my husbands, the miasma of opium smoke in the sabha by the end of the evening. And the gaming! Each night dice would be set up on boards of ivory, and Duryodhan, with Sakuni at his elbow, would challenge Yudhisthir.

Surprisingly, for all his fondness for the game, the Kaurava prince was neither a skilled nor a prudent player. He bet recklessly and lost more often than he won. Nor did Sakuni, who sometimes played in his stead, seem to have much luck. My other husbands joked about it, saying that if Duryodhan kept this up, he wouldn't have the money to build anything larger than a cowshed by the time he returned to Hastinapur. But Yudhisthir loved the games. He threw himself into them with childlike glee and made no secret of his pleasure when he won. He was not, however, used to this kind of dissipated lifestyle. He would stumble into our bedchamber late at night, reeking of wine and too excited to fall asleep. When he did sleep, he tossed and turned and cried out from nightmares. In the morning he woke heavy-headed and bad-tempered and dragged himself to the royal hall to conduct affairs of state. Dhai Ma, who had her sources, told me that he was too tired to give them his usual meticulous attention. But he refused to put a stop to all this carousing, as I suggested. I sent a message to Dwarka, hoping that Krishna could talk some sense into him, but he was off on one of his adventures—something to do with a lost gem—and couldn't be reached.

. . .

This morning was particularly disheartening, with Yudhisthir so sluggish and morose that I wondered whether Duryodhan had been adding something to his wine. Was he slowly poisoning him? Was this the true reason he stayed on? Had he plotted every step of this insidious plan a long time ago? Had he incited Sisupal to behave in a way that would lead to his death, knowing this would cause the other kings to turn against Yudhisthir? Had he realized that it would create the perfect situation for him to worm his way into his trusting cousin's heart?

My mind raced in a million directions as I stood at my balcony with my attendant women, staring blindly at the beauty that stretched out in front of me. Clearly, I had to do something to stop Duryodhan. But what? In my agitation, I paid little attention to my surroundings until one of the women said, "My queen, see who's here!"

My rooms overlooked the most beautiful garden in the palace, one I'd designed myself (although Maya had added the finer touches) to create an impression of unplanned abundance. Amidst flowering trees and shrubs with jewel-hued leaves was a large, irregularly shaped lake where many birds would come to swim. It was filled with wild lilies and its water was a brilliant blue that shone even on cloudy days. In its center rose a pavilion with intricately carved pillars depicting stories of gods and goddesses that changed even as one gazed at them. To get to the pavilion, visitors had to use one of several slender bridges suspended over the water. But here Maya had worked his mischief: though all the bridges looked solid, only one was real. The others were illusions, made of light and air and trickery, and they had caused many a visitor to end up with a drenching.

It was toward this pool that Duryodhan was making his way. He hadn't seen us, for Maya had shielded the women's balconies with a clever latticework. I hushed my companions so I could observe him without his knowledge. Perhaps this way I could learn his intentions regarding Yudhisthir.

Duryodhan loved fine clothing. Today he wore an outfit of spotless white silk (quite unsuitable for walking in gardens) and far too much jewelry and strode at the head of his retinue, who, believing themselves unobserved, acted more insolent than usual. They pointed with lewd gestures to the statuettes of apsaras, laughing so loudly that my pet doves took startled flight. Some tore off flowers and twirled them in their fingers. Others bit into fruit they'd picked from the trees, then threw them half-eaten into the bushes. Only Karna, who brought up the rear, was silent and empty-handed. His armor, which I'd heard he never removed, caught the sun, dazzling my eyes. The disdain on his face—for Duryodhan's men or for my garden?—made it clear that he regarded the entire expedition as a waste of his time. Though I tried my best, I couldn't tear my eyes from him. Disappointment and anger battled in my heart as I wished I could find a way to wipe the indifference from his face.

I was so preoccupied with Karna that I failed to notice what Duryodhan was doing until I heard the splash. He must have stepped onto an illusory bridge, for now he was floundering about in the pool. I stared, horrified, as he flailed and cursed, calling to his flustered courtiers who milled around, unwilling to jump in and ruin their own expensive clothes. My attendants burst into peals of laughter. I should have stopped them, but I couldn't help smiling myself, he looked so comical. Or was it that a part of me felt vindicated because my palace had done what I could not: brought low—if only for a moment—the man who I knew still hated my husbands, no matter what he pretended. Encouraged by my smile, one of the younger women cried out in her gay, clear voice, "It seems the blind king's son is also blind!"

I reprimanded her sharply, but the harm was done. All eyes turned to the balcony. Duryodhan glared at the latticework. I could see what he thought: I'd deliberately chosen not to warn him and then insulted him in the worst of ways, by bringing up his father's infirmity. Karna, who had stepped into the pool to help his friend, stared up, too—giving me, finally, ironically, the attention I'd been craving since his arrival. Had I acted immediately, calling out my apologies, sending down maids with dry clothes, and publicly punishing the girl who had spoken, I might have minimized the damage. But the cold fury on Karna's face paralyzed my tongue. I couldn't bear to humble myself in front of him to Duryodhan, to admit that I had been at fault, to listen in silence, with bent head, as he blamed me for my palace's trickery. What could I have said, in any case, in my defense? That Karna had distracted me from noticing what Duryodhan was doing? And so I stood struggling with my ego until the brief moment of opportunity vanished. The two friends stalked off, whispering angrily to each other, leaving me to wonder what would come of this.

. . .

In one thing my palace was no different from others: here, too, news flew on the swift wings of gossip. Not even an hour had passed after Duryodhan's mishap when Kunti summoned me to her quarters. (It made me wonder how many of my women she had bribed to be her informants.) I was surprised at the summons; since coming to this palace, my mother-in-law hadn't behaved in such an imperialistic manner. When I went to her, I found on her face that old expression, exasperation at my stupidity. For a moment, it was as though the years spun away and I was a new bride again. Politely and scathingly, she wondered how it was that I could not control my women's tongues. She recommended that I confess what had happened to Yudhisthir without delay.

"Perhaps my son can calm down his cousin and repair his insulted pride," she said. "It's too bad that he'll have to debase himself because of your foolishness, but it's absolutely essential. You don't know how vindictive Duryodhan can be, or how dangerous."

A part of me realized she was right. What she suggested was sensible; I had been considering it myself. Had she spoken differently, I would have followed her advice. After all, she knew the Kaurava clan far better than I and had survived, over and over, their labyrinthine plots. But her peremptory tone—coupled with my own guilt—made me intractable. I told her—equally politely—that I would handle the matter. Was I not, after all, queen of this palace? If I felt that my husband should be informed, I would certainly do it. There was no need for her to concern herself with such paltry events at an age where no doubt she preferred to focus on spiritual activities.

Kunti stared at me, lips pressed together in fury until they almost disappeared. Perhaps she realized that if she said anything more, the façade of politeness between us would crumble, and it would be out-and-out war—the result of which could only hurt her sons. Perhaps our clash brought home to her, with cruel clarity, that she was not in charge here. Perhaps she thought, Let her suffer the results of her folly.

I bowed to indicate our meeting was over.

I did not tell Yudhisthir what had happened. He was irritable already and hard to handle; this would make things worse. I told myself that I'd apologize if Duryodhan complained to my husbands, but he never brought the matter up. Was it because he was embarrassed? Or had Kunti made too much of what was, after all, no more than an accident? He spent his days spying around as usual and his nights gambling with Yudhisthir. Karna, too, acted in the same way as before, treating all around him with a weary courtesy. But perhaps something good did come out of the prince's drenching, for a week later, he announced that his father had sent word asking him to return to Hastinapur. At the farewell banquet, he made it a point to include me in his fulsome thanks, and I responded in a similar vein.

With the departure of the Kauravas, our lives returned to normal. And yet there was a difference. The Rajasuya ceremonies had unbalanced something, leaving behind a feeling of emptiness. Maybe all who complete a great enterprise feel this way. The mundane activities that we'd longed to pursue while the palace was crowded with guests now left us unsatisfied. Yudhisthir conducted the affairs of state with only half a heart, and in the evenings he sat in the sabha, listless, not talking. Bheem stomped about the kitchen and threw away half the dishes he cooked, complaining that they were tasteless. Nakul neglected his beloved horses, and Sahadev left unread the new books that traders brought him from distant lands. Arjun watched the mountains to the north, upon whose peaks Shiva was supposed to live, with yearning in his eyes. I tended my gardens, repairing the damage Duryodhan's cronies had inflicted upon it, but often in the middle of giving instructions, I would forget what I was saying. My eye would go to a bench where Karna had sat, a path where he had walked, and once again I would be stung that my palace had failed to impress him.

Sometimes I found myself thinking of the prophecy made at my birth. Had I fulfilled it? I'd done something unforeseen: married five kings and combined their strength so they could become overlords of the entire continent of Bharat. Surely in this I'd already made a significant mark on history? One part of me answered yes. But the other part of me whispered, Is this all, is this all that my life was meant to be?

Desire is a powerful magnet. Was my careless longing responsible in part for the invitation that arrived within the year? In it Duryodhan requested his dearest cousins to honor him with a visit to his just-constructed palace, though it was nowhere as resplendent as that of the Pandavas. Perhaps there would be an opportunity to continue the games he had enjoyed so much at Indra Prastha? He concluded by extending a special invitation to Queen Draupadi, whom his new wife Bhanumati, Princess of Kasi, had long admired and desired to meet.

This was unexpected. Wives did not usually accompany kings on their journeys. Kunti snorted at the impropriety of the idea, but my heart gave a leap.

"He's certainly been busy!" Arjun commented. "A new sabha and a new wife! I wonder what prompted him to marry again—he's got so many wives already. And sons, too. In any case, I don't want to go and gratify his ego."

Sahadev shook his head. "It's not just his ego. There's something else about the invitation—something I don't trust."

Nakul frowned. "I think he's concocting some kind of plan."

"I'd sooner trust a cobra," Bheem added, then turned to me. "Am I not right, Panchaali?"

I should have agreed at once, and emphatically. It would have ended the matter right then. Yudhisthir might have grumbled, but he would have listened to our combined voice and declined Duryodhan's invitation. What weakness made me remain silent? What dark desire?

Kunti glared at me, but carefully, so that no one else would notice. "You're absolutely correct," she said to Bheem. "Only the most foolish go looking for trouble."

Yudhisthir said, "You're all worrying unnecessarily! Duryodhan has finally realized that it's to his advantage to have us as his friends. Besides, he had such a good time when he was here. It's natural that he should want to repay our hospitality. It would be churlish to refuse."

"You're too trusting!" Kunti burst out. "Just like your father—that's always been your—"

"I think Yudhisthir's right," I broke in. "Duryodhan's made an effort to put old enmities aside. It's only right that we do our part."

What made me interrupt Kunti with words that I knew, even while speaking them, to be untrue? Was it just my annoyance at her efforts to control, once more, my husband and my home? Or was it the hope of seeing someone when I arrived in Hastinapur—just one more time—even though I knew his sight would only bring me heartache? Or was it, as Vyasa would have claimed, that I was following a destiny that had already been written?

Kunti bit her lip and said no more. She was too proud to engage in an argument with me. But she gave me a strange look, as though she realized that the words I spoke didn't match the thoughts hidden in my mind. My other husbands looked uncertain for a moment. But I'd given them good advice so many times in the past that they put aside their unease.

"We'll go," Nakul said to his brother, "since you and Panchaali both wish it. But, brother, surely you see that Duryodhan doesn't care about us. He only wants to show off his new possessions."

"Let him!" Yudhisthir said airily. "We know that our possessions"—here he waved a gallant hand at me—"older though they might be, are incomparable."

I bowed in response to this Yudhisthir-like compliment. I was already planning to pack my finest silks and most impressive jewelry and order my sairindhri to design some new hairdos. A couple of rejuvenating poultices wouldn't be a bad idea, either. I wanted to make sure that Bhanumati (or was I thinking of someone else?) continued to admire me.

"You're making a mistake," Kunti said to Yudhisthir. "At least leave Draupadi behind—it's neither right nor prudent that she goes with you."

I was ready with hot protests, but I didn't need them. "Oh, Mother!" Yudhisthir said. "You're always imagining the worst. Panchaali will be just fine. In fact, she'll make sure that the rest of us don't do anything imprudent."

. . .

Our entourage left on a beautiful spring day. My husbands rode ahead, their prancing steeds matching their impatience. Beside them, our sons spurred their ponies, equally eager to be on their way. Behind us came a hundred horsemen, bearing gifts. A curtain of fine dust rose from the horses' hooves like early morning mist. Behind it, the palace glimmered, its wavering golden domes suddenly far away. From the chariot I shared with the sullen Kunti, I leaned out to sniff the perfume of the parijat trees that lined the long driveway. I was as excited as a lad setting out on his first adventure.

"I hope the flowers will still be in bloom when we return," I said to Kunti.

She didn't reply. She hadn't spoken to me since I'd persuaded my husbands to accept Duryodhan's invitation. Annoyed, I decided I wouldn't speak to her either until she decided to get over her sulking.

I didn't know that she was right in her misgivings. That in traveling to Hastinapur we were making one of the biggest mistakes of our life. I didn't know that I'd never see this fragrant flower-laden road—or the palace I so loved—again.

games

It was a vastly different Hastinapur I came to this time—or maybe it was I that was different. Being mistress of the Palace of Illusions had transformed me in ways I hadn't realized. I was no longer intimidated by the Kaurava court, and though Duryodhan's new palace impressed many visitors with its sparkling novelties, I saw at once that it was merely a pale copy of ours, without true magic to give it a soul. Nor did the elders intimidate me. I found myself speaking to the blind king Dhritarashtra, Kripa, and even Drona, my brother's nemesis, with polite self-possession. The grandfather watched my conversations with approval in his eye, and when we were alone, he said, "Why, you've become a true queen now, equal to the best of us! You no longer care what people think of you, and that has given you a great freedom." He didn't know the shifting sands on which my freedom rested, nor that my confidence ebbed each time I entered a hall and only returned when I'd ascertained that Karna wasn't present. He didn't know how much I cared about all the wrong things.

But he was right in this: in some matters, I was equal to—or better off than—his peers. In Indra Prastha my husbands had listened carefully to my opinions concerning the kingdom, and though we sometimes argued, they followed many of my suggestions. But in Hastinapur, though the blind king sat on the throne with the elders in the seats of honor beside him, Duryodhan was the one who wielded power. He put on a polite face while they discussed treaties and laws, but ultimately, things happened the way he wanted. Dhritarashtra couldn't bear to oppose his favorite son, who would fly into a rage if contradicted and think nothing of insulting the old warriors who had kept the kingdom safe for him all these years. At such times, only Karna was able to calm him, but often he, too, was impatient with the cautious advice of the elders. Seeing this, the elders protected their own dignity and withdrew into silence. Each day they were more like ornate figureheads on a ship that had changed its course without their consent and was sailing into dangerous waters.

I didn't see any of this for myself, for Hastinapur was more conservative than our city. Although there was a covered women's section in court, we were only allowed there by invitation. My sources of information were meager, limited to tidbits Dhai Ma gleaned from the other servants, or random facts my husbands mentioned in passing. But I did learn this much: Karna had left for his kingdom just before we arrived in Hastinapur. In spite of the many messengers Duryodhan had sent, urging him to return, he had not complied.

My conversations with my husbands were brief and unsatisfying, for Duryodhan had pulled them into a whirlwind of entertainments during the day, and at night there were the infamous gambling parties I'd dreaded. This time, though, some things were different. Before leaving Indra Prastha, I'd made Yudhisthir promise to control his drinking, and he kept that promise. Sobriety helped his game. To his delight, he won even more often than before. But this meant that he was in no hurry to return home. At times this worried me, for I couldn't shake off a sense of unease, a feeling that we were in enemy territory. At other times I was glad when I thought there was still a chance that I might see Karna, though the gladness had a bitter aftertaste.

. . .

This time our rooms were not in the old palace but in the new building, resplendent, in the gaudy style Duryodhan favored, with statues of curvaceous beauties and lurid paintings of hunts and battles. They were conveniently located next to his sabha so that my husbands could go back and forth as they desired. I was not displeased with this change. It was a relief to be away from that malicious old labyrinth with its stares and gossip, its complicated histories of hate. Here I could spend my days as I wished, for my husbands were kept busy, and the boys went off each morning to play with other children or to watch jugglers and dancing monkeys. Once I'd paid my obligatory visits to the palace women, I was left with few responsibilities. It was a luxury I hadn't enjoyed since girlhood— and at that time I'd not known enough to appreciate its precious rareness. I read, composed poems, or walked in the courtyard. (I was amused to find that Duryodhan had filled it with as many of the flowers from our gardens as he could find, each crowded upon the other with little regard for aesthetics.) I had the maids bring me a light meal under the fragrant trees. I listened to birdsong. I dressed informally, in cool, thin cottons, for all the attendants in our quarters were women. I daydreamed while Dhai Ma combed my hair, and if my imagination went where it should not, I consoled myself with the thought that it harmed no one.

I was further pleased that Kunti wasn't staying with us, for though we continued to be polite to each other, matters had grown thorny between us. Since the day when I swayed my husbands' opinions about accepting Duryodhan's invitation, I often caught her watching me with narrowed eyes. I could tell that she suspected my motives in coming here, though she wasn't sure what they were. She made me feel nervous and guilty—and as a result, irritable. Fortunately when we reached Hastinapur, Gandhari, with whom she'd kept up a correspondence, invited her to stay in her chambers. "We two old women," she said, smiling from beneath that ambiguous blindfold, "have much to talk about that you youngsters wouldn't understand." I hadn't thought Kunti would agree—Gandhari's sons had, after all, tried to kill hers. But she accepted with alacrity. Perhaps the two dowagers relished this chance to complain to each other about their daughters-in-law!

. . .

Duryodhan's new wife, Bhanumati, was coming to visit. I prepared by donning dauntingly elegant clothing and a haughty expression, but I need not have bothered. She was just a girl and regarded me with such a mix of awe and apprehension that she could hardly speak without stammering. I felt a stab of anger at Duryodhan for having plucked her so soon from her parents. I also wondered what she'd heard about me that made her so nervous.

Watching her fidget with the heavy brocade that weighed her down, I guessed that Duryodhan had dictated this entire visit, including what she should wear. I brought up his name in our conversation; a painful blush spread over her pretty face. The poor girl was in love with him even as she feared him! I felt a twinge of pity—any woman who gave her heart to the egoistic Duryodhan was bound to suffer—and did what I could to put her at her ease. She responded with such gratitude that I suspected few in this palace had befriended her. Soon she was jingling her bangles, showing me her new silver toe rings and chattering about her favorite activities—eating sweetmeats, teaching her pet parrot to talk, and playing hide-and-seek with the friends who had accompanied her from Kasi. Sometimes, she confided, Duryodhan and a few of his close friends joined her in these games.

She amazed me further by adding, "Among my husband's friends, I like Karna the best. He doesn't make fun of me for being afraid of lizards, like Dussasan. And sometimes when he finds my hiding place, he pretends he hasn't seen me." Her face lit up with an uncomplicated pleasure when she spoke of Karna. Clearly, she adored him.

I was still trying to digest this information—and to ignore a foolish pang of jealousy—when she said goodbye, inviting me charmingly to come and visit her, too. At the doorway, she gave me an impulsive hug. "You're so kind," she said. "Not cruel-tongued like they warned me."

I bit the aforementioned cruel tongue to keep from asking who her cautioners were, but she carried on, oblivious. "Karna never said that, though. He took me aside and said you were noble and beautiful—and he was right." Then she was gone in a tinkling of ankle bells, leaving me without words.

. . .

Karna had returned from Anga. (This, Dhai Ma said, was in response to a taunting letter from Duryodhan that asked if he was afraid to face the Pandavas, especially his erstwhile rival Arjun.) To celebrate his friend's arrival, or perhaps the success of his own persuasive tactics, Duryodhan planned a lavish "family" banquet. This meant that all his relatives and close friends were expected to attend, accompanied by the women of their household.

I was at once excited and agitated by this news and spent much time trying to decide what to wear. Even my most exquisite sari seemed paltry, old-fashioned. Finally I ordered the royal weavers back at Indra Prastha to design a new outfit that would be unlike anything they'd made before, outstanding enough to make it unforgettable. They were to rush it to me as soon as it was completed. They promised me they would work on it night and day. It had not yet arrived when a flustered and tearful Bhanumati begged me to help her pick out appropriate clothing for the event. I arrived in her chambers to find her knee-deep in saris, each one more vibrantly colored and more finely embroidered with gold thread than the last, while sandalwood boxes holding jewels covered the entire floor. It took me the whole afternoon to convince her that she would be beautiful in almost any of them.

"But Duryodhan will be displeased if I don't dress just right," she must have said a score of times. And once, turning her wide, ingenuous eyes to me, "I want Karna to admire how I look."

Finally we decided on a deep red silk, so encrusted with gold and jewels that when she wore it I feared she would be unable to walk, and chose a set of rubies embedded in thick gold to go with it.

By the time I returned to my rooms, I had changed my own plans for the banquet. The visit to Bhanumati had opened my eyes, exposing the folly I'd been about to commit. And what was forgivable in her would be shameful in me, a woman old enough—if not wise enough—to know better. I finally faced the truth: what I wanted—even if it was only an admiring glance from Karna—was sinful. Was I not married, five times over—and worse, to men with whom Karna was at enmity? Words from our scriptures came into my mind: *a wife who holds in her heart desireful thoughts of a man who is not her husband is as unfaithful as a woman who sleeps with such a man.* I put aside the beautiful sari that had just arrived from Indra Prastha, colored like the rainbow and woven through with diamonds. I picked instead a plain white silk with a delicate border of red and gold. I informed Dhai Ma that I would wear a simple set of pearls and dress my hair only with jasmine. She clicked her tongue in disapproval, saying that I would be woefully underdressed for the occasion, that only old women wore white, but finally she complied.

Ironically, though, when I entered the banquet hall, all eyes turned to me. Among the women clustered like multicolored bouquets, I stood out in my pristine attire. Some of the women envied my creativity; others whispered resentfully, Always she must be different, always she wants to show that she's better, always she craves attention. Kunti, who had joined us for the event, gave a small snort at what she obviously considered my pretentiousness. Then she ordered me to give her my arm to lean on. Since she was perfectly capable of walking on her own, I could only surmise that she wanted to keep a close watch on me.

We had barely taken a few steps when I saw Karna, dressed simply as always. He noticed me at the same time and came to a sudden halt. For a moment I thought he would take another path through the banquet hall—it would be easy enough, among all the milling guests, to avoid me. But he did not. There was an expression in his eyes that I couldn't quite read as he took in my clothes. And that was when I realized that he and I—both in white, both almost unadorned—mirrored each other. Had such a thought lurked in my subconscious when I chose my attire? Kunti noticed the similarity at the same time. She drew in her breath, stiffening, and I wondered what she thought of our strange symmetry.

Karna had reached us by now. He bowed in a gesture that was friendlier than anything he'd offered me in Indra Prastha. He greeted Kunti first, as was appropriate, but without waiting for her response, he turned to me. "It is a pleasure to see the queen of the Pandavas looking so well," he said with a smile. "I hope her visit here has been comfortable so far."

His words of courtesy were common enough, no different from

what any courtier might say. Still, my heart pounded. Perhaps this was the chance I had waited so long for: to release the past and make things better between us. Perhaps then Karna would cease to haunt me. I readied myself to smile, to say that I hoped he had had a good journey and to ask after his health. Would it be too forward of me to state that I was glad to see him? But Kunti had tightened her hold on my arm. Her eyes went from him to me and back to him. Her face was pale and rigid.

What did she guess?

I could not afford to have my secret bared before her ruthless gaze. It would place me in her power forever. I forced my face into expressionlessness and gave Karna a bow so slight that it was worse than if I had ignored him. I swept by him without a word, pulling Kunti along. But from the corner of my eye I saw his face, the dark anger that had leaped into it. My heart twisted. I'd ruined everything! And yet what else could I have done? What ill star shone on us that made the wrong things happen—things I never intended— every time we met? Now he'd never forgive me.

Through the elaborate, unending dinner, as I ate without tasting the delicacies and smiled until my mouth ached and conversed with the women around me, not knowing what I said, I resolved it was time to return home. I would insist on it to Yudhisthir this very night. A longing for my palace shook me. I needed it the way an injured beast needs its lair—to crawl in and lick my wounds.

25

Sari

Time is like a flower, Krishna said once. I didn't understand. But later I visualized a lotus opening, the way the outer petals fall away to reveal the inner ones. An inner petal would never know the older, outer ones, even though it was shaped by them, and only the viewer who plucked the flower would see how each petal was connected to the others.

The petal of this afternoon opened like a red sigh. It was my time of month, which made me lethargic. Dressed in a light cotton that a trader had brought all the way from Bengal, I drowsed in the soft sunlight at my window, listening to the mynahs calling in the garden, feeling calmer than I had in a while. Yudhisthir had agreed (as a result of some sharp words exchanged in our bedroom last night) that it was time he ended his visit and returned to his own kingdom. He had promised to announce this to Duryodhan today. So finally I would be back in my own palace, where I could start working on forgetting the look of anger on a certain face.

I had no idea of the petal that had opened a few hours earlier in Duryodhan's new hall, where the Kaurava prince, expressing his disappointment at the prospect of losing his dear cousin so soon, had challenged him to a last game of dice. *Maybe this way I can recover a little of the money I've lost to you, eh?* And in this game—connected to all those earlier petals, shriveled now, those games played in Indra Prashtha, luring my husband in—Sakuni had taken Duryodhan's place as Yudhisthir's opponent. The petal unfurled, revealing the skill he'd hidden until now. Time after time he won until my husband—deaf to the entreaties of his brothers—lost his jewels, his weapons, and all his personal wealth. Then, goaded by Duryodhan, gripped by stubbornness, and intoxicated by the game, he began to wager things he had no right to jeopardize. And forfeited them all.

. . .

There was a commotion at the door. Had my husbands returned early? But the man standing outside my rooms, head bowed awkwardly, was—I could see it from his clothes—one of Duryodhan's attendants. I was angered at his insolence. A male servant should have known to wait outside the building and send a message through one of my maids.

I drew the semitransparent cotton closer around me. "What is it you want?" I asked in my haughtiest tones. But before he could speak, Dhai Ma came hurtling in, gasping for breath.

"Girl, girl," she cried, forgetting formal courtesies in her agitation, "terrible things have happened, things you won't believe."

My heart began to pound. Or was the pounding in my head? I spoke more sternly than I ever had to her. "Pull yourself together! Tell me clearly what the problem is."

But she had dissolved into hiccuping tears at my feet.

I glared at Duryodhan's servant. "Leave us!" I commanded him.

He licked his lips nervously and bowed. "Forgive me, your highness. I must carry out my task. Prince Duryodhan invites you to the sabha."

"To the hall?" I asked, incredulous. "But women never go there! And why would he and not my husbands send for me?"

Dhai Ma was tugging at my sari. "Because he lost it all gambling," she said through slurred tears. "Yudhisthir. First the money in the state coffers, then the palace—"

"My palace?" I interrupted, furious. "He had no right!"

Dhai Ma's lips stretched in a grimace. "That's not all. He lost the kingdom, too. Then he wanted to stop, because he had nothing else to bet against. But that fiend Sakuni said, Why, as an elder brother you can wager the other Pandavas."

"That's preposterous!" I cried. "Surely he wouldn't do that."

"He did. And lost them. Then he wagered himself and lost again. The luck of the demons was with that vulture Sakuni. And then Duryodhan said, I'll wager everything I've won from you in one final game, against Draupadi."

My head was ringing. "No!" I said.

Dhai Ma nodded, then covered her face and burst into fresh weeping.

My mouth went dry. Denials collided with each other inside me.

I'm a queen. Daughter of Drupad, sister of Dhristadyumna. Mistress of the greatest palace on earth. I can't be gambled away like a bag of coins, or summoned to court like a dancing girl.

But then I remembered what I'd read long ago in a book, never imagining that quaint law could ever have any power over me.

The wife is the property of the husband, no less so than a cow or a slave.

"What did my other husbands say?" I whispered to the servant.

"They could say nothing," he answered unhappily. "They were already Duryodhan's slaves."

My head reeled, but I steadied myself. I tried to remember other words from the Nyaya Shastra. *If perchance a man lost himself, he no longer had any jurisdiction over his wife.*

"Go back to the court," I ordered, "and ask the elders this: Is it not true that once Yudhisthir was Duryodhan's property, he had no right to wager me?"

The servant scurried away, thankful to go. I took a deep, hard breath. It was good that I was no unlettered girl, ignorant of the law. The elders would know the rule I referred to. They would put an end to Duryodhan's effrontery. Bheeshma in particular wouldn't stand for my being insulted in this way. I still had much to worry about, but at least I was saved from the indignity of being ogled by Duryodhan's cronies.

In thinking this, I was mistaken. In what happened next, the laws of men would not save me.

. . .

The incident that took place at the sabha has been sung of widely, though to my senses it remains a blur. Was it only a heart-beat before Dussasan came storming in, shouting that Duryodhan was my master now, and I must obey his orders? Did Dhai Ma try to run to Gandhari's apartments for help? Did he send her sprawling with a blow? Did he grab my hair, which no man had touched ex-cept with reverent love? I begged his leave to change into suitable clothing. Jeering at what he termed my false modesty, he dragged me down the palace corridors, before the shocked gaze of retainers. No one dared intervene. I found myself in court, a hundred male eyes burning through me. Gathering my disordered sari around me, I demanded help from my husbands. They sent me tortured glances but sat paralyzed. I could see that in their minds they were already Duryodhan's vassals, chained by Yudhisthir's word. That same word had made me Duryodhan's property. They felt they had no right to rescue me—or themselves. The blind king swiveled his head from side to side, pretending confusion, when I cried out his name. My anxiety grew, but I was still not desperate. I called to the grandfather to protect me, certain that he at least would intervene. Had he not called me his dearest granddaughter? Had he not shared with me tender confidences that he kept from others? Had he not helped me become queen of the Palace of Illusions? But to my disbelief, he sat with his head lowered.

Seeing this, Duryodhan laughed, sure of his victory. He motioned crudely at me to come and sit in his lap. And so finally, I turned my gaze on Karna. He was my last hope, the only one who had the ability to stop Duryodhan. He looked back at me, his eyes steady. There was a waiting look on his face. I knew what he wanted: for me to fall on my knees and beg him for mercy. He would have protected me then. He had the reputation of helping the destitute. But I wouldn't lower myself to that, not if I died.

He was our enemy. I had recently rebuffed his attempt at cordiality. Why then did I feel betrayed because he hadn't come to my rescue of his own accord?

I called on pride to freeze my tears to stone. I mustered all the hatred I could find within me and focused it on Karna.

When he saw the contempt in my eyes, Karna's face grew white and still, as though made of ivory. Duryodhan was laughing in triumph. He shouted to Dussasan, "Remove the Pandavas' fancy clothes and jewelry. All of that belongs to us now!" My husbands threw off their upper garments, their gold chains and armbands, before Dussasan could touch them. Karna watched the glittering mass on the floor intently, as though it could tell him a secret; his mouth stretched in a mirthless smile. "Why should Draupadi be treated any differently? Take her clothes, too."

. . .

The bards sing of what occurred when Dussasan took hold of my sari to pull it away, exposing my nakedness to all eyes. How more and still more fabric appeared until he was exhausted with tugging. Was it a miracle? I don't know. I had shut my eyes. My body would not stop trembling though I willed it to. I clutched my sari in my fists—as though I could save myself with that futile gesture! The worst shame a woman could imagine was about to befall me—I who had thought myself above all harm, the proud and cherished wife of the greatest kings of our time! Now they sat frozen as I struggled with Dussasan. The sorceress had said, When in great trouble, rest your mind on someone who loves you. I tried to call up Dhri's face. But all I could imagine was how enraged and helpless he'd feel when he heard of what had been done to me.

Then—maybe because there was no one else who could help—I thought of Krishna. He owed me nothing; we were not related. Perhaps that was why I could fix my mind on him without being swept away by the anger that arises from expectation. I thought of his smile, the way it would appear on his face for no reason. The sounds of the courtroom faded—Dussasan's grunts, the whispers of the watchers. Suddenly I was in a garden. There were swans in a lake, a tree that arched above, dropping blue flowers, the sound of water falling as though the world had no end. The wind smelled of sandalwood. Krishna sat beside me on a cool stone bench. His glance was bright and tender. *No one can shame you*, he said, *if you don't allow it.*

It came to me, in a wash of amazement, that he was right.

Let them stare at my nakedness, I thought. Why should I care? They and not I should be ashamed for shattering the bounds of decency.

Was that not miracle enough?

Krishna nodded. He took my hands. At his touch, I felt my muscles relax, my fists open. He smiled, and I prepared to smile back.

But just then another face pushed its way into my mind. I saw a different pair of eyes, hot with hate. I heard again the words with which he sealed my doom. They resonated through me like the twang of a bow that has just released a poison arrow. The punishment he'd heaped on me was so much greater than my crime.

Karna, I said to myself. *You've taught me a lesson, and you've taught it well.*

Is the desire for vengeance stronger than the longing to be loved? What evil magic does it possess to draw the human heart so powerfully to it? As I spoke, my hands slipped from Krishna's. His face wavered, dimming.

I opened my eyes. I was still clothed, and Dussasan was on the floor in a swoon. I stepped over him and spoke to the assembly in a voice like cracking ice. "All of you will die in the battle that will be spawned from this day's work. Your mothers and wives will weep far more piteously than I've wept. This entire kingdom will become a charnel house. Not one Kaurava heir will be left to offer prayers for the dead. All that will remain is the shameful memory of today, what you tried to do to a defenseless woman." I spoke to all, but it was Karna I looked at, his gaze I held. Of one thing I was glad. What happened today had stripped away all ambiguities from my heart. Never again would I long for his attention. Behind me I heard Bheem and Arjun pronouncing oaths of revenge, and the blind king's anxious entreaties as he called my name, begging me to retract my curse. Inside me Krishna's face dissolved in a red haze, but I could not—would not—stop my words.

I lifted up my long hair for all to see. My voice was calm now because I knew that everything I said would come to pass. "I will not comb it," I said, "until the day I bathe it in Kaurava blood."

. . .

What did I learn that day in the sabha?

All this time I'd believed in my power over my husbands. I'd believed that because they loved me they would do anything for me. But now I saw that though they did love me—as much perhaps as any man can love—there were other things they loved more. Their notions of honor, of loyalty toward each other, of reputation were more important to them than my suffering. They would avenge me later, yes, but only when they felt the circumstances would bring them heroic fame. A woman doesn't think that way. I would have thrown myself forward to save them if it had been in my power that day. I wouldn't have cared what anyone thought. The choice they made in the moment of my need changed something in our relationship. I no longer depended on them so completely in the future. And when I took care to guard myself from hurt, it was as much from them as from our enemies.

For men, the softer emotions are always intertwined with power and pride. That was why Karna waited for me to plead with him though he could have stopped my suffering with a single word. That was why he turned on me when I refused to ask for his pity. That was why he incited Dussasan to an action that was against the code of honor by which he lived his life. He knew he would regret it—in his fierce smile there had already been a glint of pain.

But was a woman's heart any purer, in the end?

That was the final truth I learned. All this time I'd thought myself better than my father, better than all those men who inflicted harm on a thousand innocents in order to punish the one man who had wronged them. I'd thought myself above the cravings that drove him. But I, too, was tainted with them, vengeance encoded into my blood. When the moment came I couldn't resist it, no more than a dog can resist chewing a bone that, splintering, makes his mouth bleed.

Already I was storing these lessons inside me. I would use them over the long years of exile to gain what I wanted, no matter what its price.

But Krishna, the slippery one, the one who had offered me a different solace, Krishna with his disappointed eyes—what was the lesson he'd tried to teach?

rice

 After the blind king took fright at my curse and gave my husbands their freedom and their kingdom, after Duryodhan taunted Yudhisthir for being saved by his wife and challenged him to play one last game where the loser would be banished to the forest for twelve years. After I begged Yudhisthir to ignore the challenge, after he refused me for honor's sake, after he lost as I knew he would, after we discarded our finery for clothing such as servants wear. After we said goodbye to Kunti, who stared white-faced and tearless, after I handed my crying, clutching children to Dhai Ma, who would take them to be brought up in Subhadra's house. After her accusing eyes (for she knew I could have stayed with them, I didn't have to go with my husbands to the forest, my boys needed me more). After we walked barefoot from the city all the way to the wilderness.

After all this had happened, Duryodhan and his men rode in triumph to the Palace of Illusions to take possession of it.

When they came within sight of the palace, Duryodhan released his pent-up breath. *Mine, finally!* His retainers realized then that all he'd done to the Pandavas had been for this—to own the palace he had failed to replicate, the site of his past humiliation, his present triumph. To rewrite his history. But even as he spoke a wind rose up, and as it swirled whitely around the palace, its domes and turrets began to dissolve. Duryodhan whipped his horse furiously forward until blood foamed from its mouth. Even so, by the time he arrived where the main gateway had stood, only a few small piles remained on the ground: bones, hair, sand, and salt.

How do I know? I dreamed it.

My husbands surmised that faithful servants, hearing of our misfortune, had set the buildings on fire, but I knew with bitter satisfaction that my dream was true. My palace refused to be occupied by anyone other than its rightful owners. It did what it had to do in order to remain true to us.

As we moved through the forest, I carried a pouch of salt in honor of my lost palace. At night I let the grains run through my fingers, over skin scraped raw by rocks and branches, and welcomed the sting. It would help me not to forget. In my dreams, the palace came back, at once grander and more exquisite than in life. I knew I would never find another home where I belonged in the same way.

I had another reason now for my hatred.

. . .

The forest, shadowed and feathered, was beautiful in a submarine manner. If I had allowed it to seduce me, my life might have turned out different. But to me it was merely a reminder of all that had been wrested from me. As we went deeper, I thought it watched us. Did it know we had burned down its brother? Did it resent us for it? I slept warily at night, my ears tuned to slitherings.

My husbands had no such qualms. A childlike excitement took them over. I think they remembered their early, wooded years, which were perhaps their happiest ones. With equal delight they pointed out spoor and berries, the serrated bichuti leaf that could make a man itch for hours. Can anyone blame me for being annoyed? It was almost as though they hadn't lost a kingdom!

I should have expressed more interest when they showed me a lioness with her young, or giant slugs leaving their silvery mark on fallen logs. I should have laughed with them at the antics of the orange-tailed monkeys who lived from moment to joyful moment. The twelve years would have passed faster then, and more pleasantly. We lacked no essentials. Arjun always managed to find enough game. Bheem dug up roots and shook ripe fruit from trees. Nakul and Sahadev brought me fawns to pet, and milk from wild goats. No matter where we went my husbands constructed me a cottage, airy and fragrant, lined with the softest rushes they could find, where in the early morning the sun winked through the leaf-woven roof. At times Yudhisthir sang—something he'd never done in the palace. I was surprised to discover that he had a fine, deep voice.

But a strange implacability had taken hold of me. I refused all that my husbands did to bring me comfort. I stitched discontent onto my features and let my hair fall, matted and wrathful, around my face. Each day as I served their meals, I reminded the Pandavas of how they'd failed me, and what I'd suffered as a result in Duryodhan's sabha. Each night I recited the taunts of the Kauravas so that they stayed fresh in their minds. When we blew out our lamps, I tossed and turned on my bed, the rushes suddenly as hard as sticks, recalling Karna's face, its complicated darkness as he said, Take her clothes, too. (But of this I did not speak.) Each dawn when I arose, sweaty with restlessness, I pictured our revenge: a fire-strewn battlefield, the air grim with vultures, the mangled bodies of the Kauravas and their allies—the way I would transform history. (But I couldn't bear to imagine Karna's corpse. Instead, I pictured him kneeling at my feet, head bent in humiliation. When I tried to decide on a suitable punishment for him, however, my imagination failed me again.)

Thus I won the war with insidious time, which otherwise might have softened the edge of our vengefulness or perhaps eroded it altogether.

. . .

Durvasa, that most ill-tempered of sages, had descended upon us with his hundred disciples, and they were hungry.

This was how it happened: He had visited Hastinapur, where Duryodhan had taken excellent and obsequious care of him. Pleased, the sage had offered a boon. The prince had replied that it would delight his heart if the sage visited his cousins in the forest and blessed them, too.

Durvasa had graciously agreed, and was, at this moment, bathing in a nearby river. He had given strict injunctions that food should be waiting by the time he returned.

On another day, this wouldn't have troubled me. Vyasa, who had shown up just as we were leaving Hastinapur as exiles, had handed me a cooking pot. It had special powers, he said, and belonged to the sun god. Whatever I cooked in it would increase to feed all who visited us—but only until I took my meal. At that point, the pot would yield no more food for the day.

I was suspicious of Vyasa's pot (gifts from sages, I'd learned, often came trailing complications) but so far it had borne out his claim. (Sometimes, being of a doubting nature, I wondered if it was so because our guests made sure there was always enough food left in the pot for me. But deep down I knew that this world is filled with mystery.)

Today, however, I'd already finished eating and had washed

the pot. It lay empty and shining on a makeshift shelf in my make-shift kitchen. My husbands left in haste to forage for whatever the woods might yield. I started a fire in case they were successful, though what could they find that would feed so many? Worries roiled inside me as I stared at the flames. Durvasa was known for his creative curses. No doubt Duryodhan had sent him here hoping he would burden us with some obscure, incurable disease, or metamor-phose us into exotic fauna. I imagined him smirking in the comfort of his palace, imagining our new troubles. Was Karna involved in this new plot as well? In spite of my anger with him, I guessed the answer was no. He was too proud to resort to chicanery.

Often when I was fearful and didn't know what to do, I thought of Krishna. It was a habit I'd fallen into after the incident at Duryo-dhan's court. It didn't necessarily remove my problems, but it often calmed me. Sometimes I held imaginary conversations with him. It was a good way to vent my frustrations, since he never answered back.

Today I said, "Don't we have enough sorrows already? Haven't we been tested sufficiently? What kind of friend are you? It's time you exerted some of those divine powers you're supposed to possess on our behalf!"

And there he was, sitting across the fire, smiling that charming, infuriating smile. Was my anxiety causing me to hallucinate?

"A situation in itself," he said, "is neither happy nor unhappy. It's only your response to it that causes your sorrow. But enough of philosophy! I'm hungry."

"Don't tease me," I snapped. "You know there's no food any-where in this hovel that I'm forced to live in."

"You could have remained with Dhri in your father's palace," he pointed out equably. "He's begged you, many times, in my own hearing. Or you could have stayed with Subhadra, giving her a hand with those unruly children of yours. But no! You wanted to make sure you'd be on hand to provide daily torture to my poor friends the Pandavas."

Perhaps because I was stung by guilt, I said, "That's right, give me a few more blows while I'm down. What else is a friend like you good for?"

"Peace! Peace!" Krishna laughed, holding up his hand. "I can't bear to fight on an empty stomach. Why don't you look again. Maybe there's a little something left at the bottom of your pot."

"I tell you, I washed it. Can't you see?" In annoyance I picked up the vessel and flung it at him.

He caught it deftly. "Do you do this to your husbands, too? Ah well, it'll make them that much more agile at dodging enemy arrows."

His smile was infectious. I felt an answering smile take shape on my face and changed it, just in time, to a grimace of annoyance.

"Ah, here it is," he said, removing from the pot's rim a grain of rice that hadn't been there—I could have sworn it—a moment back. "You never were any good at housework." He placed it in his mouth and made a great show of chewing. Then he made me pour him water to drink. "That was good," he said. "May all beings in the world be as satisfied as I am."

I scowled. This was no time for jokes and riddles.

Suddenly he reached out and pulled a half-burnt stick from the fire. He thrust it at me so that I flinched back.

"What are you doing?" I cried, startled and angry.

"Trying to show you something. The stick—it scared you, right? It may even have hurt you, if you hadn't been so quick. But look—in trying to burn you, it's consuming itself. That's what happens to a heart—"

I could see where he was headed.

"I wish you'd focus on the problem at hand," I interrupted brusquely. "Durvasa is about to turn us into anteaters."

"That would be worth seeing." His tone was light, but there was that old disappointment in his eyes. "But it isn't going to happen today. Look!"

I glanced behind me. Bheem was returning, bunches of bananas slung over his shoulder.

"It's the strangest thing!" he exclaimed. "I met Durvasa and his disciples on my way back. They were heading away from our hut. I thought they were lost and humbly requested them to follow me. But he hemmed and hawed and finally confessed they weren't hungry any more. He wouldn't even take the bananas. He gave a great belch, sent his blessings to all of us, and made off fast." He shook his head. "Baffling, these sages. Glad I'm not one."

I swung to face Krishna, but the spot where he'd been sitting was empty. I touched the rim of the vessel where a moment ago, a grain of rice had materialized.

"Where did he go?" I asked Bheem.

"Who?"

"Krishna."

"Krishna? He hasn't gone anywhere, as far as I know. Don't you remember, he told us he'd be busy in Dwarka until after the rainy season? What made you think of him all of a sudden when we were talking about Durvasa? Watch out! That stick is too close to your foot, it could burn you."

Bheem threw the still-smoldering stick into the fire and went off to inform his brothers of Durvasa's inexplicable behavior.

. . .

This wasn't the only time Duryodhan tried to cause us trouble. Once, pretending to examine a Kaurava cattle station, he came to taunt us in Dwaita Vana. Once he incited Jayadrath, his own sister's husband, to abduct me. Both attempts ended in failure. Duryodhan was taken captive by a gandharva king and had to be rescued by Arjun. He almost killed himself over that humiliation. And even before he reached the edge of the woods, Jayadrath was caught by Bheem, who chopped off his hair as punishment. Jayadrath had to spend a whole year on the banks of the Ganga disguised as a mendicant, waiting for his locks to grow back to a respectable length.

I was delighted at our enemies' embarrassment and didn't care who knew it, though Yudhisthir warned me it was both unworthy and unwise to make my feelings so public. I refused to listen. There were few enough satisfactions I had in my banishment. But later I would see how ignorant I'd been. The humiliated enemy is the most dangerous one. My taunting words, making their way to Hastinapur, would infuriate Duryodhan and Jayadrath. They would plan and wait, and when the time was right, strike back where it would hurt us most.

. . .

"Thank you," I said into the emptiness of the kitchen after Bheem left. Whatever had happened here, I knew I didn't deserve it. I felt humbled—and guilty. "I know you want me to drop my hatred, Krishna," I whispered. "It's the one thing you've asked me for. But I can't. Even if I wanted to, I don't know how anymore."

Outside the hut, the shal trees bent and swayed, their leaves like sighs.

tales

We had many visitors in the forest—more than when we were kings. Was it because, having lost everything, we were more approachable? Dhri came often, bringing with him colorful silken tents that he set up around our huts. His cooks cleared out a compound and prepared feast foods for us all. Musicians strummed on their veenas at dusk, sending their serene notes into the darkness. For a few days while he was with us, my husbands set down the bundle of their cares to eat, drink, and laugh together.

One time, while we were at our midday meal, Yudhisthir said, in his simple way, "Why, this is almost as good as living in a palace!"

I felt as though someone had poured scalding oil over me. The food turned to clay in my mouth.

"No, it isn't!" I cried, startling all around me by my vehemence. "Nothing can make up for the palace that I lost because of your folly."

The brightness went out of Yudhisthir's face and he left us without finishing his meal. The others looked at me reproachfully, and even Dhri pulled me aside later to say that I should guard my tongue. There was nothing to be gained by destroying what little pleasure Yudhisthir could glean from his forest existence. Wasn't he suffering enough already?

"It would be good for you if you could be philosophical like him," he added. "That way you won't torture yourself all the time." He touched my face, the new, bitter wrinkles that bracketed my mouth, and spoke more gently. "Where's my sweet sister who used to bully me and play tricks on my tutor, who used to dream about breaking out of the bonds that shackled women, who was determined to change history?"

I turned away to hide the sudden tears that welled in my eyes. Even Dhri, who had once known all my dreams and fears, wouldn't understand how I felt about the one place where I had belonged, where I had been truly a queen. To be happy anywhere else was a betrayal of my beautiful palace. I didn't want to hurt my brother, who was trying so hard to cheer us—I was sorry, already, at having ruined his feast. So I kept my thoughts hidden in the dark cave that had opened within me. *She's dead. Half of her died the day when everyone she had loved and counted on to save her sat without protest and watched her being shamed. The other half perished with her beloved home. But never fear. The woman who has taken her place will gouge a deeper mark into history than that naïve girl ever imagined.*

. . .

In an attempt to get me to return with him, Dhri brought me messages from Dhai Ma, who was failing and wanted to see me before she died. As further incentive, he brought along my sons, who lived at Dwarka and holidayed with their uncle at Kampilya and were, I feared, overly indulged in both places. Sometimes Abhimanyu, Subhadra and Arjun's son, accompanied them, shining with unselfconscious charm and his uncle Krishna's easy laughter. Arjun was delighted by his martial talents and went on for hours about how the boy knew more battle tactics than a grown warrior. I felt a twinge as I watched the warm pride in his eyes. He never looked at our son this way, though he loved him well enough. But I didn't blame him. We all adored Abhimanyu. We knew he was meant for great things.

As for my own children, I found myself awkward and tongue-tied with them. I tried to find words to tell them I loved them, that I was sorry destiny had separated us in this way. But already they were strangers, cool and distant when they weren't sulking because they'd been dragged away from courtly amusements. Perhaps their petulance also stemmed from the fact that I'd chosen my husbands over them. Which child wouldn't resent that?

Perhaps it was a mistake, but I wouldn't leave the forest, not even for a brief visit. I told a disappointed Dhri that my place was with my husbands. That I could not bear to live in luxury while they suffered the hardships of forest life. It wasn't, however, as simple as that.

What was the real reason I rejected my brother's entreaties to return with him to the simpler environment of my childhood? Why did I give up the opportunity to create memories with my children that would give them—and me—solace in the long years that stretched ahead? Why, even as I thought longingly of burying my face in her copious bosom, did I refuse to visit Dhai Ma, who had dedicated her life to caring for me and mine? Was it the fear that my husbands would learn they could live without me, that they would heave a sigh of relief at the quiet peace of my absence? Or was it a different kind of fear: that if I gave myself to softer emotions, I would blunt the edge of my vengeance and fail to achieve the destruction that had become the goal of my life?

. . .

Among all our guests, Yudhisthir most enjoyed the sages. He'd always been attracted to holy men. Sometimes I thought that if he didn't have to be a king, he would have liked to be a monk. He spent hours discussing philosophy with them. Their serenity, I'm sure, was a welcome change from my laments or his brothers' silent fuming. Unlike our friends and relatives, they neither blamed nor pitied him. Unlike strangers, they didn't come to gawk at our altered circumstance. To them, our situation was merely a thread in destiny's great pattern, something to be borne with patience until the colors of the weave changed around us. To divert our minds from our misfortunes, they told us stories of people whose sufferings were far worse.

Yudhisthir loved these tales. They appealed to his didactic nature. For weeks after a sage left us he'd go over them, drawing morals, making sure we hadn't missed the virtues they upheld. I, too, was intrigued by the stories, though I noticed that the things they led me to contemplate were not necessarily ideas of which my husband would have approved.

．　．　．

My favorite was the story of Nal and Damayanti, perhaps because of its parallels to our life—parallels that Yudhisthir didn't seem to see. (Though later I wondered if Yudhisthir understood a lot more than he admitted to. Who knows, perhaps it was a wiser way of living, allowing him to avoid a great deal of unpleasantness.)

This is the story, in the bareness of its bones: Nal the Nishad king loved the beautiful princess Damayanti. At her swayamvar, she chose him over gods. One of the gods, Kali, infuriated by this, tricked Nal into losing his kingdom in a game of dice to his brother Pushkar. (Nal did, however, stop short of wagering his wife.) Nal then begged Damayanti to return to the safety of her father's palace, but she would not leave him. When he lost his last piece of clothing, she tore her own sari and shared it with him. But he left her sleeping in a forest, believing it would be the best for her to be rid of him. They suffered apart for many years. Finally, he—deformed now, and with a false name—became the charioteer of King Rituparna, who was an expert at dice, and learned the subtleties of the game from him. Meanwhile, Damayanti, back in her father's kingdom, sent out searchers for her husband, and suspecting this charioteer to be Nal, invited Rituparna to a swayamvar. But the swayamvar was only a ruse so she could meet Nal. At this meeting, there were accusations and weeping, forgiveness and new declarations of love. Nal regained his handsome looks, challenged Pushkar to another game of dice and regained his kingdom.

The sage telling us the story said, "All through the history of the world, the virtuous have suffered for causes unseen. Learn from Nal and Damayanti to bear your misfortunes bravely. Like theirs, your evil times, too, will come to an end."

Yudhisthir said, "Look how Nal never swerved from righteousness, no matter what happened. And Damayanti never rebuked him for his losses but gave him all the support a man needs when in trouble."

I said, "And how did he repay her? By abandoning her in a forest. How was that righteous?"

Yudhisthir looked pained. The sage diplomatically declared it was time for his prayers. I went to the kitchen. But I couldn't put Damayanti out of my mind. Waking in a forest not unlike this, with only the sounds of night animals for company, how frightened she must have been—and how brave. Because she didn't go back to her parents right away. Instead, she searched for Nal for years. Once she was almost stoned to death as a witch—her, a princess who had been famed the world over for her beauty!

That's what loss can do to you, I thought, touching my own matted hair, wondering if I, too, looked like a witch. I knew, though

Yudhisthir was too polite to ever say so, that I was no ideal wife. He would have been happier with someone like Damayanti. She was a better woman than I. (But is *better* the word I was looking for? At what point does forbearance cease to be a virtue and become a weakness?) Once I returned to my father's home, I wouldn't have kept searching for my husband. And had I called for a second swayamvar, I would have made sure it was a real one.

lotus

It was Bheem's year to be my spouse, and he was determined to make the most of it.

No, not in the obvious bodily way, though he certainly enjoyed sex, the iron-limbed Bheem, and his enthusiasm left ample evidence upon my body. If I pointed out a bruise, he grew shy and penitent. He wanted to redeem himself by doing whatever I desired. That was his weakness: his need to make me happy. None of my other husbands cared in the same way. When I lost my temper, they pragmatically found themselves things to do elsewhere. Only Bheem would remain, hanging his head as I railed on, until I grew ashamed and skidded to a stop.

Bheem liked being around me. Unless I sent him away, he would hover around the kitchen, fetching water, breaking branches into firewood, fanning me with palm fronds, chopping vegetables into meticulously tiny pieces. If I'd allowed it, he would have happily taken over all my chores. He wasn't deft with words like Yudhisthir, who could hold forth on philosophy for hours. He wasn't witty like the twins or declamatory like Arjun. But when we were alone, he told me things he'd never told anyone, acting out with gestures events for which he could not find expressions. His enemies, who knew him only as a whirlwind, single-minded and destructive, would have been astonished to see it.

For instance: When Duryodhan fed him the poisoned rice pudding, the child Bheem fell to the floor paralyzed, but though he could not open his eyes, he was still conscious. He heard Sakuni's hyena-cackle, felt the creepers with which they bound him cutting into his flesh. At night, the river water was like ink. He felt his body arc through the humid air as they threw him in. He fell for days through wetness into the netherworld. The water turned to silk—or was that the snakes curling around him? Even without his eyes, he knew they were rainbow-colored. They bit him, as snakes are wont to do. Their poison canceled Duryodhan's. He sat up on a floor of green silt. Lazily, he took hold of a snake—two, three, twenty—and flung them to destruction. Someone informed the god of snakes. He rushed to kill the monster-child who was wreaking havoc among his subjects. What did he see that made him take the boy upon his lap instead and give him elixir to drink? And why did Bheem, the poisoned one, trust the king-god with his blue, striated face? He drank; the strength of a thousand elephants entered his body; the king released him into the currents that would lift him to the surface of the river so that he could go on to the heroism he was destined for.

"I didn't want to leave," Bheem told me. "When he held me in his arms, it was so much sweeter than my mother's hugs, or my brothers'. In fact, I'd forgotten them already. I clutched the king's hand and cried, Keep me with you. He closed his glowing eyes and shook his head. But before he pushed me upward, he gave me a kiss."

He held out his left hand and I saw what I'd never noticed before, a tiny red mark on the back of the hand, like a flower with two stamens, or a snake's forked tongue.

. . .

These were the times I liked Bheem the best, the quiet afternoons with only the wild doves calling in the tamarind trees, his voice soft and reflective, falling away as he stopped to think of the right word. I didn't mind if at the end of the story he took me by the hand and led me to our conjugal cottage. But even then—I confess it with some shame—I didn't love him, not in the way he longed to be loved. Looking back, I see that I didn't love any of my husbands in that way. I was a good wife. I supported them through good times and bad; I provided them with comforts of the body and the mind; when in company, I extolled their virtues. I followed them into the forest and forced them to become heroes. But my heart—was it too small? too fickle? too hard? Even during the best of our years, I never gave it fully to them.

How do I know it? Because none of them had the power to agitate me the way the mere memory of Karna did.

Did Kunti sense this, with a mother's instinct? Is that why she didn't trust me completely? But surely she knew what the sorceress told me: we cannot force ourselves to love—or to withhold it. At best, we can curb our actions. The heart itself is beyond control. That is its power, and its weakness.

My regret lies more in this: recognizing Bheem's weakness, I took advantage of it. I wept more loudly when he was around, knowing it would make him rail against Yudhisthir, thus increasing Yudhisthir's torment. When we traveled, I complained of the path's hardship and allowed Bheem to carry me, though had I made an effort, I could have managed on my own. I made unreasonable demands for impossible things, pressing to see how far he'd go to please me. (Such was the case of the golden lotus.) Ultimately, at Kurukshetra, he would kill and kill again, going against the laws of righteous war not for victory or glory, but for my sake. Yes, I broke the first rule, the unwritten one, meant not just for warriors but all of us: I took love and used it as a balm to soothe my ego.

. . .

The lotus came to me in Badari, where the Ganga is cold and crystalline. This was the time when Arjun had left us in his search for divine weapons. For months now, we'd heard nothing from him. Worry ate at us, making it impossible to rest in one place. Mingled with our concern about his safety was a more selfish thought: without him the Pandavas would never win a battle against Duryodhan.

I was sitting dejected by the river when I saw it floating on the current. Yes, it was truly golden, just as Vyasa would write later (or had he written it already?). It veered toward me as if impelled by an inner purpose. I'd never seen a flower like that, nor smelled one so intoxicating. I lifted it to my face. I felt my mind slow, my fractious thoughts subside. For a while I did not crave vengeance, nor wonder guiltily if I had sent Arjun to his doom with my weeping, nor remember a pair of forbidden eyes.

Then the smell disappeared. I looked at the flower and saw that it had faded. Its color had paled; its petals drooped; my sorrows returned full force.

I knew that the remedy lay not in finding a new flower but in what Krishna had advised me over and again: Let the past go. Be at ease. Allow the future to arrive at its own pace, unfurling its secrets when it will. I knew I should live the life that teemed around me: this clear air, this newborn sunlight, the simple comfort of the shawl around my shoulders. But because it was easier, and because I wanted the gratification of the look that would leap into his eyes, I went to Bheem instead. In silence I held up the dead flower, and in silence he bowed and set off to bring me what I wanted.

Days later he would return, his arms filled with lotuses. At night, in bed, he would weave them into my matted hair.

He said (or perhaps I imagined the words): "All day and all

night I traveled, following the flower's fragrance as a hunter follows spoor. The forest was black, studded with the jewel-eyes of stalking beasts. I blew on my conch; the four corners of the earth vibrated; the eyes disappeared. I smiled. This is the way, I thought, that I will rout my enemies on the battlefield. In a grove I came across an old monkey, his tail blocking the trail. I ordered him to clear my path, told him I was Bheem of the Pandavas, son of the wind god. He blinked in confusion and did not seem to know me. Perhaps he was senile. He requested me to push his tail off the path and continue on my quest. I bent down to flick it aside with a finger—and could not! Nor with both hands, nor with the strength of my whole body. I fell to the ground, crying, Who are you? He smiled and informed me that he was Hanuman.

"I stared at him. He had crossed the ocean in a single leap to do Rama's work! I had heard the story as a child and thought it legend. But here he stood, elder son of the wind god—and thus my brother. A god in his own right. He embraced me and said, I give you my strength. At Kurukshetra I will be with you, though none will see me except as an image on a chariot flag. He pointed me toward the lake of flowers and disappeared. At the lake I battled a thousand demon guards, killing not a few, to get you what you wanted." He lowered his face onto my breasts. "Are you happy now?"

"How did it feel," I asked him later, when we lay satiated, "to touch a god?"

He didn't answer. Perhaps he was asleep. Or perhaps there is no answer to such a question. For later when I'd ask Arjun the same thing, he, too, would be silent.

visitations

The years passed like molasses, suffocating and formless. We all labored under their sluggishness, but no one suffered more than Arjun. Yudhisthir had his morality to keep himself occupied, Nakul and Sahadev their fascination with the beasts of the forest to divert them, and Bheem his love for me that held him fast in its coils like the mythic ajagar. But quicksilver Arjun, who wanted fame more than anything in the world, who saw himself less as husband or brother or son than as hero, chafed under the restrictions Yudhisthir's promise had placed on him. He longed to battle the Kauravas and win back his honor, but he knew he couldn't, not until our years of banishment were done. Because he couldn't avenge me, he avoided me: my tangled hair, my accusing sighs, my pepper-hot tongue.

From the beginning our relationship had been troubled, with him blaming me for what his mother had ordered—my marriage to his brothers. But in the Palace of Illusions, for a blessed, magical time, we'd been at peace, both of us busy with things we loved. He'd been the commander of the city, in charge of its security. He'd traveled to the edges of the kingdom to make sure things were safe. In between, he had tournaments to perform in and his other wives to visit. Now once again, submerged as we were in the sameness of our days, the tensions surfaced. I should have read the signs, should have softened my ways. But I was caught in the coils of my own serpent, and no less blind than Dhritarashtra. Arjun began to spend longer hours in the forest by himself. He said it was for hunting, but more and more he would return empty-handed, with a distracted frown. And one morning he left us.

He had a reason, of course: the impending war, for which he needed to improve his battle skills and learn new techniques. And how could he do that, hemmed in by our rustic, rusting existence? Time gnaws on me, he told Yudhisthir. I fear I will disintegrate before the war even begins. He decided to go to the mountains of Himavan and try, through penance, to please Shiva. He would ask him for Pasupat, the divine astra that would make him invincible.

"Once I have the Pasupat," he said, "Karna is a dead man!"

When I heard that, the blood fled from my face. My knees buckled and I fell to the ground. I, who hadn't weakened so even at the moment of my great insult in Duryodhan's court. My husbands bustled around me. Yudhisthir lifted my head onto his lap. Bheem splashed water on my face. The twins fanned me. A flattered Arjun took my hands in his, even though it was not his year as my husband, in a rare gesture of affection.

"Don't worry," he said. "I go so that, when the time comes, I can restore your honor." (His words, if not totally honest about his motives, were true enough.) "Wish me godspeed."

Why did I hesitate?

My husbands thought I was too overcome with fear for Arjun to speak. They considered it sweet and womanly and assured me he would be in no danger. He was, after all, the world's greatest warrior. And his father Indra would surely be keeping an eye out for him.

Why was my heart so weak, so unreasonable? After all that had transpired, why should I care what happened to a man with ancient eyes? Wasn't he my enemy, the deadly rival of this man who was willing to risk his life to avenge me? My folly angered me, but I couldn't shake it off. To stop the voices, both inner and outer, I said, "May you be successful. May you return safely with your heart's desire."

But my voice faltered. Perhaps that is why Arjun would have so much trouble on his journey.

. . .

On Indrakila mountain, where the air is like crystal, Arjun meditated and prayed to Shiva. But Shiva did not answer. Instead, a wild boar charged at him from a copse. Arjun lifted the Gandiva bow, but as he shot, a different arrow flew through the air and struck the boar dead. Enraged by this encroachment, Arjun turned to find a man dressed in skins. He didn't seem intimidated by Arjun's threats. When Arjun in his anger shot at him, all his arrows—even his divine astras—fell useless at the hunter's feet, whereas each arrow of the hunter found its target.

"There I was, bleeding, while the hunter mocked me," Arjun would tell us later, his voice conveying his astonished outrage. "I, who hadn't been touched by an arrow since I completed my studies with Drona! I prayed to Shiva for help, but nothing happened. My heart sank."

Dispirited, he made a garland from wildflowers and offered it to an earthen image of the god in a final attempt to please him. But when he opened his eyes, the garland was gone. "I was sure the god had abandoned me," he said. "Then I saw the garland—it was around the neck of the hunter, who glowed with a golden light!"

Understanding Shiva's play, he fell at his feet. The god embraced him and gave him the dreaded Pasupat, asking only that he use it in righteous war.

But would the war still be righteous when Arjun shot the astra at Karna? Or had it swerved darkly a long time before? The blood of Abhimanyu had soaked the earth of Kurukshetra by then, Bheeshma had been made to give away the secret of his death, and Drona had been overcome not by my brother's valor but by a lie.

Enveloped in triumph, giddy with the god's presence, Arjun did not suspect any of this. "Yes!" he cried, raising his chin in that way he had, full of self-belief. Did Chitragupta, keeper of the divine books, record his promise, smiling his secret, crooked smile at the vanity of humans? Is that why Arjun, too, would fall on the mountain when we went on our final journey?

. . .

There was more to Arjun's story: How Indra and the other gods appeared, promising him more astras, to be given when the war began. How they took him up to Indra's palace where he sat by the king-god on the same throne, enjoying celestial music and dance. (I wondered if his forefathers were there, but I knew better than to ask.) How the celestial dancer Urvasi fell in love with him and asked him to satisfy her desire. He refused. (He made sure to catch my eye while narrating this part.) She cursed him. As a result he would have to spend a year of his life as a eunuch. Fortunately his father interceded. He couldn't nullify the curse, but at least Arjun could choose the year when it would happen.

There were things Arjun kept to himself. (Isn't it thus with all stories, even this one I'm telling?) But when you share a man's pillow, his dreams seep into you. And so I knew.

The very first night he was there, Urvasi came to him dressed only in a mantle of clouds. She entered his bedroom and took him by the hand.

"I burn for you," she said. "Put an end to my suffering."

Arjun turned from her, covering his ears. "You are the beloved of Pururava, my ancestor," he said, "and thus like a mother to me."

Urvasi smiled at the folly of his words. "The rules that bind earthly women do not bind us," she said. "While Pururava lived, I was faithful to him. But he has been dust for many ages, and I am free to choose the man I want. Come, let us not waste time!"

Her face shone like the moon; her breasts were pearly with the sweat of passion; the sight of her navel alone would have made kings forsake their kingdoms. What gave Arjun the power to resist her? Earlier I'd thought that it was for my sake. O vanity! Now in my dream I knew the truth. Arjun was determined to show the gods that he was stronger than their strongest enchantment, a worthy recipient of the astras they'd promised him. Against the sharp metallic seduction of instruments of death, what chance did Urvasi have?

. . .

When Krishna learned that his favorite friend would become a eunuch for a year, he laughed—the more so when Arjun glowered. "Don't you see?" he said. "It's the perfect concealment for your thirteenth year. Who'd ever suspect the manly Arjun in a skirt and veil, his mighty arms atinkle with bracelets? You should send a message of special thanks to Urvasi! Narad's always going up there— maybe he could act as your emissary—"

"No, thank you," said my husband, his manly eyebrows drawing together.

Krishna turned to me. "Even a curse can be a blessing, Krishnaa. Don't you agree?"

I nodded, but warily. He was always trying to convince me that bad luck—particularly ours—was really something else, something better in disguise. Caught between him and Yudhisthir, a woman couldn't even enjoy being miserable.

. . .

That year, our last in the forest, was filled with divine visitations. Yudhisthir had his own encounter one blazing afternoon beside a lake with a yaksha, an invisible being of power who had already overpowered his brothers. It threatened him with death unless he could provide him with the correct responses to a hundred questions. Philosophical questions, however, were Yudhisthir's forte; he forgot the danger that faced him and dived into this game of wits—and won. As a reward the yaksha brought his brothers back to life and offered him a boon. I wasn't surprised when Yudhisthir told me what he'd asked for. Victory—not in the upcoming battle but against the six inner enemies that plague us all: lust, anger, greed, ignorance, arrogance, and envy.

But his real reward was that for weeks afterward he got to ask us the yaksha's questions (and to provide us, triumphantly, with the answers when we failed). Though I professed annoyance at this catechism, I secretly enjoyed it.

What is more numerous than the grass?
The thoughts that rise in the mind of man.
Who is truly wealthy?
That man to whom the agreeable and disagreeable, wealth and woe, past and future, are the same.
What is the most wondrous thing on earth?
Each day countless humans enter the Temple of Death, yet the ones left behind continue to live as though they were immortal.

. . .

In bed with Arjun, I searched for that part of his mind where he'd stored his memory of Shiva, but when I finally found it, there was only an ocean of light in which I longed to dissolve but could not. I think I was most envious of him then. He had been in the presence of a great and blissful mystery. He had glimpsed the truth of existence that extended beyond this oscillating world of pleasure and sorrow. I lay awake all night, my soul hungering to know what he had known.

Once I complained to Krishna, "Why don't the gods appear to me? Is it because I'm a woman?"

"You have the drollest notions!" Krishna laughed. "Why do you think that should matter to the gods, who are beyond gender?"

I wanted to ask, if that were true, why our scriptures were filled with tales concerning the marriages of gods and goddesses. But I had a more urgent question. "Having embraced God, how could Arjun still care about gaining astras, no matter how powerful they were? If I'd been in his place, I wouldn't have wanted anything else."

Krishna put his arm around my shoulders in that good-natured way he had. "Wouldn't you, sakhi?" (That was what he'd taken to calling me of late: sakhi, dearest companion. I liked the appellation, though sometimes I suspected he used it facetiously.) "Then you're a lot wiser than most of us!" For a time, a smile flitted over his lips as though he were privy to a joke no one else knew.

disguise

Our twelve years in the forest were end-
ing. Now, according to the wager Yudhisthir had lost, we would have to spend
a year in hiding. If during this year Duryodhan discovered our
whereabouts, we would have to endure another twelve years in exile.

Yudhisthir decided we would spend the year in the kingdom of
Matsya, just south of Indra Prastha. "No one will think of searching
for us this close," he said. "We'll disguise ourselves and take up jobs
in King Virat's palace. I've heard his household is large and loosely
managed. As long as we don't draw attention to ourselves, we should
be safe. But no one must suspect that we know each other. If we come
across each other, we must act as though we're strangers. On no ac-
count must we contact each other. Remember, if we're detected,
we'll be forced to endure another twelve years of exile."

As agreed, I came into the city of Virat alone in the evening,
when the sky was a bruised blue. I stepped hastily, uneasily, along
the busy thoroughfare that led to the palace. Never in my life had I
ventured on a public street without an escort. With difficulty I ma-
neuvered my way around raucous peddlers pushing carts and horsemen who spurred their mounts along, uncaring of pedestrians. Men
stared at me—and who could blame them? All decent women were
safe in their homes by this time. Besides, in my sari made of flattened

bark, my crow's nest of hair that hadn't seen a comb in years, I must have looked like a madwoman. I tried to ignore their comments, tried to hide my distress. Somewhere in the shadows, dressed in the rough homespun a cook might wear, Bheem was watching to make sure I reached Queen Sudeshna's palace safely. I didn't want him to forget Yudhisthir's injunctions and come forward to help me.

To keep my mind off my own misery, I thought of my husbands. Once I was inside the gates, Bheem would make his way to the royal kitchens and ask for a job. He would prepare delicacies for men who weren't even worthy of washing the dishes from which he ate! Yudhisthir was already settled in the palace. A few days ago he'd dressed himself in a brahmin's white dhoti, fastened tulsi beads around his neck, and entered the old king's court. He said that he excelled in philosophic conversation and in the game of dice and needed a home. Virat, who loved to gamble, took him on. Now Yudhisthir, upholder of truth, would have to learn to flatter courtiers. Nakul and Sahadev were working in the king's barns. Over the years Virat had lovingly collected the finest of cows from all over Bharat. They would care for these. Taking leave of me, they'd tried to cheer me, reminding me how much they loved animals. But I knew the truth: they would be toiling in the hot sun, cleaning dung from sheds, enduring the jibes of overseers.

And Arjun, our warrior? In the inky depths of last night he'd spoken the words that would activate Urvasi's curse. By morning his hair cascaded down his back. Without mustache or beard his face looked naked. His form was lithe and slender, draped in red silk. When he walked, his hips swayed; his smile was shy yet confident. How had his body learned these feminine subtleties? There were coral bracelets on his arms. When he asked me to braid his hair, I couldn't stop my tears. He was going to be Princess Uttara's dance tutor. He, too, would live in the women's quarters. I would have to curb my emotions at the sight of his lost manhood, at the jibes to which, as a eunuch, he was bound to be subjected.

"How will I spend an entire year without even one of you to confide my troubles?" I said.

Arjun dried my eyes with the edge of his sari. Perhaps the change had been more than physical, for he spoke with a new gentleness. "You'll do it. You're stronger than you think. Remember what Krishna said when he came to bid us goodbye: *Time is even and merciful. No matter how long this year might seem, it will in truth be no longer than a year of joy in Indra Prastha.*" He'd concealed his beloved Gandiva in a sami tree outside the city, wrapping it in cowhide to keep it safe from a year's weathering. I thought of Krishna, who had driven us in his chariot to the edge of the sleeping city. Leaving us, he'd waved as nonchalantly as though we'd see each other in a week. I held fast to the two images: the wrapped weapon and Krishna's smile, cutting through the dark. As I knocked with a shaky fist on the queen's gate, readying myself to beg for a servant's job, somehow they consoled me. I would be patient. I would be brave. Even this year would pass.

· · ·

Sudeshna said: "I'm sorry to hear of all the troubles you've had, but I can't hire you. Even though you've been Queen Draupadi's attendant all these years, doing her clothes and hair. You must be good—everyone knows how bad-tempered this woman was! Is it really true that she used to throw things at her husbands when she got angry?

"You're too beautiful, that's why. Even with your torn clothes and dirty hair. Imagine what'll happen once you clean up! What if my husband falls in love with you? Or my son? Or my brother? Although I'm not too worried about my brother. He can take care of himself. You've heard of him? The greatest fighter in Matsya—maybe in all of Bharat, and the general of Virat's army? He's always falling in and out of love with my maids. He makes sure to give them enough gifts to keep them quiet, though, when he tires of them. He's a generous man, my Keechak.

"You say you're going to remain veiled at all times? And stay in the inner apartments? Never come out when any man is around? You've taken a vow not to beautify yourself until Queen Draupadi gains revenge for the way she was insulted?

"That's loyal of you, though a bit excessive.

"What's that about your husbands? They're gandharvas, half-men, half-gods? You say they're watching you at all times, even though you've been cursed and must be separated from each other? They're powerful and extremely hot-tempered? Well, that should give you plenty of incentive to remain chaste!

"I guess it's safe enough to employ you.

"That's always been my problem—I'm too kindhearted. Just can't say no.

"So can you do my hair the way Draupadi wore it for the Rajasuya yagna? Let's see—Virat's going to have a big gathering this coming full moon—some kind of poetry festival, he likes those things. How about then? And can you get rid of these spots on my face?

"Good, good! I've a feeling we're going to get along well.

"What's your name, by the way? You want me to just call you *maid*? Oh, very well, if that's what you prefer.

"Now tell me something I've been dying to know: How did Draupadi manage to control five husbands? I can barely handle Virat, and he's old! What kind of sleeping arrangements did they have? Oh yes: one more thing. Those gandharva husbands of yours—how is it, being married to them? I mean, do they have the same kind of equipment as men do?"

. . .

At times I felt the year would never end, that time had spite-fully dug in its heels. It was humiliating to be at the beck and call of a woman as feckless as Sudeshna. *Fetch my mirror, sairindhri. Make some more sandalwood paste—the red kind—and grind it smoother this time. I don't like this hairstyle. Do it over!* Even amidst the worst hardships of the forest, I'd had my dignity. Our guests had shown me respect. The people I loved had stayed in touch, even if I didn't see them often. And Krishna. Was there ever a time when he hadn't visited me for an entire year? My chest ached with a strange thirst when I thought of that. I wondered if one could die of loneliness.

I must be fair to Sudeshna: in her scatterbrained way, she was kind. She told me I could sit in her private garden whenever I wanted. *I know you're sad. It'll give you a little peace.* But perhaps it would have been better if she had been truly callous. For it was in her garden that the amorous Keechak would see me.

Sudeshna's garden was what I had expected: large, unimagina-tive, overfull of ostentatious, expensive blooms. Still, I couldn't stay away from it even though it only made me long for my own intri-cately arranged garden, where around every corner there had been a surprise: a single seat half hidden under a mountain ebony tree, a row of usir releasing their pungent odor—but only if one knew to rub their leaves. Lost now, all lost: the grove of banyans, fully grown, thanks to Maya's magic; the ketaki flowers, palest gold; the simsupa trees that whispered my name. At one end of Sudeshna's garden, I found an asoka—the same tree under which, in the Ra-mayana, Sita had borne her sorrows. When I had a moment, I sat un-der it, trying to draw upon her fortitude. She'd lifted her mind from the demonesses taunting her and sent it to her beloved Ram and found peace. But I didn't know how to do that. When I wasn't distracted by my tasks, anger filled my mind like dense smoke: anger for the Kauravas, whom I blamed for my present condition; anger for Yudhisthir, whose foolish nobility had made him their prey; anger for my other husbands, who obeyed him blindly; and anger for Karna, with whom I had no right to be angry.

This was where I met Keechak. He'd come to the garden for a tryst with one of Sudeshna's maids, but when he saw me, he waved her off.

"You're new, aren't you?" he said. He was handsome in a fleshy way, with sensuous lips. He wore many ornaments and reeked of musk and wine. "Are you one of my sister's new attendants? You're pretty!" His kohl-lined eyes roved up and down my body approvingly. My face grew hot. Not even Duryodhan had dared to look at me quite like this in his sabha, for he'd known I was a queen. Is this how men looked at ordinary women, then? Women they considered their inferiors? A new sympathy for my maids rose in my mind. When I became queen again, I thought, I would make sure common women were treated differently.

But that was a long time off. Right now, I had to deal with Keechak.

I rose coldly and walked away.

Perhaps that was my error. If I had been obsequious instead of disdainful, if I had pretended to be shy and overwhelmed by his attention, like the other women he approached, he might have lost interest in me. Sudeshna had many maids who were younger and prettier. Forest living had taken its toll on my body, and I made no efforts to rectify its ravages. But by indicating that I wasn't his to possess, I raised Keechak's hunter's instincts. From this moment, he would not leave me alone.

I wasn't aware right away of the problems I'd spawned. Other challenges preoccupied me. I was finding that having my husbands physically close to me was harder to bear than if we'd been truly separated. Catching a glimpse of Yudhisthir as he walked with King Virat, I'd cringe as he bowed deferentially. I'd hear Arjun joking with the women in the dance hall and wonder how he had the heart to laugh. Sometimes I'd look out toward the barns, wondering which of the tiny figures in yellow loincloths toiling in the muck were Nakul and Sahadev, who loved fine living. When special dishes were sent up from the kitchen for the queen and her favorite attendants, I wondered which ones Bheem had prepared, and if he knew that I wouldn't be eating any of them.

At night I'd lie on my pallet, running my fingers over the new calluses on my palms. In the dark my hands felt like someone else's. Krishna had said, When sorrow strikes you, Krishnaa—and it will strike you harder than your husbands because your ego is more frail and more stubborn—try to keep this in mind: being a queen's maid is only a role you are playing, only for a while. I repeated the words to myself, but tiredness played strange tricks on my mind. Sometimes, just before I fell into the blankness of sleep, it seemed that everything I'd lived until now had been a role. The princess who longed for acceptance, the guilty girl whose heart wouldn't listen, the wife who balanced her fivefold role precariously, the rebellious daughter-in-law, the queen who ruled in the most magical of palaces, the distracted mother, the beloved companion of Krishna, who refused to learn the lessons he offered, the woman obsessed with vengeance—none of them were the true Panchaali.

If not, who was I?

. . .

A month before our year of disguise ended, Keechak cornered me and threatened to take me by force if I would not come to him of my own will and satisfy his desire. I fled from his grasping arms to Sudeshna, but she counseled me to give in to her brother. "Who knows if you'll ever see those husbands of yours again," she said. "Or if they even exist? Make Keechak happy, and he'll make sure you have enough to live comfortably the rest of your life."

I ran then to the only refuge I could think of: Virat's sabha. Surely the king would save a helpless, abused woman. Keechak followed me there. He pushed me to the floor in full view of the court and kicked me for having spurned him. I cried out to Virat for justice, but he sat as though deaf. Only his head, bent helplessly, betrayed his shame. He knew that without Keechak's support he could not run his kingdom. When the king himself behaved in this manner, what could I expect of his courtiers? But what hurt me worst was Yudhisthir's demeanor; he gazed at me, silent and calm as though I were enacting a play.

I stared at them all in disgust. It seemed to me that time had looped back on itself, that I was back in Hastinapur, helpless once again in front of the jeering Duryodhan. When I turned my angry eyes on Yudhisthir, he said, "Be patient, lady. Your gandharva husbands will be freed of their curse soon. They'll help you then."

I tried to articulate my outrage at his words, but he stopped me sternly. Perhaps he feared exposure. "Return to the women's quarters and stop weeping like an actress!"

His words pierced me like poisoned darts. I wiped my eyes, done with entreaties. "If I'm an actress today," I spat, "who is responsible for that?"

Keechak ignored our exchange. "See!" he sneered. "There's no one to protect you here. I'm more powerful than all of them. You might as well come to my bed."

Even then Yudhisthir remained silent.

I ran again—this time to my room—and bolted the door.

Keechak laughed and let me go. He knew that no flimsy lock could keep him out. Soon enough, he'd have his will.

I bathed in the coldest water I could find, but still I burned. I couldn't eat; I couldn't sleep. After midnight, when the palace grew quiet, I searched its labyrinthine corridors until I found Bheem's sleeping quarters. I opened the door, slipped in, and awakened him. Shocked, he pleaded with me to leave. "What if someone discovers us together? What answer can we offer without giving ourselves away? And then all these months of suffering we've gone through will be wasted."

I told him I no longer cared if people found out who I was, if Duryodhan won the wager. The dangers of the forest we might have to return to were far less than the ones I faced right here in this palace. I told him of my humiliation in the court and of Yudhisthir's callous cowardice. I said, "If Keechak touches me again, I'll swallow poison."

Bheem pulled my cracked palms to his face. I could feel his tears on my calluses. He said, "Without you by my side, what use is a kingdom? I promise you that tomorrow I'll kill Keechak, even though I'm discovered."

But now that I was sure I would get my way, I grew still as ice. Together we created the plan that would destroy Keechak without betraying my husbands.

. . .

And then?

Then time rushed headlong, gathering devastation like an avalanche. In the dark of the dance hall where I lured him the next night, Keechak was pounded to death. When they found his smashed body the next morning, word spread like fire. It was gandharva magic! What else could destroy one of the foremost warriors of Bharat? A weeping Sudeshna would have had me burned as a witch, but she was too afraid of my spirit-husbands. Instead, she banished me to my quarters, which suited me very well.

But far away, the story reached the Kaurava court. At once Duryodhan suspected that Keechak was killed by Bheem. (Having been captured once by gandharvas, he knew they operated differently.) Karna suggested that they attack Virat's kingdom, at once from both north and south. He knew that if the Pandavas were there, they'd be honor-bound to help their host. If not, the Kauravas would gain a rich kingdom with little effort.

Of the battles that took place, the bards (who love to dwell on battles) have sung enough, so I'll leave them alone. Enough to say that four of the Pandavas (still disguised) accompanied Virat and routed the Kaurava army in the south, while Arjun drove Virat's son's chariot to the north. When the young prince Uttar panicked, Arjun (still in his sari) rendered the Kauravas unconscious with the Sammohan astra. The furious Duryodhan, when he recovered, declared that the Pandavas had been discovered and must return to the forest. But Yudhisthir sent back star charts to prove that our thirteen years of exile had ended on the very day of the battle. And so preparations for an even greater battle began.

But here's what I remember most clearly: When King Virat realized who we were, he fell at our feet, begging our pardon for his many discourtesies, and ordered Sudeshna to do the same. He placed us on his throne and knelt on the dais with folded palms. A sullen Sudeshna knelt beside him. She wouldn't meet my eyes. She would never forgive me for being the cause of her brother's death. But Virat, who was more pragmatic, offered Princess Uttara in marriage to Arjun. For once, my much-wedded husband (aided by a dig from my elbow in his ribs) made the right decision: he asked that the princess become, instead, his son Abhimanyu's wife.

At the wedding, we sat again on Virat's throne. I was dressed in cloth of gold and my unruly locks flowed over my back, beautiful as lava—and as dangerous. Men whispered that with my dark skin I was like a lightning cloud. I took it as a compliment. Around us sat friends and relatives who had gathered to celebrate the end of our exile, and (though no one spoke of it yet) to offer their support in the coming war. Dhri was present, and my father, and my five sons. My heart tightened as I searched their faces, trying to match names to features. But they smiled at me shyly and without resentment. Perhaps—now that they were grown—they understood our troubles better and forgave me my difficult choices.

And there in the wedding mandap was Abhimanyu, so handsome and noble, already taken—we could tell by his bemused expression—with pretty, pert Uttara. They made a good match, I thought. Soon we'd find equally good ones for my sons. The priests rang bells and chanted mantras. Sudeshna offered me chilled pomegranate juice in a gold goblet, much as I'd done for her. And Krishna? Earlier today, meeting him after so long, I'd wept, and he'd dried my tears—and then his. Now he sat behind me, so close that I could feel his breath on my neck. From time to time, as we listened to the priests' drone, he whispered an irreverent comment, forcing me into laughter.

Why did this moment mean so much to me? Was it because my ego was vindicated? Because I received, in sight of all, the respect that had been denied me these many months? Because I knew that my humiliation at the hands of the Kauravas was about to be avenged? I confess I've always found such things sweet. But there was something more: it was the last scintillation in the darkness descending around us, the last time I would be so completely happy.

preparation

We were not surprised when Duryodhan refused to honor the terms of the wager and return Indra Prastha to us. Nor— except for Yudhisthir, who had hoped for a peaceful solution— were we particularly disappointed. To tell the truth, the rest of us itched for war, for a chance to pay Duryodhan back for some of the suffering he'd put us through. That very night, Dhri dispatched messengers to our potential allies, asking for help. Our situation was grim. Hastinapur had numerous supporters already, kings whose fathers and grandfathers had befriended Shantanu, then Bheeshma, then Dhritarashtra. Could we expect them to switch generations of allegiance so easily? Many believed Duryodhan had done nothing wrong. Yudhisthir had gambled foolishly—and lost all he possessed. Now he wanted it back. Which kshatriya worth his name would acquiesce to such an unreasonable demand?

In spite of these problems, our hearts were strangely light, our blood-beat illogically elated. Finally (was it only I who thought this way?) things would be resolved. Either we'd be avenged—or it would no longer matter because we'd be dead.

Messengers were sent to every kingdom except Dwarka. We decided that Arjun should go to Krishna himself and ask his dearest friend to join us. We felt—we didn't know why, for Krishna hadn't won any major battles—that with him on our side, we couldn't fail. (It wouldn't hurt to have his notorious guerrilla troops, the Narayani Sena, fighting for us, either.)

But Hastinapur employed many spies, and so, even before Arjun set off, Duryodhan mounted his fastest steed and spurred it toward Dwarka. He knew that if he arrived there first, the laws of hospitality would require Krishna to grant his request before he considered Arjun's.

. . .

Here is what Duryodhan told Sakuni upon his return (yes, we, too, had spies in Hastinapur):

"Well, uncle, that was an excellent idea of yours, to ride through the night, driving the horses hard, changing them whenever they flagged. I reached Dwarka at noon, quite a while before Arjun got there. Krishna was taking a nap, but they showed me into his room. There was just one armchair at the head of the couch where Krishna was sleeping. I made myself comfortable in it. Soon after, Arjun walked in. You should have seen his face when he saw me! There weren't any other seats. He should have taken the hint and left. But he squeezed himself into a little space at the foot of the couch, and as soon as Krishna stirred, he bowed down, the sycophant, and did pranam. Krishna—who as you know has been most unjustly partial to the Pandavas all along—asked him what he wanted. Well, I wasn't having any of that! I cleared my throat conspicuously and, when Krishna turned, pointed out that I'd taken the trouble of getting there before Arjun, so I should get what I wanted before him. Slippery as he is, he said, But I saw Arjun first—that equals out your claims, and besides, he's younger, so you should allow him first choice. I was fuming, but I remembered what you said and held my tongue. I even managed a smile.

"Anyhow, things didn't turn out as badly as I feared. Because what does Krishna do next but announce that he isn't going to actually fight in the war. Some kind of vow he'd taken, I don't remember the details. He won't even carry weapons. Then he makes us this offer: we can either choose him, or we can choose his Narayanis (that, as you know, was the main reason I'd gone there). I was certain that Arjun would choose the soldiers, but the fool got all sentimental, saying how he wanted nothing but his dear friend's guidance and blessings, and that no army could equal that. I had to use all my powers to keep from snorting with laughter. Anyhow, the upshot is that I got myself the Narayanis—they'll be on their way to Hastinapur in a day or so—and Arjun got himself a charioteer—because that's what Krishna's going to do during the war, drive his horses, though why he agreed to it I don't know. He is a king after all, even if his lands aren't much compared to ours. Impractical fools, both of them. They deserve each other!

"Balaram? Oh yes, I went to see him right afterward. He's been a good friend ever since I took those mace-fighting lessons from him and then sent him a cartload of my best sura as thanks. Yes, it was a shrewd move. He loves his drink, does Balaram! But I did it mostly because it's a pleasure to give something fine to a connoisseur. He's always claimed I have better technique than Bheem—which of course I do. That man wields his mace like it was a giant cucumber. I thought it would be easy to persuade Balaram to join our forces, but he said he couldn't go against his brother. However, because of his love for me, he'd stay out of the battle altogether. Then he said something strange. He said, Where Krishna is, victory lies there. And he looked at me with such sadness in his eyes—as though I were already dead! I tell you, it gave me quite a turn. Made me wonder for a moment whether I'd made the wrong choice.

"I'm sure you're right: he thinks too highly of his brother's prowess. Can't blame him—they've been inseparable all through their lives, like Dussasan and myself. In any case, we've made our choice, and I never was one for regretting my decisions.

"I agree! Of course we're going to win! What was it at last count, the size of our army? Eleven akshauhini? I doubt that the Pandavas will be able to muster half that many soldiers, to say nothing of horses, chariots, elephants, and astras. The most seasoned warriors are on our side—Bheeshma, Drona, and especially Karna, a friend like no other! Did you know he's taken a vow of abstinence? He isn't going to touch meat, wine, or women until the battle is done. He's taken to bathing in the Ganga each day for purification, and if a beggar or a brahmin comes up to him at that time, he'll give them whatever they want! He believes that such acts of charity will push his powers to their peak so that he can destroy Arjun. With a fighter like him on our side, how can we lose?

"But just in case we don't win, I plan on dying with full glory on the battlefield. That would be far better than sharing my kingdom with those cursed Pandavas. For whatever my shortcomings—no, no, uncle, you flatter me by calling me faultless; I know myself better than that—I thank the god of war and death that cowardice isn't one of them."

. . .

Even bedchambers are not safe from efficient spies, and our spies were efficient indeed. Thus we knew that folks in Hastinapur were not sleeping well. The blind king started from his slumber with nightmares of mountains built of his sons' skulls. Dussasan awoke clutching his chest and screaming Bheem's name. Duryodhan drank himself into a stupor to keep from wearing out his floors with pacing. I cannot say I felt pity for any of them.

Only Karna, our informants reported, slept soundly and awoke clear-eyed to perform his daily ablutions by the river, where each day more people gathered to ask him for alms. Rumor had it that he'd given away half his wealth already. If this continued, he'd be a pauper by the time the fighting began. My husbands exclaimed at this folly, and Arjun said, scoffingly, "He always was a show-off!"

But I knew Karna wasn't showing off—he had never cared to do so. Instead, by giving to the poor, he was atoning for his misdeeds and securing a place in heaven. No matter what he said to bolster Duryodhan's confidence, I could see that he didn't expect to live past the war. Nor—my heart constricted when I realized this—did he seem to want to do so.

People love to believe that virtue is rapidly rewarded, and that agitation is the fruit of unrighteousness. But things are not so simple. For instance: Bheeshma (whom the Kauravas had chosen as their commander-in-chief) was found sitting on the white stones by the Ganga at dawn, his shawl wet with night dew. Dhri (who was to lead the Pandava army) dueled with the captain of the guard each day until he was bruised and exhausted—and still he could not sleep. Kunti had borne our years of exile stoically in Vidur's home, but now she fell ill and could eat nothing. When Yudhisthir asked her to join us in Virat's palace, she made implausible excuses. Even the blessing she sent as my husbands prepared for war was ambiguously worded. She prayed for their victory and wished that they wouldn't have to spill the blood of their brothers. ("Brothers!" Bheem cried when he heard her message. "Since when have those Kaurava vermin been our brothers?" while Sahadev wondered if Duryodhan hadn't used Gandhari to brainwash their mother.) Half-moons of dark bloomed under my husbands' eyes. Arjun (who currently shared my bed) flailed out in his dreams, speaking harshly in a language I didn't recognize, calling Abhimanyu's name. Walking out into the corridor one night, I found Yudhisthir at a window, staring at the moon-bleached grass. He, too, had dreamed of a skull mountain. But there was more to his dream: on top of the mountain was a great, glittery throne, and on it were seated the five Pandavas, goblets of victory wine in their hands. When they raised them to their lips, the drink turned to blood.

For my part, I dreamed of beasts. Riderless horses screamed their terror through my nights, the whites of their eyes gleaming in firelight. Elephants fell to their knees, trumpeting bloodily. Jackals slunk through smoke, torn human limbs gripped in their teeth. And always, a great gray owl flew through the heavy air, its wings obliterating the sky, terrifying me for no reason that I could name.

I should have tried to understand what the dreams foretold. I should have discussed them with my husbands and cautioned them accordingly. I should have urged them to step carefully on this road that would soon be strewn with death. But I didn't want to heed anything that might keep me from the revenge I'd waited for so long. When my husbands hesitantly mentioned their nightmares, I laughed.

"I didn't expect such superstition from the foremost heroes of Bharat!" I taunted them. "Of course there will be blood. Of course there will be death. As kshatriyas, isn't that what you've trained for all your lives? And are you afraid now?"

What could they do in response except commit themselves more deeply to the preparations of war?

. . .

Not to be outdone by humans, the gods were busy with their own preparations. Perhaps they were impressed by Karna's vows. Perhaps his determination worried them. In any case, they chose him for their machinations. The result became the stuff of song long before the armies assembled in Kurukshetra. Sitting in Sudeshna's balcony, winding my matted hair around my fingers, I heard it with a conflicted heart.

This is how the song went: The sun god, Karna's chosen deity, appeared in Karna's dream. "Tomorrow," Surya warned, "the king of the gods will come to you at noon, disguised as a brahmin, to beg for your gold armor and earrings. But you must not relinquish them. They alone protect you from the twin curses that follow you like beasts tracking their prey. Without them you cannot hope to defeat Arjun, or to survive the war. That is why Indra wants them."

If Karna was disturbed by this news, he did not show it. "O great one," he said, "tell me first, how did I get these amulets?"

Did the god hesitate? He said, "Your father gave them to you."

"Tell me then," Karna asked, "who is my father?" In a subdued voice, he added, "And my mother."

"Forgive me," the sun god said. "I am not allowed to speak their names. You will know them soon enough, though the knowledge may not bring you joy." At the look on Karna's face, he added, "Do not fear. You are nobly born. Your mother is a queen and your father a god. But listen carefully: tomorrow, before Indra speaks, forestall him by saying that you will give him anything but your armor. In this way, you will not break your promise."

Karna stood silent, weighing vengeance against his good name. Finally he said, "I'm triply blessed that you, Lord of my heart, have chosen to warn me. But by following your advice, I'd still break the spirit of my vow. People would say that when Karna was threatened with loss of life, he couldn't keep his word. And this I can't tolerate."

When Surya realized that Karna would not change his mind, he spoke with regret and admiration. "Do this at least: tell Indra that you know his plan. In chagrin, he will offer you a boon. Ask for his Shakti, the weapon that even his son Arjun cannot withstand. Then you might still have a chance of achieving your heart's desire."

Karna said nothing. Perhaps he wondered if Surya truly knew what his heart's desire was. So many yearnings clashed against each other inside him, he himself was no longer sure.

The next day, all went as Surya had prophesied except this: when Karna had cut the amulets from his body, Indra said, "Karna! Even I could not have done what you did. I give you my Shakti—and one other boon. As long as the land of Bharat floats on the ocean, you will be known as the greatest of givers. In this your fame will surpass Arjun's."

The song ended there. But I imagined more: as Karna walked to the palace, blood dripped from his self-inflicted wounds. But on his face there was a victorious smile, for the god had given him a boon to negate the curse the Pandava queen had laid on him a long time ago, declaring that posterity would remember only his shameful deeds.

I should have been angered at being foiled. Why then did I, too, find myself smiling?

. . .

Warriors gathered around us with their armies: Satyaki and Dhristaketu, Jayatsena, the Kekaya brothers, the kings of Pandya and Mahishmati, my father, accompanied by Sikhandi and my sons. The air smelled of molten metal, for every smithy in the land was busy forging armor. Our forces totaled seven akshauhini, and the dust from their marching obscured the sun. But our numbers were nowhere close to Duryodhan's.

At this time I had another dream.

A woman wrapped in a shawl stood beside a river, her back to me. Dawn mist rose from the river's calm skin. She started as though she'd heard something.

I realized that in my dream there were no sounds: the river ran silently, and the birds were mute.

Now I could see a man. Even before I saw his face, I knew him to be Karna. How did I know? He had none of the scars I'd expected from the cutting away of his armor. Was it the way he held himself, the way he walked? Or did some strange bond connect us even in this dream world?

The woman moved toward him, her face still hidden. I could tell that she wasn't young. She raised her hand in a regal gesture. Could it be Gandhari? But what would she want to say to her son's best friend that couldn't be spoken in the palace? Perhaps she wanted Karna to persuade her son to peace. If so, she was wasting her time!

Then I saw Karna recoil. Amazement and suspicion chased each other across his face before courtesy won and he bowed. And even before she threw back her shawl I knew it was Kunti that had come to meet so secretly with the man who boasted he was the nemesis of the Pandavas.

Kunti was weeping. All these years I'd never seen her weep. When she'd heard of my humiliation at the hands of Duryodhan, she'd pressed her lips together until they were bloodless. When we left for our twelve years of exile, her eyes had been bright with unshed tears. But always she'd been in control, the same alabaster queen who had towered over me at our first meeting in the slums of Kampilya. Today, however, tears streamed down her cheeks, and there was a look on her face of such careless abandon that I was startled. She held out her arms toward Karna as one would to an intimate, and then, as he backed away, she knelt in a gesture of supplication.

Vainly I strained to read her lips. Was she begging him not to fight against her sons? Was this what worry and age had reduced her to? Would she stoop so low, humiliating us all with her weakness? But what I saw next astonished me further. I'd expected Karna to end their meeting with a curt refusal, but he was speaking passionately, with angry gestures. What could he have to say to her? Now he was brushing tears from his own eyes. Karna! Even in the dream I felt my amazement at this. Now he was lifting her tenderly, touching her feet while she smoothed his hair. Why did he bend over her hands, kissing them?

With every fiber of my being, I longed to hear their words as they continued talking. He held up his right hand to show her five fingers. Was he referring to my five husbands? He held up the index finger of his left hand so that she was looking at six fingers. Then he fisted his left hand and dropped it as if it were a stone. Kunti burst into fresh weeping. She clutched his arm so that he couldn't release himself without hurting her. I saw her lips pronounce a word I recognized—for one's own name is a word nobody can mistake, heard or unheard. Draupadi, she'd always called me, though she knew I preferred to be addressed otherwise.

All my old suspicions of her flared up. What was she saying about me to the man who had once wanted to be my husband?

Karna grew very still. For the first time, indecision flickered over his face. After a while he sighed, as though awakening from a dream. He shook her hands off, bowed coldly, and left without a word. As I awoke the thought came to me that he hadn't trusted himself to speak.

And this, too, came to me: when I saw him in the dream, I was no longer angry with Karna. When had my feelings changed? I still wanted the war; I still longed for vengeance against Duryodhan and Dussasan. But when I thought of Karna, I only remembered the moment at my swayamvar when I'd spoken the words that turned a bright-faced youth into a bitter man.

Truly the heart is incomprehensible.

I agonized over whether to tell my husbands the dream. I sensed that what I'd seen had occurred in reality, though the reason for it was no clearer to my waking brain. Finally I decided to say nothing. I didn't want them to torture themselves by wondering why their mother had met with their fiercest opponent. They needed to concentrate on other matters now. They needed to harden their hearts against kinsmen they'd loved all their lives. They needed to pluck guilt from their souls. If they were to gain the revenge they'd promised me, they needed to proceed without being racked by the doubt that had awakened in my heart as I watched Kunti's inexplicable tears, the voice that whispered, *Could it be?*

field

By the time I arrived at Kurukshetra, the armies were already in position, for the war was to start tomorrow. My bones ached from having been jostled in a carriage all the way from the kingdom of Matsya, and for the first time I felt the full weight of my years. But no amount of pain could douse my excitement. The blood pounded in my veins. The day I had burned for, lying sleepless on my thorny bed in the forest or pounding sandalwood into powder in Queen Sudeshna's chamber—that day of vindication had finally arrived.

Subhadra and Uttara, who had come from farther-away Dwarka, were worse off than I. Uttara was in the third month of a difficult pregnancy. Though we'd all entreated her to remain at home, she had refused. She'd vomited several times in the carriage, and Subhadra had her hands full taking care of her. Subhadra had secretly confided to me that she was worried about the unborn child's safety. But looking at Uttara's face, wilted as a plucked lotus, no one had the heart to chide her. She'd had such a short time with Abhimanyu and was so much in love with him. Greeting me, she kept her eyes carefully lowered. When she raised them inadvertently, startling at a sudden sound, I saw that they were swollen from long, secret weeping. She knew she should not cry; it was harmful for her baby.

But what else could she do with the fear that grew and grew inside her until her chest felt it might explode? The fear she couldn't articulate because it might bring bad luck: What if her husband didn't survive the war?

Kunti arrived last of all. She had come from Hastinapur and had the shortest distance to travel. But she was so exhausted that when she descended from the carriage, she could barely stand. I was shocked to see how much she'd aged. Her hair had turned completely white, her face sagged, and she walked with a dispirited stoop, leaning on a cane. In the dream-vision I'd had just a few weeks back, she'd looked much more robust. Something had transpired during her meeting with Karna that had done this to her. Once again I longed to know what it was, and if it had affected Karna similarly.

Tired though we all were, when the Pandavas asked if we'd like to view the battlefield, we agreed at once. Even Kunti pulled herself together and stated that seeing the actual arena would help us direct our prayers for their safety to it more effectively. I wasn't convinced of that, but I was curious to view the site of the great adventure that was about to begin. And I wanted to spend as much time with my husbands as possible before the war claimed their full attention.

Slowly we climbed the small hillock. Yudhisthir took my arm, leaving Arjun free to take Subhadra's, sending (yes, still) a small ripple of jealousy through me. Abhimanyu tenderly helped Uttara make her way over the stony path. I watched as Ghatotkacha, Bheem's son by his first wife Hidimba, picked Kunti up and carried her. Though raised in a forest among his mother's people, the wild rakshasas, he had a sweet and pleasing personality. From the way he looked at Bheem, his eyes shining, I could tell he idolized him. A good-luck mark glistened redly on his forehead. His mother must have painted it on before he left.

Watching him made me remember Hidimba. Even after I'd

grown to tolerate my husbands' other wives, I never quite liked her. She was a tough woman who knew her own mind and followed it, uncaring of what people might think. Perhaps I was envious of that. She'd met Bheem in the forest when the destitute Pandavas were fleeing from the house of lac and married him against the wishes of her tribe. Soon after, when the Pandavas left for Kampilya, where Arjun wanted to compete in my swayamvar, she chose to remain with her people. The unexpected news that Bheem, too, had married me must have shaken her, but she took it in her stride. If she felt betrayed, no one knew of it. She devoted her life to taking care of her people, ruling them with a strict but fair hand, and bringing up her son. After we gained our own kingdom and built our palace, Bheem invited her to join us in Indra Prastha—but she turned him down politely. The one time I'd met her, at the Rajasuya celebration, she'd been courteous but cool. I'd been annoyed by the fact that, though she was from a poor forest tribe and virtually husbandless, she'd seemed so complete, so unimpressed by all I had.

Before the war, when Bheem asked Hidimba for aid, I thought she would make excuses or send a few paltry troops. She had every right. Bheem hadn't made much of an effort to stay in touch, not like Arjun, who visited his other wives regularly. (Bheem, on the other hand, had only seen Ghatotkacha once in all these years.) Furthermore, rakshasas tended to stay out of the quarrels of citified weaklings, as they called us. But Hidimba surprised us all by sending us her only son, her dearest companion, to fight alongside his father. She wasn't the kind who would have given in to tears when Ghatotkacha left. I imagined, though, that later she would weep bitterly. Did she, in the depth of her mother's heart, regret her generosity? For the first time, I admired her and felt humbled by her sacrifice.

Our lives had entered a different time. We women—no less than the men—were going to be faced by challenges we'd never imagined. The petty resentments I'd felt for Subhadra and Hidimba and the animosity I'd harbored toward Kunti were no longer appropriate. Who we were as individuals was receding to the background. What mattered more was that our dear ones were going into danger to fight beside each other. From now on, we would be united in our anxiety, in being torn between pride and concern, in our prayers for the safety of them all.

. . .

My first view of Kurukshetra was hazy and uncertain, for the sun was setting even as we reached the hilltop. In fact, what I first mistook for the battlefield was actually Lake Samantapanchaka, beside which the women's tents were pitched. In the evening light, the water looked like blood. I told myself that it meant nothing. Any lake might seem this way at sunset. But the feeling of disquiet wouldn't leave me.

Long before I saw the army, my ears were assaulted by the cacophony of animal calls. The neighing of horses and the trumpeting of elephants created a din even now, while the animals were at rest. How deafening would the noise be tomorrow in the heat of battle, when their cries would be augmented by battle yells, the blowing of war conches, and the launching of astras!

The Pandava battalions occupied the western part of the field. They would face east—a good omen, Yudhisthir said. (But would it be harder for the soldiers to begin the battle with the sun in their eyes?) When I looked down on the gathering, I was taken aback by its hugeness. I'd known the numbers, but seeing made them real in a very different way. The tents extended as far as my eyes could reach, and the tiny figures that scurried around them, busy with last-minute preparations, were too many to even attempt to count. I couldn't believe that so many men had come together to help us!

Still, I couldn't afford to feel elated. I knew that beyond our tents, past the mists that shrouded the no-man's-land, the Kaurava army lay in wait. It was far larger—eleven akshauhini to our seven—and led by Bheeshma, the most experienced warrior of our times, with Drona as his second in command. What made them dangerous was not so much their prowess in battle but the love my husbands bore them. That love would deflect the astras of the Pandavas, would make their hands shake as they aimed blows at the grandfather who had shielded their childhood, the teacher without whom they wouldn't have learned how to wield these weapons.

I narrowed my eyes and stared at the veils of vapor, trying to visualize Bheeshma and Drona, wondering whether they waited for morning with sorrow or a resigned sense of duty. But while I thought, the insidious currents of my mind changed their direction. I found myself imagining another face, the one I considered most dangerous. In my mind he stood apart from the rest of his company, gazing toward the Pandava camp, where he knew I would be. But I could not decide on the expression his face would hold.

Small fires dotted the army encampment, which looked deceptively peaceful. The cooks were preparing dinner. My brother, who had been chosen as commander of our army, was down there somewhere, walking among the men, speaking words of encouragement. My sons walked with him. I ached to see them, to hold them if they'd let me, to find out more about the young men they'd become—what interested them, what they did in their leisure time, whether they were contemplating marriage. In the last twelve years, we'd spoken to each other only a few times, and never at length. I wished they'd decided to spend this last evening with me, then pushed the thought away. Through the years of our exile, Dhri was the one who had been there for them, comforting them when they were lonely or unhappy and applauding their triumphs. He was more a parent to them than my husbands or I. It was fitting that they should keep him company at this difficult time. And difficult it certainly was; he'd confessed to me that the responsibility for so many lives lay heavy upon him. Additionally, though he hadn't said it, surely he worried about how he would fulfill the destiny he was born for, because his studies under Drona had made it clear that he would never equal Drona as a warrior.

As I turned away, I thought I heard the faint, plaintive notes of a flute, borne on a moment's breeze. Could it be Krishna's? I knew he was down there in the stables, checking on the horses he was to drive tomorrow. Until the very end, he had tried to stop the war, to mediate between my husbands and their cousins. He had risked his own safety by traveling to Hastinapur to tell Duryodhan that my husbands would be content if he gave them just five villages to live in. Anyone else would have been furious when Duryodhan mocked him, saying he wouldn't even give my husbands the amount of land that could fit on the tip of a needle. But Krishna had shrugged and smiled and slipped effortlessly from the grasp of the soldiers whom Duryodhan had ordered to capture him. And now, on the eve of a battle that might be the most devastating one our age would see, he was playing his flute! What gave him such calmness, such courage?

Arjun was explaining to Subhadra the rules that both sides would follow in this battle, rules set up by the senior warriors on each side. It was to be a civilized war, great and glory-giving and, most of all, righteous. Fighting would start only after sunrise, when the commanders of the armies blew on their conches, and it would end at sunset with a similar signal. Night was a time of truce when warriors could visit one another's camps unharmed. Wives and mothers would occupy separate camps in the rear of each army. No matter who won the war, the women would not be harmed. The battle was to be between equals—foot soldiers would fight with foot soldiers, horsemen with horsemen, and the chief warriors only with those who had similar astras. Servants, charioteers, musicians who blew the war horns, and animals would not be harmed on purpose. No one who was weaponless should be attacked, and above all, no one who had laid down his arms should be killed.

Subhadra nodded as Arjun spoke, listening carefully. Her face was alight with admiration. Arjun's eyes softened as he looked at her, and he reached out and tucked a stray hair behind her ear. How was it he never behaved with such tenderness toward me?

I knew the answer, of course: I never acted like Subhadra, though sometimes I wished I could. But I'd been with my husbands too long. I knew them too intimately. I was too critical. My eyes had bored into their deepest recesses, illumining every weakness.

Even now, the skeptic in me was wondering, how in the heat of battle would people manage to keep these laws?

Arjun's face glowed as he spoke of the nobility of this enterprise, this war unlike all previous ones, by which the heroes of our era would be recognized and remembered. I looked from his face to the faces of his brothers. They mirrored the same shining zeal. Even Yudhisthir, who had hesitated for so long, was ready. Most eager were the faces of Ghatotkacha and Abhimanyu, so sure they were entering an adventure that would imprint their names into the hearts of posterity. I couldn't help smiling as I listened to them brag to each other about how many enemies they would destroy. Some of their enthusiasm seeped into me. I lifted my face to the sky and sent forth a prayer that they would achieve even greater fame than they imagined. I'd barely finished when a star detached itself from the black fabric of night and fell. My heart expanded at this good luck sign. The gods had answered me!

I should have remembered how tricky the gods are. How they give what you want with one hand while taking away, with the other, something much more valuable. Yes, fame would come to both the young men, and bards would sing of their exploits oftener than they sang of their fathers'. But when they did so, listeners would turn away to hide their tears.

· · ·

My husbands were discussing warcraft. Should Dhri arrange the soldiers in the ocean formation or the crocodile formation tomorrow morning? Which kings should be placed at the head of the army? Who should bring up the rear? Abhimanyu begged to be allowed to lead the first charge, but his uncles felt he didn't have enough experience yet. Uttara listened to them argue, her feverish, glittery eyes filled with wonder and dread, moving from face to face, her hands clasped over the slight mound of her belly. Had I ever been so young? I thought as I wandered to the edge of the hill where a copse of trees hunkered.

And suddenly he was in front of me, Vyasa who had prophesied everything that had led us here today. In the dark, his eyes glittered, and the holy thread that lay across his chest gleamed as though carved from ice. He looked no older than on the day I met him in the banyan grove.

I felt a chill grip my chest. Why had he come? I didn't have the heart to listen to another dark prophecy just when we were beginning this great enterprise. But I masked my anxiety with formal words. "It is a delight—though an unexpected one—to find you here, respected sage. I'm glad to see you looking so well."

"A pity that the years have not been equally kind to Drupad's daughter," he replied, smirking through his forest of a beard as though he knew how uncomfortable his presence made me. "Perhaps, instead of a box of mosquito powder, I should have given you age-conquering unguents!"

Easy for you to joke, I thought in anger. You'd be acting differently if your loved ones were poised on the edge of a sword.

"Would I really?" he said, startling me. "Let me tell you where I was before this: I was visiting my eldest son, who is in some distress. I think you know him—his name is Dhritarashtra."

"The blind king? He's *your* son?" I knew I was gaping. "But I thought he was the son of Bheeshma's brother—"

"It's a long story," Vyasa said, "and some parts of it are less than flattering to my ego. I'll tell it to you one of these days. For now, let me just mention my second son's name. It is—was—Pandu."

I stared at him aghast, ashamed at how quick I'd been to judge him. His grandchildren were pitted against each other in this fight to the death! No matter which side won in the war, Vyasa had much to lose.

"How can you be so calm?" I whispered.

Vyasa smiled. "The life that you're living today is only a bubble in the cosmic stream, shaped by the karma of other lifetimes. The one who is your husband in this birth was perhaps your enemy in the last, and he whom you hate may have been your beloved. Why weep for any of them, then?"

The ideas he offered me weren't unfamiliar. The sages who visited us during our exile had spoken similarly in their efforts to resign me to my fate. I didn't disbelieve them, but I wasn't convinced. This world around me with its beauties and terrors held me too firmly in its grip. I wanted my rightful place in it. Perhaps there were other lifetimes. But I wanted the satisfaction of vengeance in this one.

"The war will work itself out the way it's meant to—the way I've set down already in my book," Vyasa continued. "Why should I grieve any more at it than if I were watching a play?" Seeing the stubborn look on my face, he stopped. "But I didn't come here to spout philosophy. I want to offer you a gift—the same that I offered to the blind king: a special vision so that you may see the most important parts of the battle from afar."

I drew in a jagged breath, trying to encompass the enormousness of what he offered. I, a woman, to view what no woman—and few men—had ever observed!

"Did Dhritarashtra accept?"

"He didn't have the courage to watch his sons reap the fruits of their actions—actions that he had encouraged with his misplaced love. Instead, he asked that I give the gift to Sanjay, his charioteer and confidant. Sanjay will tell him what occurs. By the end of it, he may be sorry, for Sanjay isn't one to mince his words! But you—are you brave enough to watch the greatest spectacle of our times? Are you steadfast enough to tell others what really happened in Kurukshetra? Because ultimately only the witness—and not the actors—knows the truth."

I hesitated. Suddenly I was afraid. For the first time, my euphoria receded and I was aware of the other face of war: the violence and the pain. Observing, I would suffer them no less than the men undergoing these experiences. And would I feel any less guilt than Dhritarashtra? Was I not, in my own way, as responsible for this war as he? Maybe it was best to wait for the couriers to bring me news, a lifetime's worth of tragedy encapsulated in a sentence.

I took a deep breath. Until the words came out, I didn't know what I'd say. "I accept your gift. I will watch this war and live to tell of it. It's only just, since I've helped bring it about."

"Don't give yourself so much credit, granddaughter-in-law!" Vyasa's smile was ironic as ever. Only later, thinking back, would I recognize the compassion in it. "The seeds of this war were sown long before you were born, though perhaps you did nudge it along a bit. But I'm glad of the choice you have made." He stretched out his arm to touch my forehead on the spot where the third eye is supposed to lie. I braced myself—for what, I didn't know. Perhaps a burst of heavenly music, a lightning flash. But his touch was disappointingly ordinary, no more dramatic than the brush of a bird's wing. I looked around. Everything was the same as before. In the dusk, I couldn't even see my husbands.

Was Vyasa indulging in a joke at my expense?

"Suspicious, aren't you? Don't worry. Starting tomorrow, for eighteen days—because that's how long this carnage will last—you'll see every important moment of this war."

He stepped back into shadow. Darkness swallowed everything except the unraveling whiteness of his beard.

"Wait!" I cried. "You say you've already written the story of the war. Tell me then, who will win?"

"Is it fair to ask the playwright to give away the climax of his play? But in this case, I'm not even the playwright—merely a chronicler. It would be presumptuous of me to reveal the end before the ordained time, O granddaughter who has learned no more patience than when I first saw you!"

With that, he was gone.

"Where are you, Panchaali?" I heard Yudhisthir call. "We must go down for our night meal now. We need to ready ourselves for tomorrow."

I allowed him to take my hand and answered his courtesies absentmindedly. We made our way by smoky torchlight to the camp. The attendants had raised up a crude structure with a roof of palm fronds that would be home for us women until the war ended. They had tried to make it comfortable with silk hangings and sandalwood incense, and had even brought in a musician who plucked at his single-stringed lute and sang softly. Still, there was an unquietness in the air, as before a lightning storm, and under the floor coverings the ground was hard with rocks so that Kunti grimaced as she sat down. As for me, I didn't care. Once I lost my palace, all places—be they mansions or hovels—became the same to me.

As we sat down to eat, my sons came in, followed by Dhri and Sikhandi. They greeted me with courtesy if not tenderness, and I knew I should be satisfied with that. There had been so much I'd wanted to say to them, but now I couldn't remember any of it. Dhri looked harried. Sikhandi, whom I hadn't seen in a great while, had grown his hair long. It gave his face ambiguity—male from a certain angle, female from another. My sons were dressed in armor, though surely there was no need for it yet. But for them it was part of this new, exciting game. I watched with fascination as the firelight played on their metal skins. I have no remembrance of what I said in blessing when they touched my feet, and strangely, though I knew I should be concerned as all other mothers were on this day, I felt no fear.

Already Vyasa's gift was working on me. It was as though I'd fallen into a river, as though I was being borne toward a waterfall, away from the people I'd thought of, until now, as my dearest kin. In the distance I could hear the rushing of water, or was it voices crying out in confusion? Soon the current would speed up, pulling me over the edge. I looked at the faces around me. They were stern and blank, carved in stone. No one noticed my consternation. Each man was locked in his own inner world where he visualized himself as the protagonist of a glorious drama.

Only Krishna, entering the tent last of all, shot me a quizzical glance. At the end of the evening, when he said goodbye, he whispered another of his cryptic statements into my ear, something about this body being like cast-off clothes, about there being no reason to grieve.

. . .

At some point that night, I found myself outside the tent, gazing at an enormous, coppery moon that hung low in the sky. I didn't know enough sky lore to tell if this was a good omen or bad. In the empty terrain where once the river Saraswati had flowed, I caught a sudden movement. At first I thought it a wild animal, but it was a woman, gathering the wild cactus that commoners sometimes eat when food is scarce. She ceased moving and stood still, watching me with wariness. Backlighted by the moon, she was scrawny-boned, her sari patched and knotted. A camp follower, I guessed, maybe the wife of one of our foot soldiers. I beckoned to her, thinking I would give her a coin.

The woman advanced a few feet, scrunching up her eyes to see more clearly. Then, all of a sudden, she turned and fled, flinging up her hands in a gesture I recognized with a shock. It was a sign against the evil eye!

I stood frozen. I knew she'd recognized me—no one could mistake my uncombed, striated hair. Was this, then, how the people viewed me? All this time I'd seen myself as the wronged one. I'd believed that the people of the country—especially the women—sympathized with me because of the insults I'd suffered at the hands of Duryodhan. That they admired me for the hardships I'd chosen to share with my husbands in exile. When I'd looked down on the huge Pandava host on the battlefield, I'd surmised that those soldiers had chosen to join my husbands because they supported our cause. Now I realized that for many of them, it was merely a job, an alternative to poverty and starvation. Or maybe they'd been forcibly conscripted by their overlords. No wonder that for their wives, I was a harbinger of ill luck, the woman who had torn their husbands from the safety of their homes, the witch who might, with a wave of her hand, transform them into widows.

How little we know our own reputations, I thought with a bitter smile.

. . .

That night my sleep was a disturbed one, but in between waking and dozing I dreamed the last dream I would have until the war ended. In it, Krishna was talking to me. When he opened his mouth to speak, I could see the entire earth inside it, and the heavens with their spinning planets and fiery meteors. He said, once again, what he'd told me in the evening—only this time I understood. *Just as we cast off worn clothes and wear new ones, when the time arrives, the soul casts off the body and finds a new one to work out its karma. Therefore the wise grieve neither for the living nor the dead.*

I searched deep inside and found that he was right. Truly, whether we won or lost, lived or died, there was no cause for grief. The core of my Self was burnished like a new sword. Sorrow could not touch it any more than rust could inhabit pure steel. Buoyancy filled me, a sense that the great drama of life was unfolding exactly as it was meant to. And wasn't I fortunate to be a participant in it?

But in the morning when I woke, my heart was despondent once again. I repeated Krishna's words to myself, but they sat on my tongue inert as stones. I could not understand why they'd made me so happy. In a few minutes, they began to break up, like a cloud picture in a windy sky, and I could not even recall them. I recalled perfectly, however, the look on the woman's face from last night. What is it in us that carves negative impressions so deeply into our brains? A terrible doubt came upon me as I saw her once again holding up her hands against me: had I pushed my husbands—and perhaps an entire kingdom—into calamity for my own petty satisfactions?

sight

The morning of the war found me tired and aching; my head felt as though it were stuffed with prickly jute fibers. All night, in between fragments of dreams, faces coalesced out of the darkness of my tent: my husbands, my sons, Dhri, and last of all, a man with ancient, unsettling eyes. When he appeared, I could not bear to lie in bed any longer. Although the sun was barely up and the war had not yet begun, I decided to climb the hill. Last night, I had informed no one of my conversation with Vyasa or the gift he'd given me. (To tell the truth, I didn't fully believe in it myself.) Now I merely instructed my maid to tell Subhadra where I was going so she would not worry. I added that no one should disturb me because I would be at prayer. It wasn't quite a lie. As I observed the war, I would ask the gods to protect the people I cared for. Would it be treachery if one of them was fighting on the other side?

As I climbed, I heard the trumpets calling warriors to readiness. The horses neighed in excitement. They knew something momentous was about to begin. I confess: my heart, too, speeded up in anticipation. If Vyasa had spoken the truth, I was to be a witness—the only witness on our side, the only woman ever—to the grand spectacle that was about to play itself out. No matter how the war ended, my role in it was something to be proud of.

But as I reached the summit, against my will my footsteps slowed. My legs would not hold me up. A great weight pulled at my eyelids. I sat down—I didn't know whether on a rock or the bare ground. I saw and heard nothing. I did not feel the sun beating down on me. As I was pulled from the state I'd always thought of as consciousness, I realized that the role I would play now had nothing to do with Panchaali's pride. The force that was entering me—I felt its pounding roughness in every cell of my body—would use me for its purpose. Too late, I was afraid.

For the rest of the war, I climbed the hill each morning and passed into this state—for want of a better word, I call it a trance. All day, I experienced neither hunger nor thirst, though by evening I was exhausted and could barely make my way down. It was during this time that my hair turned white and flesh melted away from my body. When Subhadra realized what was happening (though she didn't understand it) she sent a maidservant with me, to give me water—for that was all I could take—and bring me down safely each evening. The girl told me later that I often wept or laughed, scaring her. Sometimes I chanted in an unknown language. I have no recollection of this. But for the rest of my life, I wouldn't forget the images that came to me—those that I would try to find words for later, and those that were so terrible that I left them locked inside me.

I had expected the sight to be something like looking through a telescope, but I was mistaken. True, I saw distant scenes as clearly as though they were happening a few arm's lengths away from me—but that was the least of it. For instance: I saw silver-haired Bheeshma in the forefront of the Kaurava army, seated in his silver chariot. A golden palm tree waved on his banner. He was exhorting his troops, telling them that the gates of heaven had opened wide today to let in all that would die on the battlefield. His face was filled with vigor and a strange gaiety, and his words rang with such conviction that I believed him. But as I watched his face, it shifted and wavered, like an image drawn on water. I felt his tiredness in my own body. His heart was so heavy, I wondered that he had the strength to even draw breath. I realized then that the sight allowed me to penetrate the masks of men and look into their core, and I was at once elated and terrified. I looked up at the sky, hoping for a sign that what Bheeshma said was true, but it shone above me a blank and comfortless blue.

If war forced even a great soul such as Bheeshma to dissemble, what hope was there for the rest of us?

I saw Duryodhan pacing under his banner, a serpent in a field of gold. "Kill Sikhandi first," he instructed his generals. "No one else can destroy Bheeshma. And as long as Bheeshma leads us, we're invincible!" Under his gold crown, his face was thinner, his eyes like lighted coals as he stared at the Pandava host. But the harsh line of his lips softened as he turned toward the warriors who had positioned themselves around him. "I will not forget your loyalty," he said to them, touching one and then the other on the shoulder. They smiled back at him. I was shocked to feel love rising from them, shimmering like heat from a summer pavement, their willingness to die at his command. He beckoned a messenger close, detached a jewel from his headdress. "Give this to Bhanumati. Tell her I'll come to her as soon as I can." Then his eyes darkened, searching the field. "Where is Karna?" he asked. "One of you, go, tell him Duryodhan calls. Today more than ever I need my friend beside me."

Even in the trance, my breath grew uneven, my hands trembled with anticipation. But before I could see Karna, the vision pulled me toward the Pandava army. How puny it seemed in comparison! Yudhisthir stood at its center, under the white umbrella that signified kingship. His face was pale and drawn; in his heart he still didn't want this war. Nor did he want so many thousands to die for his sake. Next to him, guarded by our staunchest soldiers, stood Sikhandi. Bheem led one flank, Nakul and Sahadev the other. I looked for Dhri. There he was, at the rear of the formation, his bronze and silver chariot rolling through the ranks as he gave commands to various officials. My sons rode behind him on chargers.

With a start I realized that every single person I cared for in the world was gathered on this field. How many of them would walk off it when the war ended in eighteen days?

Now my eyes were caught by a strange movement at the edge of the field. Arjun's golden chariot sped past the boundary of our army into the no-man's-land. Why would he go there now, while the war hung imminent above our heads? Was he not supposed to be at the head of the army to lead the attack? I could see Krishna guiding his six white horses. How skillfully he controlled them, with the smallest flick of his wrist. With his whip, he pointed out the scions of the Kaurava army, men my husband knew as well as he knew himself. And then Arjun dropped his beloved Gandiva, hid his face in his hands, and wept.

. . .

Much has been written about Arjun's grief at this eleventh hour and what Krishna said in response to shake him out of immobility. Vyasa knew it first, dreaming it before it happened. They say he chanted it to Ganesha, god of beginnings, who penned it down. (Was it him I'd glimpsed under the banyan with his pendulous elephant head?) Others took up Krishna's words and translated them into many languages and meters. Some gave it elaborate names, but most merely called it *The Song*. It wouldn't surprise me if poets and philosophers continue to write about it until the world dissolves on the day of pralaya.

No one—including Arjun himself—had anticipated that the

bravest of the Pandavas would be paralyzed by guilt on seeing the kinsmen he'd have to kill in order to achieve victory. He was a practical man. All this time, he'd been the most impatient, the one most eager to test his skills. Who could have imagined that he would be so shaken by the thought of the devastated world we'd have to inhabit after the war had killed or maimed millions? But unless they are masters of evasion, all who begin a war must at some point face these emotions. Over the next few days, each of my other husbands would bitterly regret their part in the battle and wish it undone. But by then we would all know this: war is like an avalanche. Once begun, it cannot cease until it has wreaked all the destruction it is capable of.

When I watched Krishna advise Arjun, consoling him, teaching him how to be successful not only on this battlefield but beyond it, I almost didn't recognize the amusing, carefree man I'd known since my girlhood. Where had he learned so many philosophies? When had he made their wisdom his own?

I faithfully repeated the points he made to the other women when I joined them at night. *The pleasures that arise from sense-objects are bound to end, and thus they are only sources of pain. Don't get attached to them.* And: *When a man reaches a state where honor and dishonor are alike to him, then he is considered supreme. Strive to gain such a state.* Uttara was too distracted by her own concerns to pay much attention, but Kunti and Subhadra listened carefully and nodded in understanding. I couldn't imagine such a man of wisdom, however, far less aspire to be like him. I didn't know how to live without attachment or feel the same way toward honor and dishonor. Perhaps only when one possessed a greater treasure could one let go of this world. Krishna hinted that such a treasure was inside me—*Weapons cannot harm it; fire cannot burn it; it is eternal, still and blissful*—but the words, slippery as stones that have been left underwater a long time, slid from my fingers even as I tried to examine them. Wisdom that isn't distilled in our own crucible can't help us. Thus, though my mouth parroted Krishna's words, my will swung between remorse and revenge, and my heart wouldn't stop stinging.

But one thing Krishna said struck me directly. When Arjun asked why man found himself driven to wrongdoing in spite of good intentions, Krishna replied, *Because of anger and desire, our two direst enemies.* How well I knew them, my longtime companions—no, my masters—and their offspring, revenge! And how faithful they were! When I sought to rid myself of them, they clung to me most tenaciously.

I couldn't claim, as Arjun did after hearing Krishna's discourse, that my delusions had vanished. But I learned to watch myself. And if I wasn't able to bar anger, or her insidious cousin, irritation, from my heart, at least some of the time I bit back the sharp comments that I'd prided myself on dispensing so freely all these years.

. . .

One part of Krishna's conversation with Arjun I was unable to report. Arjun spoke of it later, though his disjointed words didn't make much sense. He said Krishna had appeared to him in the form of God.

"His eyes were the sun and moon and fire," he added. "In his body there were mountains and oceans, and the deep darkness of space beyond the stars. All our enemies—and many of our friends—fell into his gigantic mouth and were crushed to death." He shuddered. "It was terrible—and beautiful beyond description. Did you not see it?"

I shook my head. "I only saw a great flash of light, as though a divine astra had been discharged. It blinded me. I thought the end of the world had come."

"It was the end of the world—the world as I knew it," Arjun said. "Now the meaning of everything is different—our lives, our deaths, what we do in between." He stared into the distance and didn't say any more, but the sorrow was gone from his face.

I, too, said nothing, but I was deeply hurt. Why hadn't Krishna, whom I believed to be my dear friend and protector, allowed me to see his cosmic form? Ever since the war began, he'd had little to do with me. I understood that: he was preoccupied with larger events. But this was a slight too huge to ignore. I decided I, too, would have nothing to do with him until I received proof of his caring.

I decided this, but it didn't lessen the sting in my heart. I couldn't stop myself from wondering, over and over, why he considered Arjun more fitting to receive this vision. What crucial ingredient did I lack that the mystery of the universe should forever elude me?

. . .

What else did the sight bring?

My father locked in battle with Drona, both their faces rigid with old hatred. In between striking deathly blows at each other, they both remembered fragments from their shared past: days at the hermitage, sharing lessons and food, a hunt where they'd got lost in the forest together, the tears they had shed at parting. Bheem roaring as he killed Duryodhan's brothers. When the bloodlust receded from his mind, it was filled with remorse at fratricide, for no matter how he excused himself, he knew that the same blood ran in their veins. Ghatotkacha, bellowing with rage, all gentleness melted from his face, as he used his rakshasa magic to grow to gigantic proportions. When he crushed enemy soldiers under his feet as they fled in terror, his conscience cried, Is this glory? I saw Sikhandi, grown more androgynous by the moment, discharge arrow after arrow toward Bheeshma, swearing in frustration when none of them could reach him. One part of his mind was relieved that he hadn't yet committed the heinous act of killing Bharat's greatest warrior. Arjun's chariot cut through the field like a meteor, burning everything in its path—but he took care to avoid his grandfather and his teacher, not ready to kill them yet.

Thus the war went on, the physical battle outside matching the conflicts within each warrior. And yet this did not mitigate the carnage. I saw the death throes of the innocent and the guilty, and both were equally terrible. In only a few hours, the ground turned red as though the skies had rained blood. What would happen by the end of the eighteen days? I watched the pendulum of victory sway back and forth, one hour toward the Kauravas, the next toward the Pandavas, and with each swing, I searched for—and failed to find—Karna, whose heart I most yearned to read.

In the night I learned the reason for his absence. Before the war began, Bheeshma told Duryodhan that he would command the Kaurava forces only if Karna stayed off the battlefield. (Was this because of the long animosity between them? Or was it as my husbands thought—that Bheeshma was trying to protect them? Or was there a different reason, related to the dream I'd had?) Knowing Bheeshma to be the more experienced warrior, Karna had acceded for the sake of his friend—but with great anger, for this was the war he'd been preparing to fight all his life. Now he waited in his tent for Bheeshma to win—or die. My vision could not travel there, but my imagination made up for this lack. In it he paced up and down, his back ramrod straight, his weapons lying ready on the ascetic's pallet where he slept. His ears were tuned to every sound of war; his whole being chafed with impatience.

I imagined Duryodhan coming to him at the end of the day to discuss strategy and to vent his frustration with Bheeshma, for he sensed that though Bheeshma's promise yoked him to the throne of Hastinapur, in his heart the grandfather favored the Pandavas. Karna hid his own agitation to calm him, agreeing as he'd always done—the one friend Duryodhan could lean on. In case Bheeshma failed, Karna assured him, he would certainly kill Arjun. Didn't he possess Indra's Shakti, that invincible weapon? Once Arjun was gone, the Pandavas would be nothing. Why, Duryodhan could finish them off himself in a day or two!

But after Duryodhan left, greatly cheered by such talk, Karna sank onto his pallet and put his hands over his face. When he removed them—why should I imagine this?—his fingers were wet with tears.

34

secrets

 The grandfather was proving to be a problem. We'd known all along what a hardened warrior he was, and what a strategist.
But my husbands were taken aback by the energy with which he
plowed into the Pandava army, killing thousands single-handedly. He
also created troop formations that were almost impossible to penetrate: the crane with outspread wings, the intricate sea serpent, the layered mandala. Deep down they had believed (as did Duryodhan) that
he loved them too much to truly harm them. Hadn't he announced, in
open court, that he'd do his best to bring Duryodhan victory, but he
would not kill the Pandavas, because they were his grandsons, too?

"He can't talk to us directly because of his vow," Sahadev the
strategist said. "So he's sending us a coded message. Circumstances,
he's saying, have placed us on opposing sides, but even while I'm
fighting you, I'll aid you."

"Of course!" Arjun said. "Wasn't that what our uncle Salya told
us after Duryodhan tricked him into joining his forces? *He thinks
he's won, but two can play at this game. When Karna comes to the battlefield, I'll volunteer to be his charioteer, and I'll use my words to sow
discouragement in his heart.*"

Only Yudhisthir shook his head, unconvinced.

"The grandfather is made of a different metal," he said.

He was right. The promise Bheeshma had given in his youth—that he'd guard the throne of Hastinapur against all invaders—was carved into his heart at least as deep as any love that subsequently entered it. And when (following a slew of triumphs by Arjun) Duryodhan accused him of partiality to the Pandavas, he demonstrated this by fighting so fiercely that our soldiers whispered that he was Yama the death-bringer come to earth. Even the bravest of them broke formation and fled when they saw his silver chariot approaching—but that didn't save them from destruction. (Already the rules of righteous war were breaking down.) Each day, faced with Bheeshma's wrath, our forces dwindled. Each night our camp was mired in despondence as my husbands faced a fact they hadn't considered: the legends had spoken true; Bheeshma was invincible. He wouldn't kill them, no. But he didn't have to. Once he destroyed enough of their army, their defeat was inevitable.

The ninth day—when, according to Vyasa, the war had reached its mid mark—was the worst. On this day there was a great battle between Arjun and Bheeshma. But Arjun's heart was not in it. In spite of all that Krishna had said to him, he couldn't forget his childhood memories. He couldn't bear to hurt the man who had held him in his arms and comforted him through his childhood sorrows. Bheeshma, however, didn't have such qualms. He shot arrow after harassing arrow at Arjun until he bled. In between, with maddening nonchalance, he sent out astras that destroyed entire phalanxes. Finally an enraged Krishna, convinced that our army was about to perish, leaped from the chariot and, discus in hand, rushed at Bheeshma.

The grandfather dropped his weapons and knelt before him. On his face was a look I could only interpret as hope.

"And have you come to set me free finally, Govinda?" he asked. "Have I paid sufficiently for my theft?"

Krishna raised his discus, but Arjun, recalling his friend's vow not to fight, held on to him with all his strength.

"You must not break your word for my sake! That would be a terrible sin!" he cried. "Tomorrow I'll face Bheeshma as a true kshatriya faces his enemy—focused on the moment, with no memories of the past to disable him and no fear of future regrets. I swear it!"

Krishna stared at him almost as though he didn't know who he was. Then, very slowly, he lowered his weapon. When he spoke, it was to Bheeshma. "O Vasu, by your own act you bound yourself. Therefore you alone can set yourself free."

What, I asked Arjun later, did Bheeshma mean by *theft*? I couldn't imagine the scrupulous old patriarch taking anything that didn't belong to him. Why did Krishna call him by that strange name, *Vasu*? And what act was he talking about?

Arjun shrugged. The elders were always referring to mysterious events from the past that were important only to themselves. And as for Krishna, it would take an entire lifetime to figure out even a fraction of his comments. Surely I knew that!

But I couldn't let go so easily. It wasn't merely because of what Yudhisthir termed the insidious curiosity of womankind. Stories were important. Even when I was a child, I'd realized that they had to be understood and preserved for the future, so that we didn't make the same mistakes over and over. I held my questions in my mind, waiting for the right circumstance. That opportunity would arrive sooner than I expected.

. . .

Late that night, at Krishna's urging, the Pandavas went bareheaded to Bheeshma's tent. They touched the grandfather's feet and asked him how he could be killed. And he—with compassion and some relief—told them what to do.

So it was that Sikhandi was stationed in the front of Arjun's chariot, his unbound hair blowing in the wind. He challenged Bheeshma to battle, and Bheeshma laid down his bow, saying, Amba, you know I will not fight you. He did not take up his weapons again, even when a weeping Arjun shot arrow after arrow that went through him, and Sikhandi, also weeping, covered his face in his hands.

Much has been sung of how Bheeshma fell on his bed of arrows. On that day the war came to a standstill while both armies mourned side by side. Bheeshma asked for a support for his head, but when Duryodhan brought him silken pillows he rejected them. Only Arjun knew what he wanted: he shot three arrows into the ground for his grandfather to rest his head, and at that, even through his pain, Bheeshma smiled.

Bheeshma did not die for a long while. Not until the auspicious time when the sun began his northern journey would he choose to let go of his body—and that, too, only after discharging his final duty: teaching Yudhisthir the rules of kingship that Duryodhan had refused to learn from him. Meanwhile, news of the war was brought to him every day, and warriors from both sides came to ask his advice. Flocks of swans flew over him, crying in melodious voices. Men whispered that they were celestial beings in disguise, bringing messages from heaven. At night, too, Bheeshma received visitors. They came to him each alone, wrapped in cloaks of secrecy, to tell him things that could not be spoken in the company of others.

How do I know this? Because I was one of them.

. . .

I went to Bheeshma the very first night, when the moon was frail as the edge of a fingernail and sudden gusts of wind sent shadows scampering along the ground. I'd taken great care to be silent—I did not wish to be questioned by Kunti, who would have wanted me to visit him in the daytime, appropriately chaperoned. But such a visit would have kept me from speaking freely, from asking him what I'd kept locked in my heart for years: How could he—who prided himself on his righteousness, who named me his dearest granddaughter and made me believe he cared for me—have remained silent when I called for his help, when I was the victim of such grave injustice that day in the court?

Once I left the guardsmen's fires behind, I walked more easily. I didn't think I'd encounter anyone. The leading warriors of both sides, who had been with him all day, were now resting in preparation for morning—for even the fall of Bheeshma could not stop the war. In deference to the grandfather's condition, they had decided to move the battle away from where he lay and had cleared the area. But they couldn't mask the stench of rotting carcasses or hush the anguished cries of the wounded. Did the sounds wrench Bheeshma as he lay wrapped in the gauze of his own pain? Did he regret having caused much of this destruction? Or did he see it as the unpleasant by-product of his duty, a lesser evil to be endured for the sake of an ultimate good?

· · ·

I'd been wrong to assume that no one would be with Bheeshma. A man knelt by him, bent low over his feet. I heard the grandfather say—how weak he sounded—"Who is it whose tears burn me more than these wounds?" As I ducked behind a knot of shrubs I heard the man reply, in choked tones, "It's Karna. I've come to beg pardon for the many ways in which I've angered you, grandfather."

I held my breath, regretting my imprudence. If Karna discovered me, he would be livid that I'd caught him at such a vulnerable moment. What might he not do in retaliation? I doubted that, after all that had passed, he felt any tenderness toward me. Instead, with a hunter's sure instincts, he would know that the best way to get at my husbands was by humiliating me—and he would use it. What new trouble had I brought upon the Pandavas by my impulsiveness?

I should have crept away then, but I was like a bird caught in a snare. Only, the wires of this snare were made of curiosity and a disobedient heart.

Bheeshma extended a hand toward Karna. I thought I saw his fingers tremble. His breath sounded like someone was tearing old clothes into strips. He said, "I was never truly angry with you. I only chastised you for your own good—and because you encouraged Duryodhan's evil ambitions. But how can I be angry with my own grandson?"

When Karna had addressed Bheeshma as grandfather, I'd thought nothing of it. It was what everyone called him. But this reply seemed more than mere courtesy. A jolt went through my heart as I wondered what Bheeshma's reply might mean.

Karna's head jerked up. "You knew? You knew that the Pandavas are my brothers? Did Kunti tell you, too, when she told me?"

Shock dizzied me. Karna? Brother to my husbands? My brain couldn't encompass his words—words that would change everything I felt for him. Impossible, I whispered to myself. But then I remembered my dream of Karna and Kunti.

Suddenly, everything that had puzzled me began to make sense.

Bheeshma said, "I knew it a long time before that. Vyasa told me of it—but only after I'd promised to be silent. How many times since then have I wished I hadn't made that rash vow! But you know me. Once I make a promise I can't break it. Call it my strength—or my weakness."

Karna smiled without mirth. "I know. I have the same problem." Then his tone darkened. "Kunti told me she had me when she was little more than a girl. Out of curiosity she'd tested Durvasa's boon and called down the sun god. He gifted me to her—but when I was born she grew afraid of what people would say." He ran agitated fingers through his hair. "I understand how she must have felt. I don't blame her—no, I do! How could she have thrown me away, her own child, her firstborn? But worse than that, when she saw me again at Hastinapur, how could she have let me suffer, over and over, the shame of illegitimacy?" His voice grew impassioned—it was a new Karna I was hearing, so anguished, so different from the man who prided himself on his self-control. In that moment I forgave him everything he'd done while in the grip of his sorrow. "She should have told me the truth in secret—I would have kept it to myself, as I'm doing now. Just knowing it would have made all the difference. It would have kept me from making the terrible mistakes that continue to haunt my life. Oh, why didn't my mother trust me?"

With difficulty, Bheeshma placed a trembling hand on Karna's head. "I, too, wish she'd had the courage to do so. This entire war might have been avoided then. Remember the time when Yudhisthir asked for a mere five villages, saying he'd be satisfied with that? Had you known the secret of your birth, surely you would have counseled Duryodhan to agree. And because of his love and esteem for you, surely Duryodhan would have listened to you. So many men have died already—and yet I'm afraid that their suffering is nothing compared to what awaits all of you."

"I'm not afraid of suffering," Karna said. "Hasn't my entire life been one suffering after another? What stings me worse is how much I hated and envied my own brothers ever since I met them at that ill-fated tournament in Hastinapur. I, who dreamed all through my lonely childhood of having kinsmen to love and cherish! And Draupadi! The wife of my younger brothers, who, the scriptures tell us, should be like a daughter to me—I humiliated her in open court.

I knew what Duryodhan and Sakuni were planning. Out of decency I should have stopped them. Instead, because I was angry with her, I instigated Dussasan to remove her clothes! I—" His voice broke. "How shamefully I've acted! Even the most glorious death on the battlefield can't make up for it."

"The fates are cruel," Bheeshma whispered, "and they've been crueler than usual to you. But the sins you committed in ignorance are not your fault."

"I'll still have to pay for them," Karna said. "Isn't that how karma works? Look at what happened to Pandu, who killed a sage by accident, thinking him to be a wild deer. He had to bear the consequences of it for the rest of his life."

A fit of coughing shook Bheeshma; he continued with some difficulty. "It's not too late. Join your brothers. I know them—they'll welcome you and honor you as the eldest."

Karna shook his head. "No. It was too late the moment Kripa insulted me by declaring that I couldn't participate in the tournament, and Duryodhan rescued me by giving me a kingdom. He stood by me when everyone was against me. I've eaten his salt. I can't abandon him."

Bheeshma drew in a long, ragged breath. I could tell he was making a special effort to say something he considered crucial. "You've repaid him many times. You've fought his enemies, won him treasures, expanded the boundaries of his kingdom. Perhaps by leaving, you'll be doing him the greatest service. Without you by his side, Duryodhan will not have the heart to continue fighting. He'll be forced to end the war. But if you continue to support him, it can only lead to his death—and the death of all his supporters."

"Duryodhan would rather die than face defeat," Karna said. "He's not afraid to die on the battlefield—and nor am I. In fact, I welcome it. It'll end the constant torment inside my brain. It'll be the one honorable way out of a life I'm sick of, where everything has gone wrong, where I'll never get what I've always longed for.

"And as for having repaid Duryodhan, the debt of salt can only be repaid with blood. You know this! Isn't that why you fought on his side, even though you loved the Pandavas more and knew their cause to be just? And thus, though I know he's doomed—no, because of it—I must stand by him against my brothers."

Bheeshma sighed. "Go then, grandson. Do your duty, and die an honorable death. When the time is right, we'll meet in heaven."

But Karna didn't leave. He clutched his head in his hands and bent over further. "But worst still is this: even knowing what I know, I desire her! I can't forget her shining, haughty face at the swayamvar—ah, how many years has it been?"

He was speaking of me! It was the last thing I'd expected him to bring up. My hands grew clammy. I clasped them to stop their shaking and held my breath to hear him better.

"The long line of her neck," he continued, "as she raised her chin. Her beautiful, parted lips. How her breast rose and fell with passion. All this time, I told myself I hated her for humiliating me worse than anyone else has done. That I wanted revenge. But I was only fooling myself. When Dussasan started pulling at her sari, I couldn't bear it. I wanted to knock him down, to shield her from the stares. The twelve years she was in the forest, I, too, slept on the ground, thinking of her discomfort. How many times I started to go to her, to beg her to come away with me, to be my queen. But I knew it was hopeless. She was completely loyal to her husbands. My words would only disgust her.

"When Kunti told me that if I joined her sons, I'd be king instead of Yudhisthir, I wasn't tempted. But when she used her final weapon, when she said that as her son I, too, would become Panchaali's husband—I was ready to give up my reputation, my honor, everything! I had to use all my willpower to remain silent!"

My heart beat so hard that I was sure Karna would hear it. Part of my mind was furious at Kunti. How dared she offer me to Karna as though I were no more than a slave girl! At the same time, I was gratified by Karna's response. Wasn't this what I'd secretly wanted all my life, to know that he was attracted to me, even against his will? That beneath his scornful exterior he held me in such tenderness? Why, then, did such a wave of sadness break over me as I heard his words?

Bheeshma was silent. Was he as taken aback by Karna's confession as I? Finally he said, "But you did remain silent, grandson. No man can help his thoughts—but you didn't abandon your principles for the sake of the woman you desired. That's more than I was able to do."

And then, to console Karna, he gave him one last gift. He told him the story of his past life, when he'd been a demigod: Prabhasa, the youngest and most imprudent of the eight Vasus.

.   .   .

Prabhasa's new wife wanted a cow. If Prabhasa truly cared for her, she said, he wouldn't deny her this small gift. No matter what Prabhasa said to change her mind, she wouldn't listen. She stomped her dainty foot and pouted charmingly.

The cow she'd set her heart on was no ordinary one. She was a wish-fulfilling cow that belonged to Sage Vasistha. Prabhasa's wife had seen her on a beautiful spring day when the Vasus visited earth to see how humans lived.

Prabhasa knew that the sage wouldn't gift them such a valuable cow or sell her. She would have to be stolen. There would be trouble as a result, a great deal of it. But he was in love. With the reluctant help of his seven brothers, he spirited the cow away.

In meditation, Vasistha learned what had happened. In rage he cursed all eight brothers. *You must be born on earth as humans and undergo all the suffering of humankind.* When they fell at his feet, begging forgiveness, he softened the sentence for the seven older Vasus. They would be born, yes, but their mother would drown them at once so they could return to their celestial existence. But Prabhasa would have to live for many years and endure many sorrows. Because he was kinder than most sages, Vasistha added a boon: he would be a hero, a warrior feared by all.

"As you can see," Bheeshma ended, "I did worse than you—and paid for it. But I learned from my experience. In this lifetime, I never trusted women. I stayed away from them as much as I could. And even then a woman was the cause of my downfall! Take an old man's advice: put Draupadi out of your mind and concentrate on the war."

. . .

When Karna touched Bheeshma's feet and rose to leave, his face was resolute again. Perhaps that is the miracle of stories. They make us realize that we're not alone in our folly and our suffering.

"Thank you, grandfather," he said, formal once more, "for this generosity that I did nothing to deserve. It emboldens me to make one last request. Tell no one the secret of my birth—either before my death, or after. I don't want my brothers to bear the terrible weight of fratricide. And most of all, I don't want *her* to pity me."

"I see you cannot forget Draupadi," Bheeshma said. "Well, I'm not the only keeper of your secret, but I promise. With one exception: after you die, I must tell Duryodhan the truth. Selfish as he is, he needs to realize how deep your friendship ran and how painful your sacrifice was. Perhaps it'll do him some good. But I'll make sure he tells no one else. Go now—the sun will rise soon and the battle begin, and you need rest."

I did not speak to Bheeshma after Karna left. My question—which after all was about an event that was done with—was petty in comparison to Karna's present dilemma. But more important, my whole being was shaken by the secrets Karna had disclosed. The slightest jolt would break me open.

I think Bheeshma sensed my presence, but he didn't call to me. Perhaps he wished to spare me the shame that comes of eavesdropping. Perhaps he guessed my own contraband feelings. Perhaps he was preoccupied—as was I—with Karna's challenge: to face his brothers in the field tomorrow and see the hatred of unknowing in their eyes. Or perhaps, as his end grew nearer, he tired of the knotted affairs of men—and women—and wished only for peace.

I curled myself tight under the thorn bush, pressed my face into my dusty, snarled hair, and wept silently for them both, each bound to his hasty, reckless vow. How a promise—made to another or to oneself—could paralyze a life! How pride had kept them from admitting their mistakes—and thus from the happiness that might have been theirs.

Only much later did I realize I was weeping for myself as well, my own lethal vow of vengeance that had locked the Pandavas and Kauravas in their stance of enmity.

· · ·

I knew I must keep what I learned to myself, but it was difficult.

All day I managed to avoid Kunti up on my hill, but in the evening when I faced her, my heart flung itself up and down in outrage. I couldn't help staring. This was the woman who had set a helpless baby afloat on a midnight river to save her reputation, thus beginning the chain of Karna's misery. When she saw him again as a young man, she held on to her secret, protecting herself at his cost. And even now, she'd told him not out of concern for him but merely to save her sons. That's why she'd urged him to join them. To entice him further, she'd offered me up to him as a prize! Was there no end to her manipulations?

Some of my anger must have shown in my eyes, for Kunti asked me, with some asperity, if I was coming down with something.

"I knew it was too much for you, going up that hill each day. But no! Always you must do something different from the others. Maybe tomorrow you should stay with us in the tent. You're no longer that young, you know."

"I'm fine," I said shortly, not trusting myself to speak further.

That night, the talk was all of Karna. Yudhisthir announced that now that Bheeshma had fallen, Karna had joined the fight. But he'd turned down Duryodhan's offer to make him the new commander!

I gave Kunti a quick glance. Disappointment, relief, and pride slid across her face in quick succession before it took on its customary aloofness.

As casually as I could, I asked, "Why would he do that?"

"He said that Drona, as the leading elder, deserved that position," Bheem answered. "Me—I wouldn't have been so magnanimous and given up my one chance at glory. Who knows how many days he has to live?"

Arjun had been silent all evening—I guessed that he couldn't get Bheeshma out of his mind. But at this he exclaimed that he couldn't wait to duel—and kill—Karna.

I caught a stricken look in Kunti's eyes before she lowered them. Soon after, without finishing her dinner, she left for her tent, saying that the damp made her joints ache. Wallking away, she seemed suddenly shrunken.

A little of my anger faded. I remembered my girlhood sympathy for Karna's unknown mother. When Kunti gave birth to Karna, she'd been young and afraid, with no one to confide in. Could I have done any better in her place? She'd made Karna suffer, yes, but hadn't she suffered just as much? And now it was too late. If she told Yudhisthir about his elder brother, he would lose heart. The kind of man he was, he might even give up the war rather than commit fratricide. So instead, now she'd have to watch her sons kill each other, knowing that she'd brought it about. No wonder she'd tried to sacrifice me in a last effort to prevent such a calamity.

I remembered how in my dream a weeping Karna had raised Kunti up and kissed her hands. If he could forgive her—he who had been the primary victim of her fear—shouldn't I at least try?

I followed and found her lying facedown on her pallet. She'd been weeping. At my voice, she hastily wiped her eyes and glared at me.

"What do you want?" she snapped.

But for once, instead of bristling in annoyance, I heard the vulnerability beneath the pride. I told her I had a balm made of turmeric and shallaki, excellent for stiff joints. Would she like me to bring her some? She peered at me with suspicion, but finally she nodded, and so, for the first time I became her daughter-in-law—I did something for her that she hadn't demanded. I rubbed her legs until she fell into a twitching sleep, and as her muscles relaxed against my fingertips, I found that by some inexplicable osmosis Kunti's secret had become my secret. I, too, would guard it now.

Perhaps the smell of the balm had put me in a trance, for as I moved my hands back and forth, I thought I saw hanging in the night sky a great web, its glinting threads woven from our present nature and our past actions. Karna was caught in it, as was I. Others were enmeshed there, too: Kunti, my husbands, Bheeshma, even Duryodhan and Dussasan. If there was a way to escape the web, I couldn't see it. Our puny struggles only entangled us further. A strange compassion came upon me as I watched us twist and turn in the breeze.

I tried to hold on to this compassion, sensing its preciousness, but even as I reached to grasp it, it dissipated into wisps. No revelation can endure unless it is bolstered by a calm, pure mind—and I'm afraid I didn't possess that.

avalanche

Now it was Drona's turn to ride the beast of war. Drona whom I trusted less than the grandfather. Drona who cared more about victory than about the paths he needed to take to get there. Under him, the Kaurava attitude toward the battle underwent a change. Bheeshma had had his faults, stubborn and autocratic as he was. But he didn't compromise on values. He upheld righteousness and expected his underlings to do the same. And they obeyed him— if not from love then from fear. Now, without his keen and critical gaze, their morals began to disintegrate. And, as echoes from one avalanche set off other avalanches, the actions of Duryodhan's warriors affected the behavior of our army.

Drona was still a fearsome warrior, but age sat on him more heavily than on Bheeshma. Deep down he knew that, unlike Bheeshma who had been bound by his word, he was here by his own choice. It leached away some of his certitude. He'd have to make up for it by being additionally harsh.

On that first day, as he rallied the soldiers by taunting them, the sight pulled me into his mind, that place where even the most equivocal among us cannot escape truth. He was thinking that he could have left the Kaurava court long ago and returned to a life of austerities. Indeed, as a brahmin, he should have done so once he'd finished teaching the princes and received, in payment, the vengeance he so longed for. What tempted him to stay? Was it prestige? In his hermitage he would have been forgotten, but at court he sat next to the blind king, his immense, carved seat second in elegance only to the grandfather's. Was it the handsome remuneration he was paid for the military advice he provided? No. The pleasures of money and fame had long paled for him. It was love, that tricky shackle, which immobilized him.

Aswatthama, Drona's only son, had joined Duryodhan's coterie and, emulating the prince, had developed a fondness for lavish living. Drona sighed as he thought of Aswatthama the child, whose long-ago tears for the glass of milk he couldn't have had set in motion the first act of this drama. And of Aswatthama the youth, hotheaded and full of complaints, who had taken Duryodhan's side when the prince accused Drona of being too fond of Arjun. You care for him even more than for me, he'd cried bitterly. Drona, so good with weapons, had failed to find the words to tell him that everything he'd done so far, all the compromises he'd made, had been for love of him alone. One time, when Drona had mentioned the possibility of retiring from court, Aswatthama laughed, incredulous and scornful. *You want me to leave all my friends here for some godforsaken village in some backwater?* Drona, who understood the world somewhat better than the boy, knew that his presence at court and his power as adviser to the king contributed significantly to Aswatthama's popularity. And so for the sake of his son he remained, saying to himself, Another year, just another year. Until the day he found himself in a trampled field by a blood-red lake leading a million doomed men into battle for a cause he didn't believe in—and knew it was too late.

.   .   .

A long time ago, Arjun told me a story.

One day, to test their learning, Drona took the princes on a hunt. Arjun, as usual, was the star: he shot down the swiftest birds just by listening to the sound of their wings; he killed the fiercest boar with a single arrow; when the princes grew thirsty, he sent an arrow into the earth, and a cool spring gushed up.

But then something strange happened. His hunting dog had rushed ahead of him into the forest, barking. Suddenly the barking stopped. When the dog returned, whimpering, someone had shut his mouth with a muzzle made of seven interlaced arrows, shot carefully to silence the dog without hurting him. Mystified, they went to see who could have achieved such a feat. Deep in the forest they found a young man dressed in leopard skins.

"Who is your teacher?" Drona asked.

The youth fell at Drona's feet and said, "It is you, master."

Drona was taken aback. Then he remembered that, years ago in Hastinapur, a boy from a distant hill-tribe had come to him, begging to learn archery. Drona had refused, saying that he did not teach the lowborn. The boy had left without argument. He recognized the boy in this youth, now a master archer. The man—his name was Ekalavya—explained that, after Drona's refusal, he had retreated to the forest. There he made a clay image of Drona. Each day he prayed to it before practicing archery—and that is how he learned all the amazing things that he knew.

Arjun was furious. All his life Drona had promised him that he would make him into the greatest archer in the world. But here was this simple, self-taught man, already more skilled than Arjun could ever hope to be!

Drona guessed Arjun's thoughts. He said to Ekalavya, "If I'm your master, you must give me dakshina."

"Of course!" said the young man, filled with joy that the teacher was finally accepting him. "Whatever you want, I'll give it to you."

"I want your right thumb," Drona said.

Everyone around him—even Arjun—went silent with shock, but Ekalavya didn't hesitate. He sliced off his thumb and laid it at Drona's feet—and Arjun was left without a rival.

To Arjun the incident proved how much his teacher loved him. But I, thinking of the forever-lost talent of Ekalavya as I looked down at Kurukshetra, wondered if it didn't demonstrate Drona's ruthlessness, his readiness to do anything to win. What shape would that ruthlessness take over the next few days?

. . .

Though I was concerned about what Drona might do, he only captured a small part of my attention. The rest of me yearned to find out how Karna was faring, how he conducted himself in battle. But the sight controlled me and would not allow me to turn to him. What was its cruel purpose? Even when momentous events occurred around Karna, I had to hear of them secondhand.

Such was the case with Ghatotkacha's death.

Ghatotkacha, that sweet, open-faced boy, had turned out to be a savage warrior, his father Bheem's rival at destroying enemy soldiers. He had an added advantage: since he was a rakshasa, a being of night, his powers increased as the day waned. When the Kaurava warriors were at their most tired, just before the trumpets announced an end to the battle day, he would fall upon them and slaughter them. On such an evening, when it seemed as though he would never stop, a desperate Duryodhan begged Karna to put an end to his carnage. Karna hesitated. Only one astra he possessed—the Shakti—had the power to kill Ghatotkacha. But he was saving it to use on Arjun.

But a panicked Duryodhan said, "I order you as your king—do whatever you must to kill Ghatotkacha."

Karna was left with no choice. He chanted the mantra that would call up the Shakti. When Ghatotkacha saw the whirling missile speeding at him, spitting fire, he knew his last moment had arrived. Perhaps his heart quailed, but his voice was steady enough as he told Bheem to report the manner of his dying to his mother. Then by rakshasa magic he grew to an immense size. When the astra exploded his chest, he leaned forward so that, falling, he would crush as many of the enemy as possible.

By this point in the war, we had seen countless dear ones perish. But Ghatotkacha's fall made us suffer a different pain. He was the first of our children to die. Bheem looked around him with unfocused eyes, mumbling that this was a perversion of nature. That sons should be arranging a father's funeral rites, and not the other way around. My own sorrow as I tried to calm him, though real enough, was many-pointed and guilt-ridden. I feared that without the one weapon that could have protected him from Arjun, Karna was now doomed. Was Kunti, too, thinking the same conflicted thought as she rocked back and forth, keening beneath her breath?

. . .

From the beginning Drona knew that he couldn't defeat the Pandavas in open battle. He decided on a different strategy. He would capture Yudhisthir and, in this way, end the war. But this, too, was impossible as long as Arjun guarded his brother. So each morning he asked a different king to challenge Arjun to fight, luring him to a distant part of the field. Though he realized what was happening, Arjun couldn't turn down the challenge: such was the illogical kshatriya code! When he killed one challenger, another warrior took his place. Susarma, Satyaratha, Satyadharma—their names scatter in my memory as dry grass before the wind. Still, each day Arjun returned in time to protect his brother and foil Drona's plan.

Drona grew more furious as time passed. On the thirteenth day of the war, after Arjun had been drawn away again, he decided on a different strategy. He formed his army into the devastating and invincible formation known as the padma vyuha, and began to steadily advance upon the Pandava army. Even the greatest Pandava warriors could not break it apart, for a padma vyuha, shaped like a thousand-petaled lotus, can only be destroyed from the inside. Duryodhan was delighted. "What a wonderful idea!" he cried. "Now that Arjun's out of the way, no one can penetrate our war formation. Let's make use of this and wreak as much havoc on the enemy as possible. Maybe today is the day we'll get to Yudhisthir!"

Drona bowed in acknowledgment of the compliment, but he said, "There is one other person in the Pandava army that knows how to penetrate the lotus."

"Who is it?" Duryodhan asked, his euphoria fading.

"Abhimanyu, who learned it from his father, Arjun."

"We must stop him somehow!"

Drona shook his head. There was a feral smile on his face. "We can't stop him. He's too good a fighter. But don't worry. The others will not be able to follow him in. And Abhimanyu hasn't yet learned how to extricate himself from the vyuha once he enters it."

My head swam as I realized Drona's diabolical plot. If only I could send word to Yudhisthir and save Abhimanyu! But it was impossible.

Duryodhan took the costliest jewel from his crown and offered it to Drona. "Truly you are a master strategist! Even Bheeshma couldn't have conceived of such an infallible plan. So this is how we'll destroy Arjun!"

As Drona had foreseen, a desperate Yudhisthir asked Abhimanyu to break through the vyuha, promising that he and his brothers would follow close behind. I focused all my mental power on Abhimanyu, begging him to excuse himself, but I failed. An excited Abhimanyu was delighted to finally be of help to his uncles.

When Abhimanyu saluted Yudhisthir and drove his chariot into the army amassed in front of him, I shut my eyes in despair. But the sight was relentless. And so from behind my closed lids I saw it all: how the vyuha locked up immediately behind Abhimanyu; how the lock was guarded by Jayadrath, my onetime abductor who had received a boon to withstand the Pandavas as long as Arjun was not with them; how the Pandavas, unable to aid their nephew, despaired. Inside the vyuha, Abhimanyu, realizing he was doomed, decided to make his death as expensive for his enemy as possible. None could withstand him in fair fight, this boy so like his father, until finally six of their best warriors fell upon him all together, in violation of the most important code of war. Coming up behind him, they cut the string from his bow and the hilt from his sword. They killed his charioteer and his horses and smashed his chariot. Still he wrenched out a broken wheel and advanced upon them, asking only that they fight him one at a time. But they would not honor this last request. So Abhimanyu fell, his beautiful face turned toward the women's tent where Uttara waited, his eyes filled with astonishment at the perfidy of men he'd respected as heroes. And his killers—so greatly had war altered them—roared their triumph like beasts.

Who were among the killers, these warriors who trampled honor into the bloody ground beneath their feet to commit this heinous act? Drona was there, and Aswatthama, and—yes, the sight chose this moment to grant me my wish that I should observe him in action—Karna.

. . .

I remained on the hill that night. I knew that in their anguish none on the Pandava side would pay attention to my absence. I could not bear to be there when Uttara found out the news. But the cruel night air carried every sound of lamentation to me. Uttara was in a frenzy, tearing her hair and beating her breast, calling on death to come for her, too. She flung herself on the ground unmindful of the child in her womb, while the other women, putting aside their own losses, tried to restrain her. I could feel the suffering of my husbands, their rage surpassed by their excruciating guilt, for had they not pressed him, Abhimanyu would never have entered the formation on his own. Each one wished that he'd died in Abhimanyu's stead. But theirs was not to be such a quick release.

When he finally learned what had occurred, Arjun fell down in a swoon so deep that his brothers were afraid he'd perished of sorrow. But Krishna touched his chest and said, his voice stern, "Your son died most nobly. Be a worthy father to him!" Then Arjun awoke and took water in his hand and spoke a dreadful oath: If by sunset tomorrow he did not kill Jayadrath, who had prevented his brothers from entering the formation to support Abhimanyu, he would commit suicide.

I lay on the hill under the great, wheeling stars. I had no energy left for raging, I to whom rage had come so easily all my life. Fog had stained the dark; the heavenly bodies were dim. It seemed to me that with the murder—for so it was—of Abhimanyu, a glory had passed from the earth. We were firmly in the grasp of Kali, the age of injustice. The war had festered. Neither Kaurava nor Pandava would escape its infection. I wept for Abhimanyu, that guileless, golden boy who would have been king after Yudhisthir, and for all of us who loved him. I wept in fear of what would happen if Arjun failed to fulfill his vow. I wept in remorse for the part I'd played in pushing the Pandavas into war, for now I'd begun to realize its full horror. Finally I wept for Karna, who had lived all his life for honor only to lose it today. He had cut away his armor and with it his hopes of victory rather than be known as a man who broke his word. For the sake of his good name he had given up the possibility of his brothers' love. He had curbed his longing for me to stand by his friend. But now he would be remembered as the murderer of a defenseless boy.

What subversive power did war possess that it could turn even such a man into a butcher?

. . .

Perhaps it was good that Abhimanyu fell when he did. He could die believing that the Pandavas, at least, had maintained the battle code with which they'd brought him up. He didn't have to witness how, in the days that followed, they, too, swerved from honor when it was expedient, attacking the unarmed and maimed, justifying their actions by stating it was for the ultimate good. Even Krishna played his part, creating the illusion of a false sunset so Jayadrath would think he was safe—and then, when Jayadrath stood up in triumph, urging Arjun to behead him. But the worst was how they killed Drona.

After Abhimanyu's death, Drona fought like a demon, discarding every one of the laws he'd helped set up a mere fifteen days ago. Goaded by Duryodhan's poison tongue or by self-loathing, he forced his exhausted troops to attack at night, when the Pandava army had retired to rest. He turned his divine astras on common soldiers who had no way of withstanding them, transforming entire battalions into charred masses. In an attempt to break Dhri's spirit and render the prophecy of his death false, he singled out my family and killed, in one afternoon, my father and all three of Dhri's sons.

Perhaps Krishna was right in declaring that Drona must be stopped by whatever means necessary. Still, there was something shameful in the way it was done. Bheem killed an elephant that had the same name as Drona's son and announced to Drona that Aswatthama was dead. But Drona said, "My son is too fine a warrior to be killed by the likes of you! I will believe it only if Yudhisthir, who never lies, declares it to be true." Yudhisthir was caught in a terrible dilemma. But finally, weighing the lives of all the hapless men gathered to fight for him against his personal good, he gave up the virtue by which he'd lived his whole life and said it was so.

Then Drona dropped his weapons in despair, closed his eyes and sat in prayer. Seeing this, Dhri—my gentle brother who until then had not fallen prey to the insanity of war—rushed at him with his upraised sword. With all my strength I cried to him to stop—but once again I was merely an observer, helpless to intervene. Even as the Pandavas shouted that he should take Drona captive but spare his life, he beheaded the man who had, in a happier time, been the greatest teacher he'd known. Drona's blood spurted over my brother. He held up his dripping hands and roared with laughter, calling on the spirits of his father and sons to see how he avenged them. I shuddered. Bile rose in my throat. His laughter was so like that of the men who had killed Abhimanyu that had I not been watching, I couldn't have told them apart.

Thus my brother fulfilled the fate he was born for, gaining revenge and losing himself, and spawning (for such is the nature of vengeance) a further drama of hate.

wheel

When Karna became commander, some semblance of order was restored to the battle. He sent a proclamation to both sides, urging a return to righteousness. *It is certain to me that most of us shall not leave this field alive*, he wrote. *How shall we behave, then, in these last days? Would you rather the gods welcome us to the loka meant for heroes, or do you wish to be banished to the tortures of narak?* Perhaps the warning about hell struck a chord in the hearts of the kings, for in the next days they extended a grudging chivalry to each other.

For his part, Karna practiced his own philosophy. I sensed that he bitterly regretted his part in the death of Abhimanyu, that moment when in the blood-heat of battle he forgot himself. Perhaps in recompense—or because of the secret that clawed at him from within—he spared, one after the other, Sahadev, Nakul, Bheem—and most important, Yudhisthir, when he had them at his mercy. In this one instance he was disloyal to Duryodhan. He was careful not to rouse their suspicion, though, and taunted them mercilessly before he let them go. Only I saw the way he gazed after them in sorrow and tenderness.

The common soldiers adored Karna. Thanks to him, they no longer lived in constant fear of the pitiless astras that could, in an eyeblink, turn a disciplined battalion into a writhing mass of agony.

They could rest at night without worrying that they might be attacked without notice. But mostly they loved him because, in the evenings after the other maharathis had retired to their tents, he walked among them. He offered solace to the wounded and made sure they were given what comfort was available. To those who would go into battle the next morning, he spoke bluntly and honestly, man to man. *I cannot promise you safety, but this much I know. Whoever wins—Yudhisthir or Duryodhan, he will take care of the families of those who fight faithfully in this battle.* Such was the power of his conviction that men who were ready to desert changed their minds. I wonder if Duryodhan ever knew that it was Karna's words that held his dwindled army together in its last moments. This was how things stood on the seventeeth day of the war, when Karna and Arjun faced each other.

From the beginning it was clear that this duel was unlike their previous encounters. It would end only when one of them died. By unspoken consent, soldiers on both sides stopped their skirmishes to watch. (If they lived, this would be the story they'd tell their grandchildren.) Vyasa has written that the gods themselves came to see this amazing fight. I believe him, for though I couldn't see them, I felt an electric presence in the air, a deep, if impersonal, sadness.

As for myself, I prayed desperately for the sight to be taken from me—at least for the duration of this duel. Whatever its outcome (and already I guessed what it would be), for me there was only pain. But the sight, inexorable, descended on me clearer than ever so that it was as though I were in the midst of the fighting, close enough to hear every indrawn hiss of pain.

Vyasa describes it as a glorious battle, equally matched, each hero countering the other's astras with unconcern. This was certainly true of Arjun. For the first time, I felt his concentration, pure, exhilarated, the way he focused on his task as if it were the one point of light in a drowning darkness. Who could resist admiring a talent so absolute and deadly? Not I, even as my heart twisted in fear of what would happen to Karna.

As Karna ordered his chariot to be driven up to Arjun's, his face was equally calm. But I felt the storm of agitation that swept through him. He was not a man to deceive himself. He knew already that, having used up the Shakti, he could not defeat Arjun. He knew that Arjun was determined to kill him. But it wasn't the fear of death that shook him. Nor did his charioteer, Salya, the uncle of the Pandavas, manage to dispirit him by extolling Arjun's greatness. No. Karna was debilitated by his own knowledge. Because where Arjun faced a hated enemy, Karna was facing his younger brother.

Had Kunti realized this would happen? Had she told him her secret on purpose, so that when the moment arrived, he wouldn't be able to focus his entire will behind the arrows he let fly at the son she loved more?

Still, Karna was a true warrior—and a true friend. He gave the battle everything he had. He quenched Arjun's fire arrows with his storm arrows. He invoked the Bhargav astra, named after his guru, powerful enough to wipe out tens of thousands of warriors. When Arjun neutralized it with the Brahmastra, he invoked the Nagastra, the deadliest missile he had left. It turned into a poisonous serpent and sped toward Arjun. Who knows what might have happened if Krishna hadn't intervened? He spoke a word to the horses. They knelt in response, lowering the front of the chariot. The arrow passed through Arjun's jeweled crown, disintegrating it, but Arjun's life was saved.

I noticed with relief that the sun was setting. The duel would have to be called off until the next day. I let out a breath I'd been holding for so long that my lungs burned. My entire body ached with tension. But I'd been granted a reprieve! Tonight, I decided, I would do what I should have done much earlier. I would tell my husbands the truth about Karna. Many would hate me for doing this. Perhaps it would sway the outcome of the war against us. Still, I couldn't bear to watch my husband killing his brother without knowing what a terrible thing he did.

But as I waited for the commanders to give the signal for the armies to withdraw, Karna's chariot suddenly tilted sideways. One of his wheels was embedded in the earth—strange, for they were on high, hard ground. Karna jumped down to free it, but he failed. His face grew pale; his brow was beaded with sweat. He was remembering the brahmin's curse: *You will die when you are helpless*. No! He couldn't perish like this, so pitifully, without a chance to fight back! Still struggling with the wheel, he called out to Arjun to remember the code of honor and give him a moment to ready himself.

Before Arjun could respond, Krishna turned to him. "Don't do it! This is the man who instigated Dussasan to humiliate Panchaali in the royal court, in the sight of all! Did he think of honor then?"

No! I cried. No matter how terrible that incident had been, I didn't want to be the goad Krishna used to prod Arjun into killing Karna.

Rage flashed across Arjun's face, but he hesitated. He was thinking that he didn't want to be remembered as a warrior who attacked an unarmed opponent. He wanted people to know that he was powerful enough to kill Karna in a fair fight.

"He butchered your son, who was fighting off five other men. He approached him from the back and cut the strings of his bow," Krishna continued. "What would the shade of Abhimanyu feel if he saw your misplaced mercy now?"

Ah, Krishna! He knew the exact note he needed to play upon the flute of our passions! Arjun's jaw hardened. He raised his bow.

Karna saw the look on his face. He dropped the wheel and began to chant a mantra—a simple one to bring him a weapon, any weapon, but almost immediately he faltered. He realized what was happening. The cruelest curse, his dear teacher's, was taking effect. *Your knowledge will fail,* Parasuram had raged, *when you need it the most.* He knew his time had come. He raised his hand in a gesture that an observer might have taken as a plea, but I recognized it as one of forgiveness. Arjun released his arrow. It sped through the air like a comet, trailing unhindered fire. Just before it reached its mark, Karna smiled.

. . .

What did I feel, seeing Karna fall? Part of me was glad that the unbearable tension of the battle was over. Part was relieved that my husband had won, that he was safe. Part realized that we were now very close to achieving the vengeance I'd craved—though it gave me no satisfaction. Part was thankful that this dreadful war would now end—for without Karna, what hope did Duryodhan have? Part sorrowed that a great warrior and a noble soul had died. But the part that was a girl at a swayamvar facing a young man whose eyes grew dark with pain at her words, the part that didn't owe loyalty to the Pandavas yet, couldn't hold back her tears. Regret racked me. How might Karna's life have turned out if I'd allowed him to compete that day? If he'd won? The longing that I'd suppressed all these years crashed over me like a wave, bringing me to my knees. He'd died believing that I hated him. How I wished it could have been otherwise!

Vyasa writes: *At the moment when Karna died, the sun plunged behind a cloud so dark that people feared it would not return. Despite the brutality of his death, his face held an enigmatic smile. A divine glow left his body and circled the battlefield as though searching for something before it discarded this world.* Some have doubted his words, but I can vouch for their truth.

But here's something Vyasa didn't put down in his *Mahabharat*: Leaving the field, the glow traveled to a nearby hill, where it paused for a moment over a weeping woman. Before it soared into the sky and disappeared, it grew into a great radiance around me. A feeling emanated from it that I have no words for. It wasn't sorrow or rage. Perhaps, freed of its mortal bondage, Karna's spirit knew what I hadn't ever been able to tell him.

When the glow faded, I was left with a strange comfort, a belief that this was not the end of Karna's story.

owl

After the death of Karna, I didn't want to climb the hill again. I was no longer interested in the war. I didn't want anyone to realize this, so I continued to go up there. But once there I would lie on the ground and close my eyes and try to send my mind far away. I realized now that the main reason I'd accepted the sight from Vyasa was for the opportunity to watch Karna the way I never could in real life, to decipher the enigma that he was. Now I understood him—his nobility, his loyalty, his pride, his anger, his uncomplaining acceptance of the injustice of his life, his forgiveness. But the weight of this knowledge that I could not share with anyone was crushing me.

We'd hoped that with Karna's death the war would end, but Duryodhan refused to give up. How could he? As he declaimed to Aswatthama, the only friend he had left after Karna's fall: Having been emperor of the earth, having tasted life's pleasures to the full, having stamped on the heads of my enemies, how can I now go with joined palms to my hated cousins, begging for mercy? For once, I understood him and agreed. Any end other than a death-by-battle would have been an anticlimax to the Kaurava prince's furious life.

I shut my eyes, but as I'd feared, the sight did not release me. And so I saw Salya, last of the commanders, fall to Yudhisthir's javelin. With his final breath he sent a blessing to his nephew, not knowing that in doing so he burdened him further with guilt. I saw the last of the Kaurava chariots explode, the last of the horses and foot soldiers die. Now only four warriors were left: Duryodhan, Kripa, Kritavarma, and Aswatthama. The wounded, heart-sore king entered a lake, chanting a mantra that would allow him to rest underwater for a time. But spies informed the Pandavas of this; they arrived at the lake and challenged Duryodhan to a final confrontation. I saw the Kaurava prince leave his sanctuary, impelled by the pride that had always been his downfall.

And so the last battle took place at Samantapanchaka, a place once considered holy but now laid waste by war. Around my husbands the land stretched sick and discolored, great, gaping holes torn into its side by the blasts of astras. The few remaining trees were leafless skeletons. There was no sign of the many birds and beasts that had roamed here peacefully just a few weeks ago. Only vultures sat on dead branches, waiting in eerie silence. This was what we had done to our earth.

. . .

Nakul said: "You know how Eldest Brother is, very noble and admirable, only sometimes he doesn't think things through. So he tells Duryodhan, You're alone here and tired out, and there's five of us against you, which isn't fair. Why don't you fight a duel with one of us—you can choose the person you want to fight, and you can choose your weapon, too. Whoever wins will rule Hastinapur.

"We stared at him, quite horrified. We knew that none of us except Bheem was equal to Duryodhan, not if he chose to battle with the gada, which of course he would, it being his favorite weapon. Krishna was furious. He told Eldest Brother, You're a fool. Millions of men have died in the last few days to protect you from Duryodhan. Your brothers have faced the greatest dangers to secure your victory. Panchaali has wept and prayed for this moment through thirteen years of hardship and humiliation. I myself have manipulated dharma to help you. Now you throw it all away with one grandiose gesture? You know that Duryodhan learned gada-yuddha from my brother Balaram, the world's greatest mace fighter. No one in the world can beat him at it. You should have just killed him when you had the chance.

"Things could have gone really badly, but we were saved by Duryodhan's arrogance. He said, Not one among the lot of you is a fit opponent for me, other than perhaps Bheem. I invite him to duel me. In this way, when I kill him and gain back my rightful kingdom, I'll have the satisfaction of having fought a good fight.

"We breathed a sigh of relief, but our joy was short-lived. As soon as they began, we could see how good Duryodhan was, how lightly and gracefully he sidestepped Bheem's blows, how cannily yet viciously he struck. We remembered what our spies had reported: Years back, he'd had his armorers make him an iron statue of Bheem. Every night he practiced on it, and with every strike his hatred of our brother grew. He'd even had it brought to Kurukshetra. Today, he'd called upon all of that hate to fuel his strength. Our Bheem didn't have enough malice in him to counter that force.

"They fought for an hour. Two. Bheem was getting tired, I could tell. Duryodhan hit him so hard in the chest that he staggered and almost fell. Recovering, he hit Duryodhan on the shoulder with all his strength. It was a blow that would have shattered anyone else's bones. But Duryodhan didn't even wince. We remembered another report: Before the war started, his mother, Gandhari, asked him to come before her naked. (Out of modesty, though, he wore a loincloth.) She undid her blindfold and sent the power of her penances into his body, making invincible whichever part her eyes touched.

"What chance did Bheem have against that?

"Even Krishna was looking worried as he watched the fight. He whispered something to Arjun, who caught Bheem's eye and slapped his thigh. The gesture—it looked familiar. Then it came back: that shameful day in the sabha when Duryodhan had bared his thigh and invited you to come to him. Bheem's oath that he'd take revenge. And he did! He barreled ahead, thrusting his gada at Duryodhan. Duryodhan jumped high to evade him, but Bheem had been feinting. He whirled and struck, catching the tops of Duryodhan's thighs, and, with a sound like a lightning crack, broke them. The duel was over.

"We were delighted but dismayed as well. Bheem had violated the most important law of gada-yuddha, hitting Duryodhan below the navel. There was sure to be consequences. Indeed, the skies grew dark. The earth shook. You must have felt it, even here in the women's tent. Balaram—did I tell you he'd joined us?—was livid. He came after Bheem, threatening to kill him, and stopped only when Krishna grasped his arms and begged him to calm down. Before he left, he told him, Because you cheated so despicably, Duryodhan will be glorified and remembered as the best of fighters. He will reach heaven, whereas you'll face everlasting shame.

"Bheem lowered his head in deference to Balaram, but his back was stiff with stubbornness. He said, I stand by my action. I did it for Yudhisthir, whom Duryodhan cheated of his heritage, and for Panchaali, whom he insulted the way no woman should ever be. What kind of man would I be if I hadn't kept the vow I made for her?

"What did Krishna have to say to all this, you're asking?

"When Duryodhan cursed him for teaching us the unfair tricks by which we won the war, he smiled and said, I take care of my own—in whichever way possible. The moment when Panchaali gave up struggling with Dussasan and called on me to save her, in that moment your death warrant was signed. If there's sin in what I did, I'll gladly shoulder it for her sake.

"What happened? Why are you crying? Did I say something wrong? Now you're laughing? Ah, women! I'll never understand them!"

. . .

That night, following the ancient laws, we stayed in different places. Krishna and my five husbands lay in the vanquished Kaurava camp, as winners were expected to do. Dhri, Sikhandi, my five sons, and the handful of soldiers that had survived the massacre slept in the Pandava camp. I longed to join them. There was so much I wanted to say and to hear from each of them. Above all, I wanted to touch my boys, to feel their arms and legs and faces, to run my hands over their wounds. Only then would I fully believe that the horror of this war was over and that they'd survived it. I swore that I would be a better mother from now on, giving them all the attention they desired, repairing the relationship I'd sadly neglected these past years. But for one more night I had to be patient and remain in the women's tent.

All of the women were too excited to sleep, so late into the night we prepared for the victory feast. It would be tinged with sadness, yes, but at least this terrible war was at an end. Even Uttara was in better spirits. The baby had kicked for the first time today. We took that as a blessing sign. As I rolled balls of sweet dough for frying, I silently thanked the gods that amidst all this devastation, the people I cared for most (all except one) were alive. I was so much more fortunate than the other women: Subhadra, Uttara, Kunti, far-off Hidimba who by now must have received news of her only child's end. And Gandhari, who would soon be bereft of every one of her hundred sons. A dark thought uncoiled my mind: I who was a major cause of so much destruction had no right to be so lucky. I talked and laughed louder and busied myself with the details of the feast, but it wouldn't leave me.

When at last I went to bed, I was overtaken by a dream unlike any I'd ever had. In it I was transformed to a man—who it was I didn't know, though I could feel his hopeless rage. Was it Duryodhan? No. I moved, slithering on my belly through the night to avoid detection. I made my way across a barren plain to a broken body and wept over it. It was the Kaurava prince—my prince, barely alive, still in agony. How unjustly had he been reduced to this pitiful state! I promised him revenge (that word so familiar on my parched tongue) and crept to the base of a tree in a frenzy of thought. I had no army, no chariot, no horse, no father to guide me (ah, they'd butchered him). My two companions, wounded as I, overcome by exhaustion, slept beside me. But despair would not let me rest. I stared into the tangle of branches overhead where I could see a nest of sleeping crows. As I watched, an owl materialized in the dark sky. It swept down, its wings like smoke. (Where had I seen it before?) It was as silent as the death it brought. It killed every crow in its sleep, then disappeared into the satisfied fog.

I clenched my jaw in glee. I knew what I must do. I shook my companions awake. When they saw my face, they feared I'd gone mad. Be calm, Aswatthama, they begged. But it was not a time for calmness. I told them my plan. By the horror in their eyes, I knew it was good. They resisted, but I reminded them of our oath to our prince. When I led the way, they followed, and I knew they would obey.

. . .

I awoke in the women's tent, screaming and thrashing. Failing to calm me, my attendants ran to fetch the other queens. Kunti declared I was possessed by an evil spirit and called for red chilies, which she burned over a flame, making us all cough. Subhadra splashed water on my face and chanted prayers. Uttara watched from the doorway, her arms wrapped around her belly, disquiet on her face. I pushed past them all, not caring that I was still in night-clothes, and shouted for a chariot, for the guards to come with me. My face must have convinced them of my urgency, for they rushed to fetch their weapons. Even Kunti fell silent. But it was too late. The night mists were lifting. I'd wandered too long in the maze of the dream.

When we reached it, the Pandava camp was ablaze. A few servants ran here and there, wailing, trying to drag out bodies. Our guards put out the fire and helped assemble the dead. They brought a man to me. He fell at my feet, gibbering with terror. Through soot and bruises I recognized him: Dhri's charioteer. Dhri had told me once, I'd trust him with my life. Through the carnage of Kurukshetra, he'd managed to keep my brother safe.

He told me that Aswatthama had crept into the camp and overpowered my sleeping brother. When Dhri begged him to give him a chance to die fighting, he'd laughed a maniac's laugh and started to strangle him.

Choking, my brother had entreated, At least kill me cleanly with a weapon and give me an end that's fitting for a warrior!

Aswatthama replied, What end can be more fitting than this for a man who killed his guru when he'd dropped his weapons? I'll make sure you die in a way that will ensure your passage to hell.

He kicked my unconscious brother until he was dead.

"He was as strong and bloodthirsty as a rakshasa," the man cried, "and like them he struck silently at night. By the time we realized he was in the camp, he'd already killed your brother Sikhandi, and all five of your children. If only he'd killed me, too—"

My ears refused to hear any more, or maybe it was my mind that stopped. I walked to where they'd laid the bodies. Dhri's face was so swollen and discolored with bruises, at first I couldn't recognize him. I sat and placed his head on my lap. I asked the guards to place my dead children around me, to bring Sikhandi. His long hair had been torn from his head. I ran a hand over his lacerated scalp, too numb to weep. My sons' mouths were O's of blood, open as though they were still screaming.

A part of me screamed, too, but without sound. Why should this happen to me now, after all the other things I'd suffered already—just when I thought my troubles were finally over? But a part said, She who sows vengeance must reap its bloody fruit. Have you not had a hand in turning Aswatthama into the monster he is to-day? But the largest part of me refused to believe what I saw, what I touched. It waited for them to disappear the way dream images do in the morning. When they didn't, my mind detached itself from my body and flew away. I was a girl again in Kampilya, behind a curtain, whispering to Dhri the words he didn't remember from his lessons. Later, on our lonely terrace, I hung on his words as he explained to me the rules of righteous war. I watched Sikhandi walk across the marble floor of my room toward me; I heard him tell me the pain of his past life as Amba. At our gates, I held his callused hand and begged him not to leave us yet. Older, I ran after my children in the gardens of the Palace of Illusions, scolding them for some childhood naughtiness while they dodged me, laughing. One of them plucked an aparajita flower and stuck it in my hair. I gathered him in my arms. I would never let him—any of them—go.

But a flute was calling me, sweet but insistent, refusing to allow me to rest. I cried to be left in peace. I was too weary; the world was too hard. But its haunting notes snared me and tugged me back across a chasm. When I awoke (is *awoke* the word I'm looking for?) Krishna was passing his hands over my face.

"Be strong!" he said. "Such is the nature of war, and you're not the only one to feel its lash. As a winner, you can't take the easy way of oblivion. Many responsibilities will be waiting for you. We'll speak of this again—but for now I must leave you. Bheem has already gone in pursuit of Aswatthama. Arjun and I must help him, or else Aswatthama will kill him, too."

In this way the chariot of vengeance, which requires no horses or wheels, rolled on.

. . .

They found Aswatthama by the Ganga, where he'd fled after informing the dying Duryodhan of what he'd done. Aswatthama fought Arjun with the one-pointed strength of desperation, and when it was clear he couldn't win, he loosened upon the world the terrible Brahmaseershastra with the command, *May the earth be rid of the seed of the Pandavas.* Arjun countered it by sending his own astra.

Vyasa writes: *As the two flames coursed along the sky, oceans began to dry up and mountains to crumble. Men and beasts screamed their terror, for the fabric of the world was about to be ripped apart. Watching from the edge of the tale, I was forced to intervene, though that is not my preference. I stepped out between the flames and raised my hands. By the power of my penances, for a moment the astras were rendered immobile. I chided the two warriors for forgetting themselves and their responsibilities toward the earth-goddess. I demanded that they recall their weapons.*

Arjun obeyed, but Aswatthama the tainted (as he would be known from now) no longer had the power to pull back his astra. As he gabbled useless chants, it aimed itself at the unborn child in Uttara's womb. In the women's tent, they saw the sky begin to burn. The air grew too hot to breathe. They didn't know what came at them, or why. Subhadra threw herself in front of Uttara—Uttara, who carried within her the only hope of the Pandavas—and cried out to Krishna. The last thing she felt before fainting was a wall of misty coolness around them. And Pariksit, whom Yudhisthir would place on the throne of Hastinapur thirty-six years later, was saved.

. . .

When Bheem returned, he placed in my hand Aswatthama's most precious possession, a fabled jewel that had been set in his forehead in the golden days of his life by the gods. It had the power to protect its wearer from weapons, disease, hunger. I stared at the gem as it sparkled many-hued in my palm, its edges bloodstained because Bheem had torn it from him. Once I would have felt delighted at having acquired an object so unique. I would have placed it in a position of pride in the Palace of Illusions. Today it held no more meaning than a lump of clay. Worse: each of its shiny facets seemed to hold the face of one of my loved ones in the throes of death.

I wanted to fling it from my sight, but I knew that Bheem had fought hard to wrest it from Aswatthama, hoping to console me. To please Bheem I gave the jewel to Yudhisthir and told him to wear it in his crown. He took it, but on his face was a strange lassitude, and I could see he accepted it only because he thought it would bring me satisfaction. I grew light-headed; it seemed that time rippled around me like wind on water. I saw that this was how we would live out the next decades, dragging ourselves from one expected action to the next, hoping by meticulous duty to bring each other some small measure of happiness. But the comfort that duty proffers is lukewarm at best. Happiness, like a mischievous bird that hops from branch to branch, would continue to elude us. Duryodhan's last words to Yudhisthir echoed in my ears: *I'm going to heaven to enjoy all its pleasures with my friends. You'll rule a kingdom peopled with widows and orphans and wake each morning to the grief of loss. Who's the real winner, then, and who the loser?*

pyre

Constant, pitiless, ever-increasing, the stench assaulted us as we made our reluctant way to the battlefield to deal with our dead. I pressed my lips tightly together to keep from vomiting. Where earlier soldiers had built their cook fires, now funeral pyres were being lighted—so many that the vista in front of us was covered in a haze of smoke. I blinked my stinging eyes. The chandaals whose job it was to burn bodies rushed from fire to fire, shaking their cudgels and yelling at mourners to keep their distance. Dressed only in loincloths, their faces streaked with soot and sweat, they looked like the guards of hell. But when I glanced past them, a strange sight met my eyes. The battlefield was filled with white shapes. In my confused numbness they looked like snowbirds, the large wingless ones poets sometimes sing of that live at the far northern edge of the world where neither herb nor grain grows. They moved uncertainly, like creatures that have lost their way in a storm and emerge from it to find themselves in a strange, frightening terrain. From time to time they emitted sharp, wordless cries. It took me a moment to recognize what I was looking at: not birds but widows who had traveled from Hastinapur and Indra Prastha—and who knew how many other cities of Bharat. Who had congregated here to do what nature never required of bird or beast—for it is only we humans that create such tragic duties for ourselves: to identify their dead and perform their final rites.

It was soon clear that they would find the first of the tasks impossible. The kings and commanders who had died in duels, though mangled, were recognizable. But the sons and husbands of these women—the common soldiers who are the first casualty of every war—had been annihilated by astras, or crushed to pulp beneath chariots and stampeding beasts. There was nothing left of them but heaps of rotting flesh.

When the women realized that they would not be able to view the bodies of their loved ones, they grew frenzied with despair. Some called down curses so vituperative on my husbands' heads that I shuddered. (Strangely, they didn't curse Duryodhan. Perhaps his death had absolved him in their minds. Or perhaps there's no satisfaction in cursing someone who can't hear you.) Others tried to kill themselves with the weapons that were strewn about the field. Still others threw themselves onto the pyres stacked with bodies. Their tormented cries as their white garments charred to black were more unbearable than all the death screams I'd heard in battle. My own despair receded as I watched their agony.

A horrified Yudhisthir ordered the guards to stop the women from harming themselves, to bring them to him. It wasn't easy. Crazed with fear and grief, the women fought the guards with whatever strength they had left. Some threw themselves down into the bloody mire and refused to move. Some tried to run away. Some called on their dead husbands' spirits to save them. They didn't trust Yudhisthir. They didn't want to come anywhere near him. Wasn't he the one who caused their husbands' deaths? Wasn't he the one who made them widows? Who knew what he'd do to them now?

At first the guards were taken aback by the ferocity of the women's attack. They tried to reason with them. When that failed, they resorted to force. How long can unarmed women resist a battalion? They were finally gathered in front of a makeshift dais where Yudhisthir assured them they had nothing to fear. He vowed that they would suffer none of the evils that befell the women of a defeated city. He offered them food and water, and a safe place to rest while the dead were taken care of.

But the women wailed and cursed, their grief replaced by rage. They didn't want his charity! Having taken everything from them, did he think he could appease them by something as paltry as refreshments? They beat their breasts and asked him to murder them, too, and thus spare them the bleakness of widowhood and its endless humiliations. If he was too cowardly to kill them, they cried, at least he should allow them to die an honorable death on their husbands' pyres. *We will die!* some of the more militant among them cried. *Which man here dares to anger the gods by denying us the final right of a faithful wife?* They broke away from the group and rushed at the pyres. Others followed them, keening as they went. Threatened with divine anger, the guards tried to stop them only halfheartedly; many of them pulled back, reluctant to intervene. Soon, if a quick remedy wasn't found, there would be a stampede, followed by mass suicide.

Aghast, Yudhisthir stared at what was happening. If it had been a battle, he would have known what kind of command to give his men. But here he was at a loss, paralyzed by guilt and compassion and the ancient and terrible tradition the women had invoked. I could see on his face a further concern: the tragic death of so many women at the very beginning of his reign would be a stain on his kingship, a devastating karma for him to bear. But neither he nor my other husbands knew how to prevent it.

When I climbed onto the makeshift dais, my intention was only to stand beside Yudhisthir because he seemed so alone. But to my surprise, the women stopped fighting to get to the pyres and turned toward me. Was it the unexpectedness of seeing a woman up there? Or did they know my story—all the way to the last bloody night, for that's how swiftly stories can travel? I wondered if they were thinking that I deserved everything that happened to me. I remembered how, even before the war began, a woman had made the sign against the evil eye at me. How much more reason did these women have to hate me now. My palms grew sweaty as I looked at their hard faces. My eyes burned, but I could not weep. Since my children's deaths, tears had deserted me. My mouth was dry, as if stuffed with cotton. I knew that if I stood there much longer, I'd be unable to form any words at all. And this one moment of opportunity, this one moment when I had their attention, would be lost.

Before this, I had never addressed a crowd, though I recalled Dhri's tutor discussing, earnestly and at length, the importance of powerful words. He'd said they were the sharpest and subtlest of weapons. It was crucial for rulers to use them correctly, swaying their audience with the appropriate intonation, tugging at their hearts as a master musician does his lutestrings, mesmerizing them until they obeyed the speaker blindly.

But even if I'd been capable of such manipulation, I didn't want to, not with the images of my dear dead still floating in front of my eyes. Instead, I started too fast and too loud and did not know what I would say. I found myself mentioning the bereavement we shared— for I, too, like them had lost a father and brothers. I admitted my guilt about the part I'd played in bringing this war about and asked for their forgiveness. When I spoke of the children, my voice broke and I had to pause. I told them that unlike me, who was left childless, they had a responsibility toward the sons and daughters they had left at home. Who would take care of them if the women killed themselves? I was not sure what I said after that; I spoke as though in a trance. I think I said, In spite of grief, we must live for the sake of the future. For the sake of the future, I promised them, I would take their children (for certainly I would have no others) as my own and make sure they lacked for nothing.

I'd started to address the women as a queen might her subjects, but as the words formed in my mouth, I spoke as a mother among mothers, and together we wept.

. . .

It fell upon me, the wrenching task of guiding my husbands to our dead. There was no one else who knew what I longed to forget: where and how they'd fallen, what their dying gestures had been. I pointed out the mangled bodies: Ghatotkacha, who in the extreme pain of his end had thought only of our good; Uttar and his father Virat, who had sheltered us in our distress, not knowing the ultimate cost of that hospitality; my father, his eyes open in death, his mouth drawn back in a grimace of disappointment, for he did not live to see the vengeance he had spent his entire life planning. Reaching the mutilated corpse of the young Abhimanyu, I described to my husbands how bravely he had fought even when overwhelmed by so many experienced warriors and saw pride mingle with the sadness on their faces.

But as we proceeded, I grew confused. Which of the dead should I single out, and which should I ignore? What of Salya, uncle to the Pandavas, who had helped us the best he could even though he was tricked into fighting for Duryodhan? Drona, his headless body twisted in his chariot, who had once taken their child-hands in his and taught them how to bend back their first bows? I looked into the blood-encrusted face of Lakshman Kumar, Duryodhan's son, his eyes wide with surprise as though he hadn't expected death to win this game of tag, and it blurred into the face of one of my boys.

And now we came to Karna's body. I kept my face averted, but it seemed my heart would burst from agitation. I couldn't bear to think that there was no one to mourn this great and unfortunate warrior's passing. His friends were all dead, Kunti could not claim her kinship with him, and I could not express my grief. My husbands remarked casually on the smile on his face. Why, Nakul asked, did his body not give off a stench like the other corpses? Arjun spoke magnanimously of his valor, for it is easy to praise those you hate once you have killed them. When Yudhisthir said, I wonder who his parents really were, and if they know he's dead, I couldn't bear it. I fell to my knees and said, "Husbands, you must cremate every warrior who died in Kurukshetra with due honor. You must pour ghee into the fire for them all, and offer rice and water so that their spirits may be at peace."

Yudhisthir agreed at once, but as he called for arrangements, we heard a voice behind us.

"No," it cried. "You have no right to touch my sons, whom you butchered along with their loyal friends. I will not allow you to offer prayers for them and thus lessen the punishment that awaits you in this life and beyond. I will take care of my own dead."

It was Dhritarashtra. He had always been stalwart and tall in spite of his infirmity. But overnight he'd aged—spine bent, hair grayed, forehead marked by grief's ravages. But Gandhari, who led him by the hand, stood taller than ever. The anger on her face, ice-white as the scarf that covered her eyes, frightened me more than her husband's outburst. Her years of prayer and abstinence had given her great power. Would she use it now to harm my husbands? I reached for Yudhisthir's arm to warn him—but I was too late.

Everyone knows what happened next. How the old king, with piety on his tongue and murder in his heart, pretended to accept Yudhisthir's apologies, his promise that he'd be a son to them. He held out his arms in a gesture of forgiveness, calling first for Bheem, who had killed every one of his sons. But once more Krishna saved us. He pulled Bheem back and gestured to his servants to bring out, instead, the iron statue upon which Duryodhan had so often vented his hatred. Dhritarashtra tightened his arms around it until he crushed it. Then he wept with genuine regret—for hidden behind the anger and envy, there still remained some concern in his heart for his brother's children.

Seeing this, Krishna explained his ruse and reminded the king that the Pandavas had been pushed unwillingly into war by his own son. "The least you can do to make up to them for all they've unjustly suffered at Duryodhan's hands," he said, "is to truly forgive them and give them your blessing, so that their hearts might find peace."

Dhritarashtra obeyed Krishna, but something broke in him as he touched my husbands' heads with the tips of his reluctant fingers. Perhaps the knowledge that until his death he would have to eat Pandava salt was too much for him. From that day on, he spoke little and gave up all kingly luxuries. He ate only once each day and slept on the bare floor, and though Yudhisthir entreated him many times to take his place as king in Hastinapur, he never again entered the sabha to sit on the throne he had so coveted.

And Gandhari? She was wiser than her husband. She knew that her sons had brought about their own downfall. But even wisdom is no match for a mother's pain. When Yudhisthir touched her feet, her rage manifested as fire, burning his fingernails black. And when Krishna snatched him away, she poured that rage on him.

"You were the mastermind behind my sons' destruction. Because of that, your own clan will destroy itself in the span of a single day. On that day, your women will weep just as the women of Hastinapur are weeping now. Then you'll know how I feel."

I stared at her in shock, but Krishna said, with his usual equanimity, "All things must end some day. How can the house of the Yadus be an exception?" Then his voice grew stern. "But tell me, aren't you responsible for this war, too? Who indulged Duryodhan when he was a boy, instead of punishing him for the things he did to his cousins? Who couldn't bear to banish Sakuni—because he was your brother—from the palace even though he was an evil influence on Duryodhan?"

Gandhari bowed her head.

Krishna continued more gently, "Duryodhan broke his word again and again. He took from his cousins through trickery what was justly theirs—and then, after they'd fulfilled all the conditions he'd placed on them, refused to return it. You know this yourself. Isn't that why, when Duryodhan asked for your blessing just before he went to Kurukshetra, you didn't say, 'May you win'?"

Gandhari was weeping. Krishna put his arm around her shaking shoulders. "Instead you said, 'May righteousness prevail.' I know it was difficult for a mother to pronounce those words. But you did the right thing. Now that your words have come to pass, how can you hate those who were merely the instruments of universal law, which ultimately must restore that which was out of balance?"

She turned to him then, sobbing against his chest. "Forgive me! That terrible curse—I want to call it back!"

"There's nothing to forgive," Krishna said as he led her to her tent. "Whatever you pronounced—even that was part of the law."

. . .

But what I remember most clearly are Krishna's words to the blind king when he insisted on cremating his dead by himself: *You call them* mine, *and you call the others* theirs. *For shame! Hasn't this been the cause of your troubles ever since the fatherless sons of Pandu arrived at Hastinapur? If you'd seen them all as yours to love, this war would never have occurred.*

Wasn't it the cause of my troubles, too? Of every trouble in this world?

. . .

We'd thought that the day was done with its surprises, but it had kept hidden in its recesses one final secret. As the Pandavas stood holding lighted brands, ready to begin the cremation of our children, Kunti came to them. Her eyes were bleak. Her voice held a quiet and terrible resolve.

"Wait," she said. "You must begin the ceremony by paying respect to your eldest brother." And as they stared in amazement and growing shock, she told them—though it was a lifetime too late—the truth about Karna.

ash

After the war, the cremations. After the cremations, the remains given to the Ganga. It was there by the river, the last sift of ash and grit pouring from his fingers, that Yudhisthir fell into his depression. For thirteen years his life had been directed to this moment like an arrow released from the bow of a master archer. But when the arrow has shattered the target, what is left for it to do?

Though we all entreated him, Yudhisthir would not leave the riverbank and come to Hastinapur for his coronation. For weeks he sat staring at the devastated land where nothing would grow, thinking of the millions whose death-anguish had poisoned the air. But most of all he brooded on Karna, his own brother whom he'd hated for so long.

I stayed with him during those weeks, for I was afraid to leave him alone. Each day we'd discuss the same things, over and over, as though his mind were stuck in a rut too deep for it to climb out of.

"How delighted I was when he fell!" Yudhisthir said. "In my selfish glee I ignored the fact that on that very day he'd spared my life—and before that, the lives of Bheem, Nakul, and Sahadev. Why didn't I guess? Why didn't any of us guess? We rushed to view his corpse. We laughed and shouted our congratulations to Arjun, even though we knew he'd killed him unfairly. Ah, the terrible sin of that fratricide will fall on me, not Arjun, for he only did what I wanted him to!"

My own regrets resurfaced as he spoke. If only I'd told him what I knew earlier, how much heartache I could have prevented him now! But I couldn't afford to wallow in remorse. I needed to help Yudhisthir. In all our years of marriage, I'd never seen him so dejected—no, not even when I was insulted in Duryodhan's court.

I ignored the sting of that thought and said, "You acted from ignorance, not malice."

But he refused to listen. He held me by the shoulders, his fingers digging into my flesh, his gaunt mouth working. "How could my mother, so wise in everything else, have kept such a matter secret? How can I trust her again?"

There was a time when I'd have gained a certain pleasure from hearing him speak thus of the woman who, more than any of the other wives, had been my rival. But even the thought of such pettiness was distasteful to me now. A knot had unraveled in my heart when I saw Kunti at Karna's funeral. She looked so worn, so ashamed, so beaten down. Besides, guilt flooded me at Yudhisthir's words. I, too, had kept the same secret that his mother had. How furious might he be with me if he discovered this?

I said, "It's not for you to judge your mother's actions. Who among us can know how terrified she must have felt when Karna was born?"

But Yudhisthir had sunk once again into grief and didn't hear me.

Anxious at his continued apathy, my other husbands and I took him to visit Bheeshma. Perhaps, we thought, a philosophical discussion with the grandfather would cheer him. We knew how Yudhisthir loved such things. The dying Bheeshma put aside his own pains to teach him the art of kingship: *A ruler should know how to conceal his own weaknesses. He should choose his servants carefully. He must cause dissensions among the noblemen in his enemy's kingdom. He should be forgiving, but not excessively so, for then men of evil heart would take advantage of him. His innermost thoughts must be concealed even from his nearest ones.* Yudhisthir listened respectfully enough, but even Bheeshma could not shake off his numb despair.

Finally Krishna took him to task. He pointed out that while Yudhisthir was indulging himself with melancholy, bandits were terrorizing his helpless subjects at the edges of the unraveling Kuru kingdom. Ah, Krishna! He'd appealed to the one thing Yudhisthir couldn't shake off: his duty. He allowed himself to be led back to the city and crowned, though he took no pleasure in it.

I didn't blame him. It was hard for anyone to find pleasure at Hastinapur. The palace, which in Duryodhan's day had been filled with a frantic, garish energy, had turned dank and funereal. The few retainers that were left—perhaps in deference to the old king and queen—wore mourning and walked with a hushed step. I ordered them to dress in coronation clothing. They obeyed me fearfully, the festive attire hanging askew on their bodies. How I missed Dhai Ma then! Her raucous curses would have jolted them into action. I made my own servants pull down the heavy, dust-filled drapes and throw open the windows. I called my women to comb out my long-tangled hair and rub perfume into it. Still, all around I smelled, inexplicably, funeral incense. As I breathed it, I felt as though I was sinking into the morass of depression that had claimed Yudhisthir. The night before the coronation, I stood at my window, unable to sleep. It saddened me to think that this was the place where I would be living out the rest of my life. What I had said to Bheeshma a long time ago as a new bride still held true: it would never be home to me.

On the day of the coronation, my greatest challenge was to enter the throne room again. At its threshold my footsteps faltered, sweat sprouted in my armpits, my breath grew uneven. I had to use all my willpower to step into the room that had been the scene of my greatest humiliation. The task must have been harder still for my husbands. Their memories were worse than mine. To see a loved one in pain is more wrenching than to bear that pain yourself. The war had taught me this. However, we knew we had no choice. The throne of the Kurus had sat in that sabha for generations. We couldn't move it, not at this time, when we needed the help of tradition to stabilize a foundering kingdom.

Once again Krishna—who else!—came to our rescue. From his own palace he sent us cooks and gardeners, musicians and dancers, even his favorite elephant for Yudhisthir to ride in the royal procession. On coronation day, he brought the entire Yadu clan—and they, not knowing the doom that hung over them, cheered us with their simple pleasure in good food and fine wine, their feckless antics. Without them, we couldn't have borne the empty seats that stretched on both sides of the throne, seats that—out of respect or guilt—Yudhisthir would leave unfilled. On the right, Bheeshma's; on the left, Drona's; in the raised alcove, the ornate throne specially carved for Duryodhan; next to his, severe in its simplicity, the chair Karna had once used.

. . .

Hastinapur after the war was largely a city of women, widows who had never dreamed that the survival of their families would depend on them. The poorer ones were used to working, but now that they were without male protection, they found themselves exploited. Affluent women, pampered and sheltered until now, were the easiest victims. Men would appear from nowhere claiming to be relatives and take control of the family fortunes. The women became unpaid servants. Sometimes they were turned out. They were too afraid—even if they'd known how—to apply to the king for justice. I'd see them on the roadside, often with children in their arms, begging. There were others that I didn't see, but I heard of the street corners they frequented at night, selling the only thing left to them.

It was a terrible situation—and it saved me.

I knew how it felt to be helpless and hopeless. Hadn't I been almost stripped of my clothing and my honor in this very city? Hadn't I been abducted in the forest and attacked in Virat's court when men thought I was without protection? Didn't I, even now, mourn my blood-clan—dead, every one of them? And if I wasn't careful, might I not turn into one of these women—empty-eyed, capable only of churning through futile memories?

It was time I shook off my self-pity and did something. I resolved to form a separate court, a place where women could speak their sorrows to other women.

At an earlier, more arrogant time I'd have tried to do it by myself, but now I asked Kunti and Gandhari for their aid. They acquiesced; together we approached Yudhisthir. A chamber was set up in the women's palace with thrones placed on the dais for the dowagers. Subhadra and I sat below. I invited Uttara, too, to help us. I had expected her to refuse, for she was in the late months of an unwieldy pregnancy, but to my surprise, she agreed. Often she was the most perceptive one, seeing directly into the heart of a problem. Perhaps it was from these sessions that the unborn Pariksit, alert within his mother's womb, learned his judicial clarity, so that in time he would be compared to Rama, that most impartial of kings.

Only Bhanumati declined to join us. She returned to her father's kingdom, and who could fault her? With the death of Duryodhan (and Karna, said a voice in my head), what was left for her in this palace that had always made her feel like an outsider? On the day she left, as she climbed into her chariot dressed in white, her forehead bare, her arms stripped of the jingling bangles she had once so delighted in, she raised her head for a moment to send me a look of smoldering hate. At that, guilt—never too far away—speared my heart. How the war had changed the naïve girl she'd been, eager to please, happy with the littlest things! For the sake of that girl—and the man we had both loved silently, though perhaps in different ways—I prayed that she would find a measure of peace in the home of her childhood.

. . .

The court by itself wasn't enough to help the women. Yudhisthir had given us permission, but that was all he could afford to let us have. The coffers of Hastinapur had been depleted by the Great War. But unless we had the power to enforce our rulings, who would obey them?

We were at a loss until Uttara came to us—it was just a few days before Pariksit's birth—followed by two maids carrying a chest. With a start we recognized its ornate carvings—it contained her wedding jewelry. She threw open the lid and said, "I have no use for this anymore. Use it to help those who are more unfortunate than I."

The sale of that jewelry allowed us to hire scribes to interpret the law and a queen's guard to carry out our judgments. By itself, it might not have been enough, but Uttara's action galvanized us all. We scrounged around, collecting our own jewelry and palace furnishings that weren't essential. Kunti surprised me by donating artifacts she'd held on to all these years, things that had belonged to Pandu. All this allowed us to set up the destitute in homes of their own and buy merchandise to start businesses for them. In time the women's market became a flourishing center of trade in the city, for the new proprietors took pride in their goods and were canny but fair in their dealings. We trained those who showed interest in learning to become tutors for girls and young boys. And even in the later years of Pariksit's reign when the world had passed into the Fourth Age of Man and Kali the dark spirit had gripped the world in his claws, Hastinapur remained one of the few cities where women could go about their daily lives without harassment.

snake

This is the nature of sorrow: often it fades with time, but once in a while it remains lodged below the surface of things, a stubborn thorn beneath a fingernail, making itself felt every time you brush against it. (How well I knew this, for random events would startle me into the memory of a pair of ancient eyes.) In Yudhisthir's case, the thorn moved deeper into him with time, festering as it went. At court he was just and compassionate. In the royal apartments, he was kind and undemanding. But he brooded incessantly on the many lives that had been destroyed because of what he considered his ambition. Even after Hastinapur grew back into a prosperous city where people flocked to live, much as they had once done in Indra Prastha, we never saw him smile.

It took the birth of Pariksit to change that.

The day Uttara went into labor was a stormy one. Kunti said the sky wept because it knew how hard the world was to a father-less child, and when the labor continued for many hours, she added that perhaps the baby knew this, too, and that is why it was reluctant to be born.

I bit my lips to keep in an angry retort at such negative words, but Yudhisthir said, "Mother, you are wrong! As long as I have breath in my body, this child will never feel the lack of a father." He shocked everyone by entering the labor hut, a place traditionally barred to men. He laid his hand on Uttara's forehead as one might with a daughter and called out Pariksit's name (for Krishna had already decided what it was to be). Was it in response to his yearning that the baby came soon after? Even before he'd been cleansed in a ritual bath, Yudhisthir took him in his arms and kissed his head. As I watched the look on his face—tender, reprieved—I realized that I would no longer have to worry about him.

My other husbands, too, showered Pariksit with the frustrated fatherly love pent up in their hearts. Preoccupied with their troubled destiny, they'd had little opportunity to spend time with their own children. When they finally thought they would get to enjoy their company as young men, our sons were snatched from them. They swore not to let that happen again. But more than that, perhaps, they treasured Pariksit because we had so nearly lost him.

From the time Pariksit was in swaddling clothes, my husbands spent hours planning his education. They were determined to mold him into the perfect king, the one in whose hands they could leave Hastinapur without worry, the one who would redeem their sins with his goodness. As soon as he could stand, Bheem began to teach him the first moves of wrestling; Arjun had an infant-sized bow designed for him; Nakul sat him on his favorite horse and walked him around the courtyard; Sahadev taught him how to speak to animals; and Yudhisthir told him stories about the lives of saints. For his naming ceremony, they invited all the important sages and gave away more wealth than they could afford. They begged Vyasa to officiate at the ceremony and then pestered him to tell the child's future until he admitted to them that Pariksit would be a powerful and virtuous king.

But before he left, Vyasa drew me aside. "Watch the boy's temper," he said. "It'll get him in trouble if he isn't careful."

My mouth went dry. "What do you mean?"

Vyasa shrugged. "Just what I said: the boy's temper might be his downfall."

A pounding began inside my head. Here was history, repeating itself once again. But this time I wouldn't let Vyasa's riddles ruin Pariksit's life. I grabbed his arm, though I knew it was most inappropriate for a woman to touch a sage. "Speak clearly for once."

Looking at my face Vyasa must have seen I wasn't going to let go until he satisfied me. "Very well," he said. "There will come a day, a sweltering summer day not too many years after you are gone, when Pariksit—still a young man—will go on a hunt. Separated from his men, he'll get lost in the forest. He'll be hungrier and thirstier than he'd ever been in his life. That's when he will stumble into Sage Samik's ashram and see the sage sitting at the entrance to his hut. He'll ask for water. But the sage will be too deep in meditation to hear him. Thinking the sage was slighting him, Pariksit will be furious. He'll find a dead snake nearby and throw it around the sage's neck and depart.

"The sage will still know nothing of this. But his son, returning to the ashram in the evening, will be enraged at this insult to his father. Being hot-tempered himself, he'll take holy water in his hand and use up the power of a lifetime of penance to pronounce a curse. *May the man who did this to my father die in seven days of a snakebite.* Waking from his trance, Samik will be filled with consternation. But the curse will be too strong to recall. He'll do the only thing possible: send a warning to the king of his impending doom."

"You can't stop now!" I cried when my heart had slowed enough for me to speak. "What happens next?"

Vyasa shrugged. "Here the path forks, as it often does with destinies. Pariksit could be overcome by vengeance. He could destroy the sage's hermitage and all in it, and then drown himself in revelry until he died. Or he could realize the wrongness of his conduct, ask forgiveness, set his affairs in order, and spend his last days in holy company. It'll depend on how you bring him up! In any case, you'd better arrange an early marriage for him if you want the Pandava lineage to continue."

I could tell, by his tone, that though he wasn't unsympathetic, he didn't consider the matter particularly calamitous. To him it was like watching a game to see what the outcome might be. Perhaps that's how it feels when you've predicted the deaths of millions. His indifference made me livid.

Vyasa deftly rescued his arm from my slackened grip. "Ah yes, one more thing: keep this knowledge to yourself."

"Why?" I cried. "And why didn't you tell my husbands? They, too, need to know of this terrible doom that is lying in wait for our family so they can take precautions."

"I only tell people what they can stand. Knowing Pariksit's fate now, just when he's recovering from his long dejection, would break Yudhisthir. And his brothers wouldn't be able to bear that. But you—I've always known you to be stronger than your husbands."

Before I could recover from my surprise at that statement, he was gone.

. . .

I wanted to ask Krishna's advice, but he seldom visited us nowadays. Perhaps he needed to take care of his long-neglected kingdom. Perhaps he wanted us not to depend on him overmuch. Perhaps he felt he'd completed what he needed to do for us. So I followed my own uneven counsel, watching Pariksit carefully, disciplining him whenever he showed signs of anger. In this I was alone. Kunti and Gandhari doted on him, and even Subhadra, who had been much stricter with her own son, could not refuse him anything. How could

I blame them? There would be no other child in the palace in their lifetime. And as for Uttara, he was the only reason she'd held on to life when Abhimanyu died.

I urged my husbands, at least, to be firm with Pariksit, but they only accused me of excessive harshness—unbecoming, they said, in a grandmother. They showered Pariksit with every luxury they could imagine. Scores of attendants hovered around him. He was always in a royal lap. I doubted that he even knew the meaning of the word *hunger*—or *thirst*.

When I pointed out that a more disciplined upbringing—like their own—would prepare Pariksit better for kinghood, they smiled indulgently. Yudhisthir said, "Let him enjoy his childhood, Panchaali. I don't remember a single day when my mother didn't remind us that we had to make our dead father proud."

The others nodded.

Sahadev said, "Every moment of our life, we knew our goal."

Nakul said, "Everything we learned, every conversation we had—it was for that purpose alone: to help Yudhisthir reclaim our father's kingdom."

Bheem added, "I could never eat a meal without thinking, This food must make me strong enough to wrest the kingdom away from Duryodhan when the time comes."

Arjun said, "I never had a night of unbroken sleep. I'd get up in the dark while everyone else was resting to practice archery—because otherwise we might not win."

"Do you want Pariksit to grow up like that?" Yudhisthir asked.

Gagged by Vyasa's injunction, what could I say?

. . .

So much indulgence would have ruined another child. But Pariksit was an introspective boy, soft-spoken, with dreamy eyes.

Though his uncles crowded his life with lavish entertainments, he preferred simplicity and quiet. To my surprise, in spite of my strictness he was fond of me and often sought me out. But perhaps it is vanity on my part to think so! He had the gift—like his granduncle Krishna—of giving his undivided and courteous attention to whomever he was with, making them feel he loved them especially. In any case, I enjoyed his conversations, which were filled with wisdom beyond his years. A chord of subtle sympathy resonated between us. Except for Dhri during my childhood, I had never found anyone who so instinctively understood how I felt—and accepted it. Sometimes a powerful urge would rise in me to confide in this boy things I'd never been able to tell anyone—yes, even my feelings for Karna. But always I bit my tongue to stop myself. I had no right to burden a child with my murky confessions. His future would be hard enough!

Pariksit had one intriguing habit: if he came across someone new, he would approach him and gaze intently in his eyes. Once I asked him why.

"I'm trying to find someone," he said shyly. "I don't know who he is. He was the most beautiful person I've ever seen—except he wasn't really a *person*. He was tiny, about as big as your thumb. His skin was a beautiful, shiny blue. He stood between me and a huge burst of fire and smiled—and the fire faded. Maybe it was just a dream."

I stared at him in wonder, this child who'd been brushed by the elusive Mystery I'd been trying to grasp all my life. The tiny being he described was very like the Cosmic One mentioned in the scriptures. Could it be Krishna that he'd seen in this guise, the infinitesimal counterpart of the vision that had overwhelmed Arjun at Kurukshetra?

Subhadra had told us, over and over, that Krishna had saved

Pariksit's life when Aswatthama's astra came to destroy him. She was convinced it was because he was divine. I believed the first part, but the skeptic in me was unable to accept the second. Having special powers didn't necessarily make one into a god. And yet a part of me longed to believe, for the sake of the serenity it might bring my storm-swept heart.

I waited impatiently to see what Pariksit would do when Krishna came to visit us next. I trusted his intelligence, his child's clarity of vision. If he recognized Krishna as his savior, my doubts would be put to rest. But when Pariksit saw Krishna, he treated him just like his other granduncles, except he was more reserved with him because he hadn't seen him in so long. He bowed and recited a formal welcome, but soon he got over his bashfulness and sat close, examining with delight the many intricate gifts Krishna had brought him from Dwarka and describing in detail the antics of his pet monkey.

. . .

Did I say Pariksit delighted all our hearts? Not so.

As time passed, the blind king grew more reclusive. He seldom left his chambers, where he paced restlessly, counting his prayer beads, though they did not seem to do him any good. On other days he sat in front of the windows that looked out toward Kurukshetra, remaining there long after the sun set and the maids brought in the lamps that he could not see. Each time we visited him, he appeared to have shrunk further. He sighed often, drawn-out wisps of recrimination. Though he was polite to my husbands, he couldn't forgive them for being alive when his sons were crumbled ash. I felt his resentment for them emanating, a black oily smoke, from each pore of his body. He must have resented Pariksit as well, for through him Pandu's lineage would continue to flower while his had withered already. Pandu, whom he'd always envied for getting what should rightfully have been his: the kingdom, the prettier wives, popularity and acclaim. Even his death had been exciting, meteoric, not the aching blankness that drew a little closer to Dhritarashtra each day. Pariksit must have sensed this, for though he was fond enough of Gandhari, he refused to accompany us to Dhritarashtra's rooms. When forced, he stood behind us, stubbornly mute, and escaped as soon as he was able.

Only Yudhisthir, that perpetual innocent, was surprised and dismayed when Dhritarashtra announced he'd had enough of palace living. It was too painful. There were too many memories. (Did he send one of his accusing sighs toward my husbands as he spoke?) Death was almost upon him, and he wished to prepare for it by moving to a forest hermitage. Yudhisthir begged him to reconsider; he remained righteously adamant. But perhaps I'm biased. Perhaps he'd truly set his heart on the next world.

Certainly it was so with Gandhari. When she announced that she would accompany him, under her blindfold, her thin, ascetic's face blazed with conviction. I was sorry to be losing her. She had traveled past grief to wisdom. Observing her gave me the hope that one day I, too, might complete that journey. When I was stricken by the memory of my dear dead ones, I would go to her rooms and sit by her. She would place her hand on me, and somehow I would be calmed.

But what shocked us most on the day of departure was to find Kunti standing beside Gandhari, holding her by the arm so she could guide her. She bade us goodbye, and no amount of pleading could change her mind.

"Mother," Yudhisthir cried, "why do you want to leave us now, when we've finally gained back our father's kingdom? Isn't this what you wanted all your life? Don't you want to see your great-grandson sit on this throne one day?"

Sahadev, her favorite, threw himself at her feet. "Are you angry with us?"

She smiled and shook her head and gave us all her blessings. She allowed my husbands to escort her to the hermitage so that they wouldn't worry overmuch. But she didn't explain her decision, choosing instead to remain an enigma that would haunt her sons. Is it ungracious of me to think that she knew, by doing so, that she would remain in their minds long after she was dead?

For months my husbands grieved over Kunti's departure, discussing it over and over in a vain attempt to comprehend it. They asked me what might have caused it, but for once I didn't know. In recent years, I'd deferred increasingly to her. (Kurukshetra had cured me of the longing to control things. Perhaps it had cured her, too, for she no longer tried to impose her will on me.) And though she—like us all—sorrowed for the dead, I thought she had come to terms with loss. After all, she was luckier than most: five of her six sons had lived.

It was only years later, when my husbands and I set out on our own final journey, that I understood her motivation.

reed

 Panting, the messenger fell at the foot of the throne. His clothes—once white to symbolize mourning—were dirt-stained and torn. His disheveled hair and bulging eyes gave him the look of a madman. His chest heaved as he tried to speak, but no words emerged from his mouth, only guttural cries that we couldn't understand. We knew him, however, by the emblem he carried: he was a royal messenger from Dwarka, Krishna's city.

A concerned Yudhisthir called for water and potions to calm his terror. He spoke in broken stutters, the news leaving his mouth halting and lame like a beggar who knows he will be unwelcome. The Yadu clan was annihilated. Balaram was dead. No one knew where Krishna was, but it was unlikely that he was alive. Overnight, Dwarka had turned into a city of mourning, peopled—like Hastinapur after the war—with children and widows. But this was more shocking, for we were in a time of peace, our complacent minds unprepared for such a tragedy.

A part of me refused to believe this devastating news, but another part, dark and pessimistic, knew it was true. Hadn't I, deep inside, been waiting for just such a calamity ever since Gandhari's terrible curse at the death fields of Kurukshetra? At first every time I'd looked at Gandhari, I'd remembered it and shuddered, hating her. Each day, I'd offered flowers and water and prayed for Krishna's safety. But the years passed—ten, twenty, twenty-five—without incident. Gandhari grew bent and mild-mannered and spent her time increasingly at her devotions. Slowly, the curse slipped further and further back into my mind, coming to rest among other might-have-beens. As Gandhari and I became friends, I hoped for her sake that she, too, had forgotten about it. It's embarrassing to be the author of a curse that promised annihilation only to fizzle out like a damp firecracker!

But once again death had leaped upon a loved one just when I believed him to be safe. How ironic that Gandhari's curse should come into effect when she had outgrown her anger and was finally at peace.

My mind couldn't encompass the fact that Krishna was no more, that he wouldn't suddenly show up, as was his habit, with his teasing grin, to take care of whatever was troubling me. A huge emptiness yawned beneath my feet, ready to swallow me. I remembered the sorrow I'd felt at the yagna when I'd thought Sisupal had killed him, but this numbness was worse. There was, however, no time to indulge in grief. No time even to hold ceremonies for the dead. Rumor was that brigands were gathering around Dwarka already. If they struck, who would hold them back? Yudhisthir dispatched Arjun to the city that Krishna had built with such care at the ocean's edge. He was to find out who had caused the massacre and punish them appropriately. Then he was to bring back the women and children to Hastinapur. We can't assuage their sorrow, Yudhisthir said, but at least we can provide them with a refuge.

As we waited, rumors flitted around our ears like dusky moths. (Later we would realize there were bits of insidious truth in each of them.) The Yadu warriors had died because of an ascetic's curse. A great serpent had come out of the sea and swallowed them when they went to visit the pleasure gardens of Prabhas. The rushes on the seashore had turned by demon magic to arrows. These flew at them, striking them dead at the slightest touch. The Yadus had drunk a drugged wine that caused them to go mad and turn on their own. A traveling minstrel sung about how Krishna was killed in a copse by a hunter who had mistaken him for a deer, but this was so blatantly impossible that we chastised him and sent him away with the paltriest of remunerations.

Each day we sent our attendants to the palace rooftop to watch for Arjun, but each day they returned shaking their heads. Why should it take him, the greatest living warrior in Bharat, so long to accomplish a task that, though sad, was simple enough? Around us there were disturbing omens that the world order was falling apart. Owls shrieked at random through the day, and the skies were filled with smoke though there was no fire. Arriving at the altar to adorn the deities, the palace priest found the tracks of dried tears on their stone cheeks. At sunrise, instead of the crowing of roosters, we heard the cries of night creatures: coyotes and she-jackals. On the day when, from the women's terrace, I saw crows attacking an eagle, pecking at him until he fled, I knew that Krishna was truly gone.

. . .

When he returned, for a moment no one recognized Arjun. His hair had turned white. His face was haggard, and his ribs formed tense ridges under his skin. His eyes darted from side to side, reminding us of the messenger from Dwarka. He swayed on his feet and spoke in a cracked voice, calling on death to take him. Before Yudhisthir could catch him, he crumpled in a faint. Only then did we realize that he hadn't brought anyone back with him.

When he regained consciousness, Arjun said: "They killed each other, the fools! I don't know what insanity came upon them. They'd gone to spend a pleasure day at Prabhas, all the men of the Yadu clan. Perhaps they drank too much. Perhaps the sun was too hot. They began to insult each other about the part each had played in the war, though Krishna had made them promise never to bring it up. Soon, everyone started taking sides. A fight began—it didn't end until every one of them was dead! Everyone except Krishna's charioteer. He's the one who told me all this. He told me this, too: the Yadus weren't carrying weapons—they were there on holiday, after all. They plucked the rushes that grew on the seashore and threw them at each other, but the rushes turned to javelins—can you fathom this?—and pierced their hearts.

"No, Balaram didn't die there, nor Krishna. They didn't join the fight, though they didn't try to stop it either. I don't understand why. They could have done it easily. Everyone respected them.

"I don't know. Perhaps they were disgusted by the folly of men who'd once been such great warriors. Perhaps they knew it was time for things to end. Balaram walked to a deserted beach where he went into a trance. Daruk saw the life-breath leave his mouth in the shape of a white serpent and enter the sea. Krishna saw it, too. He didn't weep, though he had loved Balaram most dearly, in spite of their disagreements. He said to Daruk, Go back to the city. Send word to the Pandavas. Tell them to save the women, if they can. There was a grove of trees nearby. He lay down, half hidden by the tall grass. That was where the hunter's arrow found him. Yes, he was killed by a mere hunter, our Krishna who had once dazzled me with his immense cosmic form! I wouldn't have believed it either if I hadn't seen his body with my own eyes.

"Can you imagine the grief in Dwarka? Krishna's wives threw

themselves at my feet, crying, Bring him back, we can't live without him. We wrapped him in yellow silk, his favorite color. He was still smiling—you remember that smile? I had to place his body on the pyre. How my hand shook as I struck the flint. When the flames rose, many of his wives threw themselves into the fire. No, I didn't stop them. If I weren't honor-bound to bring you this news, I would have done the same. All my life, he'd been next to me, guiding me, putting up with my ignorance. How can I tell you how it feels to remain in the world when he's no longer here?

"I gathered the others and started for Hastinapur. Barely had we stepped out of the city gates when we heard a great roar behind us. Turning, we saw a tidal wave rushing toward the city. It crushed the beautiful golden domes of Dwarka. There's nothing left there now but swirling foam and seaweed.

"The worst was still to come. As we were traveling through the forest, bandits fell upon us. I reached for my Gandiva, but I couldn't string it. I tried to invoke an astra. Not even the simplest of summoning chants would come to my mind. I remembered my brother Karna, the way I'd killed him, and wondered if this was retribution. But it was more. With the death of Krishna, my spirit—or whatever you'd call that which had made me great—had withered away. The bandits took the women and their gold—I couldn't stop them. I who in my day have made an entire phalanx of warriors flee from a single arrow! The women cried, Save us, save us! I could do nothing. Truly, it's time for me to die."

Afterward, Arjun wept. The tears pooled in the sunken pits under his eyes. His chin, stubbled with white, quivered. I couldn't bear to look. I had never seen him weep like this. Yudhisthir, too, was weeping. So were the others. Watching them, my heart was torn apart by loss, by the realization that, like Krishna, my husbands' life purpose was over. Having purged the earth of evil, having changed the course of history, having raised a child to be a true king, they had rendered themselves unnecessary.

Now Yudhisthir held Arjun's shaking shoulders, the bones that stood out under the loose skin. He said, "Brother, you're right. It's time for you—for all of us—to die."

42

Snow

I stood under the archway of the main gates, its old, old stones, and gazed back at Hastinapur one last time in farewell. Its tree-lined avenues shimmered in heat haze like a scene out of a dream. Twice before I'd left this city. How different it had been each time.

The first was as a naïve bride whose heart strained after all the things she wanted: adventure, love, queenship, a palace to call her own. I made sure to wear my finest clothes and all the gold I owned so that the eyes of onlookers would be dazzled. I held tight to the side of the elaborate, impractical chariot Dhritarashtra had given us to hide my nervousness, for I wanted the people of the city to remember me as heroic, majestic. The woman around whom history would gather itself. I wanted them to make up stories about the beautiful Panchaali, to weep because I was leaving them for something better.

The second time I was on foot, clad in the rough garments a servant might wear. My hair hung loose about my face, already snarling. I no longer possessed any jewelry—my husband had lost it all at dice—but my eyes glittered like diamonds. My face was hard with hate and remembrance. Hadn't I possessed the most beautiful palace in the world, which Duryodhan had wrested from us by trickery? I lifted my chin high. I wanted the people of the city to remember the way I'd been humiliated, the curse I'd pronounced. I wanted them to cower under my slashing gaze, knowing that subjects must ultimately pay for the sins of the rulers.

But today, like my husbands, I was clad in beaten tree bark, attire of those who have renounced worldly life. I wore no gold. I had given all my jewelry away. Indeed, beyond what I wore, I possessed nothing. Behind me, Pariksit wept, and his new wife, and Uttara and Subhadra, and further behind (as I had once so bitterly wished) I heard the laments of the people of Hastinapur, their sorrow at losing us. But I no longer required their tears. It baffled me that as a younger woman I'd thought such a thing would make me happy. Now I wanted nothing—not even from Pariksit, whom I'd come to love more than I'd ever loved my sons. I sent a good thought toward the city, but I felt oddly detached from it, from all that had been my life until now. I was struck, suddenly, by how brief that life was compared to everything around me: the marble buildings, the flowering flame-blossom trees, the cobblestones smoothed by generations of feet, the indigo haze of the distant mountains. Perhaps this was how Kunti had felt, like a tiny boat rocking unmoored on the shore of a huge ocean as she waited with vague interest to see where the current would take her. There was an unexpected freedom in finding out that one wasn't as important as one had always assumed!

But as I stepped beyond the gateway, a traitor wind brought me the scent of parijats, that old smell out of my garden in the Palace of Illusions—and with it a regret. Why hadn't I planted it here in Hastinapur? Like the firework stars that the court magician had ignited on the night of Pariksit's coronation, that single regret exploded in my heart, filling it with showers of burning sparks. I wasn't ready to let go of my life. How amazing it seemed to me with its victories, its adventures, its moments of glory. Even the shame that had struck like hot iron, branding revenge into my brain, seemed suddenly precious in its uniqueness. I wanted to live it all again—with more wisdom this time! I wanted to put my hand on Yudhisthir's arm and ask him to wait another year, a month, even one day. I hadn't taught Pariksit's wife how to make mango pickles with the secret ingredient that would keep them fresh for a decade. I hadn't commended Uttara on the strength she'd grown into. I hadn't asked Subhadra's forgiveness for the many ways in which I'd tortured her. And Pariksit! How much there was to tell him! I should have confessed to him all the mistakes I'd made that I didn't want him to repeat. I should have disobeyed Vyasa and warned him of the dangers that lurked in his future. But it was too late. Already Yudhisthir strode ahead, his face still as glass, my other husbands following him, steadfast, as they had all their lives.

Even then I could have changed my mind. They'd all asked me to stay back. Pariksit claimed he needed me to guide him, especially with my husbands gone. The women wept, saying they would miss me. Why did I have to go? they demanded. If it was a religious life I wanted, I could live it right here in Hastinapur. Didn't they have temples and priests? Wasn't every holy festival royally celebrated in this city? Didn't the most famous sages visit us regularly? My husbands, too, asked me to remain. They feared for my safety. The path they were to follow, up into the secret recesses of Himavan, was too treacherous. No woman had ever attempted it. If I fell by the roadside, Yudhisthir warned, my husbands could not stop to help me. Such was the implacable law of this final journey they had chosen to undertake.

The more people dissuaded me, the more determined I became. Perhaps that has always been my problem, to rebel against the boundaries society has prescribed for women. But what was the alternative? To sit among bent grandmothers, gossiping and complaining, chewing on mashed betel leaves with toothless gums as I waited for death? Intolerable! I would rather perish on the mountain. It would be sudden and clean, an end worthy of bard-song, my last victory over the other wives: *She was the only consort that dared accompany the Pandavas on this final, fearsome adventure. When she fell, she did not weep, but only raised her hand in brave farewell.*

How could I resist it?

. . .

The sages guided us to the base of the Himalayas. There they left us, for only a person who had given up the world forever was allowed to embark on the road that stretched ahead. We knew little about it except its name, which seemed ominous (though Yudhisthir repeated it with relish): mahaprasthan, the path of the great departure. We had no idea of what it held. Even Arjun, the most widely traveled of my husbands, had not come this way before. The sages had told us that the road ended upon a sacred peak, a place where earth met the abode of the gods. There a man who was pure enough could push past the veil that separated the worlds and enter heaven. The scriptures declared it to be the most glorious of experiences. But those who were not as holy, the sages warned, would be prevented from proceeding beyond a certain point. The mountain would make sure of that. With melancholy relish, they described avalanches and hidden craters. Man-eating snow beasts.

When he heard of the veil that could be crossed, Yudhisthir's eyes sparked with an interest I hadn't seen in them for a long time. I knew what he wanted: to enter heaven in human flesh! It was the latest of the impractical goals he'd run after all his life, with us in tow. I wanted to point out that we were dressed flimsily, in clothing made of bark. Our feet were bare. We carried no food, as was the custom when one embarked on mahaprasthan. We had no means to protect ourselves should the snow beasts happen to be real. (Yudhisthir had declared that weapons were a sign of ego and persuaded my other husbands to lay them down.) It was clear that we wouldn't last long enough to reach any peak, sacred or otherwise. That did not worry me too much. I had accepted that we would probably die on the mountain. (An end by freezing, I'd heard, was less painful than some others, and not too different from floating into sleep.) But what I resented was this: when we fell, our failure would be ascribed not to a physical limitation but a moral one.

. . .

The path was narrow and untraveled, cluttered with sharp rocks and choked with snow and slush. Not too many people, it seemed, were desirous of leaving the world behind! In a few hours, my feet were lacerated, though because of the cold they didn't bleed. Nor did they hurt much. Already I'd begun to lose sensation in my feet. But my other senses were heightened. I'd never been one for appreciating the wilderness, preferring the shaped and contained beauty of my garden. Nature, whom I'd encountered often enough in my wanderings, had always seemed my enemy, her only purpose to add to my discomfort. But today I couldn't keep my eye off the peaks, the way the light slid and shimmered along them, turning them into different shades of gold as the day grew older. There was a sharp sweetness to the air. I breathed it in great gulps, holding it until my lungs ached, and still I couldn't get enough. Did it smell like the incense Vyasa had once sprinkled on a fire to make it speak?

I shook my head to clear it. I knew that the ether of the mountains could make one hallucinate. Already it was hard to advance, to lift my feet from the snow that sucked at them. Still I smelled the incense, and along with it I heard the chirping of birds, though we were too high up to encounter any. I called to my husbands to ask if they noticed anything. Only then did I realize that they'd gone far beyond me. Arjun was the farthest ahead, scouting the path for danger, closely followed by Nakul and Sahadev. But Bheem and Yudhisthir, conversing as they walked at a more leisurely pace, heard me and stopped. Bheem turned—he was coming to get me—but Yudhisthir put a forbidding hand on his arm. He was reminding him of the law. Once on the path, you couldn't retrace your steps, no matter what happened.

Resentment flared through me. Rules were always more important to Yudhisthir than human pain—or human love. I knew then that he alone would reach the gate of heaven, for among us only he was capable of shedding his humanity. I wanted to tell him this, one last outburst that he would remember even in heaven. But the bitter words dissolved in my mouth the way the far peaks were dissolving into evening. What use, even if I was right? On the nearest mountain, the snow had turned the color of the lotus I'd once made Bheem pluck for me. I hoped he recognized it and rejoiced in what we'd been: the strongest man in the world, who for the sake of love rushed into danger; the woman born of fire whose glance had the power to make him smolder with imprudence. It was a good memory on which to end a life.

. . .

When I stepped from the path into the air, I heard my husbands cry out. As I fell, behind me there was a confused commotion. Bheem, I guessed, was scuffling with Yudhisthir, trying to get past him to me. But Yudhisthir would win, as he always did, because Kunti, in her efforts to ensure their survival, had trained his younger brothers to obey him without question. Bheem was sobbing. Would the others weep when they heard? Surely even the callous Yudhisthir would shed a few tears! Hadn't I been by his side all these

years, through good times and bad? But no. I could hear him mur-
muring consolation, reminding Bheem of their greater goal. It was
both infuriating and mortifying. Perhaps that was why, when the
thought came, I did not try to push it away: *Karna would never have
abandoned me thus. He would have stayed back and held my hand until
we both perished. He would have happily given up heaven for my sake.*

I hadn't fallen far. Just a few arm's lengths below the trail jutted
a lip of rock cushioned with snow. I landed there. My breath was
knocked out of me, and my left arm was twisted under my body,
but—perhaps because of the cold, or because I'd deliberately chosen my fate—there wasn't much pain. I could have scrambled up to
the path somehow—but for what? To listen to another of Yudhisthir's sermons? Better to lie here, in relative peace, and gather
my last thoughts.

Perhaps the mountain air carried sounds farther than normal, or
perhaps I imagined the words. For though they must have traveled
even farther by now, I could hear Bheem and Yudhisthir talking.

"Why should she fall?" Bheem asked, his voice rough with
tears. "Why couldn't she walk any further? Was it because her
woman's strength gave out?"

And Yudhisthir replied, in that dispassionate voice of his, "No,
Bheem. It's because although she had many good qualities, she had
one major fault. As do each one of you. Like her, you, too, will fall
when you reach the level beyond which that flaw can't proceed."

"Panchaali?" Bheem exclaimed. "I don't believe it! Why, she
was the most devoted of wives." (I smiled through numb lips at his
words, generous Bheem who had forgotten the many times I'd berated him, the many difficulties in which I'd landed him.) "What
fault could she have had?"

"She married us all. But she loved one man more than everyone
else."

"Who was it?" I could hear the longing in Bheem's whisper.

In that moment, if I could have chosen where love fell, I would have given it to Bheem. I consoled myself with this: at least I'd kept my feelings hidden from my husbands. I'd spared them the pain of knowing who it was that occupied my innermost thoughts through these years. Whose admiration I'd longed for, whose taunts had hurt me the worst. At whose death all colors were leached from my world.

"It was," Yudhisthir said—and then he paused.

He knew! The secrecy I'd prided myself on—he'd seen through it. Lost as he was in his world of ideals, I'd never credited him with much perception. But I'd misjudged him. My heart constricted as I waited to hear what he would reveal. What he would accuse me of. I was surprised to discover how tense I was. I'd been wrong in thinking I wanted nothing more from the world. Though I wouldn't see them again, my husbands' final opinion suddenly mattered immensely to me.

Yudhisthir let his words out in a rush. "Arjun. It was Arjun. She cared most for him."

He had spared me. He'd chosen kindness over truth and uttered, for the sake of my reputation, the second lie of his lifetime!

Thus in my dying hour Yudhisthir proved that he had loved me all along. In doing so, he left me at once grateful and ashamed for the many bitter words I'd directed at him, and those I'd held festering inside.

Bheem gave a resigned sigh. "Can't really blame her, I suppose," he said. "Him being such a great warrior, and so good-looking, too. Why, even the celestial dancers at Indra's court couldn't resist him!"

How easy he was with his forgiveness where I was concerned, how magnanimous! I wished I could tell him how much I admired him. And my other husbands, too—each had his strength, his tenderness. Nakul with his jokes, Sahadev with his consideration, Arjun who had never hesitated to stand between us and danger. When I'd had the chance to appreciate them, I'd spent it venting my dissatisfaction. Now it was too late.

"What are the flaws that will cause the rest of us to fall?" Bheem asked.

"Sahadev's is pride in his learning, Nakul's is vanity for his good looks, Arjun's is his warrior's ego, and yours is your inability to control yourself when you are angry." Yudhisthir spoke calmly as always, but this time I caught the sadness beneath. It was a lonely life he'd led all these years, set apart even from those he loved most by his passion for righteousness. I'd been foolish to let it infuriate me, to wish that he would give up his stiff, silly principles. Righteousness was his nature. He couldn't give it up any more than a tiger can give up its stripes. And because of it he would go on, abandoning his dearest ones in the moment of their death, to the ultimate loneliness: to be the only human in the court of the gods.

fire

The last of the footsteps have passed beyond my hearing. The light on the hills has dimmed, or is it my vision that's fading? My body, too, seems to be fading, parts of it floating away: feet, knees, fingers, hair. It strikes me that, like every home where I've resided, this body, too—my final, crumbling palace—is beginning to fail me.

How shall I spend these last moments of my life? Should I remember my mistakes and practice contrition? No. What use to berate myself now? Besides, I made so many errors, I wouldn't even get past my childhood! Should I forgive those who harmed me? Should I ask forgiveness of those I'd harmed? A worthy enterprise, but fatiguing, particularly since they're all dead now. Perhaps I should recall the people I loved and send them a prayer, for prayer is one of the few things that can travel from this realm to that next, amorphous one. Dhai Ma with her ribald jokes, her loud, affectionate scoldings; on her deathbed she'd bolted upright, delirious, calling for me. Dhri of the conscientious eyebrows and startled laughter, my first companion; he was murdered because of a war I helped cause. My boys that grew up without a mother; the way they'd greeted me after my years in the forest, wary respect in their eyes for the legend

I'd become. Pariksit with his searching glance; I'd failed to answer his question and end his search; I'd failed to warn him of the calamities that lay in wait for him. And Karna who was born under an ill star, who sat alone in the midst of a jeweled court, his eyes filled with a bitterness that I'd put there. Torn in two by his love for me and his hate, he had sacrificed himself rather than give in to Kunti's temptation: *You, too, could be Draupadi's husband.* Would he feel vindicated right now if he knew that in the hour of my death I thought of him rather than my husbands, wondering again, one last time, whether at my swayamvar I'd made the wrong choice?

But the faces swirl away even as I call them up—perhaps because I've hurt them, because I've betrayed them all in some way. They merge into each other, then into the blackness that has covered the sky, and I'm left alone. Left alone to die on a frozen hill! I, whose life had been a rush of attending to the needs of my five husbands—how ironic that at the moment of my own final need not one of them should be with me!

A long time ago I'd asked Vyasa's fire-spirits, Will I find love? They'd assured me I would. But they'd lied! I'd gained glory, yes, respect and fear, yes, even admiration. But where was the love I'd longed for since I was a girl? Where was the person who'd accept me completely and cherish me with all my faults? Self-pity (that emotion I've always scorned) rushes through my being, what's left of it, obliterating my heroic resolutions as I realize this.

It begins to rain, if one can give that name to the icy needles piercing my face—the only part of my body that remains with me. To distract myself from the pain I place my mind on how Krishna had loved rain, how once when I visited Dwarka he had called me to the wet balcony to show me peacocks dancing in the downpour.

"About time you thought of me," he says.

Amazed, I try to turn toward that beloved, familiar voice, but I can no longer move my head. I think I catch, out of the corner of my eye, a glimpse of yellow. Or is it merely the force of my desire?

"So now you think you've imagined me! I'm quite real, I'd like you to know. But what are you doing here, lying in the snow in this awkward and downright unqueenly posture?"

"I'm trying to recite a prayer," I tell him with what little dignity I can muster. "But the problem is, I can't recall a single verse."

"You probably didn't know too many of them to begin with!"

He's right—I've never been one for formal rituals. Still, I want to tell him off—as I did so many times—for his ill-timed levity. But annoyance takes too much energy. "I'm dying, in case you didn't notice," I say, in a tone that is, for me, fairly mild. "If I don't put my mind to praying, I'll probably be whisked off to the fires of the underworld—if they're real. Are they? You should know, being dead already."

"They are and they aren't," he says, "just as I am and am not dead." I see that he hasn't lost his old habit of speaking in riddles. "But don't think of hellfire now. And if you can't remember a prayer, don't let that distress you. Think instead of something that makes you happy."

I consider my life. What was it that made me joyful? What made me experience peace? For I guess that's the kind of happiness Krishna means, not the wild up-and-down of the wheel of passion I'd ridden all these years, delighted one moment, distraught the next. Certainly none of the men or women I'd been close to had given me that type of joy—nor I them, if I were to admit the truth. Even my palace with its strange and beautiful fantasies, the palace that in some way I'd loved more than any of my husbands, the palace that was my greatest pride, had ultimately brought me only sorrow.

There's the lightest of touches on my head, Krishna's hand, I imagine—for I can't see it—moving in a soothing motion such as a mother might use to comfort a fevered child. Though here, too, I'm mostly imagining, having had no mother, and having relegated most of the mothering of my own children to other women.

"Can't remember," I say, the words beginning to knot up in my mouth. Soon, I know, I'll be unable to form them. I don't want to die with the question that had bothered me for so long still pent up within my chest, so I ask, "Why didn't Bheeshma help me in the sabha even when he saw how much I suffered?"

"How your mind leaps, like a drunken monkey! Bheeshma thought too deeply about the laws of men. It paralyzed him. He wasn't sure whether you were already Duryodhan's property—in which case he had no right to intervene. But sometimes one has to drop logic and go with the instinct of the heart, even if it contradicts law."

I want to agree, but a treacherous lethargy is taking me over. I recognize the signs, and though all this while I'd resolved to be brave, I find that I'm suddenly terrified of this dissolution into nothingness. Don't let go of me, I try to tell Krishna. For some reason I don't fully understand, it's crucial that he keeps touching me when I die. But I can't bring out the words.

"Don't worry," he says as though he'd heard. "Focus now: you have work to do. Take another look at your life. Are you sure you can't remember a single happy moment?"

And, unexpectedly, I do.

I stand beside Krishna's chariot at the gates of Hastinapur, handing him a cool drink of coconut water before he leaves for Dwarka. I complain that we hardly see him nowadays, that perhaps we were better off when we were wandering in the forest because there he came to us more often. He says, You needed me differently then. But in my heart I'm with you just as much! When he smiles, there are wrinkles at the corners of his eyes, strands of white in his hair, the first soft footfalls of age, hastened by the war he let himself be pulled into for friendship's sake. Love takes me in a wave even as I pretend annoyance. Don't wait so long next time, I tell him. I won't, he says. I'll come when you're not expecting me. I watch him ride away. The winter sun lies soft as a shawl around my shoulders. If someone were to ask me, at this moment, what I wanted, I would say, Nothing.

I don't know that this will be the last time I wave him goodbye.

Other memories follow, tumbling like fallen leaves in wind. They're in no particular order, for here I am, a child in the courtyard of my father's palace, chasing after a butterfly that evades me, getting sweaty and teary until Krishna holds out a hand. The butterfly lands on it, and silently he extends it to me. And I, understanding something beyond my years, don't grab but instead gently stroke, once, the dusty yellow wings.

Here's one in Indra Prastha, in our great hall, where Krishna is pretending to read our palms, my husbands' and mine, only when it's my turn, he makes me double over with embarrassed laughter by prophesying a hundred and fifty children. Here's one where I've prepared a meal for him myself, waving away the services of our many cooks—something I don't do even for my husbands—and he's complaining (falsely, of course) that the food is too salty. And here I'm showing him my garden—which is the most beautiful garden on earth, which would be perfect except for the fact that I haven't been able to find, anywhere, a parijat tree to plant. He smiles and extends his fist, and when I pull it open, it holds a single seed. I'll plant it, and it will grow into an entire grove of parijats.

Here's a more somber moment when I'm going from Kampilya to Hastinapur after my marriage. All of a sudden I'm afraid of leaving behind the walls that I'd chafed against all these years as though they'd imprisoned me. Of exchanging the company of my dearest brother for that of husbands who are strangers. Krishna takes me by the hand—how familiar the gesture, though I'm sure he's never done this before—and guides me to Yudhisthir's chariot. He helps me up, whispering that it'll be a great adventure—and when I hear him say so, that's what it becomes. Here, years later, after the Rajasuya yagna is tarnished by Sisupal's blood, we sit shrouded in gloom. But Krishna will not let us mope. He claps his hands and calls for the servants to bring lamps, more lamps. In their glowing halo he assures me—for though he speaks to my husbands it's me he looks at—that Sisupal brought his death upon himself, that throughout the incident we behaved honorably, that if a curse should follow, it will fall on his head rather than ours.

And here's one I'd forgotten all this while:

In my year of disguise, I stood one evening on a small, seldom-used balcony in Queen Sudeshna's palace. I'd escaped there for a moment of peace away from her nagging demands, from Keechak's hot eyes that raked my body more boldly each day. I hadn't seen my husbands for days, not even those fleeting, distant glimpses that left me so frustrated. I still had months to live out like this, lonely and beleaguered. Despair swirled in me like ink, drowning my heart. In my confusion I wondered if all this suffering had descended upon me as punishment because in my heart of hearts I had been unfaithful to my husbands. Perhaps it would be easier to throw myself from the balcony, to end it all right now. It would be only a minor tragedy. My husbands would weep a while in secret, but when our year of disguise ended, they'd shake off their sorrow and busy themselves with fulfilling their destiny.

The balcony looked out onto a narrow street frequented mostly by vendors or servant maids hurrying from one great house to another. But today a group of horsemen—strangers by their garments—were riding down it. Perhaps they'd lost their way. I drew my veil partway over my face, as was the custom for women in this city. I need not have bothered. Busy arguing about directions, the men did not notice me. They spoke in the accents of my hometown. Nostalgia shook me as I listened, and I had to suppress the inappropriate—and dangerous—desire to call out a greeting. They had passed me by when the last man looked up at me. It was Krishna!

Such a thing was impossible—but there he was, a peacock feather waving cheerily in his turban. He neither spoke nor gestured. But a current of consolation coursed through my body as we exchanged glances. Over the next months that glance would remain with me, as palpable as a warm hand slipped into mine, reminding me that I wasn't forgotten. It gave me the strength I needed to survive, to hold back from acts of desperation that might have exposed us all.

It's only now I see that he'd always been there, sometimes in the forefront, sometimes blended into the shadows of my life. When I thought myself abandoned, he was busy supporting me—but so subtly that I often didn't notice. He loved me even when I behaved in a most unlovable manner. And his love was totally different from every other love in my life. Unlike them, it didn't expect me to behave in a certain way. It didn't change into displeasure or anger or even hatred if I didn't comply. It healed me. If what I felt for Karna was a singeing fire, Krishna's love was a balm, moonlight over a parched landscape. How blind I'd been not to recognize it for the precious gift it was!

I have just one question now, one yearning. I want to remember the very first time. The moment when he entered my life—what happened then? What were his first words to me? How did this love, the only love that is here to uphold me at the moment of my death, begin?

How will I ask with these frozen lips?

But he understands. I feel his breath, warm and perfumed with a scent I do not know, on my forehead. And the memory comes.

I was surrounded by redness, though I wasn't in a room. The walls undulated, gave off warmth. I had no body, no name. Yet I knew who I was. Someone spoke to me encouragingly, in a familiar voice, telling me that it was my turn now. I must go forth to do my duty. But I held back. It was so comfortable in this place. So safe and undemanding. Also, I was worried by the enormousness of my task.

Can I really change history? I asked. What about the sins I'll incur, being the cause of so much devastation?

The voice was as gentle as a brook wending through pebbles. Try to remember that you are the instrument and I the doer. If you can hold on to this, no sin can touch you.

Instrument, I repeated. Doer. It sounded simple enough, though I suspected that it would become more complicated once the game began. I asked, What if I forget?

He said, You probably will. Most of them do. That's the beguiling trick the world plays on you. You'll suffer for it—or dream that you're suffering. But no matter. At the time of your death I'll remind you. That'll be enough.

A force pushed me forward, loving yet implacable. I felt myself gliding through the redness, taking on form as I went. I had arms and legs now, jewels around my neck. I was wrapped in gold cloth. It was getting hotter. I had to hurry. Smoke from the fire made me cough and stumble. Under my feet, the stone was slippery from the ghee the priests had poured into the flames for a hundred days, the air acrid with an odor I hadn't smelled before. The name for it came to me as I stepped out, dizzying me: *vengeance*. My brother gripped my hand so I wouldn't fall.

Everything's turning to snow-dust, even my brain. But with the last of my strength I formulate a thought: *That was the yagna fire out of which I came into this world! Were you there with me even then, before I took on this birth?*

I feel him smile. He's glad I made the connection in time.

I did forget everything, didn't I? Made a mess of things?

There's something else I want to ask, but it's hard to focus because thoughts are passing through me like water through a sieve.

"You did what you were supposed to. Played your part perfectly."

Even when I got furious? When I held hatred in my heart? Loved the wrong man? Tortured the ones closest to me? Harmed so many people?

"Even then. You didn't harm them that much. Look!"

Above me there is light—or rather, the absence of darkness. The mountains have vanished. The air is full of men—but not men exactly, nor women, for their bodies are sleek and sexless and glowing. Their faces are unlined and calm, devoid of the various passions that distinguished them in life, but with some effort I recognize each one. Here's Kunti and my father, finishing up a conversation. Here's Bheeshma, floating amicably beside Sikhandi and Dhai Ma. Duryodhan is positioned between Drona and my brother, all of them smiling as though at a recent joke. Four of my husbands are here (Yudhisthir must still be toiling up the path), along with Gandhari, who holds Sahadev close as one would a young child. Spread out behind them are countless others, their bodies erased of the wounds that killed them at Kurukshetra, their faces evincing the satisfaction of actors who have successfully concluded their roles in a great drama.

Is this real, or am I seeing things?

Krishna gives a mock sigh. "Skeptical to the last! It's real enough, though *seeing* isn't quite the word for it. You're going to have to learn a whole new vocabulary for all the things you'll be undergoing shortly. For now let me just say that each person experiences this moment differently."

Am I dying? I ask—with admirable equanimity, I think.

"You could call it that."

I wait for fear to scrape my spine with its frozen nail, but it surprises me by its absence. Is it because this moment is so different from what I've always imagined death to be?

"You could also call it waking," Krishna continues. "Or intermission, as when one scene in a play ends and the next hasn't yet begun. But look—"

In front of me floats a tall, spare form, gold glinting on his chest, his ears. He bends forward and holds out his hand. The expression on his face is one I never saw on it in life—serene, affectionate, content. I hesitate, wondering what my husbands would think, then realize it doesn't matter. We are husband and wife no more; nor is Karna (if I can still use that name for this being with his joyous, patient eyes) any longer the forbidden one. I can take his arm in view of everyone. If I wish, I can embrace him with all of myself.

But first—for in a moment human inquiry will become irrelevant—I must ask Krishna the question that had slipped from me earlier, the question that has plagued me all my life.

Are you truly divine?

"Will you never be done with questioning?" Krishna laughs. Like the small brass bells tied around the necks of calves, that sound will remain with me even when hearing has gone. "Yes, I am. You are, too, you know!"

I try hard to comprehend what he means. I know it's critical that

I do so. But his words baffle me. I don't feel divine. With this body dissolving away, my thoughts fraying, I feel as though I'm less than nothing.

Krishna touches my hand. If you can call it a hand, these pinpricks of light that are newly coalescing into the shape of fingers and palm. At his touch something breaks, a chain that was tied to the woman-shape crumpled on the snow below. I am buoyant and expansive and uncontainable—but I always was so, only I never knew it! I am beyond name and gender and the imprisoning patterns of ego. And yet, for the first time, I'm truly Panchaali. I reach with my other hand for Karna—how surprisingly solid his clasp! Above us our palace waits, the only one I've ever needed. Its walls are space, its floor is sky, its center everywhere. We rise; the shapes cluster around us in welcome, dissolving and forming and dissolving again like fireflies in a summer evening.